33+ Hot, Explicit & Taboo Sex Stories (4 in 1):

Forbidden Erotica Collection for Adults- Horny Threesomes, MILFs, First Time Anal, Lesbians, Gangbangs, BDSM & More Fantasies

By: G.G. Goode

Goode Publications

Table of Contents

Book 3

I Cum When You Cum

Book 4

Taboo, Explicit& Forbidden Sex Stories For Adults

Dirty Erotica- Threesomes, MILFs, First Time Anal, BDSM, Cuckold, Femdom, Submission, Lesbians, Gangbangs, 69 (Orgasmic Collection)

Written By:
G.G. Goode

- Goode Publications -

Submission For House Keeping

Luciana woke up before her alarm rang. She turned it off prematurely to avoid waking her flatmates. Padding over to the shower, she let the water wash over her as briefly as possible to freshen up. She wouldn't have the luxury of enjoying a long bath until her shift was finished and she had access to the bathroom at a more reasonable hour. Even then, irrespective of how mindful she'd been not to consume an excess of hot water in the morning, Luciana guessed there'd be little left to fill the bath when she returned home, with the other five flatmates having had their showers.

She pulled the plain black dress with white trim on the arms and collar over her head, then wrapped a white apron round her waist. Slipping into her black work shoes, she acknowledged they were comfortable like a pair of well-worn slippers, which was welcome in her line of work, but knew they were the least racy attire ever to grace a pair of feet.

Luciana spun in the mirror. There were many women in uniform that the opposite sex found irresistible, but Luciana could honestly say in regard to her dating that being a housekeeper was hard going. She genuinely felt like the least sought-after woman in the city. Maybe if it had been some cutesy French maid outfit her love-life would be more exciting, but a respectable housekeeper at the New Victorian was made to look as bland and uninteresting as possible. Her job was to clean and behave as if she wasn't visible to the hotel's customers.

In some ways it was quite soul destroying, but it paid the bills, and she had a LOT of stories from her encounters over the years. The New Victorian had only recently opened so Luciana had yet to experience anything too unusual. However, she knew it was only a matter of time before that changed. Walking to the underground, she embarked on the same 40-minute commute to the inner-city hotel she travelled daily. She took the staff entrance, missing the grandiose frontage of the building. When you come through a back door in a brick wall it really could have been any hotel.

"Banana for my love," offered her camp friend Arnold.

"Has it been anywhere suspect?" she asked.

"Darling, even if it had, it has a skin on it. Peel and enjoy."

"Maybe not," she passed it back to him.

"Lucy, I'm joking. It's fine."

He peeled the banana and took a bite.

"See!"

She looked dubious.

"Have the muffin if you must. It's sealed."
Luciana snatched it from him. Leaning in to give Arnold a quick thank you kiss, she stopped herself and paused her lips from pressing on his.

"Maybe not. I don't know where that mouth has been all night," she teased.

"I'm concierge, Lucy. I organized the shenanigans. I don't get to take part. Anyway, shift's finished. Richard's taken over. I'm off home to bed – alone!"

"Don't use all the hot water."

"You best come home in a better mood if you want me to cook and serve you the finest wine this evening."

He opened his jacket to give Luciana a flash of the bottle of wine he'd tucked away.

"My mood's lifting already," she laughed.

"Pre-Shift House Keeping Meeting starting at 7.45am" came the announcement over the speaker.

The housekeeping team assembled as their manager painstakingly ran through the same schedule he did every morning. Luciana was relieved she'd been allocated a standard floor that wasn't exceptional – no famous visitors, no penthouses or hot tubs.

"Should be able to get in and get this done and get outside to real life," she thought.

"Share cleaning?" she suggested to her floor partner, Min.

"No. Separate. I feel hungover, I need to go at my own pace," moaned Min. "I won't be any company for you. Besides you'll make me feel bad if I need a little snooze. Leave me be today."

Luciana nodded amiably. Min never minced her words. It meant you always knew where you stood with her. If she was feeling fondly toward you, you'd be encased in an abundance of her affection. However, when she was in a mood like today, it also meant that was probably her last verbal exchange with Luciana for the shift.

The girls loaded up their trolleys.

"Hey, fill it up. Take as much as we can. I don't want to have to come back down," ordered Min.

Luciana loaded the two trolleys from the linen cupboard. Min lent on the wall looking pale and tired. Without asking for further help, Luciana filled the drawers of the trolleys with all the incidental bathroom bits.

"Let's go," she said, giving Min a shove to move her from the wall and propel her to a walking pace.

Min followed her. As the lift opened on their floor, Luciana heaved both trolleys to the middle of the corridor.

"You do that end and I'll do the other," she suggested, indicating the different directions.

Min huffed, "I hate orders."

"It's not an order. It's what you wanted."

Min thought for a moment or two, then hugged Luciana.

"Oh yeah, so it was."

"So, we'll meet in the middle?"

Min nodded.

"Yeah. Remember to call me though if I sleep too long," warned Min.
"How long should I let you sleep?"

"One hour for a power nap. Two hours if you want to do some of my rooms as well."

Luciana rolled her eyes knowing she'd be picking up Min's slack. She wheeled her trolley to her end of the corridor. Preparing herself, she went to grab the clipboard with detailed notes on which rooms required cleaning and which rooms had late check outs or weren't to be disturbed. The folder was nowhere to be seen.

"Shit," she cursed under her breath, realizing she must've left it on Min's trolley.

She jogged down to the opposite end of the floor, but Min and her trolley had disappeared.

"You have got to be kidding me," she thought.

"Min. Min," she hissed under the door on her left. "Min, are you in there? Are you awake?"

She tried the door gently, but it was locked. Could she really have gotten in and fallen asleep that quickly? Luciana looked at the opposite door. It was worth a try.

"Min," she hissed again under the door on her hands and knees.

Still no reply.

Luciana tried the handle and it opened. Relief washed over her. Leaving the door on the latch, she walked into the main bedroom.

Min wasn't there.

Luciana's hand flew to her mouth. She shuffled back from the doorway trying to analyse the scene in front of her.

A woman lay spreadeagled on the bed in her underwear – hips propped up by pillows. Luciana could see ropes round her wrists and ankles securing her to the bed posts. She noted the girl was not gagged and wasn't screaming for help so must be complicit in the set up.

She could only see the back of the man. Some middle-aged, portly man in loose plaid boxer shorts. Luciana knew she should silently leave the room to return to work. Despite her racing heart and the pressing schedule of the day, she wanted to know what would happen next. She kept herself as close to the doorframe as possible so as not to be visible to the two participants but to also allow herself an unrestricted view of the live porno.

The man sat on the mattress with a pair of scissors. He snipped the band from the front of the girl's bra, and it sprung open revealing two very small breasts. Dragging the open scissors down the white skin of her stomach, the girl wriggled in response at the cold metal on her body. He dug the scissors under the elastic of her outer thigh to slice through her panties. The same action was repeated on the other side of her briefs. His hand went into her crotch to roughly tug and release the torn underwear. Putting them to his mouth, he inhaled deeply then rubbed them over the girl's face.

"I think you should taste what I taste."

Luciana kept watching as the girl nodded her head and willingly opened her mouth. The man stuffed the panties into her throat. Luciana suspected the woman could easily spit them out if she needed to but clearly didn't want to. The man stood up and headed toward the entrance where Luciana was. Shuffling to the side, she prayed the man was too engrossed on the task in hand to detect her nearby presence. Fortunately, he didn't come out the door. She heard a plastic bag rummaging. It went silent. She could hear the springs on the mattress depress as he crawled back onto the bed. Luciana slowly moved back to put half her face to the door. The man was placing clothes pegs on the girl's nipples. She writhed as they tightened on her erogenous zones.

"Remember, sex dolls can't talk," said the man to his slave.

He seemed to be working between her legs. When he stood from the bed to admire his handiwork, Luciana was able to as well. He'd placed clothes pegs on the lips of her pussy and one seemed to be hanging from her clit. Luciana's thighs tightened at the thought of how the girl must be feeling. She watched as he flicked the pegs, taking them off only to snap them back on. Throughout the pegging and unpegging the girl on the bed watched with a contorted expression. She didn't even close her eyes to try and block herself from the small torture she must've been experiencing.

Luciana darted away again as he got off the bed. She wasn't as cautious knowing that he appeared to have everything he required within the room. A number of objects were placed at the end of the bed. Luciana didn't know if she was curious or turned on. He produced a black, rubber item which appeared to be shorter than an average vibrator and was shaped like a rounded pyramid. Luciana watched as he squeezed a bottle of lube on his hand then smeared it over the girl's behind. Hoping he'd ease it in, she was unsurprised when he forced it in with one sharp push. The girl's hips bucked high. The man stroked her thighs in a calming way which also seemed to communicate that the girl was in no way to verbally express how she felt about her treatment.

He held up a vibrator. Luciana sighed, deciding it didn't look too intrusive. The man grabbed a clear sheet and wrapped it round the vibrator increasing its girth. As he wound gaffer tape at the base to secure the covering on the vibrator, Luciana could hear loud pops. Squinting, she realized he was enhancing the smooth surface of the vibrator with bubble wrap. She smiled at the creativity and decided the girl was actually in for a real treat. Lubing the bubble wrapped vibe, as he had with the butt plug, it slid into her in one attempt.

The girl looked stuffed. Luciana felt a tinge of jealousy. It was a sadistic picture that screamed sexual delectation. Once again, the man emerged off the mattress to admire his handiwork and shared the same thought as Luciana in regard to the scene he'd created.

Luciana realized he still had some tool or toy in one hand. Satisfied he'd perfected the set-up, the man's thumbs ran over the tiny box. Her keen ears detected a buzzing. He clearly had a remote control for the vibrator and had started it. The girl on the bed squirmed furiously. Luciana wondered if the bubble wrap may have dulled the sensations the vibrator could produce, but the way the man knowingly worked the control, it clearly had a lot more functionality than just vibrating. As he manipulated the various buttons, she could see the girl sweating to limit the response of her body, but soon enough she was jerking on the bed. Her hands went to grip the bed post to try to regain a modicum of control of her body."

"No," bellowed the man, leaving the girl to orgasm intensely on the bed again and again.

Luciana could see the man's hard on against his boxers. He was definitely not her type, but the display was so steamy, she wanted to come in and wank him off as a congratulations for serving up an abundance of sensuality this early in the morning.

The man pulled down his boxers and Luciana got the full view of his thick, stubby cock. Part of her was repulsed but another part of her was now so invested in what she'd been watching she wanted to know how it finished. With every morsel of self-control she possessed, Luciana forced her head to turn and return to the entry door to the room. With painstakingly slow movements she opened the door as silently as she could and closed it behind her.

"What are you doing in there?" snapped Min. "That room's not to be done."

"I know!"

"How'd you know? We forgot our clipboards. I had to go downstairs and retrace our steps to find them."

"I know from what I walked in on. Those two need to think about using the "Do Not Disturb" sign."

Min's anger dissipated as suddenly as it flared up.

"Why'd you say that? What'd you see?"

"Not what I was expecting," laughed Luciana.

"What were you expecting? Another dirty, empty room?"
"Actually, I was expecting to find you sleeping, Min. Like you said you were."

"I needed to find a room I could sleep in and without knowing which rooms needed cleaning I wasn't able to do that. Hence, I found our folders downstairs. Then I came back up and I'm checking all the bloody rooms to give you your clipboard and you're nowhere to be seen. Now I won't be sleeping at all."

Luciana glanced at her watch. Min was right; they were going to have to work at double-speed to get these rooms finished in the allotted time.

"I'm sorry. I had the most bizarre experience. Come to dinner at mine tonight and I'll fill you in."

"I need sleep!" yelled Min. "Work, home, bed. Tell me some other time. How interesting can a hotel room be?"

Luciana took her clipboard and returned towards her half of the corridor. Entering the nearest room that needed cleaning she went to the toilet. As she pushed her panties down, she saw how wet the crotch was. She'd clearly enjoyed the BDSM scene more than she'd anticipated.

When Luciana got home, as promised Arnold had dinner and wine waiting for her.

"Where is everyone else?"

"I don't know. On shift or out enjoying themselves. They aren't as refined as you and I," winked Arnold.

"You would not believe the day I've had."

"Let me guess. Someone had been smoking in room 208. The toilet in 333 had skid marks. A used condom was on the floor of 524."

"Bleurgh. I'm trying to eat. Those are part and parcel of the job. Something actually interesting happened today. And you have to promise to keep it to yourself because I don't think I'd have a job if it ever came out."

"Oh, do tell. I'm so intrigued. I promise I'll never tell a soul," teased Arnold.

Luciana went on and described in detail her morning.

"Why didn't you just walk out?" asked Arnold. "Why stay and watch?"

"Curiosity I suppose."

"But it must've been obvious what was going on from the way the girl was trussed up."

"I guess. Put it this way. It's one thing to read the books. It's another thing seeing it being played out in front of you."
"Sounds hot!"

"It was," confided Luciana.

"Is it something you'd be interested in?" he probed.

"No, not for me. I prefer to be in control if you know what I mean," she tapped her nose with her index finger.

"You picked up a few tips?"

"Oh yeah, put me in a BDSM club and the boys would be running scared with my imagination," Luciana giggled.

"is that so?"

"Don't believe me?"

"Au contraire."

Arnold tapped his fingertips on the table while musing over an idea.

"What?" she asked.

He studied Luciana carefully as if weighing up whether or not to share something with her.

"What?" she pressed.

"No, it doesn't matter. I don't think it's up your alley."

"Try me!"

"No," said Arnold decisively.

"At least tell me what you were going to say. You know how annoying it is when someone starts something and doesn't finish it."

He sighed.
"I was only going to say, in my role as concierge you're aware I get a lot of requests."

"Yes," she prompted.

"Some requests are from business guys that…. well the whole French maid thing."

"Like I said, I'm not really into the whole submissive scene."

"If you let me finish, what I was going to say is some requests are from wealthy, powerful business guys looking to be dominated by a woman in a housekeeping uniform. The thought of someone so unmistakably lower than them in terms of class and status is a big turn on for these types of men."

"There are guys like that?"

"Loads. And if I can organize it then there's big money involved."
"I'm not a whore and -"

"You don't have to sleep with them. They want to be humiliated. It doesn't have to be sexual. I'm not a pimp. I'm your best friend."

"How much are we talking?"

"Depending on the client thousands."

"And how much would I keep?"

"Wow, you actually think I'd rip you off. I'm the hook up guy. Ten percent."

"$1800 of $2000 isn't the worst payoff."

"I believe I could get $5000 with the right client. But you can't run off or get scared half-way through or not turn up because you've had a change of heart. It's my reputation at risk," said Arnold practically. "These are important clients. If I fail to deliver it reflects badly on me. Then I lose out because people won't trust me to honor my word or think I'm incapable of providing the service they need. Reputation and tips are essential to my living."

"I know. I would never do that to you," promised Luciana.

"Where are we on this then?"

"Let's do it!"

Arnold was true to his word. One Tuesday afternoon when Luciana was off roster, she received the text with the time and room number. As she fussed over what to wear, she remembered it had to be her housekeeping uniform.

She got to the room fifteen minutes earlier than her client's expected arrival. Arnold had left her uniform hanging in the bathroom. Already showered, she slipped it on hastily. There was a soft, black sports bag on a table. Luciana unzipped it. Her eyes widened at the black, leather, and chain toys within. Her client had provided her with a toy-box to assist the session.

There was a sharp knock on the door. Luciana jumped. Her legs felt wobbly.

"This is not how a dominatrix behaves," she chided herself mentally. "It's acting. Pull yourself together and start earning."

Opening the door, she was shocked at the man standing before her. For some reason, after the scene she'd witnessed while cleaning, she'd thought it was only fat businessmen into the sub-dom play. This man was drop-dead gorgeous with wavy blonde hair and a face that should be on the cover of a magazine. He was so dreamy and knowingly available. Luciana couldn't help herself. Standing on tippy-toes she kissed his lips, lingering slightly.

"I'm not sure-" started the man.

"Quiet!" ordered Luciana.

His rich baritone was as enticing as his looks. She didn't actually want him to be quiet. She wanted a moment to sort her head out to take charge.

"I've stumbled at the first hurdle," she internally berated herself. "That kiss was way too romantic. He is nothing, I am everything. Except he's bloody perfect and I want him to marry me."

Luciana stopped the school-girl giggle climbing up her throat.

"Undress," she said simply.

"Are you sure-"

"I said undress," she snapped.

Every time he opened his mouth she fell out of character. She walked up to him to stare him straight in his beautiful navy eyes.

"I don't want to hear anything again from you, pig. Do as you're told or leave. I don't want to be wasting my time with someone – something so pathetic."

His eyes lit up and he smiled.

"Lose the smile and lose your clothes. Last warning."

The man undressed. Taking the time to hang his suit. Luciana was in awe of his swimmers physique. She wasn't a whore by any stretch, but she was entitled to enjoy herself. She hitched her uniform up slightly and sat on the one-person sofa. Swinging a leg over an arm rest, her hand delved straight into her panties to rub the juices that were bursting from her pussy. Completely naked, the man stood where he was waiting for instruction. Luciana wanted to bring herself to climax, but remembered she was here for his pleasure, not hers.

"Go to the bag," she barked.

She pointed to the table.

"Take out the ankle cuff spreader and put it on," Luciana commanded.

He sorted quickly through the toys. Taking out the two-foot metal bar with leather cuffs on either end, he attached the cuffs to each ankle.

Luciana walked over to the bag and grabbed the ball- gag mask. Placing the ball in his mouth she went behind him to tighten the leather straps.

"That's better. Now I don't have to worry about you interrupting. Get to the ground, little piggy."

Awkwardly he went on all fours. Luciana grabbed a leather flogger from the bag. The handle fitted her grasp perfectly. She gently swished the braids over his back and buttocks. She could hear him groan through the gag. Flicking her wrist with a little force, she let the flogger thwack against his buttocks. He wriggled his arse.

"I'm not here for your enjoyment."

She flung the flogger hard against his lower back and buttocks. There was no happy moan as he inched forward on his hands to try and distance himself from the force of the leather braids. Luciana laughed.

"That's right. Run, little piggy."

Ankles spread, restricting his movement, he tried crawling away. Perversely Luciana followed whacking the flogger hard against him, leaving angry red marks. She followed his attempts to elude her, smacking harder and harder each time. She realized her pussy was dripping. Dropping the flogger, she let him move a few more inches, grabbing his blonde hair hard she pulled his head back. She yanked again before releasing him.

"Don't move."

She moved to stand in front of him. Gently her hand caressed his face. His eyes were wide in wonder. She knew he didn't trust her momentary kindness. Grabbing his hair again she pulled his head under her dress and shoved her cunt against his face – rubbing against him for her own satisfaction. She released him. Pushing his head to the floor, she angled him, so he was looking directly at the sofa she'd been sitting in earlier.

"Hands between your legs," she whispered in his ear.

Adjusting his shoulders, he placed his hands between his legs. Luciana squatted behind him and placed a wrist in the two cuffs that were placed in the middle of the separator bar. Hands and ankles cuffed; he was secured to the spot.

Luciana grabbed a dildo from the floor and returned to her sofa. Legs spread again she inserted the dildo in and out of her pussy. She fucked the dildo like she wanted to fuck the man but stopped herself before climax. She knew he was hoping she'd make herself come. Luciana was determined not to give into his expectations. Covering the space between them in a few strides, she crouched down and undid the straps of the ball-gag mask. He wheezed, taking in as much air as possible into his lungs.

"Open wide," instructed Luciana, confident he'd caught his breath.

He opened his mouth and hungrily took in the inches of dildo she forced into his mouth. She could hear him sucking contentedly as she rummaged through the bag. Luciana grabbed two more items. As he continued mouthing the dildo, she inserted the smallest ball from a string of anal beads into his arse. He whimpered.

"Do not let go of my dildo."

Looking around she saw he'd stopped enjoying her juices on the dildo and was now biting it hard; desperate to follow her orders and also accept the anal beads.

The beads increased in size each time she popped one in. The first four he accepted without too much trouble, but as the size increased, he ground his teeth into the rubber cock and grimaced. By the time the tenth bead was forced into his arsehole, he looked in pain. Luciana gave a small tug on the ring at the end and heard a whine.

Assessing the wooden paddle, Luciana let him get accustomed to the beads and uncomfortable position. Satisfied she'd be able to use it competently, she cast her eyes over his ripped physique. She noticed the dildo had fallen from his mouth. Walking over she put her foot on it.

"Bad, bad boy."

She kicked it away. He looked up at her apologetically. Luciana took the paddle to his buttocks. There was no warm up this time. She knew she didn't have a lot of upper arm strength so couldn't do any serious damage, thus letting herself spank him with gusto.

"Please," he begged.

Luciana was consumed by her need to dominate the man. She had to have him.

"I told you not to talk," she said. "I don't care what rules or arrangements you made with the concierge, I'm in charge here."

She unshackled his wrists from the ankle separator bar.

"Get on the bed."

As quick as he could shuffle with the restrictive bar on his feet, he managed to lay on the bed. As tacky as they were, Luciana grabbed the pink fluffy handcuffs from the bag and attached one to his left wrist. She manipulated the chain through the intricate carving of the bed to secure his other wrist.

Like the man she'd watched days ago when cleaning, she got off the bed to survey the scene. Ankles separated. Hands secured. Cock hard. Climbing on the mattress, she sheathed him with a rubber. He shook his head emphatically.

"Don't talk," she reminded him as she straddled and sank on his eight rock hard inches of pink.

She rode him with gay abandon, rubbing her clit and orgasming furiously on his dick. As the electric sensations from within her pussy stimulated his prick, he too bucked his hips. Luciana looked down to see him biting his lip to not scream out to claim his own climax.

"Job well done," she thought. "Might have overstepped the boundaries. Might be considered a whore taking money for sex. Might have also fucked the most beautiful man I've ever laid eyes on."

She leapt off him. She hadn't really any clue how to finish this or what etiquette was required. Deciding to stay in character, she decided to free him and let him clean up the carnage.

Unlocking the cuffs, she freed his hands. His eyes caught hers before she could escape making eye contact with him. Reaching up, he pulled her face to his and kissed her warmly and firmly. It was a perfect kiss. "I really wish we'd met under different circumstances," he said.

"Except you think I'm a whore," she thought.

"Me too," she agreed.

Her voice was barely a whisper.

"Everything about you is perfect. I wanted to stop you from going through with this. To rescue us from this sordid arrangement so we might've been able to explore a potential future."

"Oh."

"Some other life," he smiled kindly.

Luciana walked out the door; tears pricking her eyes. She got as far as the concierge desk before bursting into tears wondering why fate played the cruelest tricks.

Car Park Coupling

"Boy, this place is awesome. I've never been anywhere this fancy in my life!"

David smiled patiently, mildly embarrassed by the enthusiasm of his young guest.

"Who even knew a buffet could have lobster and sushi and noodles and steak...and have you even seen the desserts?" the girl rattled on.

"Who knew?"

She was sweet enough. It was moments like these though he realized she was probably a little too young for him. Actually, that was unfair. She was inexperienced and had a very different upbringing and lifestyle to his. You couldn't expect too much commonsense at twenty-three. She brought a lot of joy to him. When you are forty-five, life can become dull. David felt like a lot of what he saw from day to day was grey because he'd done it so often before. However, having Riley by his side meant that he could see life through fresh eyes. Experiences were different. It was as if it were the first time for him as well as Riley and that was possibly half her appeal.

The other part of her appeal was that she was absolutely stunning. Riley had the whole American college girl, cheerleader style going on – though she was not American and had never been to college. Still she had a trim figure, big boobs (an enhancement he was now paying the loan off for), platinum blonde hair and inquisitive blue eyes. She was proving to be a costly endeavour but knowing that everyone was staring at her and wondering how he got so lucky was a nice return on his investment. As for the fact that she didn't have any higher education, David thought in the long term it might be for the best. His intellect would mean over the forthcoming years he could mold her to ensure she was always aware that she was never going to get any better than him if in ten years' time she felt the twenty plus year age gap was a problem. It also meant her career options were limited. No chance in her becoming a highflyer and leaving him behind. And no chance she would ever have a man of his stature sweep her off her feet again.

"Did you know you could go back multiple times so you can taste everything?" he asked.

"Well Duh David, I'm not an imbecile. I know what all-you-can-eat means."

"Yeah, but we don't want you eating everything. Can't have you getting fat. That would not be a good look on you."

"If you want a special dessert later, you'll happily watch me eat every dessert I want right now."

Cheeky was cute. Tolerable at her age, but he didn't want the sassy attitude turning into disrespect.

"There's plenty of other girls who'll give a special dessert without the threat of becoming a whale." Her face dropped. He saw the hurt expression. It stung to see her ego knocked but it was for the best – in the long term she'd thank him. They'd be happy together if she didn't rail against his wishes.

"I was kidding."

"Treat yourself to one dessert," offered David, thinking himself generous.

"No. It's okay. You're right. I've had loads and maybe you'll take me here again sometime so I can save myself for dessert."

"I'm sure I will," he placated. Grateful she'd understood the need to compromise and not get into a habit of becoming gluttonous.

There was a definite change in the mood at their table. Riley pushed the remaining food round her plate.

"Sometimes David says the meanest things," she thought. "I wonder if my friends have a valid point about dumping him. If you care about someone it shouldn't matter what size you are."

It wasn't David's condescending and controlling manner that bothered her friends the most. It was the fact he was married. She'd had many a heated argument with her close circle regarding the nature of their affair. But it was just that – an affair. Riley didn't see it going anywhere. How could it be when he was married. It had an expiry date, and she was happy to see it play out; especially given he'd paid for her boobs and was taking her out to lavish places like the New Victorian hotel where her friends would be more likely to be working at than dining in.

She badly wanted to ask David if his wife was overweight, but was worried it might annoy him. Giggling to herself she had an urge to ditch David and hide in the toilets so she could come back out to make the most of the buffet and eat every single one of the desserts on offer. As satisfying as it would be, she was thinking long term. His ever-ready credit card for any of her whims and fancies made him a lot easier to tolerate when he was obnoxious.

"Did your wife make the mistake of indulging in dessert over the course of your marriage? Am I her punishment for letting herself go?"

She decided to risk it. David's eyes narrowed.

"That topic is off limits."

Riley shrugged but smirked inwardly knowing she'd pushed the right button to stab him pointedly in response to his callous attitude.

"We may as well leave if I'm not having any more to eat."

"I didn't say I wasn't having dessert," snapped David.
David left the table to examine what treats were on offer. He didn't even like sweets, but Riley was coming at him in a manner he didn't like. He'd made a decision to include Riley as a significant part of his life but when she acted like a spoiled brat he wondered if it was a healthy choice. He stared over at her. She smiled and waved brightly. She winked at him – the same way she did when she knew sex was on the cards – and he felt his cock hardening. He dropped his plate.

"Let's go have dessert upstairs."

Riley followed him out of the buffet knowing she'd had a little win in using her feminine allure to prevent him from having a dessert as well.

David smiled proudly as he opened the door to the modest but luxurious hotel room. Riley bit her tongue from saying it was a huge step up from the dingy joints he normally bought her to for sex. He certainly hadn't been a cheapskate taking her to lunch and booking a room at the New Victorian hotel.

"It's so cute and quaint," she cooed. "Everything is so new but looks so old fashioned. It's adorbs!"

"Well, I'm glad you like it. It's the best in town."

"Yeah. Me and my flatmates were intending on hitting the stripper show on payday," confessed Riley.

"Is that actually your sort of scene?"

Riley watched as he undressed. No sense of foreplay or seduction needed as far as he was concerned.

'Hanging out with my squad will always be my scene. The strippers are a one off – just some fun for the girls."

"Don't you have fun with me?"
She studied his pudgy body. He wasn't overweight, but he had no real physical conditioning. Watching some hot studs reveal their best moves as they undressed on stage was going to be way more memorable than going to the city's fanciest hotel and only being allowed to pick at the buffet before having vanilla style sex in what she guessed to be the hotel's cheapest accommodation. Still David had unwittingly paid for the tickets to the stripper show – with backstage meet and greet – so Riley decided to do the right thing.

"Always," she replied.

She walked toward where he sat on the bed like a sultry catwalk model. Wriggling her body in a smooth motion in front of him, she let him put his hands on her hips. Slowly she lifted her crop top jumper over her head. His tongue was licking her tanned flat stomach. Continuing dancing a little longer as she ran her hands through her hair and down over her torso, she gyrated and then performed a slow sexy twist to slip out of her skirt. Semi-naked, she stopped for him to drink in the view. Her eyes flickered downward and she saw the short, stubby penis standing to erection in a rubber sheath. She hoped a blow job wasn't on the cards that afternoon. Riley was intending on getting away with the speediest most perfunctory sex possible.

David began humming a tune; bopping his head slightly waiting for the strip tease to continue. Reaching round her, he squeezed a buttock as a sign of encouragement. Riley shook her head and quickly grounded herself. She wanted to tear her bra off but slowly unclasped it and let each strap fall from her shoulder. She leant forward to shake the bra off and covered her bosom with her hands. When she returned to an upright position, she was completely naked apart from her panties. David tried to pull her hands away. His impatience was irritating. He knew nothing of sensuality.

"He's not even worthy of me giving this lap dance my everything," she thought.

When he made a further attempt to move her hands, Riley let her breasts be exposed. He squeezed them like a schoolboy seeing his first pair of tits. He opted for a grab and squeeze which elicited no pleasure whatsoever for Riley.

"Make them jiggle," he commanded.

"They'll jiggle fine when I'm riding you 'Daddy-O'."

Riley pushed him in the center of his sternum to indicate he should relax back. He went down immediately, only to bounce straight back up.

"I want to see your cunt."

Annoyed, Riley bobbed down, pushing her underwear as she went and stood up completely naked. She widened her stance and raised her hands up above her head as if forming the letter "X".

His banana fingers flicked her labia. He strummed the lips back and forth before giving them a hard pinch.

"You aren't wet," he complained.

"I am now."

Riley took his hand and placed it on her crotch. She positioned his fingers so that when she manually directed the motion of his hand to rub around her it was pleasurable, and the juices finally flowed.

"That's a good girl," he sighed, leaning back.

She purposefully mounted him. As hard as he was, he needed direction to get inside her. Reaching between her legs she grabbed his shaft roughly. He inhaled sharply. She pinched the head of his cock between her finger and thumbs.

"Tit for tat," she thought.

Blocking the eye of his cock with her thumb she pressed down hard and when she released felt the pre-cum oozing from it. With his bum hanging slightly over the edge of the mattress she was able to cup his balls. At first, she held them lightly as if trying to guess their weight in her hands. Then she pulled down and gave the sack a sharp twist while letting her palm slide up and down his shaft, lest he realise it wasn't a sex trick but rather a little spite on Riley's part.

Riley moved up and onto his cock. With some slight movement she was able to slip the tip of his dick into her slit. She settled on his stick. Hands on his shoulders for balance, Riley tried to inch the unremarkable prick in as far as it could go. Once she felt David wriggling his own hips to get in her she realized he was in as deep as he was able to reach. All she needed to do was start the motion. David would take control from there.

David was aware how promptly he climaxed with Riley and hoped he'd eventually get used to her pussy so it would take more than minutes to complete the act. The snugness of her slit, with him being able to access and spread her arse cheeks enlivened his pace. Within a short few motions of diving into Riley, his cock exploded swiftly.

"That was that then," thought Riley, knowing she'd be using a vibrator to finish herself off.

"I was hoping we might go again later?"

Riley raised an eyebrow.

"I have to pop out for a meeting, but I've booked the room for the entire night. Enjoy it," he said.

"Will wonders never cease," she thought.

"How long will you be?" she asked.

"My schedule is no business of yours."

Fully dressed David left without another word.

"There is a car park I can direct you to ma'am, but we do have a complimentary valet service."

The boy prayed he sounded friendly and helpful as the lady in the car appeared highly agitated.

"I'm not actually a guest so is that service even available to visitors? I don't know what to do. What will be quicker? I'm running late. I have to meet someone at the bar."

She was way too foxy, for Jacob not to play the white knight in shining armor.

"Honestly ma'am, if you pass me the keys and take this token, our team will look after the rest. No cost, no fuss. I can even take you directly to the bar if you aren't familiar with your way round the hotel."

Faith didn't have time to focus, but the voice was warm and confident. Her gut said to trust the young man. Impulsively she leapt out of the car and gave Jacob the keys.

"But I need you to take me to the bar too."

Jacob slid a token in her palm and passed her keys to a colleague to deal with.

"Follow me."

He placed his hand on her elbow to ensure she didn't trip on the small stairs leading into the hotel reception.

"Do you know which bar you're going to ma'am?"

"There's more than one?"

"There's quite a few at the New Victorian. Our hotel has some of the best features of its time. The bars we have include-"

"Just the reception bar," she snapped, immediately regretting her tone.

"Well, you're in luck. It's on this floor and straight through here.

Jacob walked her across the reception area to a cozy snug area that had the feel of an English pub.

"I'll see you later?" she asked apologetically.

He nodded politely.

"You absolutely will be, you fiery little MILF," he thought.

Faith walked in and saw David drinking. She couldn't remember the last time he'd taken her out for a drink. She couldn't remember the last time she'd seen him outside of the home. Maybe this was a small gesture to indicate he thought their almost unsalvageable marriage was worth saving.

She smiled and he kissed her cheek.

"Hi Darling, sorry I'm late," she began.

"That's fine. I haven't been waiting too long."

"Good. I'd hate to inconvenience you."

"You might have though. Why the delay?"

His tone was icy.

"I wasn't sure where to park the car and -"

"Faith, this hotel is now a focal point of the city. It's not some tucked away B&B off the beaten track. It's an actual architectural landmark, but you couldn't find it?"

"That wasn't the problem so much as parking."

"Because the multi story car park behind the building wasn't a dead giveaway."

"I must've missed it. I was distracted. Worried about being late."

"Yes well don't go on about it," he snapped.

Faith smiled nervously. David was short tempered and impatient at the best of times but today he seemed very on edge and anxious which weren't normal personality traits.

"Was there something you wanted to say?"

Faith used her softest, most compassionate voice, not knowing it was only flaming the fans of David's anger.

"Well obviously Faith or I wouldn't have asked to see you, would I?"

"You might feel better if you just come out and say it, David."

"I might? Well yes, I might. But you might just find you don't feel better once I've said."

Faith's stomach dropped. A wave of nausea washed over her. Something ominous was coming.

"I'm sure I'll be fine."

"You're sure you'll be fine, are you Faith? Well Faith, how fine are you going to be when I tell you we're over. I'm leaving you. The marriage is done. Do you still feel fine now Faith?" he sneered.

A flicker of shock crossed Faith's face as she processed the news, but she didn't feel like vomiting. It was as though a physical weight dropped off her. Her chest suddenly felt lighter when she breathed. She shook her head and shoulders as if flinging off the shackles from this bad mistake that had been dragging on for years.

"Well David, that's wonderful. I'm happy for us. I can see we'll both benefit from this."

"Putting on a brave face?"

"Not at all. We ran our course. We have two lovely children who you might see a little more of if you don't feel obligated to busy yourself at work so you can avoid being in the house with me."

"I wasn't busy at work. I'm in love with another woman. I need to be free to marry her."

Faith threw her head back and laughed with gay abandon.

"Oh David, poor thing. I do hope she knows what she's getting into with you. Still, I wish you the best. It's even more reason to be cordial and sort out the divorce as quickly as possible."

"I'll be in touch. I'm staying at my flat in town."

David stalked off. Rubbing her chin, Faith smiled.

"Good, I'm glad you're gone," she thought.

Unexpectedly tears pricked her eyes. She didn't want David. She didn't want to be married to him a moment longer. But she didn't want someone leaving her because they found her physically repugnant.

"Is this all I am now? A forty-something mum, with two college kids that don't need me and only a part time bookkeeping job to keep me employed," she thought. "It doesn't paint an attractive picture to any prospective suitors."

She grasped the drink David bought her and she threw it down in one go. Then realized he'd bought her a sugar free soft drink. He couldn't even stretch to splashing the cash on an alcoholic drink when telling someone he'd been married for twenty years that he'd been having an affair and was leaving them. David's tumbler remained untouched. Faith finished that and was rewarded with some kind of drink that included a double shot of dark rum.

She looked at the girl behind the bar who smiled comfortingly.

"One on the house?"

"Best not. I'm driving home. I don't suppose you'd be able to direct me to my car?"

"Sure. Go out the door and turn right for the lifts. The car park floor will be marked on the button,"

"Thank you."

Faith followed the directions. She entered the car park. It was full of cars but not a valet in sight. Faith immediately realized the confusion. She should've just gone to the front of the hotel where the valets were and given them the token to bring the car directly to her.

"I'm telling you mate – she was unreal. Totally out of my league. But still a yummy mummy that needed me to give her a good seeing too."

Around the corner of the car were two valets. One stopped mid-sentence. Faith clocked the loudmouth as the one who'd been helpful earlier.

"I've been ever so silly. I'm lost and I need to locate the valet station so one of you can pick up my car. Jacob gave her a cheeky smile – wondering if she knew he'd been talking about her.

"I can walk you to your car and we can save you going back and forth. You can just drive out."

"Fantastic. Jacob is it?" she asked reading his badge.

"At your service ma'am."

His friend waved and walked on.

"Just need your token to identify where you're parked."

Faith offered the token in her hand. Jacob's hand went over hers and he drew it slowly off her palm while keeping eye contact. Faith flushed and felt a damp patch on her underwear.

"I think he's flirting with me," she thought.

"That meeting wasn't too long."

"There wasn't a lot that had to be said to be honest. There's only so many ways you can say it's over."

Faith covered her mouth. She couldn't believe she'd revealed that to a stranger.

"What a loser!" scowled Jacob.

"I suppose I am."

Jacob stopped.

"Not you – him. You look like you stepped off the cover of a magazine."

She laughed.

"We're at your car."

Jacob held up the keys and pressed a button for the car boot to open.

"Nothing to put in there," giggled Faith, reaching up to pull it down.

Jacob stood behind her to put his hands on her waist. She froze.

"You can say no," he whispered in her ear.

Faith turned and reached to put her hand through his brown curly hair. His skin felt so young and unblemished on her palm as she stroked his face. This probably wasn't the right thing to do, but sometimes you needed to do the wrong thing to feel right.

"This is silly," she stopped.

He put his hands on the open boot and stepped closer to her, pushing his stocky, muscular body against her. Jacob was only an inch taller than Faith in heels, but the brown waves that framed his face and the stormy blue eyes set on his chiseled face was hard to resist.

"How old are you Jacob?"

"I'm twenty-one"

"I have an eighteen-year-old daughter and nineteen-year-old son you know."

"I didn't but that's pretty sexy."

"Jacob, I'm too old for games."

"This isn't a game, it's...whatever you want it to be. Let's call it a little pick-me-up."

With that, Jacob lifted her and sat Faith on the edge of the inside of the car boot.

"Stop thinking and over analyzing and let your body do whatever it wants. I only want to serve you," he promised.

She tilted her head for a kiss. It was stupid but she would've sworn he tasted young. His hands were on her thighs, rolling up her skirt as she lost herself in his luscious lips. He shoved inexpertly at the material.

Faith raised her bum so he could roll the skirt to her hips. The car was parked in a private area, but she felt exposed with a stranger gazing at her semi-naked body.

"This is somewhat wonderful," murmured Jacob.

All Faith could think was that she didn't have a thigh gap, All Jacob could think was how wonderfully soft and tantalizing it was to touch and manipulate her flesh to finally touch her wet pussy.

His breathing was heavy. Faith lay down and raised her feet on the edge of the boot to completely expose her pussy. Looking downward, Jacob started undoing his trousers. As he pushed the waist band of his boxers lower and slid on a condom, Faith couldn't help but admire the length of his prick. Long and in his prime, it was so erect it almost went to his belly button.

He put his hand over her panties and rubbed her clit.

"Can I take these off?"

"Of course." replied Faith breathily.

Possessed by his need for her, Jacob tore them off. He brought them to his face to inhale deeply.

"Can I keep them?"

Faith nodded, feeling both bemused and besotted.

"I want to make you come," he said boldly.

"Keep doing what you're doing."

Jacob let his thumb slip in her juices to run it over her clit. He varied the speed of the circles and pressure he put on her bud. Every so often he'd stop to lick his fingers; making sure Faith could see what he was doing.

Faith felt like there was a flood between her legs. She was close to the brink. All he had to do was penetrate her and the orgasm would be upon her.

"Jacob,' she pleaded.

"Tell me how you want me to fuck you," he demanded.

"Fuck me how you want me."

Jacob threw her legs over his shoulders. His fat head burst through her slit causing her to cry aloud. Biting back her scream, Jacob hesitated momentarily to check she was okay.

"For God's sake don't stop," she growled.

 Dragging her onto his mighty shaft he slammed into her repeatedly. Fast and furious so his balls were slapping against her. Faith's hands were searching the boot of the car to try and find something to steady herself.

Jacob stopped suddenly.

"I wanna see your tits. I wanna make them bounce."

She unbuttoned her blouse. Jacob reached in to pull her bra down and reveal the breasts Faith thought were droopy from breastfeeding, but he saw as fulsome and feminine.

"Fuck me hard!"

With full permission granted, Jacob got lost in the feelings and delight of mastering a MILF and adding her to his list of conquests. It didn't take long for him to finally reach his climax. Grabbing her hips, he took a final thrust – stabbing so hard she cried in pain at the length of him hitting her cervix and eliciting a new range of sexual thrills she'd never encountered. He stood there a moment; eyes closed, brushing one hand across her breasts, leaving the other to rest on the thin strip of hair on her pubis.

"Literally the best," he affirmed as he withdrew from her to assist her out of the boot and cover her modesty while she arranged her clothing to something more presentable.

"You've made an old lady very happy," she joked.

Now both fully dressed he kissed her again.

"Can I give you my number in case you're ever in need of a pick-me-up again?" he asked.
Faith nearly snatched the phone from his hand to enter her number in his mobile. He rang the number she'd entered and winked when it rang in her handbag – that was one number he wouldn't be ghosting.

David had been riding the glass elevator lift for some time in a bid to calm him down. Faith's reaction to ending their marriage had been nonplussed. It was as if it was an out she'd been waiting for forever. Still, she didn't have some pretty young thing waiting for her, like he had his little pocket rocket waiting for him and tonight he'd make her commit fully.

Finally departing the lift on his floor, he opened the door to their room.

"Hey," greeted Riley, not looking up from her phone.

"Can I have your attention please!"

She dropped her phone dramatically and stared at him expectantly.

"I need you to be serious."

"Fine, David, I'm serious," she said, sitting cross-legged on the bed and adopting a more neutral expression.

This wasn't how he intended to do it, but David's judgement was clouded with red. Instead of executing his original plan he decided to blurt it out now. He needed to know her answer – to be happy with his earlier decision.

"I've just told my wife I want a divorce so I can marry you."

Riley's face went pale. He hoped it was from disbelief.

"You want to marry me?"
"That's what I said. Here," he thrusted a ring-box over to her.

"Oh David, no. No, no, no. This was just a... I never thought you were serious...We were never meant to be forever. We were filling in time till you found your next fling or started appreciating your wife again."

"But we're so great together,' he spluttered.

"No, we're not. You like having a trophy on your arm and I liked you buying me things, but come on. I need a big dick, a man that knows how to please a woman, someone that has sex with me because they love me, not to make themselves feel better about being middle-aged. I want someone that runs riot with me at the buffet. Someone who'll eat all the desserts together with me and then collapse in bed together in a food coma – not some arsehole who dictates what size I should be."

Riley got up and grabbed her backpack. There was nothing more to say.

"See you never!" she called as the door slammed behind her.

Cashing In On Curiosity

The blue sky moved slowly. The clouds were fluffy and white on the idyllic blue backdrop. A perfect summer sky. Walking along the canal, Rachel noticed an abandoned gondola. She began crossing a picturesque bridge but stopped in the middle to lean on the rails to admire the Italian brick structure of the shopping mall.

"You'd have no idea what the time is if you got lost in here," she thought.

There was a large town clock further down the mall which you could use if desperate, but the beautiful surroundings were designed to help people forget the time.

Rachel inhaled deeply. There was no smell of nature. No fishy waft from the canal. Everything was artificial. As if somehow a little slice of Venice had been relocated into the New Victorian hotel. The moving sky and water, the colors and detailed reconstruction were enthralling to a first-time visitor. However as someone who worked day in and day out of the mall it felt fake. It felt like a trap. In essence it was. Go to the casino, win big, then go to the mall and spend all your winnings on gold or designer labels.

She walked into a women's fashion shop.

"Just in time for the rush."

"How can there ever be a rush if the house always wins?" asked Rachel.

"That's a good question and one I don't have the answer to. All I know is this job keeps our fridge full and a roof over our head."

"Don't you ever find it a bit depressing. Preying on people's addiction?"

Becky considered Rachel.

"If we worked in the casino maybe. They definitely exploit people's addiction and vulnerabilities. But we're retail. People only come here if they have the money to spend. We don't offer credit cards or loans. If you win you spend. If you lose you go home. I sleep with a pretty clear conscience."

Rachel kissed Becky's cheek.

"I know you do. It feels a little empty at times."

"Rachel, we flunked out of high school. We're lucky we have jobs. And there are opportunities to learn here and step up the ladder. I'd say we've landed on our feet being employed here," consoled Becky.

"We're lucky we have each other."

"Sure we are," agreed Becky absentmindedly.

"I hate it when you do that," said Rachel, trying to keep her voice light.
"Do what?" sighed Becky.

"Dismiss us. What we have."

"I don't dismiss us," laughed Becky. "You are literally my favorite person in the whole wide world. Why are you being such a prickly pear today?"

"I'm not. I just think we're as fake as the faux Venice out there."

"What is this about really?" enquired Becky.

"Us. We're lucky to have each other. I'm your favorite person. Mum this is my best friend. Dad, this is my flatmate. Always forgetting to tell anyone we're so close we share a bed together."

"You're feeling insecure?"

"I'm not feeling insecure. We've been together since 9th grade. But, here at work, you treat me like a friend."

"What do you want me to do? Ravish you on the counter?" grinned Becky.

"Maybe. If it meant people knowing what we mean to each other."

"Rachel, private relationships are exactly that. They're private and stay out of the workplace. You don't see married couples getting it on when they're at work do you."

"Fine. I just feel like our relationship is so private only you and I are aware of it."

"Does it matter who knows if we're happy."

"But I'm not happy," shouted Rachel.

A few faces from the assistants in other shops pushed their faces to the windows or looked out the door to get a view of the bubbling argument.

"What can I do to make you happy."

"Say we're together. Tell people I'm your girlfriend."

"Why do you need a label?" exasperated Becky.

"Because it's been years. I hang around and I'm always a friend."

"That's because I'm not sure what I want and who I want."

"What?" Rachel was beginning to wish she'd never broached the topic.

"I don't want to call you my girlfriend because I'm not sure I'm a lesbian."
"You don't have to say you're a lesbian. There are a million labels to pick from. Pan-sexual or - "

"Rachel, I don't feel a need to define myself. I can't define myself," snapped Becky.

"Well, we've been together for 7 years. You've never had sex with anyone else. You can be pretty certain of your label..."

"That's the whole point. How can either of us say we're lesbian if we've never slept with a man."

A silence fell between them. It felt as though hours were passing by, but if either Rachel or Becky were able to see the clock then they would see it was only minutes. Becky sent a silent prayer out for a customer to come in, but nothing came back.

"I didn't know you wanted to sleep with a man," Rachel admitted quietly.

"I don't. If I'd wanted to, I'd have done it. That's how you should know I'm in love with you. But because we've been together forever and only with each other we've never really been tested. We've never tried anything new or different."

"Is this a roundabout way of saying you want to break up?"

Rachel's question sounded defeated.

"No," said Becky, smilingly lovingly at her. "This is me asking you to be open minded."

"You want an open relationship. You want to fuck around?"

"It's not even that. I don't want to wave a rainbow flag and put a label on myself. I want to make sure we're right together. I love you but I don't want to go through our relationship wondering what if? I don't want you going through our relationship feeling like I settled with you and then insecure I am always looking for something else."

Rachel pushed aside her personal hurt and realized it wasn't an unreasonable point of view.

"If you want a hall pass you have one."

"That's not how I want us to do this. Aren't you curious in the slightest? Wouldn't you like to try a guy before putting all your eggs in my basket?"

"I don't think I like boys, but now you've said it out loud. It'd be nice to know I tested my label," said Rachel thoughtfully.

"Then this doesn't have to be an open relationship or hall pass scenario. What if we both spend a night with a guy? Did the deed. Then after having that experience made an informed decision on how our relationship goes forward."

"So, you're saying going forward it might change?"

"I hope not, but we have to be aware it's a possibility," said Becky bluntly.

"How do we even arrange this?"

"Easy. We exploit people's vulnerabilities. Find a big winner in the casino who's high on the win and offer him a threesome. No man is going to turn down two women and we get the chance to explore our sexuality"

She was right it would work.

"One stipulation," said Rachel.

"I'm listening."

"Afterwards we go home together, and you let me make love to you. Then in the morning you can decide if you're still bi-curious."
"Deal," agreed Becky offering her hand.

Rachel shook it.

After their shift finished the girls "borrowed" two designer outfits and accessories from the storeroom of the shop they worked in. They convinced their colleagues from the cosmetics store to provide them with the free make-up service usually reserved to encourage customers to make a purchase. Heading down the various escalators, as they set foot in the casino, they were confident they could turn more heads than the swarm of professional gold diggers that frequented the venue each day.

"How do we even know who the high rollers and big winners are?" asked Rachel.

"I've given Liam the heads up that we need a sexy, single winner. He's going to text me the best table to go to when he's found someone that fits the spec."

Liam was a mutual friend who worked as a croupier. Rachel couldn't help but think that Becky's sudden compulsion to have an encounter with a man was not completely spur of the moment. She'd obviously thought about it long and hard and planned it out in her head. Given Liam's willingness to assist, she suspected that Becky had talked it over with other people as well.

Becky's phone vibrated. She pointed her finger at a table. Rachel followed her, nodding at Liam who was dealing cards to the people at his table. She could see the man who had stacks of chips in front of him. Glamorous female vultures hovered round the table to see how the next game of blackjack would unfold. He won and the chips were doubled again.

His appearance in a Bond-style tux was smooth and sophisticated but the over-the-top reaction to his win suggested he wasn't an old hand in the casino. Becky and Rachel clapped politely at his win. Becky could see various women coming closer to swoop in and collect titbits from this fresh, young winner. She grabbed Rachel's hand, forcing herself next to the winner.

"Wanna party, big boy?"

"The name's Simon, but big boy is also appropriate – if you get my drift."

Rachel wanted to laugh at the absurdity of the invitation, but the man snaked his arms round their hips and started to the cashier's desk to cash out his chips.

"Try and make an effort please," whispered Becky as they waited. "He's currently minted and looking to show off. We could lose him very quickly if someone prettier and more tactile comes along."

"The things we do for love," thought Rachel.

Winking at Becky, Rachel linked her arm through Simon's then whispered in his ear.

"Let's get up to my room."

By the time they arrived at his upgraded room, the staff had warmed the hot tub and surrounded the small pool with plenty of champagne buckets. Not wanting the dresses they couldn't afford to be damaged, the girls literally stripped off as they walked through the room. By the time they reached the hot tub they were in their bras and panties.

"I must be dreaming," murmured Simon as he watched the young women sink into the tub. He disrobed and hopped in the tub with them. The girls sat on either side of him. Rachel had to admit he was a fine specimen of a man, if you liked bodybuilders with boyish good looks. Becky was already latched onto his lips. Rachel's hand touched the smooth, tan skin of his collarbone and let her hands explore his torso. He felt so different to a woman. Soft but firm at the same time – hard muscles with a weight she imagined to be comforting if crushed on top of her. She moved her hand to his muscular thighs to drag her nails on the inside of his leg.

Moaning, he released Becky for air then turned his face to Rachel. She kissed him. The lips were eager, and the tongue was like a washing-machine. She could sense he was drunk and determined to make the most of his good luck at having landed a big win and two lovely ladies for the night. As her hand crept further up his thigh toward the bulge in his boxers, Rachel's fingers brushed against Becky's. Becky was clearly determined to become accustomed with cock tonight.

A wave of jealousy washed over her. Undoing her bra, with the assistance of the water, Rachel was able to straddle Simon. In doing so she pushed Becky's hand from his hard-on. Leaning back, her breasts lifted from the water. Simon's mouth latched onto them. Rachel smiled pointedly at Becky as his tongue licked and explored the flesh of her rounded bosom. Grinding on his erect cock to tease Becky, she couldn't help but feel her slit tingle at the thought of it filling her up.

"Hey Simon, we'd both like a little action but we're not mermaids. How about letting us see what feels so good down there," suggested Becky.

"One girl's attention is fun, but two girls would be ideal," thought Simon.

Lifting himself out of the hot tub, he let his boxers float off. He sat on the edge of the tub - legs spread wide with eight inches ready and waiting for the girls whose names he didn't even know.

Becky looked longingly at the erection and began to lick the shaft from base to tip. Rachel saw Simon's body shiver in response. She felt Becky's hand hold hers and incline her toward Simon. Shifting her small frame, Becky ensured there was enough space for Rachel to get in on the action. Rachel closed her eyes to share the pink prick with her lover. The erection was hard and smooth and even in the cold air she could feel it pulsating under her tongue. She followed Becky's lead by tasting the length. When Becky wrapped her head round the mouth of his dick, Rachel bobbed down in the water to open her mouth to suck on Simon's balls. As they filled her mouth, she closed her lips and tugged them down slightly. Simon grunted in excitement. Rachel was pleased it was her affection that was generating his primal groans.

Becky released Simon from her mouth to take Rachel's place in tending to his sack. Rachel stared at the swollen dick. The small slit in the top of the head oozed a clear liquid. She licked it and was surprised at the saltiness of it. Like a snake, her tongue flicked out and around the dome. Simon's hand went to her head. He held her until Rachel opened her mouth and took in the bulb. She didn't hate his dominance, so found herself moving inch by inch down the shaft. As she swallowed him, he held her head and thrust his hips upward. The erection shot deep in her mouth, causing her to gag. The fat dick deep in her mouth had her nipples buzzing and her pussy wet.

She looked up at Simon.

"Let me ride you," she mouthed.

Simon lowered himself back into the hot tub. Becky swam to the other side at the sudden change in position. Before she could get involved, Rachel was back straddling Simon.

"Ease me on," Rachel said audibly.

Becky couldn't believe Rachel was getting the cock first when it was her that was so desperate to try.

Simon's hands were on her hips. He let Rachel place her pussy lips over the head of his prick. Holding tightly, he pushed through. Rachel's hands gripped like a vice as he forced the head in. She squealed as he burst through. She was tight and felt brand new to him. Looking at her face, she was biting her lip and nodding; encouraging him to plant himself inside her. He pulled her down his ample shaft gradually – letting her tight cunt stretch and encompass him. He kept his hands on her hips to keep her on him once he was fully inside her.

Rachel was enamored by how organic and satisfying Simon's dick felt inside her. She circled her hips round the base of his shaft so that his cock would stimulate her internally. As she felt the pain of her first invasion diminishing, she was able to rock back and forth on him. As the pace increased, she was able to lift up and down his shaft until they were in a state of active fucking.

Becky felt like an outsider but realized Simon had pretty base needs. She returned next to them. Arms resting on the hot tub edge, the seat was wide enough for her to kneel on in a doggy position.

"Don't forget about me," she reminded him.

Simon looked at her and grinned at her wriggling arse. He lifted Rachel off him then swept aside to stand in the hot tub behind Becky. Working his shaft between her pussy lips and with no idea it was her first time, Simon let his hands grab her shoulders as he forced his eight inches directly into her pussy. Rachel saw Becky's face contort at the action and rubbed her back.

"Get next to her so I can swap between the two of you," he proposed.

Rachel liked the idea. It should've been like this from the beginning. The two girls next to each other being serviced accordingly by the man. She climbed on the seat, placed her arms on the hot tub edge and mirrored Becky's position. Becky turned her head to catch her eyes. The two girls kissed as a peace-making gesture between one another. As Rachel was enjoying her lovers lips, she felt the shaft diving into her cunt. The ramming of the rod in and out of her was divine. He put in a minute on Rachel and returned to Becky and so forth. The girls were blissfully squirming on his cock, turned on at the thought that they were sharing the same dick.

As Rachel bounced up and down his shaft, Becky mouthed at her, "Don't let him come!"

Simon's pace built. His hands secured even tighter on Rachel's hips. She thrust backward to force him off.

"Time for us to go," giggled Becky, grabbing Rachel's hand to help her from the pool.

The girls ran back into the hotel room to collect their bits and pieces. Simon stood bewildered in the hot tub with a rock-hard cock that needed its ending.
"Think of us as modern day Cinderellas," shouted Rachel as they ran from the hotel room half dressed.

They were able to find a nearby public toilet to change so they didn't call any attention to themselves as they returned to their shop to replace the dresses and thank their colleagues for not letting onto their boss that they'd borrowed the items.

Back in civilian attire, the girls left to go home. They stood quietly at the bus stop, pretending to check their phones to avoid the conversation.

"You still up for fulfilling your stipulation?" asked Becky, when her bus app told her there'd be a ten-minute delay.

"Sure. Why have you changed your mind and turned already?"

Rachel meant to say it playfully but suspected it sounded bitchy.
"No. I thought you might be tired and want to leave it till tomorrow that's all," replied Becky sharply.

Rachel sidled up to her.

"Sorry. It's been a weird night. I don't know how I feel, let alone how you feel. But I do want to make love to you."

"Well, can you try and believe me when I say I want you to make love to me?"

Rachel knew Becky well enough to know she wasn't lying. They linked arms, waiting in companionable silence for the bus to arrive and take them home. Back in their familiar flat, Rachel was gripped with fear that she couldn't really compete with the hot tub setting or that she didn't possess the energy to please Becky in bed. Trouble was, she'd made such a scene about it she couldn't back out now.

"Want some dinner?" she offered Becky, trying to buy herself more time.

"I'm only after dessert and I'm pretty sure you're serving that up in the bedroom," purred Becky.

"It's now or never," thought Rachel, taking Becky's hand and leading her straight into their bedroom.

She slowly lifted Becky's shirt over her head. Kissing her lips, she expertly removed her bra. Rachel sat on the edge of the bed and tugged Becky over. She unbuttoned her jeans to watch them fall to the floor. Becky climbed naked over the mattress. Rachel stood and took a few steps from the bed to perform for Becky. Seductively she removed her dress, pushing the shoe-string straps over her shoulders and letting the light material slither down her body. Her hands went behind her back as she released her best assets from the basic cotton bra. She let her breasts swing and happily observed Becky staring at them. Knowing her curvy feminine body was Becky's main physical attraction to her, she did a 180 then swayed her hips as she rolled the tiny briefs over her booty.

Kneeling onto the mattress where Becky was sitting, she placed her nipple between Becky's lips. Becky sucked and let her hand move between Rachel's thighs. Her fingers went between Rachel's labia. Becky sucked harder on the nipple excited by the sensation of Rachel's wetness. Rachel got on all fours, forcing Becky to lie back. Pulling her tit from Becky's mouth, she let her bosom dangle in Becky's face. Becky spread her legs. Rachel moved one leg between Becky's. She pushed her knee up to Becky's crotch. Becky began grinding against it. Rachel could feel how drenched Becky was rubbing her pussy against her leg.

Moving her entire body between Becky's spread legs, she backed down the mattress to look at her lover's pussy. She confidently let two fingers slide into the slit. Becky moaned as Rachel inserted, twisted, then pulled the fingers from her. She buried them in again and continued letting her roam round her pussy. Expertly Rachel located Becky's G-spot and stimulated it until Becky was pleading with her to stop. Taking her to the brink, Rachel stopped before she could climax.

She slithered up Becky's slight frame trailing kisses from her mound lazily up her torso, eventually stopping at Becky's small apple sized breasts. She opened her mouth wide. As easily as she'd taken in Simon's balls, she was able to take in all of Becky's tit. She bit firmly on the soft plump skin, causing Becky to whimper in delight. As she sucked and nibbled the breast, Rachel began rubbing herself against the thigh of Becky's she had straddled. She squeezed her thighs tightly round Becky's to rub her mound hard to build friction between her clit and Becky's upper leg. She forced her teeth harder on the breast and used a hand to pinch and squeeze Becky's free tit. As Simon hadn't bought them to climax, she was keen to ensure both Becky and herself were satisfied. Releasing Becky's breast from her mouth, she kissed her deeply, giving her nipple a final pinch to make her squirm. She nuzzled her neck. Taking little bites round the sensitive neck skin elicited a series of delighted sighs from Becky.

Snaking back down her, Rachel shifted her weight to indicate to Becky to part her legs to let Rachel between them. Rachel crouched to study Becky's pink pussy. She let her thumbs go to the labia and spread them wide. She could see her clit was engorged. Flicking her tongue over and around her clit, Becky moaned loudly. Rachel didn't want her too frustrated too early, so took her lips to the red slit which had been visibly aggravated by Simon's dick. Slowly she began to draw an outline of every geometric shape she could remember from school. Becky's hips were bucking as the tongue teased her slit with a series of different lines.

Rachel crawled to the edge of the bed to pull out a drawer from the base of the bed where they kept their sex toys. She grabbed a double ended dildo. It had the length to stretch into both their slits but wasn't ridiculously thick like an obscene sex toy only a hardened porn star could physically accommodate. With a deliberate unhurried pace, she began inserting the vibrant, orange colored flexible rubber into Becky's pussy. Becky squealed with gay abandon. Placing her feet either side of Becky's hips, Rachel was able to move her bottom to seat herself between Becky's open thighs. Declining slightly Rachel was able to bend the dildo to insert it into herself. She only needed a few inches in slit after Simon's earlier fucking. Sitting at an angle, she grasped the middle of the dildo between their two pussies to move it back and forth. It was the perfect controlled thrusting. Becky raised herself on her elbows so she could see the dildo moving in and out of her own pussy and also in and out of Rachel's.

Becky's eyes lit up at the vibrator Rachel held in the hand that wasn't working the double-ended dildo. Rachel's thumb hit the button on the base and the vibrator started buzzing. She placed it on her own clit to allow Becky's excitement to grow at the sight of her pleasuring herself. As Becky started panting, she placed the vibrator on Becky's clit. Becky fell backward on the bed to let Rachel work her pussy. Doing her best to bring them to a joint climax, Rachel continued mutually fucking them both with the dildo and teasing their clits with the vibrator, stopping the second she felt herself close to climax or sensing Becky was.

Suspecting they were both ready, Rachel turned off the vibrator then yanked the dildo from their holes and tossed the toys on the carpet. Angling her legs round Becky, she pulled Becky to her in a scissor position. She could feel the heat from her pussy. The second their mounds met the girls rubbed against one another's pussy. Becky was first to reach her climax, kneading furiously against Rachel's hot cunt. As soon as Becky started moaning and writhing, Rachel ground hard and reached her own delicious climax.

The girls languished between each other's limbs as they caught their breath and allowed the electric sensations to subside.

"Okay you win," conceded Becky. "It's better with you. It'll always be better with you."

"Told you so."

"You proved yourself to me today. After tonight I can see we are in it together forever. I'm kind of looking forward to calling you my girlfriend."

As Rachel licked her lips enjoying the sweet intoxicating taste of Becky's pussy, she thought about Simon's prick and the easy delight it bought her.

"I think you're right though – we don't really need labels to define us. Let's just see how things pan out. We've started something tonight – let's not rule it out just yet."
Becky couldn't describe the odd feeling in her stomach but would later learn it was regret.

Conference Room 69

Josie woke up a minute before her alarm went off. Taking her phone, she disabled the alarm before it could wake her husband. Slipping out of bed, she put on her dressing gown and left the master bedroom to head down the stairs.

"Hey team, up and at 'em. It's another happy day at school."

She heard moaning from her children and knew they'd be back into their pillows snoring within minutes if she didn't take action.

"Come on."

She walked into her eldest daughter's room and pulled the duvet off.

"Mummmmmmm," screamed her sixteen-year-old. The blonde hair and blue eyes made her look angelic, but she was already proving to be a little devil in and out of school. She was not to be trusted ever with going to school unattended because Josie would only be the recipient of a call on her lunchbreak from the headmaster asking why Carrie was not at school. When that happened she'd be stuck coming up with an excuse for her daughter's truancy while in a panic that Carrie might be off somewhere with a teenage Romeo becoming a teen-mum or worse yet already pregnant and auditioning for a cable channel reality TV show about teen mothers.

"I'm up, I'm up," protested her youngest son, Cody. "Not likely I was going to go back to sleep with Satan incanting in there is it?"

Josie smiled. Younger kids were normally troublesome and attention seeking, but he had an easy nature and good humor. He wasn't quite blessed with his father's good looks to be a middle school ladies' man, so was infinitely less trouble than his older sister. She ruffled his hair.

Josie raced up the stairs. Her husband was already showered and dressed.

"I've got an early start," he reminded her.

"I know. We talked about it last night. I'll drop the kids off on my way to the training session."

"Where's that happening again?"

"At the New Victorian. If the conference rooms are up to standard, we might be able to convince the bosses to throw the Christmas party there."

"At the prices they charge? Good luck!"

He kissed her quickly on the cheek, smacked her bum playfully, then padded silently downstairs, calling goodbye to the kids on his way.

Josie rushed to get herself suited and booted for the training session. Most people would be using the excuse of being out of the office to dress down, but Josie thought it was more of a reason to look professional and business-like as they were ambassadors for the firm in a public place.

For once the kids were on time and there were no huge issues with forgotten lunches or last-minute excuse notes for Physical Education. Mindful of the time, Josie didn't want to risk a call regarding absenteeism so made sure the kids were through the school gates for a good five minutes before continuing to work.

She pulled into the car park that was constructed to cater for all the hotel's visitors.

"Josie!"

Her smile brightened instinctively as she recognised the voice.

"Elijah!"
Elijah jogged over. He was wearing a three-piece-suit that looked bespoke. It clung to his frame and accentuated his broad hips and narrow shoulders.

"What perfect timing," he laughed. "Now I don't have to deal with the social anxiety of being the first or last person to go in."

"We're a team," said Josie lightly.

"We are," grinned Elijah, placing a friendly arm round her shoulder.

"Did the terrible twosome cause any disasters this morning?" he asked.

"They didn't. In fact, they were so agreeable I'm worried now I missed something."

"Don't be so suspicious. Even teenagers have the odd good day."

"Does yours?"

"Never. Teenage life is so dramatic. I don't even need to watch soaps. I get the kids to tell me about their day."

"God he's perfect," thought Josie. "Family man, perfect work life balance…lovely wife. Maybe he's not always perfect," she conceded.

There were many work functions that started out as conference, training, or bonding days that always ended with Josie and Elijah overstepping the boundaries of their respective marriages. It wasn't that Josie didn't love her husband and she knew Elijah loved his wife, but when you spend fifty hours a week sharing an office with someone – How do you not get attached? How do you not discover everything about them? How do you not develop your own special bond? How do you not learn all your shared common interests? How could the familiarity not become attractive?

There had always been the questionable brush of fingers as he lent over her keyboard or their bodies touching as they moved past each other in the corridors of the office. Little incidents that were innocent but exciting. But at work functions, when the booze was flowing, when partners weren't present, where secluded spots could easily be located - that's when there'd be an illicit kiss. A fumble. Playful touching to see who was most turned on. Actions for which she would throw her husband out of the house for if the situation was reversed. Josie wasn't sure how she and Elijah justified their relationship, but butterflies were already swarming her stomach for the day ahead.

The guilt never lasted long enough for her to openly broach the subject of their relationship directly with Elijah. She had a feeling labels and commitment might sour the entire friendship and she liked the way things currently were.

"Is this going to be a scintillating professional learning experience or a countdown to the free booze for enduring 7 hours of people talking at us?"

"Six hours and fifty-nine seconds," began Josie.

"Six hours and fifty-eight seconds," continued Elijah.

They walked in the building, greeted colleagues and navigated to their assigned conference room.

In all fairness the company couldn't be accused of being mean with funding – it wasn't only an elaborate venue, but the trainer was engaging and made sure the session was interactive and presented in short blocks with plenty of tea and coffee breaks.

Josie was careful to ensure she and Elijah didn't select each other for every activity. Even during lunch she'd kept her distance and sat with 'the girls' as opposed to the rest of middle-management. The office thrived on gossip and she didn't want her and Elijah being a hot topic – ever. She had a feeling they had aroused suspicion with their general closeness, but nothing had ever been publicized. Her company had family values. It liked to include partners and children at suitable functions and wouldn't take kindly to any scandal – especially extramarital affairs.

Not that she and Elijah were having an affair. They merely liked to be flirty and had occasionally blurred the lines of friendship. Despite deliberately avoiding Elijah for the majority of the day, she was relieved when they were led into a function room with a small portable bar and a DJ in the corner so the attendees could let off steam.

"What's a girl like you doing in a place like this?"

Josie took the glass of wine offered by Elijah.

"How cheesy!"
"I thought I might get you to play along. Wondered where the evening would go if we were strangers in the night."

He sounded amused, but she detected meaning to the words.

"Strangers don't always have the best sex," winked Josie.

"Damn, girl! Are you making a play for me?"

"In your dreams!"

"You certainly are. It's the best place that we meet," he confessed.

His smile was full and reached his eyes, but Josie thought her heart might break. She was in love with him. She had been for some time. It didn't mean she didn't love her husband. She just wanted to open her heart and let Elijah in – even if for a night.
"I'm sorry. I didn't line my stomach. It's the drink," he appeased her dismayed look.

Josie felt tears prick her eyes. She swallowed down a hard lump in her throat, squeezed Elijah's forearm and hurriedly left the room.

"Josie, wait. Where are you going? You don't even know your way round this hotel"

Elijah's hands were on her shoulders. He was a giant of a man. At six foot five she was dwarfed by him; even in heels. He pulled her back into him and she fell against his hard chest. His hands slipped to her waist to drag her closer.

"I didn't mean to upset you," he murmured in her ear.

"You didn't upset me. This – our situation – upsets me. It will always be like this. We'll only ever meet in our dreams."

Elijah took her hand and tried the door of the nearest conference room. Surprisingly it opened. Closing the curtain on the door's windows, he turned the light on. It was the room they were occupying earlier. The set up remained the same in regard to the tables and chairs, but all the refreshments had been cleared away.

"Think they've finished here for the night," he guessed.

He spun her to pull her into his embrace. Gazing down he kissed her tenderly, like a feather brushing her lips. Josie opened her eyes; his chocolate brown eyes and full lips were set perfectly on his structured ebony face.

"We need to take the opportunities life presents us to make moments that we can remember forever. Right here and now. That's the seed for our dreams, Josie."

Josie stroked his face, contemplating his words.
"I know you're right."

She yanked his shirt out and ran her hand under every ripple of muscle on his torso. He stood secured to the spot letting her hands caress him. Josie went to his belt buckle to start undoing it. She could see a healthy nine inches pushing at the whitest of white boxers. She pressed the back of her hand against his hard on. Pulling the boxers down she was greeted with a fleshy, dark shaft. Her fingers went round the girth of the base and she had a sudden urge to ride him. She wanted to feel close to him, but lust had her wanting the big black cock inside her. She gripped his length.

"Josie, I don't think we can."

She stopped. Embarrassed. She'd never gone this far with him, but what else had he wanted taking her into a locked room.

"I'm so sorry," she blustered.
"Me too," he said.

His chest heaved and relaxed. His expression was of a man trying his hardest to remain in control.

"Cheating is horrible," Josie conceded. "And I love my husband and you love your wife."

"Yeah I do," he paused. "But what is cheating?"

"Having sex with someone that's not your partner," she replied instantly.

"And what's sex?"

"You're a grown man with children, you shouldn't be asking that. Penis enters vagina – can result in kids without protection."

They both laughed at the absurdity of the question.

"See if cheating is sex and sex is penetrative, if you and I were," he coughed to cover his fluster. "According to your definition if I don't penetrate you then it's not sex. And if it's not sex, it's not cheating."

Josie kissed him. His semi was hardening to its former fully erect state.

"That works for me."

Elijah took off his blazer, vest, and shirt and folded them neatly into a makeshift pillow. He kicked his trousers and boxers aside. Josie was in awe of how sculptured he was. How daunting his dick was.

"Strip down for me," he requested, stepping in to help her carefully fold each item of clothing she discarded.

He smiled bashfully as she removed her skirt and panties.

"Lie down, rest your head on my stuff," he suggested.

Josie used his folded clothes as a pillow. Elijah stood over her and then got down on all fours. His prick dangled precariously close to her mouth. Josie's hands wrapped around it and guided it to her lips. She licked the head liberally. Letting her tongue run under the rim. She used both hands to grasp and squeeze the shaft.

Elijah spread Josie's legs. The pink plump lips of her pussy were too inviting to resist. His thick tongue parted them, and she squirmed at the intimate invasion from his mouth. He lapped up and down until he had her clit bursting. Sucking on it, he buried his face right into her – pushing his nose at her slit. He wanted to have her juices covering his face. He wanted his face to fuck what he considered to be her beautiful wonderland.

As Elijah tended to Josie, she wanted to return the physical sentiment. She opened her mouth to receive the head of his cock. It stretched her lips wide. She was mindful to widen her jaw, so her teeth didn't cause any damage. Josie sucked on the dome as if she were a toddler having her first lollipop. He tasted extremely different to anything she'd ever had in her mouth. Excited, she tried to take more of the length down her. With her hands still on the shaft she was able to control how deep he went.

As Josie spread her legs wider and wider to make sure her pussy was fully exposed for Elijah's attention, he was able to grip her thighs to keep them open to easily tease the entrance of her cunt with his tongue. Pressing his tongue at the slit, she was thrilled as she started to grind down hard – insinuating that he should enter. He forced his way in there. Fortune favored Elijah with a long dick and a long tongue. He was able to use his tongue like a dildo and poked it in and out of her. The more juices that gushed from her over his face, the more his tongue thrust in a fucking motion.

In the midst of Elijah fucking her pussy with his tongue, Josie lost herself in the moment and forgot the act she was performing on Elijah. Elijah however had been delighted to be invited into her throat. Thinking she was letting him take charge as her hands were no longer wrapped around his shaft to control the depth, Elijah took it as an opportunity to test Josie's limits. He inched deep into her throat. The feeling of her throat gag and reject the cock had him close to the edge but also sensitive to her limits. After her throat clenched and outed him, Josie would gasp for breath before wantonly beckoning the prick back into her mouth.

Height was a bonus in this situation. Elijah had the ability to move a little further along from Josie's cunt. He could see her pink anus on show. He let his tongue dance on the rim and heard Josie squealing in delight. His licks became thick and slow on her arsehole. He used the tip of his tongue to swirl and tease her. Her body didn't know how to react – thighs thrown open but buttocks clenching. Elijah continued and pressed the end of his tongue so hard that it popped into the opening of her arse.

In response Josie's hands immediately gripped and spread Elijah's buttocks. She dug her nails in hard. Elijah loved it. He released her anus and buried his face back into her wet pussy and began thrusting his hips. His dick went low into her throat. He pumped hard. Using her mouth as he would have her pussy. Josie's eyes watered. She loved the intimacy; the monstrous cock filling her throat resulting in her grinding her clit against Elijah's face. But occasionally he went so deep she thought she might vomit instead of gag.

Elijah was near but it was imperative that Josie had the same intensity of climax. He licked furiously as he rhythmically thrust into her mouth. Returning to her clit, he let the thickness of his tongue cover and push on her bud. He knew she was seconds away from bliss. Elijah took a final deep plunge into her mouth and stayed buried deep.

Josie was shocked. Vibrations were emanating from her clit and she was consumed by tremors that would soon propel her to orgasm. Elijah's dick was welcome but as much as she wanted him in there and the thought turned her on, air was escaping her lungs. With her throat stuffed with dick she was unable to gasp for breath. She bucked and pushed at Elijah's thighs. She tightened her hands into fists and pounded at his hard, powerful thighs.

Elijah held his prick a moment longer. When her entire body jolted in need of air, he released his load and allowed his cock to swallow in her throat. As soon as his prick released the pressure on her entire being, Josie came - in tandem with the white release of Elijah's ejaculate. It was sexy having his cum drip into her mouth and on her lips.

She wasn't sure if it was seconds or minutes before they were recovered enough to change positions to be able to face each other. She crept up to him.

"That's cute," said Elijah.

He traced his cum over her lips.

"Better than any lip gloss," he joked.

"I'm not sure if we did the right thing or the wrong thing," said Josie doubtfully.

"We did what was right in the moment. Long term. I'm not sure. I know how amazing you feel now. I appreciate how your body fits so well with mine. It's hard to walk away from that."

"We don't have to walk away from each other," she panicked.

No, but the next step from this. Isn't that cheating?"
Elijah let the question hang between them as they stood and dressed.

"How do you want to play this for now?" asked Josie.

"I can go home, you go back in and enjoy what's on offer or if you'd rather go home first, I can hang around for a bit."

"I look like I've been dragged through a hedge backwards. You still look pretty unwrinkled so I might go straight away if you don't mind."

"Absolutely."

Elijah gave her a kiss and unlocked the door for Josie to leave. He took his phone from his breast pocket. Seventeen missed calls from his wife. He dialed her number.

"What's going on? Where have you been?" his wife demanded.

"Misha, I had work, remember?"

"Your father didn't pick me up from chemo."

"Shit! He probably forgot. I shouldn't have asked him with everything going on with Mum. Where are the kids?"

"They're in a cab on their way over to pick me up. They at least don't forget about me the minute I'm out of sight."

"Alright, I'm a terrible husband."

"Why couldn't you answer?"

"I was caught up in a work thing, but I'm on my way."

Elijah felt like the world's worst human being.

Josie was on a high when she got home. She felt sure her car had cloud wheels and she must've floated home. She shouted hello to the kids as she headed to her en-suite.

"Where are you going?"

She stopped short at the sight of her husband, Anton.

"Hey you," she smiled falteringly.

"How'd today go?" he asked.

"Good. Well, a tad boring, but parts were useful. Same old, same old to be honest."

"What was the hotel like?"

"Grand. It doesn't feel like a new building, but it's impressive."
"Reckon you'll get them to have the Christmas party there?"

"No. You were right about how expensive it is."

"I thought you'd stay a lot longer and come home a lot drunker," he laughed. "I can't remember the last work function you went to where you were home at a reasonable hour. Normally I'm up all night worrying you've run off with someone more interesting and better looking than me."

"Don't be silly-"

"Let me get to the punchline. Then I look in the mirror and realise that'll never happen," he joked.

She forced a laugh.

"It IS lovely to have you home," he said sincerely.

Josie knew that kind of voice and knew what he was after.

"The kids are downstairs."

"Occupied with takeaways and Netflix. We're two floors up with lust and desire."

She did still love him. She did still want him. He was the polar opposite of Elijah. Nordic. A giant Viking with white, blonde hair, and blue eyes. His hand snaked round her waist and he dragged her close. Her crotch pulsed. Elijah had been the entree. Would it be so bad to have a main course?

Anton's lips brushed hers; the taste he didn't recognize was Elijah's ejaculate. His tongue dove straight into her throat where less than an hour earlier another man's cock had staked claim. Josie felt dirty – morally, physically, and sexually, but it didn't deter her. Maybe she wanted to get caught. Maybe she liked the idea of arousing Anton's suspicions.

His lips never left hers as he unzipped her skirt. It slipped easily from her hips. He dropped to his knees. Josie threw a silent prayer to the universe that the garments had not been involved with the action from that evening. As he inhaled, she knew the risk was too great if Anton wanted to taste her.

"The kids might interrupt," she reminded him to break the spell of her tantalizing cunt. "Let's make it PG."

He nodded, taking his time to admire her rounded figure as she stood.

"Suck my cock?"

He was undoing his trousers. Josie was fearful she might get lockjaw.

"That's not PG. Saturday when they're both out I promise you'll get the whole shebang."

He tugged down his gym shorts and yanked his pink prick from the side of his briefs.

Josie lay on the bed. She turned to her side and batted her eyelids. Lifting her leg, she let her primed, juicy lips gleam invitingly. Anton edged into bed behind her. He held the ankle that was raised. His cock poked and probed; attempting to break into her slit. Josie reached between her legs and grabbed the inquisitive dick. She guided it into the space he was searching for. He had a long, thin prick. Affectionately known as the pencil. While it didn't spread her hole wide like she envisioned Elijah's would, it went deep and even in shallower positions made her gasp for more.

"You're so wet and ready. I've never known you to be this lubed up."

He slid smoothly in and out of her hot pussy. Josie was worried the unhurried pace might be because he was wondering why she was flooded, having had her pussy stretched by Elijah's tongue. Aware she'd be bringing him deeper and there would be a stinging sensation as he stabbed into her, Josie dropped her leg anyway to let it wrap behind Anton. He groaned and plunged further in. Josie gritted her teeth. The hunger for his cock to be buried in her was departing as she found herself focusing on not alerting Anton to anything peculiar about her stipulations on this current engagement. Anton was nibbling her neck as he continued ramming his hard-on into her like a jackhammer. He loved seeing every grimace on her face as his cock hit hard.

The hand not supporting his head, dropped onto Josie's soft stomach. He went down into the already dripping pussy. She bucked when his fingers found her clit. It was raw from the excessive force of Elijah. She wanted to scream at him to stop, but quietly endured the two fingers rubbing her bud roughly.

"I need you to cum for me to cum," he said in her ear.
Josie closed her eyes and tried to be in the moment. Tried to appreciate the hot, warm, kisses and nibbling of her neck. Tried to appreciate the long, satisfactory dick delving inside her. Tried to appreciate the fingers so determined to bring her to climax.

They'd been married a long time. Could she pull off faking an orgasm to end the sex?

She rolled away from Anton.

"I'll finish you off,"

There was no need for any lube, just expert rhythm and pace. Her hand wrapped around his erection and moved up and down. Anton's eyes were shut but he didn't seem anywhere near ejaculation. She worked his shaft laboriously. Josie couldn't bear the thought of taking anything else in her mouth, so resorted to licking his balls. A smile finally spread across Anton's Face. Relieved the end was in sight she continued vigorously.

"That'll do," said Anton.

"I can get you there," she said, between mouthfuls of his balls.

"Please stop. I couldn't make you come, you can't make me come. There's a first time for everything I suppose."

She noted the cool of his voice.

"I'm tired," she explained.

"Me too."

He stopped at her apologetic face.

"I'm sorry. I'm just disappointed I couldn't get you there. Makes me feel like...I'm doing something wrong," he confided.

"I'm sure it happens to everyone. Everyday life gets in the way."

"You felt pretty fired up at the start."

"Anton, you didn't do anything wrong. For all I know, I might've been doing something wrong."

"You're probably right," he sighed. "I'm going for a shower."

She remorsefully watched him head to the shower. Her phone vibrated. Unlocking the screen, she saw a text from an unfamiliar number. When she opened it, a picture began downloading – a picture of Elijah naked and on top of her. The accompanying text read, "Tongues will wag."

Her hand flew to her mouth to stop the uprising bile.

It was only a matter of time before Anton knew exactly what his wife was doing wrong.

Keys On The Table

"Oh, to be sixteen again," bemoaned Clare wistfully.

Her three companions followed her gaze to a nearby table where a young couple in the first bloom of love sucked the straws of their milkshakes. The boy had one hand covering his girlfriend's and scrolled through his mobile device with his other. The girl gazed adoringly at him but when his attention wasn't returned, she began posing and preening while taking selfies on her phone.

"Not exactly love's young dream," laughed Nathan.

"Oh, but we were once that couple," said Clare.

"None of us were," argued Abigail. "When we were that age, we didn't even have mobile phones. I don't think even the big brick phone my Dad carried thinking he was Mr. Technology was capable of sending texts. When we were sixteen and on a date, you had to be into the person. We didn't have the option of being connected to the rest of the world while on a date."

"That makes me feel great," said James. "There I was thinking you enjoyed being my high school sweetheart when in fact you would've preferred to be updating your status on some silly app."

"I loved being your high school sweetheart, almost as much as I love being your wife. It's different for young people now. There's so many options and an array of ways to meet people. The need to get to know someone and develop a connection isn't as important now as it was then because the pool of potential partners is-" Abigail faltered trying to find the word.

"Well, it's an ocean now, not a pool, right? There really are plenty more fish in the sea,' Nathan concurred with his best friends' wife. "And no, I don't wish I'd cast my net any further," Nathan reassured his wife, Clare before she could take offence.

"I wasn't claiming they were Romeo and Juliet. I was simply reminded what it was like to be in the flushes of young love. When everything and everyone was new. I wouldn't change a thing but I'm not so old that I don't remember how exciting it was the first time you took me out," said Clare pointedly to Nathan.

"Nathan was trying to get in your pants, not trying to get wifed-upped," ribbed James. "I shared a dorm with him at college. He only put a ring on that finger to lose his virginity."

Nathan laughed as his wife peered closely at him.

"James has had enough to drink and is starting to rewrite history. Might be time we called it a night," deduced Nathan.

"It's been lovely catching up with you two though," admitted Clare enthusiastically. "You guys don't come into town as much now."

"James is an old man," winked Abigail. "He likes country life, but he's not used to socializing."

"I can socialize with the best of them. I can party till I drop," insisted James. "Did I say that out loud? I sound like such an old man."

The four of them giggled. Tonight, had been a welcome blast from the past. They'd gone down memory lane taking in a movie at the struggling cinema they'd frequented when younger, and finished off at their favorite retro 50s diner.

"Come on we'll walk you home," offered Clare. "I'm desperate to have a gander at this new hotel."

As they walked a few blocks, the New Victorian dominated both street and skyline.
"No wonder we had such a cheap night," observed Nathan. "It must be costing you a bomb to stay here."

James stared up with his friends at the massive building. If a building had a presence or personality, the New Victorian's was intimidating.

James slung an arm round his friend's shoulder.

"Come inside. Let's have one for the road."

"Neither of us are driving in this state," said Nathan wryly.

"Then let's carry on the party. You two can get a cab back."

The girls' exchanged looks. With both of them having babysitters for their respective children, they were more than eager to not cut the night short.

The doormen opened the doors as they approached.
"Wow, it's really happening here," observed Clare taking in the sounds and flurry of people.

"There's a nightclub, casino, a theatre-" promoted Abigail.

"Alright girls. Rein it in. We were easily the oldest people at the diner tonight. Let's not make a spectacle of ourselves by getting pissed and embarrassing ourselves in a nightclub in front of a bunch of twenty-somethings," warned James.

"He has such a way of making a girl feel special," said Abigail.

Nathan gave Abigail a hug round the waist.

"The man's a fool. You two girls sparkle more than any of the women in this place and there's a lot of sequins going on."

Abigail held Nathan's eye for a moment. The intensity of the complement increased the longer they refused to break their gaze.

James pushed them toward a free table with low couches.

"Let's get in and get drunk."

Abigail sat across from her husband James but next to Nathan.

James threw the key fob on the table so the bar person could get the room number to charge the drinks to their room. The conversation flowed easily but the shared moment between Abigail and Nathan hung unspoken between them. Clare was happy to be merry. Taking in the surroundings, she didn't notice the sexual tension emanating from her husband and best friend.

"It's getting late," said Nathan, checking his watch. "It's time we made a move."

He stood to go.

"You can't possibly drive. You said we'd get a cab," Clare reminded him. "Give me those keys before you have any more foolish ideas."

As Nathan handed the keys to Clare her fingers missed. The keys fell on the table next to James' hotel key fob. Everyone looked, knowing what it was a known practice for.

"What's happening then? You looking for a bit of the 70s wife swapping, old buddy?" said James extra-loudly hoping to break the ice.

The group laughed nervously. Not one of them found themselves objecting to the suggestion made in jest.

"I suppose we should go up to the room. You said you were keen to have a peek, didn't you Clare?"

Clare found herself nodding and letting James' hand slide onto her lower back.

"I'll lead the way," said Abigail, taking Nathan's fingers in hers as they headed to the elevators.

Everyone trouped a single file into the hotel room behind Abigail. Clare thought the furnishings were as grand as the exterior of the hotel. It appeared very stately.

"I prefer something more modern," said Abigail. "It's perfectly cozy I suppose. Which is fine as we're only sleeping here one night."

"Might be doing more than sleeping," jibed James, not wanting to lose the momentum created downstairs.

Abigail was on the same page as her husband. She didn't stop to join him or her best friend on the sofa. Rather she led Nathan directly to the bedroom. The four-poster bed was the main feature.

Nathan let Abigail's fingers slide from his. She was certainly eager, but he hadn't really had time to contemplate the entire scenario. If it went wrong - if minds were changed or if performances were disappointing - the four of them were flushing away a twenty-year friendship. He and James had buddied up in their school years – along with Abigail. Abigail was slipping his sports jacket over his shoulders.

"She's a bit keen," he thought. He turned to look at her as she hung his coat up. She was a trophy wife; continuing to look the part even after two children. Abigail was five foot ten with a slim frame which was accentuated by a figure-hugging designer label. As she prowled toward him, he was hypnotized by the voluminous brown hair with even darker eyes.

"You have no idea how long I've wanted to do this," she confessed.

Nathan dropped his head to allow her lips to meet his. They were hungry. The kiss was ferocious. He felt her tongue in his mouth as her hand rubbed his crotch. His cock was begging him to abandon any contemplation of the consequences of seeing this night through.

He grabbed her wrist.

"Should I have asked James' permission? Should we have checked in with Clare?" he asked pointedly.

"I guarantee you James doesn't have a problem. Clare had every opportunity to voice an objection."

It was simpler for him to agree with Abigail's answer rather than give it any further thought.

Abigail positioned herself to face one of the posts of the bed. She raised her arms over her head and widened her stance. Nathan could see the zip at the back of her dress. He unzipped it slowly. It would've been fun to rip it roughly off her, but Nathan wasn't sure she'd still feel as wantonly toward him if he damaged the expensive outfit. He tugged the material clinging to her body, so it slid down. He was surprised to see she was wearing no underwear whatsoever.

Reaching to her front, he let his hands trace the outline of her bony body. He liked that Clare had a little meat on her, but there was something sexy about a woman who followed the trend of near anorexic catwalk models. As he got to her mound, his finger danced on the bare skin. His dick hurt from his pounding erection. He slipped a middle finger between her labia into the clear sticky wetness. She moaned, pushing her arse against his erection. He doodled idly in the dampness, slowly dry humping her arse. Abigail could feet Nathan grinding between her buttocks.

"You'd enjoy that a lot more if you didn't have your clothes on," she said lightly.

Nathan clumsily stripped off, grateful Abigail wasn't able to see the display of what he guessed was akin to an excited schoolboy losing his virginity. He placed his cock between the cleft of her buttocks and pulled her close. He simulated sex. Keeping one hand on her hip to secure her close, his other hand raced to return to her pussy. With trepidation, his fingers wandered through warmth and wetness to locate her clit.

The moment he pushed on the bud, Abigail pushed back harder against him.

"Don't make me wait, Nathan."

She rotated ever so slightly round the post and lifted her leg to place a foot on the mattress. Stepping back Nathan could see her plump lips hanging down – glistening and encouraging entry. Nathan grabbed the base of his prick to let it slide between the wet excitement she elicited for him. She bent lower. He took his cock then lazily slipped it into her slit. Her need for him was a turn on but her pussy had clearly been well used and stretched over the year as it wasn't as tight as Clare – who'd birthed him three children.

Abigail was used to thicker girths. Nathan was a nice length. It was fun having a cock that reached deep inside her to brush her cervix wall. Abigail was an exercise freak and that meant exercising all parts of her body. As Nathan thrusted in and out of her robotically, she took the time to practice tightening her pelvic floor. Nathan was lost in the feeling of another pussy when he felt the muscles within Abigail's cunt tightening and releasing round his cock. It was a trick he'd never experienced. He felt himself stiffening within her in reaction to the teasing of his dick. Grabbing her hips, he slammed into her. Abigail grunted as his length rammed in and hit the cervix wall repeatedly and roughly. Done with such force there was little pleasure in it for her.

"Not too soon," she ordered, to snap him out of his rhythm.

Nathan pulled out. His prick so hard it nearly reached his navel. Abigail turned to face him.

"Onto the bed. Let me ride you like the stallion you are."

Nathan almost laughed at how unreal her words were.

"She's been reading way too many romance novels," he thought.

Abigail was surprised to see Nathan's cock soften. She put it down to her suddenly stopping the action to reposition him for her comfort.

"Lay on the bed," she suggested.

Nathan went to the side of the bed and sat down. Swiftly, he positioned himself in the middle of the mattress with his head propped up by the pillows. His hand went to his dick to work it back to a fully erect state.

"I'll do that."

Abigail curled up next to him on the lower half of the bed. She took his cock in her hand and licked the head. The pre-cum from the slit on the top of his prick was sweet. She ran the fleshy dome over her lips as if it were a giant lipstick. Admiring the inches in her hand, she took long licks all-round the shaft from top to bottom. As Abigail expected, he hardened quickly. She licked his balls, gently grazing her teeth across them. Nathan's thighs quivered. She didn't want to bring him to orgasm yet. From seemingly out of nowhere she produced a condom to slip on his rod.

Abigail sat up. In a swift motion she swung a leg across to straddle Nathan. She let his cock slide between her pussy lips for a moment or two and then let the shaft bounce up straight to permit her to mount it.

Nathan's hands were gripping tight at the bed covers. He was close to the brink from the attention lavished on his prick. He watched as Abigail rode him. She caught his eyes, staring at him intensely as she yanked at the hair on his chest while speeding up the pace. Nathan's hands went to her hips to hold her firm to blast into her. The solid bounce of her breasts and the wince of her face as he hammered into her was rewarding.

Abigail began to contract on him deliberately. Tightening and releasing the cock, she shifted slightly to shallow the penetration and force Nathan's cock to rub her g-spot. Slowing her rhythm, she was able to bring herself to climax. Nathan finally reached his release after she began convulsing on his dick. His climax was quick and not as intense as he'd have liked, but he wasn't going to let Abigail know that.

She rolled off him. They stared at the ceiling.

"What now?" he asked.

She was quiet; wishing Nathan might hold her hand or display some kind of affection toward her.

"We see if James and Clare have finished and call you guys a cab."

She kept her tone friendly, trying to keep the mood the same as it had been in the diner.

Nathan hopped off the bed and dressed.

"I need to check on Clare."

He went out of the room, leaving Abigail to make herself respectable. Clare ran to him and held him close. Nathan kissed her head. He looked at James who smirked at him.

"Good night?" asked James.

Nathan nodded. He wasn't sure how to respond.

"Don't think any of us anticipated the turn of events," continued James.

"No," agreed Nathan without emotion. "I should get Clare home."

James winked at him.

"I'll call a cab?" he offered.

"There'll be plenty downstairs," replied Nathan. "The concierge can call us one if the rank is empty."

James went over to shake Nathan's hand. He forced a kiss on Clare's cheek.

"Till next time we're in town."

"I'll call you tomorrow, Clare Bear."

Abigail's voice sang out from the master bedroom. Clare closed her eyes to muster the enthusiasm to return the farewell.

"Please do."

The couple stepped out of the hotel room to hastily make their way to the elevator.

"Did you want a go straight home or shall we have a drink at the bar," asked Nathan.

"I need a drink," said Clare.

They entered the bar. Nathan ordered their drinks while Clare found a secluded table.

"Are you okay?"

"Dumbstruck is the word I'm searching for," said Clare.

"Want to tell me what happened?" enquired Nathan.

In her head, Clare revisited her evening after Abigail accosted her husband.

James smiled at her uncertainty.

"Everything's fine," he reassured her.

"Is it?"

"It will be."

"Why don't we make the most of the complimentary champagne the hotel has laid on. It might help you relax."

Clare watched him fill two glasses. He chose to sit on the floor rather than the sofa then patted a spot next to him on the carpet for her to join. She wasn't sure what was happening or how she felt about everything so was glad the alcohol was available to take the edge off. Sinking the whole glass, she tried not to imagine what was going on with Nathan and Abigail. James immediately refilled her glass.

"Are you trying to get me pissed so you can have your wicked way with me?"

"I'm hoping you won't need alcohol to want me to have my wicked way with you."
The compliment was much needed. Clare knew Abigail was the stunner between the two of them. She always felt like a dowdy housewife in comparison; despite juggling her family responsibilities and a rewarding career as Nathan's Executive Assistant. She was also fully aware that everyone saw her as a mousy Executive Assistant. Folks were always shocked when they discovered she was Nathan's wife. Nathan was quite the heart throb at college and that hadn't changed throughout their lives. She'd always been confident in his love so was proud to watch women make fools of themselves over her handsome husband. Now it seemed Abigail had her hands on him, and she didn't feel quite as confident in the monogamous relationship. The crushing reality of how easy it would be for Nathan to up and leave her left a bitter taste in her mouth. James' crude attempts to bed her were exactly what her ego needed.

She turned her head to his. James was by no means unattractive. Yes, he was out of shape, but Dad bods were in. He didn't have the idol looks of her husband, but he was always cute. His appeal was helped by his cheeky smile and the dangerous glint in his eyes. Clare suspected he could talk any woman into bed.

Their lips were less than a centimeter apart.

"Trust me. Let me make you feel like the goddess you are. I want to ravish you in all the ways you need to be."

Clare tilted her head to let their lips touch. She was stunned at how sensual the kiss was.

"Stand up," muttered James.

Clare obediently followed his request. Looking up adoringly, James knelt. His hands ran up her legs, under the dress until his thumbs were slipping inside the elastic of her panties. Firmly he pulled them down to fall to her ankles. She stepped out of them.
James patted the sofa in front of him. Clare sat down modestly. His hands ran up and down her calves and went to her knees which were clamped shut. James' hands were large. She saw his muscular arms flex as he forced her knees apart. She tried closing them, but resistance was futile. Keeping them spread, his face went between her legs and straight to her cunt. He poked his tongue between her lips. She gasped. Her husband was the only man she'd ever slept with. Having someone else explore her intimately was thrilling. His tongue drew all sorts of squiggles around her wetness. He did his best to plunge his tongue into her slit. Clare spread her legs wider and slid down the sofa.

Pleased she was opening up to him, James' arms went to her thighs to pull her to the sofa's edge. He sucked on her clit, nibbled her pussy lips playfully then returned to teasing her entrance with his tongue. Clare was moaning audibly.

With some exertion James stood up. He unbuckled his trousers and shoved them downward with his underwear. Clare's eyes widened at how thick his cock was. Without thinking her fingers went round the shaft. She could feel the blood pulsing through it. It throbbed under her touch. Clare worked it slowly. She'd never laid eyes on such a thick dick.

Forgetting about her husband, Clare needed it inside her pussy. She bunched her dress under her hips to allow her to spread her thighs as wide as she needed to. Squatting, James attempted to dip his cock in her. He licked his lips as he saw her slit tighten. Lowering his squat, he grabbed her ankles to lift them to his chest. He spread them wide, so her cunt was gaping. Forcing the head of his cock into her she bucked at the stretch. She was a lot tighter than his wife. Nathan was a lucky man to have this on tap every night. James began to inch into her. He mightn't have had the longest cock, but he definitely had one of the widest.

Keeping her ankles spread far apart, he was able to see his shaft sink inside her. James smiled at the sight of her hands turning into fists to accommodate his girth. He started to slide back out of her slowly to watch her pussy tighten even more. He let his head stay inside her before beginning to glide into her again.

Clare wanted to relax so she could get used to the thickness of him, but her body was unwilling. Each smooth insert was a form of blissful torture. James was making it slow and deliberate to have that effect. She cried out when his head popped out, pulling her slit wide.

James' thighs were in agony. He didn't have the strength to continue squatting.

"Lay on the floor."

Clare was far more willing now she knew what the reward would be for her pussy. She lay down and immediately raised her legs to James' chest. He spread her by the ankles again and dipped the head in. She exhaled slowly. Controlling her breath. He pulled his cock straight out. Clare gasped in delight. James let the head of his shaft repeatedly dip in and out of her cunt. Not once did her pussy loosen or relax. Deciding she'd had enough treats, he plunged in one more time and then fucked her. He let his shaft move at a pace that suited him. Her whimpering confirmed she was happy to receive the dick forcing its way in and out of her.

Her legs slid from his shoulders, making the penetration shallower. James was unable to get lost in the sensations of her tight cunt. He was distracted in keeping her legs secured over his shoulder and trying to find his rhythm.

Letting her legs drop, he turned her on her side into a semi fetal position. He forced his cock into her slit. It was even tighter with her having one leg on top of one another. His thick dick opening her spread pussy was delectable enough but in this position, Clare felt dizzy as his angry, needy prick essentially forced its way into her slit.

James rammed inside her. Once in, he started with small shoves of his hips to bury himself inside her. He persisted with the motion until he could feel her entrance was finally beginning to stretch to fit him. As her slit slackened he was able to pull his shaft out further and further. The sight of his cock going in and out was the visual he needed to let his lust loose on her. Hips jerking harder, he gradually built up the pace until he was fucking her like a common whore. Lost in his own enjoyment, James had to force himself not to tear at her dress. He dislodged from her slit to regain some self-control.

Repositioning Clare on her back, he lifted one leg up to sling over his shoulder and let his dick dive back into her. He gyrated his hips as he moved so his pelvis rubbed her clit. As he ground on her clit he unwittingly climaxed and spurted inside her. Clare was moaning in ecstasy – one leg wrapped his waist, the other over his shoulder as he fuckcd her into orgasm. Pulling out, he saw his cum seeping out her tired slit. He dipped his fingers between her legs to smear the white cream round her inner thighs.

There was a sound from the bedroom. Clare sat up abruptly, rolling her dress down. She sought her panties and flung them in her handbag. James stood and deftly did his pants up. Sitting innocently on the sofa he could feel his dick harden at the image of the cream pie Clare was nursing between her thighs. His best friend strode from the bedroom to signify the night was at an end.

Clare wasn't sure Nathan actually wanted to hear about what her and James got up to. She had no way of gauging his reaction upon learning, however unintentional, that another man had come inside his wife. Plus, if she told Nathan what happened would her punishment be to hear every sordid detail about what took place between him and Abigail?
"For the sake of our marriage I'm not sure we should go there," Clare replied to Nathan's question relating to her and James.

"You could be right," he said kindly. "Although I very much doubt it impacts on James and Abigail's relationship."

"I don't think that was their first time at the rodeo," said Clare shrewdly.

"Really?"

A comfortable silence fell between them. Clare could see Nathan replaying his scene with Abigail trying to determine if her theory was correct or not.

"You really think they've done the whole partner swapping thing before?" he asked incredulously.

"Absolutely. They moved to the country. It hasn't got the bustle of the city. It's quiet. They have to find ways to fill in time. And there's plenty like them that moved out there. I bet there's a whole club or something."

Nathan's loins stirred.

"You've no inclination to follow them?"

He laughed as he said it, but Clare knew he'd have an estate agent hired and be looking at schools for the kids if she so much as nodded her head to the possibility of moving to the country.

"Not my scene," she said coldly.

"I'm teasing," laughed Nathan.

"Are you?"

Nathan laughed nervously. He remembered the disappointment of Abigail's loose pussy. That was never a problem he'd had with Clare and it wasn't something he wanted disappearing from his sex life any time soon.

"I promise you I am."

"I'm a jealous wife Nathan, you know that. You had your hall pass tonight. If this is something you want to get caught up in, it'll have to be with someone else."

There was something sexy about a possessive woman – particularly when she was fiery enough to make good on her threats.

"I promise you I don't," he repeated emphatically.

She smiled in relief.

"Are we ever going to see them again?" she asked.

Nathan shrugged.

Clare's phone vibrated.

"Had a great time tonight. We must do this again. You two REALLY need to come visit us in the country sans kids," read the text.

Clare showed the phone screen to Nathan.

"Told you!"

The Tools Of A Cuckold

When Sophia walked into the bar almost every man's jaw dropped. No matter how enamored they were with their own wives, girlfriends or first dates, Sophia was a head turner. Even the envious women took a moment to admire her beauty.

While she didn't look her age, Sophia was comfortably into her forties. She had the glamorous appearance of a movie star from Hollywood in the 1930s. She adopted the figure hugging, floor length gown that was designed to show off the pale skin of her back, neck, and shoulders. Sophia was every man's dream.

Which meant whatever bar she went to, she would be showered with attention and offers from men who were single and men who wanted a night away from their wives. Her accessories matched her outfit, but there was barely any requirement for the matching clutch she carried as Sophia had yet to buy a drink or meal with her own money.

She'd yet to venture to the bar of New Victorian, but was hunting fresh blood so decided to give the city's newest hotel a whirl to see what breed and quality of men it attracted.

"Lots of men trying to impress their dates," was her initial thought.

She headed over to the bar and sat on a stool as if she were the owner, purveying the room for the right opportunity.

The barman looked familiar. When their eyes met, he opened his mouth to greet her. She immediately put her fingers to her lips to signal a shush to him. The boy stepped back, stung that she was embarrassed to acknowledge him in public. His manager caught his eye.

"Professional, mate. If she doesn't want to know, she doesn't want to know," the manager advised him.

"It's nothing bad-"

"Discretion, mate. I said if she doesn't want to know, she sure as hell doesn't want me knowing."

Licking his lips, the manager's eyes roamed her from head to toe.

"But once she's gone, I want to hear everything," insisted the manager.

To avoid any interaction between the two, lest the woman feel uncomfortable in their establishment, the bar manager headed toward her to take her order. He was also keen to see if he could be the object of her interest for the evening.

"Can I get you a drink ma'am?"

She smiled sexily from her bowed head and looked coyly up at him.

"Actually, I'd like to get the lady a drink. With her permission of course."

The bar manager forced a smile, knowing he couldn't' compete with rich clientele.

"Espresso martini, thank you," replied Sophia.

She took great pleasure in looking the man up and down; making it obvious she was deciding if he was worth spending time with or not.

Caramel skin, brown eyes, and close-cropped hair on a heavier frame, she knew instantly from the cut of his suit that he could afford her attention for the evening.

"Do I get a name?" he asked.

"Sophia."

"That's beautiful. A beautiful name for a beautiful lady."

"I do hope your conversation is more engaging than your pickup lines."

He smiled self-consciously but liked the attitude.

"Okay I deserve that, and I owe you another drink for the cheesiness."

"Are you trying to get me tipsy?"

"Only if you want to be tipsy."

She sipped her cocktail while watching him order a vintage red wine. The man had taste. That was another box ticked.

"And what do I call you?" she asked.

"Tyrone."
"A beautiful name for a beautiful man," she laughed.

Tyrone was flattered. From the corner of his eyes, he could see his work mates. They'd been attending a training session in a conference room earlier and had decided to stay back and enjoy the facilities of the hotel. He knew his team were jealous she'd accepted his offer of a drink.

"Don't tease," he objected, trying to recover a little dignity.

"Most men like to be teased to the point of frustration. No?"

"Depends on the kind of teasing I suppose."

"There's many kinds of teasing. Word play,"

"Foreplay," finished Tyrone.

"So brash and so vulgar, Tyrone."
Sophia pushed her glass away to make as if to move.

"Don't go!"

She cast a withering glance his way.

"I can make it up to you?"

"How?" Sophia enquired.

"However you want?"

"However I want?" she repeated.

"Within reason."

Tyrone had a feeling he'd underestimated Sophia or rather he'd over-estimated his charm.

"Boundaries. They're so restrictive are they not. Don't you like a woman who'll try anything?"

"Game on," he thought.

"I do and for the right woman I can be a man who'll do anything," Tyrone promised.

"For me to be able to test this and not get arrested, perhaps we should take this conversation elsewhere."

"I can get us a cab back to mine," he proposed.

"Oh no, no, no. I don't want a bachelor pad and I need to feel safe."

Sophia raised her eyes upward to the floors where the hotel rooms were located.

"This is going to hurt my credit card," thought Tyrone. "But she was a woman worth losing a paycheck on – especially with half his workplace watching.

"I'll sort it out and be right back."

Sophia watched him leave. Reaching into her clutch she took out her mobile phone and sent a message. It was time for the evening to begin.

Tyrone returned. He tried to keep calm and cool and not run at her like an excited puppy waving the key to the room.

"Shall I order some champagne for the room?" he asked masterfully.

"That would be wonderful."

She linked her arm through his and let him direct her to the room.

"I can definitely get used to these hotel rooms," thought Sophia. "They would make a very satisfactory home away from home."

"Tell me Tyrone, what are you expecting to happen tonight."

"Whatever you want," came the automatic reply.

"Shall I tell you what I want?"

He nodded mutely.

"I want you to make love to me. I want you to savor me. I want you to worship my body knowing this is the first and last time you'll ever have it. I want you to bring me to the pinnacle of pleasure."

It was exactly what Tyrone wanted to hear but the possibility of him not meeting her needs and wants had beads of sweat forming on his brow. But Tyrone was never one to not step up. Imagining himself as quite the ladies' man he was eager for the challenge.

Sophia walked the room's perimeter, opening all the curtains.
"Maybe you should keep them closed, with everything I'm going to do."

"Or maybe we should give the people a show. If anyone can even see in here at this altitude. But it's fun to put on a show is it not?"

Tyrone grabbed Sophia by the wrist and circled her into him. His lips met hers. At first, he merely pecked her. She tasted sweet and expensive. Sliding an arm behind her neck he dipped her to kiss the pale skin of her neck. She was feather light in his masculine arms. He released her to a standing position expecting her to be flushed by the romance of it all, but she remained unruffled.

He sucked his lips and walked round Sophia struggling to work out how he could remove her dress without damaging the precious garment. Sophia lifted an arm and he saw a zip. Pulling it down, she gracefully stepped out of it.

"Girl, you blow my mind," wowed Tyrone.

Sophia resisted correcting his language because at forty-five it was quite nice to be thought of as a girl. He could feel his hard on stretching the seam of his zipper and was worried the sight of Sophia in her lingerie might burst the material. Dropping to his knees, he was acutely aware of the importance of following Sophia's precise instructions.

She stepped away from him. Walking toward the bed she teasingly removed her lingerie. She did it so effortlessly Tyrone momentarily wondered what her day job was. She stood in front of the king-size mattress.

"If you are going to worship me, let us do it fully naked like the Adamites."

Tyrone didn't know who the Adamites were but if they got nude to worship – it might have encouraged him to attend church more regularly with his wife on Sundays. It's hard to be graceful when you have the powerful build of an ex-rugby player, so Tyrone focused on speed rather than sensuality as he got out of his clothes.

Sophia was pointing at his erection.

"My, my, that is a real object of beauty. Is that how I make you feel?"

He nodded – mute again.

"Then come here and worship me."

Tyrone walked gradually to her. Kneeling, he lifted a foot to kiss each pedicured nail. He licked her slender calf. He used his free hand to tend to her alternate foot – stroking it, then running up the golden tan skin of her leg. Raising his hands, he moved them behind Sophie to grab her buttocks. Squeezing firmly, he inhaled the soft skin of her hairless mound. He was frightened if he spoke it would break the mood and Sophia didn't behave like someone who could forgive careless errors if she had a scene painted a particular way and it didn't go to plan.

His hands moved to grip her small hips to sit her down on the bed. Spreading her thighs wide he was able to place his face between them and flick his tongue out to explore until it landed on her clit. As soon as he made contact with the bud, Sophia lent back on the bed resting on her elbows and widening the spread of her legs. Her gleaming lips parted, and Tyrone was able to relax into treating her orally. As he let his tongue lay at the base of his vulva and worked its way up to flick the clit repeatedly, a sharp noise from outside had him sitting bolt upright.

He thought Sophia would be too, but she remained comfortable and stared at him as to why he had stopped.

"Did you hear that?" he asked, startled.
"What?"

"Like a noise on the balcony."

"Probably cats."

"I'll close the curtains."

"Close the curtains then go," she ordered sitting up.

Tyrone looked incredulously at her.

'Or finish making love to me."

"You really like to think you're in charge, don't you?" he enquired with a tone of annoyance.

"Then show me who's in charge Tyrone."

Tyrone stood up. His large, brown cock was demanding and throbbing. Grabbing the base, he slapped it hard across Sophia's cheek and slapped the other side before she had time to recover. Her hand flew to her cheek, but he could see the blush of excitement rising from her neck. Reaching under her buttocks he flung her up the mattress.

Her eyes challenged his. He took her ankles and put them on his shoulders.

"You best be wet if you're going to survive this," he threatened.

The words elicited a gush from between Sophia's thighs. His girth was astounding, and Sophia tweeted delightfully as he shoved the hard-on in her. Her ankles locked behind his neck, allowing Tyrone maximum penetration. He pounded her up the bed till her head was knocking the headboard. She grunted and groaned like a whore rather than a lady as she tried to breathe through the rough sex.

Flipping her over, he climbed on top of her, covering her entire body.
"Do I need protection?"

The last thing he needed was having to confess to his wife a one-night stand resulted in a mini-Tyrone.

"No, I'm on birth control."

He put his legs over hers to force them open from the ankles. The power of his legs from years of rugby had them separating without any real resistance. She raised her hips and dipped them so the dome of his prick could find its way back in. Sophia groaned. It wasn't purely the fat cock stretching her cunt, but feeling the weight of a real man crushing her that turned her on. Tyrone pounded a little longer and then released his load.

"Keep them wide," he ordered, as he stood up.

Lowering the focal line of his eyes to her pussy he was able to see his cum seeping out of the raw, red slit he'd brutally dominated.

"Yeah, that's how I like it."

He took another step back to admire his handiwork. He wasn't sure what made him do it, but a sixth sense caused him to turn his head to the window. A face was staring in.

"What the fuck!"

Naked and vulnerable he thought he was going to have a heart attack.

"Who the fuck are you? What are you doing?" he shouted at the window, feeling foolish as he tried to put some clothes on.

Sophia drew herself up from the bed and walked over to where Tyrone was jumping on the spot. He wasn't sure whether he should attack the guy for being a peeping tom or run from the bizarre scenario and hope no one – not his friends, family, and especially not his wife – ever heard of this.

"It's a maintenance man. He must be doing some work on the balcony."

"He's not fucking working. He's perving on us."

"Don't you think that's sexy? He's not doing any harm. Poor little worker bee."

Sophia walked to the doors leading out on the balcony.

"Let's invite him in."

She slid the door back.

"Nah, fuck this," said Tyrone.

The maintenance man came in grinning happily. Some short, little, nothing of a man, with ragged red hair and thick glasses.

"You're lucky I don't knock you into the middle of next week little man. Fucking peeping Tom."

"You're lucky I loaned you my wife."

Tyrone looked to Sophia who was unmoved. His mind was only just beginning to process what was going on.

"I don't have time for this," mostly dressed, Tyrone walked out the door leaving all his dignity behind.

"Look at this."

Sophia sat on the edge of the bed and rubbed her thighs to a creamy glaze. Keeping her legs wide she let her husband watch as the last droplets of Tyrone's ejaculate spilt from her cunt. She scooped it up and deliberately let a droplet fall from her finger to her tongue. Striding to her husband she wiped the remaining cum on his upper lip.

"That seemed nice. Did you enjoy it?"

"It passes the time while you're at work."

"I'm glad it made you happy. Shall I take you home now?"

Sophia could see his erection and knew he was looking for a release.

"Not yet. I have one more appointment this evening."

"Another one? Is there a particular location where me and my toolbox need to be?"

"What time does the pool close?"

"9pm."

"Then I would find some work to do by the pool."

"Can you make it different this time?"

"If that's what you like. I'll see you by the pool house. I need to put a little work in on this one."

Sophia left her husband and spent an hour in the bathroom, recreating the look she'd first entered the hotel with. She retraced her way back to the bar. It was close to closing time when she walked in. Sophia took a bar stool.

"Hi Benny," she softly greeted the bar boy she'd silenced earlier when attempting to engage Tyrone.

"Hi, Mrs. Cavendish," he smiled slightly, still hurt from her casual disregard.

"Can I apologize to you for earlier?"

"There's nothing to apologize for," he insisted, remembering he was obligated to be professional.

"Of course there is. You're my son's best friend. I've known you since you were – what?"

"Six."

"Over fourteen years then. Of course, there was no excuse for me not saying hello, let alone pretending you didn't exist."

"I'm sure you had your reasons."

Benny had seen her leave with Tyrone. He was young but he knew that Mrs. Cavendish was a complete MILF and the guy she left with wanted to engage in activities that you had to be horizontal to enjoy and not vertical.

"You were so cute when you were six and now... Now you've grown into quite the man. How did I not notice that?"

Benny flushed. Mrs. Cavendish was an incorrigible flirt. He'd been madly in love with her since he was thirteen, but she'd always treated him like he was six. He felt his chest puffing out at her flattery.

"I'm not sure because I've half lived in your house since I first met Rafe."

"Ahhh but even with Rafe in college he'll always be my little boy."

"I am definitely not a boy and I'm definitely not little," flirted Benny.

"Benny, so cheeky. Let me see. Give me a twirl."

"Boys don't twirl. They posture."

Benny adopted a pose he'd practiced in the gym that tensed all his muscles to make for the perfect selfie when sending pics online.

Mrs. Cavendish laughed.

"Your uniform doesn't do you justice. I see only the barest hint of all the time you spend working out."

Benny scowled.

"Well one day I'll give you the full show if you like," he said boldly.

"I'd like that very much, Benny. What time does your shift finish?"

"You mean tonight?"

Benny realized Mrs. Cavendish wasn't teasing. His best friend Rafe crossed his mind. But Rafe didn't have to work to put himself through college so it was unlikely he'd ever find out. He thought of Mr. Cavendish. He was a decent man who loved his wife and had always treated Benny as part of the family. Could he really do something so selfish and self-indulgent?

"I mean now," said Sophia, reaching over and putting her hand on his arm.

Benny glanced at the bar. It wasn't spotless, but the tills had been counted, emptied, and the monies secured in the safe. He could always start his shift early tomorrow if he felt too guilty that it wasn't immaculate.

"That works for me. Where will we go?"

"I know somewhere private."

Sophia walked Benny to the lifts. Pressing the button for the fourth floor, Benny realized they were headed for the pool. It was a safe call. The pool was closed, and it'd only be the two of them. Pre-game nerves were starting to settle in. It was one thing fucking a silly college girl when you were drunk at a party, but it was another thing fucking your best friend's mother when you were stone cold sober, and she was an absolute Goddess.

Steam rose from the pool.

"We could try the hot tub?" suggested Benny.

Sophia continued down to the sauna. She opened the door.

"Here I think."

Benny nodded. Wherever they chose wouldn't be overly comfortable but whatever happened it was going to be a blast.

Sophia smiled kindly at Benny and untied his bow tie. Deliberately she slowly unbuttoned his shirt buttons. Pushing his shirt off she looked at the firm, rippled torso. Her hands ran over the muscular shoulders, down his pecs and six pack and delved into his pants.

Benny shivered at her touch. He looked down and watched Mrs. Cavendish's hands undoing his pants and drawing them downward. Benny stood there in his white boxers; the pink head of his dick peeping out. The door to the sauna opened. Benny's hands flew to his groin.

"Darling, come in. "I'm just getting started."

Benny raised his eyes and saw Mr. Cavendish – in the standard maintenance uniform of a blue shirt and navy dungarees.

"Don't mind me, Benny. I'm here for the show," he said in a small voice.

"I'm so sorry," stammered Benny.

"I should've been here earlier, but I had a job to finish off. I can maybe sit on this."

Mr. Cavendish upturned the water bucket to create a makeshift seat.

"Sir, I can only apologize."

"Benny boy, you've done nothing wrong," assured Mr. Cavendish. "But I will be disappointed in you if you reject my wife."

"I couldn't. I wouldn't. She's beautiful."

"Then show me how I might make love to a beautiful woman."

Benny looked down at his now flaccid penis.

As the men had been talking, Sophia had stripped to sit on the lowest bench of the sauna watching the exchange in amusement.
"Sit down, darling," cajoled Sophia.

Benny sat on the bench. Reaching into the hole of Benny's boxers Sophia's hand grasped his cock. He moaned. Not sure what to do or how to react.

"I'm sure I can get you harder."

Sophia knelt in front of him and put the semi-erect penis between her red lips. Benny's eyes fell to see her womanly arse spread, making her waist appear even tinier. As he hardened at the sight, he looked up and caught Mr. Cavendish's eye, who was nodding expectantly. Benny closed his eyes and focused on the firm sucking of Mrs. Cavendish's mouth.

"Now I think you're ready."

Benny knew he was. Leaning back into the higher sauna bench for support he widened his thighs. His seven-inch cock was rock hard and ready. Mrs. Cavendish crept on top. Squatting on the bench either side of his legs, she kissed him passionately. He'd thought she'd feel softer, but her lips were as firm and as hungry as they had been working his shaft. She lowered herself till her wet lips were able to tease Benny's prick. She bounced – seeking the head of his dick. Benny held his length firm until she landed and the dome spread her slit. Hands clasping the bench, under the bizarre circumstances, Benny thought it best that he let Mrs. Cavendish take full control of the sex.

Sophia began bouncing up and down. It was a strain on her thighs, but she knew the squatted position meant her husband had a nice view of her booty – spread and bouncy. It was also nice to tease the boy. Dipping low to take the full length of him but other times dipping shallowly so it was only the head of his cock that had her pussy's attention. It was a precarious game. Benny was young and she didn't want him coming too quickly.

Sophia stood on the bench and dragged Benny's head to her pussy. She had a tight grip on his hair to keep him firmly in place and gyrated against his face. Jumping to the floor easily in her four-inch heels. She grinned at how wet and dazed poor Benny was. To prevent Benny from focusing too much on her husband, she wasted no time in sitting backward onto him.

Benny's muscular arms reached down to lift Mrs. Cavendish and place him on his cock. This time his full shaft shot inside her. She squealed at the sensation of the satisfactory seven inches going deep. Benny lifted her legs to place them outside his own spread thighs to restrict her movement even more. She was stuck on his rod now and he was in control of the penetration.

Sophia wriggled to encourage Benny to take action. Lifting his hands under her upper thighs he began to lift her on and off his cock. This time he was able to dictate pace and depth. He started with lifting her off completely, so that his purple dome split her entrance each time he plopped her back on it to slide down his sword. He could feel her thighs quivering. He continued placing her on and off his cock because he enjoyed her little grunts each time he ploughed in, but he did, of course, want to reach his own climax.

He lifted her faster and faster on his cock creating a pace that matched his desires. His muscles were aching. He switched to holding her raised and steady so he could buck his own hips to delve in and out of her. It had all started so frantic, but he wasn't sure he'd be able to finish off. Sensing that his arms were tired Sophia began grinding and dipping her hips to encourage Benny to plant her back on his prick for her to slide up and down at her preferred pace. As she did her pleasingly plump breasts wobbled. Benny's hands reached for them to let them juggle in his hands. He nibbled her ear lobe. Sophia's head went back – now she was in paradise. She slid a hand between her legs and pushed her labia apart. Her fingers traced up, down, and around her pussy, edging closer to her clit but never quite making contact.

She looked at her husband who was mesmerized and hard.

"Come on," he mouthed.

Sophia yanked Benny's hand and took it to her wet cunt. She covered his fingers with her own and teased her clit until she was on the brink.

"I'm gonna come, I'm gonna come," he warned.

He was close to shouting – aware he was too young to be a father.

"It's fine. You can cum inside me. I'm on the pill,"

Benny thrust hard. Sophia could feel the cum filling her. As it did, she manipulated his fingers on her clit to bring her to her own climax. Benny moaned at her orgasm and his cum dripped from her onto his thigh. He felt his cock stiffening again. Cum dropped from her

"I think you've both had enough for one evening. I know I have," said Sophia simply.

Benny remembered Mr. Cavendish was in the room. He felt nauseous. Pulling on his trousers, he scurried out of the sauna, apologizing repeatedly as he left.

"He didn't even give me a chance to thank him," said Mr. Cavendish ruefully.

"He has no interest in you little man," Sophia reminded him haughtily.

"I don't suppose he does. But thank you, darling."

"The pleasure was, as always, mine."

Mr. Cavendish put his hand in Sophia's.
"Will the boy let on to Rafe?"

"No. It's never a good idea to fuck your best friend's mother under any circumstances. He won't tell a soul."

Mr. Cavendish nodded.

"I think I would like a permanent residency here," mused Sophia.

"Then you're lucky I don't earn a maintenance man's wage," laughed Mr. Cavendish.

"Darling, you're a wealthy heir playing with his parent's money."

"One day we'll own this hotel," he reminded her. "Until then, isn't it more fun to play make believe."

Cavendish rattled his tool bag and kissed his wife, making an impulse decision to hang onto the Maintenance man's uniform for future adventures. Tonight, had been all too easy.

Cooking Up A New Climax

Chloe's eyes rolled open. She wasn't convinced she'd even slept. She'd been stuck somewhere in the state between falling asleep and waking up. What had actually gone on last night? Closing her eyes, she did her best to recount the evening.

Work had been work. Busy, stressful, shouting, sweating. That was the deal when you worked in a kitchen. It was demanding. More demanding than when a teenage Chloe was considered a great Olympic hope for mid-distance running. She'd worked her way through the system; from independent fast-food outlets, to being a kitchen porter and then up the ranks of various restaurant kitchens. Everyone had been keen to get involved with the New Victorian. Not because it was predicted to be one of the best restaurants in town, but because if she got into the flagship restaurant, she'd be working under world renowned Head Chef Oliver Dunmore.

The hiring process was unlike any other. Chloe was glad she'd used her earnings from the thousand different food industry jobs she worked to eventually ensure she graduated culinary school. HR were happy with her qualifications, so she got an immediate foot in the door. However which eatery within the New Victorian hotel she was placed in was a different matter. Oliver Dunmore insisted on full control of the restaurant. She'd been up against not only some of the best chefs in the city, but people had come from all over the nation for a coveted place on Oliver's team.

Chloe landed the job. Alongside her experience, she was creative, had a discerning palate, an unremitting work ethic and could follow instructions. That's what Oliver wanted most. People that listened and did as they were told because under his micromanagement, they were able to produce what was soon to be awarded Michelin star food.

"Work, work, work…. What happened next," she pondered internally.

Drinks. Drinks and drugs. For the most part Chloe had the youth and drive to keep up in the kitchen, but she was only human. Some shifts were more demanding than others. Some rosters required an unnatural amount of time. A little sniff of white powder to help keep her energy levels up and maintain her focus wasn't the worst thing in the world. A few drinks to relax and go crazy when time permitted was worth it sometimes – even if her sleep suffered as a consequence. Drug and alcohol misuse was a known problem with kitchen brigades. The fact there was little to no drug-testing going on made it almost feel acceptable. Almost.

It wasn't her style or scene, but hell it felt amazing. There'd been the usual post-shift glass of wine that even routinely Oliver would partake in. Afterwards they'd decided to carry on the party. They went to a dingy little basement pub that was the opposite of the glamorous New Victorian, but was a grimy little scene that screamed sex. You could almost smell the testosterone competing with the estrogen when you entered the club. Chloe remembered the hairs on her arm raising as she became intoxicated by the crowd of people with only one objective - to get laid.

She remembered a small booth she'd been squashed into.

Next to Oliver.

He'd come as well.

At first, he'd sat there quietly as everyone chattered randomly about the inanest topics. Oliver was tall and skinny. He was slightly under six foot but appeared taller. His gangly appearance was down to how emaciated he was.

"Never trust a fat chef," she'd drunkenly declared.

Oliver smiled.

"And if you want your restaurant to make a profit, always hire a skinny chef. They won't eat all the food."

The other four people squashed in the booth laughed as if it was the funniest comeback ever. Chloe appreciated his sense of humor but didn't think he'd appreciate people kissing his ass when they weren't at work.

His hazel, feline shaped eyes met hers. He was quite striking really. His head was shaved. He had fine bone structure and the jet-black beard on his pale skin was an eye-catching contrast. She smiled at his unappreciated looks and thought no more of it. He was like an emotional robot. On the one hand he had a fierce temper that no one wanted to endure, but then he was completely detached from everyone and didn't appear to have any real close bonds or connection with anyone.
A hand slipped between her thighs. She looked down and realized the long fingers could only be Oliver's.

'How's my best Chef de Partie?"

"She's -" Chloe paused, internally debating if Oliver's gesture was sexual or not.

It wasn't the fact he was her boss that meant she didn't consider him a sexual being, but the fact he behaved with disinterest in men and women alike.

"She's?"

"Wondering why your hand is on her leg?"

"Shall I take it off?" he asked.

"No."

"I'd like to take you somewhere and kiss you," he declared.
"Wow, you really put it out there don't you?"

"You either want me to kiss you or you don't. It's your choice."

Chloe stopped. There were still people in the booth, but they were either too drunk or too high to acknowledge what was occurring.

"There's always ramifications unfortunately," she said hesitantly.

"No. Never. It's a kiss. That's all."

"Okay. I'll play. I do want you to kiss me."

"Good. I also want to fuck you."

"Woah. There's people here," laughed Chloe in mortification.

"Again. Who cares? Do you want to fuck or not?"

"This will spill into work."

"Not for me. And not for you. You work for me and you know the rules. You leave your personal life at the door when you enter my kitchen."

"You do always say that," concurred Chloe.

He was sexy enough. And what a story – to say you slept with a first-class internationally famous chef.

"I want to fuck you," she said simply.

The second she'd given him a direct answer was the second he waved a casual hand at their colleagues in the booth to indicate he needed to get out. She trailed after him. They went straight to the street. Oliver made no attempt to show any affection once outside in the crisp air of the early morning. He flagged a cab on the empty streets without issue. Chloe was all too aware of the distance between them in the back seat of the cab. The atmosphere was still – it lacked any bristling sexual tension. Chloe wasn't even sure the sex was going ahead.

The car arrived at a stunning set of new build flats in one of the trendier areas of town.

"Inside, inside," instructed the crisp British accent.

Chloe followed him through reception and to the lifts to zip up to the penthouse floor.

"Look like they're paying you what you're worth," she said lightly, hoping to convince him to engage.

"It's not only the food I produce when my name's attached to a venue. It's my entire brand. It gives immediate value and popularity to wherever I work."

Chloe ambled round the sparsely furnished suite – he was clearly a fan of minimalism. Oliver watched her. She could feel his eyes studying her every movement. Maybe it was still game on.

"Am I right to take a shower?"

"No."

"What?" snapped Chloe.

She bit her tongue to control her tone. "It's only we've both done a 12-hour shift and been sitting in a sweaty club, I thought you might prefer for me to freshen up."

"On the contrary. You're exactly how I want you."

Chloe reached and rubbed the back of her neck, letting her straight hair fall in even curtains. However calm his voice was, he had the stare of a predator who'd finally found an easy dinner.

"And where exactly do you want me?"

He pointed in front of the island bench.

"In the kitchen. How predictable," she mocked.

He let her saunter over with her put-on swagger.

"Right here."

His finger directed a point on the tiled floor between him and the kitchen bench. Chloe stepped on the imaginary mark, lifting her chin to await his kiss. Oliver pulled her blouse from the waistband of her jeans to take it straight over her head. Holding her wrists above her head for the satin top to float down from, he let his tongue trace a line from the inside of her wrist, down her forearm, upper arm and into her armpit. She was suddenly semiconscious that the deodorant she'd sprayed before leaving work had worn off some time ago. Oliver growled as he nuzzled her armpit.

"He seems to be enjoying himself," thought Chloe.

He repeated the same action on her other arm and licked the sweat from her armpit. Dropping her wrists, as her arms dropped, he spun her round to face the bench of the marble island. Unclasping her bra, he pushed it over her shoulders for her to finish removing. Oliver was unfazed by her petite breasts. Rubbing her nipples unconsciously, he stopped to let his index fingers slide under the small weight of the breasts. Her breasts fell over the fingers. Dragging them from under her tits he tried to capture the sweat from the space where her bosom touched her chest. She could hear him sucking each finger. Chloe's face contorted, thinking it was pretty gross that all he wanted to do was taste her bodily odors.

She felt his hands fumbling with the crotch of her jeans. Feeling anything but sexy, Chloe didn't really feel in a position to walk away from sex now and decided it was best to let him get on with it. The sooner his kink was satisfied the sooner she could relish a shower in the comfort of her own home. With gusto, she pushed her jeans and underwear down in one swoop to step out from them.

"Back to your mark."

Oliver was as particular toward sex as he was to food. She sensed him falling to his knees. Before she could protest his hands were on her buttocks and he parted them enough so that his tongue could run up and down her crack. Chloe had an urge to vomit but the foreign sensation was actually quite pleasurable. As still as a statue, the thoughts of disgust were pushed aside as his tongue lapped her cleft like a dog at its water bowl on a summer day. He pushed against the entrance of her arse and she immediately straightened – tightening her buttocks. That was a step too far for Chloe.
Oliver's disapproving huff echoed round the flat, but he refrained from forcing it on her.

His hands went between her inner thighs to direct her to widen her stance. Chloe eagerly obeyed his directions knowing what was coming. Not unexpectedly, but certainly more welcome Oliver sniffed her crotch from behind. Chloe lent forward over the bench to permit Oliver better access to her pussy. His tongue darted between her labia. She dipped her hips to encourage him to explore. Oliver licked her slit and she groaned. She squatted to increase the pressure of Oliver's tongue on the entrance to her cunt. Oliver's mouth tried to take in her entire quim. Chloe could feel his teeth grating on her pussy lips and gnawing at the edge of her pubic mound.

"Won't you please just fuck me?" she pleaded.

She could hear Oliver standing and suspected he was freeing his cock to finish the deed. She felt his dick lay between her pillowy buttocks. It was almost a dry hump, but she felt his shaft harden as he continued sliding his prick in her crack.

She squealed as the head of his cock stabbed at her arsehole.

"Wrong hole," she yelped.

Oliver sighed again. She heard him spit in his hand and realized he was masturbating to get hard again. He was clearly turned off by hearing the word no.

"Turn round," he said shortly.

Obediently, Chloe spun round to face him. His hazel eyes held no emotion. As he masturbated in front of her, his free hand tapped the kitchen bench. Using her hands, she lifted herself to sit on the bench.

"This is quite sexy," she thought as she laid back.

Back to his full length, Oliver hauled her to the edge of the bench. He stood up straight to direct his cock into her slit. It went in and he did a few lack luster thrusts before realizing he wasn't going to plunge as deep as he wanted.

"On the floor quickly."

Chloe jumped down and laid on the floor while he wrapped up. Oliver grabbed her legs and heaved them over his shoulder. His expression was one of irritation as he guided his dick into her pussy. He started slowly to make sure he was deep. The thrusts were slow and deliberate, and Chloe finally felt sensual. He built up a rhythm quickly.

"Can you make yourself come, I need to finish."

Chloe slipped her hand between her legs and rubbed her clit in the way that she knew best. With Oliver plundering her so smoothly, she only had to close her eyes to let the flashes consume her before her expert hand brought her to a hasty climax. The second her vaginal muscles started clamping and tensing round his cock, Oliver reached a silent peak.

Removing himself from her, he didn't offer any assistance to help Chloe from the floor.

"Stay the night, but don't shower," he offered as he discarded his condom.

Chloe couldn't afford a taxi so crept into bed with him. There was a world between them, and Chloe wasn't sure she'd even sleep with the genuine threat of falling off the mattress and cracking her head on the dresser.

"Oliver's flat. That's where I am," Chloe was finally able to recall after retracing the events of the night. She stayed on her side wondering if there was an easy escape from the flat without Oliver knowing.

The rustling of the sheets meant he was awake already. She could feel him turning toward her. His breath was beside her ear. She tried relaxing in order that he might believe she remained asleep. A hard fleshy sword pressed against her buttocks.

"He has got to be kidding," she thought. "Can this guy not take a hint?"

The shaft nestled between her buttocks.

"He knows I'm pretending. How do I reject him without making work super awkward?"

The dome of his cock slipped to the rim of her arse and was insisting again. Chloe had no real choice. She began coughing and hacking as if she had some kind of serious lung condition. Her body wracked and his cock slipped away.

"Are you okay?"

She held up a hand and forced the barking a little longer.

"Respiratory problems," she revealed, tears falling down her cheeks from the exertion. "I didn't take my meds last night and clubs like that only exacerbate the issue. I'll be fine."

"I'll arrange a cab to take you home. Have the day off," insisted Oliver, worried he was to blame.

"I couldn't possibly," protested Chloe.

Days off weren't really an option as part of the kitchen brigade.

"Honestly we can cover you. I'm sure one of the Commis Chefs is dying to step in and show me what they can do."

Chloe didn't really like the idea of someone stepping into her shoes for the night and being better than her, but she'd started this charade so was committed to finishing it.

"I'll make it up to you," she offered.

"Perhaps."

Oliver gave her a look and they both knew how he wanted her to make it up to him.

"Me and my virgin ass are getting out of here now," thought Chloe.

She couldn't get out of the flat and into the cab quick enough.

Oliver shook his head. It was not the night he had been hoping for. Most girls didn't dare to disobey him. If anything, they were desperate to impress and would compromise themselves and their values if it meant him lavishing a modicum of attention on them.

"Fuck!" he shouted, knowing he could be himself and was no longer on show.

He hated not getting his own way and he'd been desperate to bust open that virgin hole. He rubbed his forehead wondering if there might be another chance down the line to pop Chloe's anal cherry or if he'd been too obvious with his fetish.

Kitchens were clean and sanitized. Oliver preferred his sex to be at the other end of the spectrum. He liked dirty girls and he loved dirty sex. The idea of corrupting Chloe had his morning glory returning with vengeance. He scowled at the agitation of his blue balls. As he made his way to his immaculate shower, he toyed with the idea of releasing his frustrations so he could concentrate at work. A wave of guilt spread throughout Oliver as he acknowledged keeping Chloe from her usual routine prevented her from managing a medical condition that had never once revealed itself when she was at work. The feeling dissipated as he realized her absence did create a potential opportunity for him to use his status to relieve his carnal urges. One of the Commis Chefs would have to cover Chloe's station. While the kitchen was dominated by male staff, there were two young girls he'd employed to indulge the equal opportunity demands of the HR department of the New Victorian staffing requirements.

With renewed vigor, he got ready for the pending shift. He didn't believe in sexual harassment, but he did believe there was nothing wrong with a little give and take in the workplace if everyone was satisfied with the final outcome.

By the time he arrived at the kitchen, the staff were already prepping for the lunchtime rush.

"Kayla, Tegan, into my office," he barked, giving a nod to acknowledge the rest of the busy team.

The two girls walked in with trepidation.

"Please sit."

They sat – as meek as mice.
"Chloe is off tonight. I need someone to fill in. I was wondering if one of you girls wanted to step up."

They nodded in tandem.

"Are both of you keen? Or just one of you? Who wants to do it?"

Oliver was unaware that his reputation precedes him with women. Gossip flowed freely when he wasn't around, and the community of chefs was small enough for girls to talk about what kind of kinks Oliver had.

Kayla was already shaking her head.

"You don't want an audition? I'm disappointed Kayla. I thought you had a little more drive than that."

"I'm sorry, Chef. I don't feel I'm confident enough yet to step in and I don't want to hold the team up or ruin service by taking on something I'm not capable of accomplishing to your standards."

It was a fair point and Oliver believed it.

Tegan knew if she didn't do it one of the boys would and she hated the thought of being overlooked. But she also knew what Oliver was expecting in return for the favor. Unlike Kayla, Tegan did have career aspirations and she was prepared to sacrifice her morals in order to get the advances she needed.

"I'd like to try out."

Oliver met her eyes.

"Are you sure? I can be exceedingly demanding if I'm handing someone an opportunity on a plate."

"I'm up for the challenge," she affirmed with a wink.

A smile played on the corner of Oliver's mouth.
"You can go Kayla."

"Good luck," she muttered to Tegan, squeezing her shoulder encouragingly.

"Did you have something in particular you wanted me to do, Chef? Something I need to cook up at Chloe's station."

"I know your skills, Tegan. You'll be adequate. Impress me tonight and the next opening we have could well be yours."

"Thank you, Chef. Shall I go back to prepping?"

"If you want to. Unless you'd like to thank me. There's a lot of guys out there that would've liked this chance."

"How would you like me to thank you?"

Tegan stood up and walked to the front of the desk to face Oliver.

"She knows the game," he thought.

"Have I pleased you giving you Chloe's job for the night?"

"Yes, Chef."

"Do you want to please me?"

"Yes, Chef."

Tegan pushed down her baggy black and white hounds-tooth patterned pants to reveal red French knickers. She sat on his desk and unbuttoned her chef's white to reveal the matching bra.

"How do you want me?" she asked boldly, looking directly in his eyes.

"Not facing me," he smiled.

Tegan turned away and placed her hands on the desk and wiggled her arse in his face. She was slimmer and less curvy than Chloe, but Oliver only wanted a tight arse. He suspected this was familiar territory for Tegan. He slapped her arse cheek firmly; hard enough to leave a red mark to let her know he was there for business. He could feel his cock already erect. He was possessed with the thought of ramming it in her.

Ripping her panties down, he grabbed his dick and pushed hard at the hole. Tegan whimpered.

"I haven't actually done this before."

Oliver grinned wickedly. He spread her cheeks to see the little pink bud, quivering in anticipation. Licking a finger, he let it run up and down the cleft of her buttocks. She shifted her stance to grab the far edge of the desk. He sucked his thumb. As close to tenderly as Oliver would get with sex, he pushed the tip of his thumb into her arsehole. Tegan stiffened in response and tried to slow her breathing to accept him. Oliver's free hand caressed her buttocks as he eased his thumb in.

Tegan was aware of the pain but also aware how queer her body felt with the thumb planted firmly in her arse. She felt her pussy wetten in response. Oliver didn't move his thumb but left it there a few moments longer. She wondered if her hole would become accustomed as quickly to his dick as it did his finger.

Slowly he withdrew his thumb. Tegan's gasp was audible as she had a second where she felt like she lost all control of her rectum. Oliver sucked his thumb like a happy toddler.

"Let's start prepping you properly."

His tone was both light and menacing. His tongue circled her arse and Tegan relaxed into his adoration. She gyrated slightly to signal she was ready for more. Oliver licked his index and middle finger on his right hand. He needed to stretch her entrance so that the dome of his head would enter her without trouble. Similar to what he'd done with his thumb, he popped both fingertips into her arse. Tegan was thrilled and shocked all at once but held back any verbal reaction. The tips waited until she settled and then he wriggled the length of the fingers into her.

She cried in delight.

"Shhhh," he warned.

He let his fingers stay still and then jiggled them to stimulate the inside of her arse. Her head was swimming with the new phenomenon that was overpowering. She worried her legs wouldn't hold her for the full duration. Slowly Oliver began withdrawing the length of his fingers but let the tips remain embedded in her entrance.

He licked the index and middle fingers of his free hand and brought them to her hole. He placed them inside so all four fingertips slipped inside. He leaned near and blew on her arsehole. Tegan shivered and found she was trying to withstand the girth pulling at her entrance. Tugging, he'd spread her rim and then began working in all four fingers. Each time he widened her rim, he'd force the fingers a little deeper inside her. When the four fingers were in securely, he began spreading them to stretch her deep within.

"I don't think I can take much more," she begged.

Tegan felt completely out of control. Even though she was wet and wanted to be fucked, she hated that she didn't know what to expect. It was like losing her virginity again.

Oliver released his four fingers quickly. He saw her arsehole seize shut to recover from the invasion and bliss. He couldn't afford to let the muscles tense again. Sheathing his cock, he spat on his hand and rubbed it round her ring.

"Hold tight," he whispered.

Tegan tried to ground herself, but the force of the head of his prick forcing open her arse was not something she could ever have prepared for. She released one hand from the desk to cover her mouth to smother the scream of ecstasy.

Oliver forced his seven inches directly into her hole. The snugness of her arse was infinitely more rewarding than any pussy. As he had done previously, once inside her he remained still. Every muscle twitched and tickled his dick as her arsehole stretched to accommodate the foreign body within.

Tegan returned to having both hands on the far side of the desk to prepare for the force of his thrusts. Oliver put his hands over hers and pressed his clothed body against her nakedness.

Softly and restrained he rocked his hips. Tegan thought he'd be like a wild animal, but the gentle motion where he inched in and out was bearable. As he continued at the same pace it became more than bearable – it was enjoyable. She moaned slightly.

From the sound and feel of her Oliver knew she was able to satisfy his end goal. He started withdrawing and left the dome of his shaft at the entrance. He slid smoothly into her again and repeated the action. The tug of his cock's head at her entrance had her getting louder.

"Quiet," he reminded her.

She simmered slightly so he pulled his cock completely from her. Tegan felt her nipples harden as the entrance was stretched by his exit.

She widened her legs, wondering if he'd plough her pussy now. Oliver went straight back to her ring. He forced his way in and built-up a pace. She was stretched enough so that any resistance was not unpleasurable for him. Hands on her hips he blasted into her. He bit his lip, imagining himself in a porn movie. Slamming into her, he forced her head to the desk and held it there with one hand.

It was all very intense, but Tegan reveled in being treated like a piece of meat. His need for her was dizzying. She loved each time the slams got harder and faster. He was seeking his own release and she felt on the brink of her own. As he came hard with a final thrust, Tegan felt a strange orgasmic sensation radiating from inside her arse as erogenous spots were stimulated from Oliver's cock. Electric euphoria coursed through her body. She hadn't even been aware there was such a thing as an anal orgasm, but it was even more intense than a vaginal one.

She felt his dick deflate in her until it slipped out as they both caught their breath.

"That thank you was greater than my gift to you," conceded Oliver. "It seems I'm now in your debt."

"What does that entail?"

"I'm not sure yet, but trust me when I say I don't ever neglect to fulfil a debt."

"You're a man that keeps his word then?"

"Always," he answered sincerely.

"I suppose I better get back out there."

"Don't you dare until you're clean. My kitchen has standards. You can use my shower."
Scooping her uniform up, Tegan slipped into the shower. She checked her phone to see a text from Chloe.

"You won't believe the night I've had," it read.

"You won't believe the morning I've had," replied Tina, punching in the response on her keypad.

A series of question marks were returned instantly by Chloe.

"I've moved up a rung on the ladder. Whatever you didn't do last night has given me the game advantage in kitchen wars."

Tegan added a wink and smiley face to the text to let Chloe know she was only half-joking.

Chloe looked at her phone then looked at her cupboard. Should she make the effort to go into work so Tegan can't step in her shoes?
"No," she decided.

It was a cutthroat game. If Tegan was prepared to go to those extremes to get up a rung on the ladder, then as far as Chloe was concerned, she'd earned it and deserved to enjoy it.

Serving Up A Threesome

Emily groaned as the alarm on her mobile phone sounded, shattering the peaceful ambience of the bathroom. The stillness of the hot water was broken as Emily was forced to stand up and step out of the free-standing tub to cross to the room to the counter to turn the alarm off. The large bath sheet that wrapped round her small frame felt fresh and cozy. Turning the alarm off, she placed her hand on the mirror to wipe away the steam. She admired her reflection, knowing her flawless skin shaved ten years off her age. Emily happily would've wiled away more time in the tub, but knew her skin would pucker and she wasn't sure exactly how the evening would turn out so didn't want to risk looking like a prune when her husband eventually got home.

She flung off the towel deciding to air dry in the seclusion of her empty house. One of the few perks of being infertile was there were no children to invade her privacy or make demands on her daily schedule.

"Which is why I look so fabulous for thirty-five," she declared aloud.

Taking a twirl in front of the full length mirror she mentally congratulated herself on her self-discipline. Her breasts were perky, and her figure remained slim. Everything about Emily's appearance was immaculate and near-perfect. However, with no job and a very rich husband, Emily could afford the luxury of a personal trainer and allow for regular visits to the relevant beauticians and hairdressers to ensure she remained in peak physical condition. She turned away from the mirror lest she become too mesmerized by her own appearance – like Narcissus and his pool.

Emily took herself into her dressing room. She sat on the plush pink chair and pulled it closer to the mahogany vanity to conduct her pre-makeup skin care routine.

"I wasn't always this image conscious," thought Emily. "But how else do I ensure George's eyes remain trained solely on me."

There had been a time when Emily was a flourishing PA at the law firm where George was an associate. Life had been very different back then. She'd be an independent party girl with eyes on a big career. Sharing a flat with friends and earning a generous salary she'd certainly been living her best life.

"Not that my lifestyle isn't to be envied now," she reminded herself.

But it certainly wasn't what she'd been dreaming of as a young girl and, truthfully, it wasn't really what she and George had planned either. They'd both wanted the children and the family home. Emily happily gave up her career because she wanted to be a stay-at-home mum. Her aspirations of being on the PTA and ensuring her kids were well rounded with a score of hobbies and sports for her to chauffeur them back and forth to stopped abruptly when she discovered the unfortunate news that both her and George were infertile. Maybe there would have been a shred of hope if just one of them had problems, but with both of them barren having kids naturally wasn't on the cards.

There was the niggle again. The smallest tug of anger toward her husband. It wasn't as though adoption or fostering weren't an option. In fact, they were both viable choices to have children in their lives given she didn't have to work, and her husband had a mammoth bank balance.

George was old school. He only wanted kin with his own blood running through their veins to inherit his wealth. Emily tried persuading him for some time but realized early on he wasn't going to change his position and if she didn't accept it, she was in for a long and unhappy marriage.

So that's what she did. She accepted she wasn't going to have kids. She also accepted that George was a red-blooded male. If he'd found her enticing enough to make moves on in the office way back when, there was every chance the day would come when another young girl would catch his eye. Emily had no intentions of losing George. If he left her, she knew she'd be entitled to half of everything and maintain her lifestyle, but the emptiness of not sharing a life with him would be unbearable. The thought of starting over, trying to find that connection and unconditional acceptance all over again was a burden she didn't want to bear.

"And that's why I do this. It isn't vanity. It's making an effort to maintain a happy marriage and that is nothing to be ashamed of is it, Arya?"

The miniature red and white husky tilted her head curiously at Emily as if mulling over what Emily said.

"It's nothing to be ashamed of at all," affirmed her husband's voice with a note of laughter.

Emily spun round and saw a cheeky smile on his face as he leaned against the door frame of her dressing room. All six foot four of him was irresistible. As George entered his forties, he'd only become more handsome. It was so much easier for men. Men improved as they aged, whereas women fought the good fight to cling to their looks after thirty. His jet-black hair had length to it, and he looked adorable when he ran a hand through it to slick it back. His blue eyes still danced when he looked at her. The wolfish grin of desire made everything worthwhile. That they were still magnetically drawn to each other after ten years of marriage was no small feat. They were each other's world and in that moment, Emily knew she wouldn't change a thing about their relationship.

"And I am a very happily married man," he continued, as his long legs strode determinedly toward her.

His lips brushed her shoulder.

"Can't that wait a little longer," he murmured in her ear.

The huskiness of his voice turned her on as much now as it had when he'd first taken an interest in her and insisted on her staying behind at work when they'd first met.

Emily's eyes darted to the mirror so she could see the time of the grand clock from the bedroom reflected. It was 6pm.

"What time's the restaurant booked for?"

"Not till 8pm."

He was already trailing kisses from her ear down her neck. Emily turned her head to catch his lips softly.

"If you can manage a quickie, I'm all yours."

George scooped her from the dressing stool and carried her to the bed. As long as he remained in such good condition, she would always feel like a princess in a fairytale. He placed her on the bed then moved to the end of the bed to take in the full view of her naked body. He appreciated how lithe and lean her body was. Smiling at her perfectly cute pink pedicured toes, his eyes devoured her long slim legs and settled on the landing strip on her pubis.

His hands went to her ankles and he began to part them as he crawled between her legs. Bending his head toward her pussy, he inhaled deeply to get drunk on her feminine scent. He blew out softly and saw small twitches of her pussy as it involuntarily reacted to his attention. Continuing for a moment more, George was aware of the time and leapt forward and clamped his mouth onto her clit.

Emily's hand tightened and pulled the sheet. She could feel his teeth, pinching ever so gently on her clit and tried to stay in place lest the pain increase if she struggled against the bite. He sucked firmly on the bud eliciting a juicy release from between her plump lips. Releasing the fleshy button, George's tongue went straight to her slit. It forced its way as deep into her hold as possible. Emily could feel all her nerve endings reacting, but was in a state of near delirium to worry about her contracting anus. Tonguing the entrance of her pussy, he took a long lick to taste her liquid pleasure.

George swirled his tongue round her clit. Emily felt the firm tip of it taunting her. She ground down on the tongue to let him know she was keen to climax. George puts his thumbs either side of her labia to part them. He lapped furiously at her cunt until her thighs started to shiver. Knowing how close she was to the edge, he stabbed his tongue in her slit. He wriggled it deeper and deeper inside. Convinced he was in as deep as he could go, he released her labia. He let one hand cover her mound so his thumb could encourage the clit to push his wife over the edge. As his tongue thrusted and she fucked his face, he slipped his free hand underneath her buttocks. Emily wanted what was coming but it wasn't something on their regular sexual menu so tightened her arse in anticipation. Lightly touching her rectum, George's index finger tried to enter her behind. She was tight so it required a degree of persistence on his part. Once the tip was inside her arsehole, he heard Emily gasping. He smoothly interested the full length of the finger. Emily's hips were bucking. George knew from here it would be easy to bring her to orgasm. Wiggling his finger inside her arse to stimulate the delicate nerves within, he thrust his tongue one final time in her cunt and returned to her clit. Emily writhed and eventually gushed in delight as her entire body was wracked with delicious convulsions.

Emily felt exhausted from the strong reaction to her husband's attention down south. She wasn't sure she had the energy for sex or even helping George to reach his own peak. Fortunately, George was aware of her need to recuperate. Rising from between her legs, George backed off the bed and stripped off hastily. Emily was envious of his naturally muscular physique that didn't require any gym time that she was aware of. George let her eyes drink in his nakedness before slithering up her body.

He kissed Emily deeply and athletically changed positions, so he was straddling her torso. Reaching behind, George's hand returned to scoop the juices from her pussy to lube his dick. When it was satisfactorily glistening, George slid it between her breasts. Emily's breasts were ample, and she reached to hold them tight together to give him the friction he required to come. Looking down to see the head of his cock popping out the top of her cleavage then disappearing down into them was the visual George needed to ensure this session met the time restrictions placed on it. He pumped his prick faster and faster. When he saw Emily's tongue stick out to catch the pre-cum dripping from the top of his head, he felt his own thighs quiver in anticipation. Watching the scene before him was more rewarding than any porn clip.

His hands went to Emily's breasts and he squeezed them so hard, the action was almost cruel. Seeing Emily wince had him one step closer to the end, He tweaked her nipples between his thumb and forefinger and Emily yelped out loud. The sound had George squirting out as he grunted in satisfaction. Watching the sticky, thick white liquid drip across her neck, George took a minute to admire his handiwork before speaking.

Emily looked good with his ejaculate on her. Idly he smeared the ejaculate dripping round her neck. He massaged it in.

"I'm not sure that's going to stop wrinkles on my neck."

"It might", chuckled George. "Do you still have time to do your make-up?"

"Probably if I rush," said Emily agreeably. "But I'm going to need a shower as well now."

"I'll join you."

"It's hands-off affair or we'll never make this restaurant."

Being practiced with doing her own make-up, Emily was still able to make herself as stunning as she intended to. A text alert beeped on her phone.

"Taxis here," she called to George.

He stepped out, looking the epitome of men's fashion with a simple open collared shirt and blue suit which accentuated the colour of his eyes. Emily opted for a classy red designer dress. It dropped off her model-esque frame and showed the right amount of flesh.

George offered his arm. She linked her arm through his and headed out to the cab.

"Where are we going again?" he asked as they settled in the back of the vehicle for the drive.

"The New Victorian."

"Oh right, the new hotel."

"I feel tired now. I hope I can muster up the energy to enjoy it," said Emily softly.

She rested her head on George's shoulder.

"I hope the dining isn't too fine because I'm starving now. I don't think I can handle minuscule portions," growled George.

"You may have to settle for a cheeseburger on the way home, because we are booked into the restaurant, not the buffet for the riff-raff."

"I have the appetite of the riff-raff, so I'd have been happy to slum it at the buffet."

The car pulled out. Having paid in advance, they were able to step out and admire the building.

"I'm impressed. We did well to invest here."

"Did you invest here?" asked Emily.

"We did."

George sounded pleased with himself.

"So, we're like owners of the hotel?" mused Emily.

"It doesn't work exactly like that, but I'm hoping that's the kind of treatment we'll be getting tonight."

As the main doors were opened for them, both George and Emily were in awe of the impressive open reception area. It was buzzing with life on a Thursday night. George scanned the signage to locate the restaurant and took Emily to the elevator. The glass elevator took them to the very top of the hotel. They were met by the Maître d' who greeted them as if they were the owners, which made Emily wonder just how significantly George had invested in the hotel.

Their table was situated in one of the domes that formed the top of the corner turrets of the hotel structure. The seclusion of the table tucked away in isolation and the view of the city made for an exceptionally pretty and romantic setting.

"This is something else," observed Emily.

"Isn't it just," agreed the waitress.

Emily smiled at the waitress and then realized how stunning the girl actually was. She appeared to be of mixed heritage – somewhere from southern Asia. Olive skinned, with a curvaceous figure and plump pink lips; her chocolate brown hair matched the dark richness of her eyes. Without being aware she was doing it, Emily's eyes darted to George. He was as approving of the waitress's good looks as she was.

"There's no real crime in looking," she chided herself mentally to stop herself from being hurt by George's obvious attention to the girl.

"I don't suppose you get much time to enjoy the view if the restaurant is this busy," said Emily directly to the waitress to bring the conversation back to her.

"I'm enjoying the view of such a beautiful couple far more than the city lights," replied the waitress, before leaving them with their menus.

Emily was stunned by the comment and didn't know whether to take the girl seriously or not. She gave George a look as if to say, "Did that just happen?"

"It did," answered George. "And she's either looking for a big tip or has impeccable taste."

Emily laughed and put the comment to the back of her head, but the waitress was a permanent fixture during their three-course meal with all the wine they were knocking back. What Emily found perturbing was that she didn't feel jealous of the girl. Under other circumstances she would be annoyed by anyone brazenly flirting with her husband in front of her, but the girl's flirtatious interactions seemed to be shared between them.

"Alright, I'm going to have to say it," said George in a low tone. "I swear that waitress has been flirting with you the entire evening. She obviously fancies you and I kind of like it."

Emily literally scoffed on her drink.

"Please."

"I'm serious. Another man would react differently to me. I thought I was all worn out from earlier, but I might be inclined for round two when we get home," he teased.

The waitress returned with George's credit card and receipt tucked in a leather bill presenter.

"I do hope you enjoyed your evening. It would certainly be lovely to see more of the two of you in the future."

George and Emily exchanged a look as the waitress turned and sashayed away, her black skirt hugging her hips and accentuating the sway of her curves. Smiling, George opened the folder and saw some scribble on the back of the receipt.

"If you don't want the night to end, I'll see you in Room 407 at 11pm," murmured George under his breath.

He passed the note to Emily. She read it and her eyes widened. George tried to gauge where she was with this invitation. Emily scrunched the paper up and slipped it in her handbag.

"Should we go?"

George got up silently and escorted Emily out, keeping his head down to avoid eye contact with the waitress. Once outside, Emily turned to him and suggested a drink at the bar.

"What are you thinking?" prompted Emily, when George returned to her with a non-alcoholic beverage.

"I think I was right about her fancying you."

"She might just be trying to get to you through me. Women are devious," noted Emily.

"Is that really the vibe you got?"

"Actually no. And she was beautiful."

George thought Emily's final statement was odd. It was as if she wasn't closed off from the idea. The thought of him in bed with two women was a dream come true, but he also had no intention of jeopardizing the long-term state of his marriage with a rash decision.

"It's certainly a night that's been good for both our egos."
"It could be a night that we never forget," mused Emily.

"I don't want you having any regrets so it's probably best I get you home."

Emily closed her eyes. George knew she was choosing her words carefully and giving their predicament a great deal of thought.

"Opportunities like this are few and far between. If this is something we both want, I'm not sure it'll present itself so organically again any time soon. And I bet we won't get another invite from Angel if we stand her up."

"Wow, you even took the time to memorize her name," teased George.

"It's 10.45pm. Should we be making our way to room 407?"

"You wish is my command."

They took a slow walk to the hotel room. George tried the handle on the door, and it opened without the need for a key or card. The room was as gloriously furnished as the hotel reception and restaurant. George and Emily sat on the couch where three glasses and a bottle of champagne were set up. The door to the bathroom opened and Angel, the waitress, walked out wearing a stunning piece of lingerie. The white lace accentuated her brown skin.

"You must've been pretty confident we were going to show up to go to this effort."

Emily could feel her throat was dry and the words sounded unnatural coming from her mouth. Angel knelt in front of her. He hand caressed Emily's cheek. She gazed deeply into her eyes.

"Some people are worth making a fool of yourself over."
Before she knew what was happening, the soft round lips of Angel's were on hers. Emily's eyes closed instinctively so she could be consumed by the kiss of this beautiful girl. Angel slipped the straps of Emily's dress over her shoulders. Another kiss went on the base of her neck. Angel's hand expertly unclasped her bra. Her gaze on Emily's breast was adoring. She kissed the round bosom and then sucked on a nipple. Her other hand massaged the neglected breast and every so often teased the nipple.

Emily was frozen. Everything seemed to be happening too fast. Aware that Emily wasn't responding, Angel continued sucking on her nipple and slid her free hand between her own thighs.

George could see Angel pleasuring herself and decided to step in to reassure Emily. He undressed keeping his eyes glued on the sensual scene unfolding in front of him. Once naked, he pushed the table aside to get behind Angel.

Angel could feel George's nakedness. His hard cock was pressed between her bouncy buttocks. His hand went over hers and followed the motion as her fingers danced on her clit. George's hand went under the lace to get to her pussy. Angel threw her head against the back of his chest and grinded against his hand. Her slippery clam was ready and waiting for whoever wanted to do whatever to her.

As Angel released her breasts from the lingerie, Emily was able to see George was now actively involved. She wasn't sure how she felt about her husband getting another woman off in front of her. Angel was pushing her behind back further and further. George backed away to take Angel by the waist and help her onto all fours. Emily didn't have time to object. She watched as George grabbed his shaft, sheathed it with one of the condoms Angel had laid out enticingly alongside the champagne and slid straight into Angel's pussy.

Emily wasn't quite sure what to do with herself. She felt exposed and ignored at the same time. Initially this felt amazing but with George's involvement she felt very much on the outskirts. A slapping sound bought her back into the room. George was slapping and leaving a red hand imprint on Angel's buttocks as he slammed into her.

Emily realized she only had one weapon in her artillery. She slid her dress and panties off and took Angel's chin so that she was forced to look up at the hours of work Emily had devoted to her slim figure. Angel's eyes went from glassy to focused. She licked her lips. Emily placed her foot on the side of the nearby table to stretch open her manicured pussy for Angel to see. Angel immediately dived forward and began licking the spread slit.

George's cock had been abandoned. But watching someone else lick out his wife kept him rock hard. He rubbed Angel's crack, moving down to her slit and then pushed two fingers inside her. Angel groaned into Emily's vagina. Emily held her head in place so that Angel couldn't divert her full attention back to George's finger fucking.

George's eyes met Emily's.

"I need you," he mouthed hungrily.

He nodded his head over to the bed. Indicating that they needed to move the action somewhere a little more comfortable. Emily released Angel from her task. She walked straight to the bed. With Angel free from Emily's pussy, George plunged his rod back inside her and cupped her pendulous breasts as he slammed back and forth into her.

"Come."

Emily's command had George withdrawing before he came inside Angel. He went over to lay in the middle of the king-size mattress. Before Angel could take control of what was happening, Emily squatted onto George's cock and began to bounce.

"You take his face. I've already had that this evening," directed Emily.

Angel removed her remaining lingerie and then mirrored Emily by squatting on George's face. She rubbed her wet pussy over his face, pressing on his nose. George's tongue was out, lapping at her sweet juices. Catching Emily's gaze, Angel sat to smother George's face with her ample thighs. Emily slowed her bounce down and lent across George's body to connect in a kiss with Angel again. This time she let her tongue delve into Angel's mouth. Her hands reached over to hold her heavy breasts. She let her hands trace the curves of Angel's figure. Lost in the kiss, Emily finally broke away when she saw George's hands gripping Angel's thighs to try and release for air. She put her hand on Angel's shoulders to drown George in pussy for just a moment longer while she rapidly built up her pace on his cock.
Only when George thought he might die in sexual bliss as he felt a tight pussy flying up and down his prick while he drowned in Angel's juices, did his ejaculation come. The might of it was such that he was able to break free from Angel's quim and gasp for breath.

Angel wasted no time in hopping off the bed and heading straight to the shower.

Emily was still straddling George. He half sat up to pull her tight to him.

"You okay?" he whispered in her ear.

"I am." She paused. "What happens next?"

"I don't really know."

"What happens now is I kiss you and you goodbye and leave you here to enjoy the delights of the room," advised Angel, kissing both George and Emily sensually on the lips.

"Are we allowed to stay?" asked Emily.

"Perks of being an investor in this place."

She winked at them.

Emily looked at George and he winked knowingly at her.

"Are you a perk of this place as well?" she asked the waitress.

Angel smiled.

"Of course. Whenever you want me to be!"

She left the room.

"That's quite the perk." said Emily, processing whether she was annoyed or excited by George's bold move. "How'd you know I'd go for it?"

"I didn't. And I wanted it to be your decision, but happy birthday darling."

"If you're hoping I'll return the favor for your birthday…. you might just be right."

First Night Nerves

The atmosphere was engaging each and every sense to the point of over stimulation.

The almost primal roar of excited women of all ages filling the venue to capacity were drowning out the smooth, sexual R&B tunes blaring from the sound system. The hormonal buzz was palpable. Estrogen emanated from the pores of what appeared to be an all-female crowd. Olivia could feel goosebumps raising on her arm. The tingling sensation of her skin was a reaction to the waves of different moods and desire generated by the women surrounding her. The extreme range of anticipation ran from absolute desperation to a fevered thirst for the next man to appear on stage. Olivia struggled trying to control her own temperament to something mid-scale. On stage was a blazing electrical light show matching the beats pounding from a nearby amplifier, but when she turned her head away from the spectacle, she was met by a sea of animated expressions she wasn't able to discern between. Her chest rose and fell heavily. The temperature was rising even though rationally she knew this was a new building and couldn't possibly be without air conditioning. She reached out to grip her glass, grateful for the beads of condensation from the ice in her cocktail. She allowed herself a long sip, knowing that most of the alcohol was considerably watered down by melted ice. The taste of peach schnapps and cranberry juice was a welcome relief to her tongue. She felt as though she could taste the sweat and heavy panting from the aroused strangers.

A hand on her leg diverted her attention from the claustrophobia settling in.

"Enjoying it, love?"

She nodded vigorously at her Aunt while mouthing, "Sure am."

What she wanted to say was, "Not as much as you."

Olivia wasn't the type to rain on anyone's parade, let alone her Aunt whose hen party she was attending. She knew going to a male strip show was a given for most hen parties, but the whole eagerness to drool over chiseled torsos during a seductive dance felt demeaning. Taking in the room again, Olivia realized she was in the minority. Shaking her head, she flung her arm round her aunt to give her a squeeze. There was nothing wrong with a little silliness and a lot of fun. Olivia had the feeling her Aunt's friends thought she was a prude or had a giant stick up her backside. Whilst she couldn't quite submit to emulating the screams of a teenage girl to encourage the next act to grace the stage, she did permit herself to match the drinking pace of the women in her party and clapped amiably to add to the noise to encourage the stripper.

When he finally came on stage Olivia acknowledged he was worth the wait. Lean and six foot two. he had the perfect body definition without looking like an ape on steroids. A grin played on her lips and she was grateful her aunt had insisted on arriving early to ensure they were as close to the action as possible. He leapt off the dais to prowl the audience, hunting a lady to join him for his dance.

The stripper's green eyes lit up at the sight of her hen's party. Although there were plenty of bachelorette celebrations to choose from, he was acutely aware that picking a middle-aged soon-to-be-bride might provide better entertainment and reactions from the show-goers. He put his hand out and took Olivia's aunt's fingers. She could hear her aunt's squeals and the raucous laughter from the surrounding people. Given her demeanor throughout the performance thus far, Olivia thought her aunt would've shot up there faster than a speeding bullet. Suddenly she was coquettish and refusing the invitation. The performer allowed her a moment more in the spotlight before kissing her hand gently then letting it slip from his.

"Choose Liv. Take my niece up," her Aunt boldly suggested. "Heaven knows she could do with the attention."

Olivia was mortified. A red bloom flushed her cheeks as she imagined the entire crowd could hear the comment. She furiously waved her arms to signal this was not something she was prepared to do.

"Oh, go on, love. It'll be fun. I can't do it, or my Arthur would be furious, but when are you going to get a lad like that grinding on you again?"

Olivia wanted to argue that Arthur would be fine with her Aunt going up. Hell, they were in their 60s and it was Arthur's third time down the aisle. It was highly unlikely the stripper would be asking a woman close to retirement to forgo her nuptials and runaway with him. With the crowd impatiently chanting, Olivia didn't have time to present this argument. Besides, her Aunt had a point. Olivia knew she wasn't exactly in demand on fashion catwalks so the chances of her having a hot guy dance for her were in fact few and far between.

"Okay, let's do it," she conceded.

The stripper smirked at her. For the first time she was able to take in his face. He had a jawline you could grate cheese on, and his eyes were a shade of sea-green that Olivia had only ever seen in travel blogs to pacific islands she would never be able to afford to visit. Dropping her head to the floor so she didn't embarrass herself by tripping up the stairs to the platform was the only way to dampen the queer sensation she felt in her stomach. The stripper gently guided her to a stool center stage. She had to disconnect herself from what was going on if she was going to avoid the shame washing over her. Most women in her position would be overreacting and making the most of the opportunity, but Olivia was crippled by anxiety.

"Hey, Look at me. Things are about to hot up!"
Olivia instinctively raised her head at the dulcet tones of the stripper. Her eyes were waist level. She could see the outline of his cock straining at his leather pants.

"This is just obscene," she thought. "That's got to be close to 8 inches."

She wanted to look away, but she was mesmerized by the form of the crotch in his pants. A lump formed in her throat, proving hard to swallow down. She forced her eyes upward only to be met with the sight of his flattened stomach. It was as if an Italian renaissance sculpture had come to life and transported himself to the 21st Century.

Processing the beauty of the man in front of her, Olivia didn't have time to resist when he took a few steps away from her and lifted her from the seat. She relaxed – relieved it was finally over.

Except it wasn't.
Olivia realized she was being assisted to lay on the floor. This was what he meant about things hotting up. She internally cringed knowing he was going to simulate sex with her. It was beyond her to derive any pleasure from this public embarrassment. Her breathing was hot and heavy – not from the sexual playfulness, but from the reality that Olivia hadn't actually had sex yet and was completely overwhelmed. She didn't have a clue what to do or how to behave. Her body was like a doll. She could only let the stripper manipulate her into the positions he required for his dance. Just as she was inventing ways to disassociate from what was happening, she felt a hand on her chin and her face was tilted to meet those deep green eyes.

"Trust me. If you relax you might enjoy it."

But she couldn't. She shut her eyes as she heard the horny crowd screaming in delight. She could feel his near naked body getting closer and closer to hers. His face was lowered to hers as the gyrations became slower. Her eyelids fluttered open as his peppermint breath was on her face. He was smirking again, and she felt giddy at the sight. There was a throbbing below and Olivia wondered if he could feel the heat radiating from between her legs. She had an urge to put her arms round his shoulders and pull him close to her. She wanted to feel him grinding against her. He was so close - almost touching her but not breaking any boundaries.

"I wonder if there are rules to this," she thought. "Probably. He's treating me with respect. Well as much respect as you can when you're essentially a sex doll for entertainment purposes. It definitely would be against the rules for me to touch him. I'm sure that's like a client stripper unspoken code."

As he reached his performance climax, Olivia let her pelvis gradually move upwards. The length of the cock she'd been studying earlier rubbed against her pussy. She'd never wanted a man more in her life.

But it was over, and he'd finished. He was kissing her on the cheek and presenting her with a rose. She was greeted by a stagehand dressed in all-black who was directing her back to her seat. As she sat down to the cheers and jeers from the hen party, she was unable to analyse her feelings and emotions. Now she felt jittery and on edge. Olivia couldn't think straight.

"But that's the stress of being up on stage. I'm not cock hungry or anything," she thought as she rubbed her eyes in a bid to bring herself into the present situation.

The remainder of the show passed in a blur. Olivia felt still in the action. She was greatly relieved when she realized the seats were emptying and the crowd was thinning out.

"I took plenty of photos to put on your socials," shared her Aunt wickedly.

"Oh God, No."

"Sweetie, it's good to have the memories to look back on."

"I don't think I'm ever going to forget tonight," stammered Olivia.

"Got the heart pumping did he?"

"I'm not really someone who thrives on attention. So, a public scene like that certainly did get my pulse racing. But not in a good way. I thought I was going to have a heart attack up there."

"You certainly were the inevitable duck out of water," chuckled her Aunt.

"I'm sure I looked like a complete idiot."

The butterflies had long departed Olivia's stomach. She now felt like vomiting at the realization that her escapades had been seen by hundreds and probably more if people were sharing photos and videos over social media. It may all be lighthearted, but Olivia was traumatized at the thought of people witnessing her awkwardness and reluctance to enjoy playing with a hot man.

"Liv, any of the girls who went up there tonight looked foolish. Whether they were embarrassed or over eager or trying to play it cool. I can't think of any woman that could go up there and come back with their dignity completely intact."

"I know you're trying to make me feel better, but you're not."

Olivia's Aunt sighed. There was no cheering her favorite niece up. The auditorium was nearly completely empty.

"What do you think of this place? It's fab isn't it? It's nice to have a hotel in town that offers so much." It was idle chit-chat, but Olivia didn't want to continue replaying the evening in her head and suspected her Aunt wasn't enamored with having to spend her hen's night consoling her niece. Taking part in the conversational pleasantry, Olivia took in the theatre located in the basement of the hotel. Now the show was over, and the audience were gone, it was devoid of the abundance of life it had contained for two hours.

"Well, we've only seen the theatre so far. I mean, it's looking abandoned now, but they put on a great show. Everyone seemed to have a blast."

"Everyone except you," her Aunt guffawed.

"Can we not do this?"

"Liv, it's like this. You can overthink this for the rest of the night or come and explore with me. Apparently, there's a nightclub here."

"A nightclub? Evidently the New Victorian has got it all."

"It's the city's grandest hotel," mimicked her Aunt from the famous adverts that had plagued all media sources months before its opening.

"You go on. I'll join you. I need a bit of time on my own to get my head back into party mode."

"Well, I don't want you getting lost."

"In the city's grandest hotel?" teased Olivia to reassure her Aunt that she really was okay. "I'm sure there'll be plenty of staff to help out if I need directions. Anyway, I bet I'll hear the gang long before I see you given the noise we were making tonight."

"Very true."

Her Aunt planted a kiss on her head.
"I best enjoy my last night of freedom from Arthur. Come find me on the dance-floor."

Olivia watched her Aunt walk back up the aisle and out the theatre. She was now the only person left. Standing, Olivia took a step back to take in her surroundings. Most new buildings felt either minimalist and sterilized or were over-the-top and desperate to be eye-catching. The nod to Victorian architecture was to be admired and gave the venue its own character. Tracing her fingers along the intricate wall designs, Olivia heard voices in conversation coming from the stage.

Ever the introvert she studied the red carpet. Forcing herself to be interested in the plush maroon carpet and ignore any direct eye contact with the folk intruding on her time-out. She felt the rush of the small group pass her by as they too headed out to explore the hotel.

"You know there were tickets available at an extra charge if you wanted backstage access to the boys."

Tightening her hands into fists, Olivia knew it wasn't a tired usher trying to get her out of the theatre to close up for the night. She also knew she couldn't ignore the person trying to engage her in conversation.

"I didn't know that, but that's not why I'm still here," she replied, taking her gaze from the carpet up to the face talking to her as social convention dictated.

Olivia knew what was under the white shirt and she knew the bulge behind the zip on the denim jeans. She focused on his chin to avoid eye-contact.

"Then why are you still here?"

The green eyes lowered a fraction to meet her gaze.

"Just recovering," she mumbled.
His eyes were penetrating, and she felt faint.

"I don't think so."

He stepped closer to her. Olivia remained silent. His fingers laced into hers.

"Do you want this?"

Everything was about consent nowadays. In normal situations the constant need for verbal questions and answers to clarify communication took away from the sexiness of acting on impulse. In all fairness though, given his job and how badly a roomful of women wanted him, she couldn't blame him for wanting an answer.

Did she want this though? She was twenty-two years old and had never had sex. Olivia couldn't think of any particular reason why she'd kept her virginity intact. It wasn't as if she had strict religious beliefs. She'd been raised to respect herself and had a strong sense of self-esteem, so she'd never fallen victim to peer pressure or the need to seek a man's approval to establish how attractive she was to the opposite sex.

"Am I a romantic at heart?" she thought. "Am I waiting to be in love to give myself to someone? Or am I just waiting for someone to stir the urge in me, so I give into that carnal desire? Is losing your virginity for lust a lesser reason than losing it for love?"

"Yes. I want this," she said aloud.

Her brown eyes finally met his. The electricity sizzled between them and as his mouth covered hers, she understood the need she felt for him had not been one sided. His breath was still fresh, and her knees buckled slightly when his tongue moved into her mouth. One hand cupping her cheek she felt a burst of dampness flood her panties.

She did want this.
As the kiss deepened, his free hand went to her waist and unbuttoned her jeans. Olivia immediately wished she'd worn something more feminine or at least more accessible. His hand cupped her pussy and she moaned in his mouth.

In the deep recesses of her mind Olivia wasn't sure it was ideal to lose her virginity in a place so public where they risked being interrupted or worse arrested. But the need to have him fill her was so overpowering any common sense or logic was abandoned.

Wantonly, she pushed down on his hand as it pressed against the sheer material of her panties. Her clit became engorged as she rubbed to be pleasured. When the material of her panties lifted and two fingers slipped between her wet lips, Olivia felt she might explode. A thumb crept in and she was amazed that he could feel her pulsating clit as he pushed it like a button rhythmically and in time with the contractions. Olivia wasn't sure where to take things. The jeans were too tight for him to pull down to access her properly and yet that's what had to happen.

The stripper alerted Olivia to her unintentional selfishness. Grabbing her hand, he placed it on the cock straining at the seams. The heat and outline already felt familiar to her.

"If you want this. Show me."

Instinctively Olivia's hands went to his belt. Undoing the belt was nowhere near as difficult as she dreaded it would be. The leather moved easily through her hands as she freed it from the buckle. The moments taken to unbutton the stripper's jeans gave Olivia time to remember the specimen of man in front of her. Without encouragement, she lifted his shirt over his head. While he shrugged the shirt off, her hands felt the smooth olive skin. She traced the outline of his pecs. Stepping closer to inhale his scent, she was fighting an urge to taste him. Olivia shook her head to free herself from her self consciousness. She licked his chest and began dropping to her knees. As she lowered herself, she let her tongue trace his six pack. She nipped the prominent hip bone that led to the designer band of his boxers. His hand touched the top of her head for the briefest of seconds before the slight pressure was released.

Olivia wasn't sure if she was ready to taste his dick, but he smelt so good. She knew he'd showered recently from the aroma of a coconut milk shower gel and yet she was driven to taste him as she recalled the strong essence of his masculinity from the sweat that had dripped on her while she was underneath him on stage.

She tugged at his boxers and felt them, and his jeans fall easily. Olivia had never seen an actual prick so close up. Despite how frightening the pale purple sword with veins running through looked, her tongue flicked over the head of it. Hearing the stripper groan she let her tongue brush the length of the shaft and was rewarded as his moans became more audible.

Olivia stood up. Keener and more needy she hurriedly removed her own jeans. Her tongue had sent a message to her slit that he would feel as good as he tasted. The stripper effortlessly wrapped his erection in a condom.

The stripper bunched her panties to one side and lifted her. Olivia was immediately concerned that she was too heavy, and this was like a scene from a movie that when executed in real life failed dismally. The stripper however was confident and reached down to grab his cock to let it slide in. Any worries about how amiss this was going to go were abandoned as the head of the dick forced against her slit. She yelped in pain and let herself slide down the strong muscular thighs.

The pace didn't falter. Almost as if they were on stage again, the stripper guided her to the floor. On her back he was in complete control. He parted her legs and knelt between them. Rubbing the round head between her drenched lips he tried again at the entrance of her pussy. There were no rules now. As he penetrated the hymen, she dug her fingernails into his shoulders and bit his collar bone hard.
He moaned and kept his movements smooth and slight. Taking his time, he began to inch his length into her. With every inch that went in, he would pause and withdraw slightly leaving the tip in and then slide in again going a little further each time.

Olivia was on a knife edge between pleasure and pain. When he finally stuffed the entirety of his shaft inside her, he kissed her and enjoyed the tightness of her newly breached pussy clinging to his cock. He could feel the muscles beginning to relax around his girth and then started a slow rhythmic drive. She would routinely drag her nails into his flesh and bite hard into his shoulder but the newness of her was a turn on. The stripper had enough experience with backstage artists and slept with enough eager fans to know any visible marks on his body could be disguised for his next performance.

Olivia was enthralled with how wet and stretched her slit was. As his pace picked up to plough into her deeper and rougher, she forgot the pain and focused on how much they needed each other in this instance. She wrapped her legs around his waist to lock him in. The stripper bucked and she tightened her grip. Thrilled she was enjoying the ride, the stripper let himself go. As he brought himself to climax, he ensured that his pubis rubbed Olivia's to ensure her clit got the attention it required to have her moaning and convulsing in unknown bliss.

When he finished, he landed an affectionate kiss on her lips.

Olivia lay there dazed and confused. As she let the new sensations subside, she realized the stripper was already getting dressed. Following suit, Olivia forced herself to her feet and began dressing.
"All good?"

It was an odd question to be asked after something so intimate had taken place.

"Sure, I guess," she replied, matching his detached but friendly tone.

"Looks like you'll have another good story to tell the old girls when you find them."

Olivia only found the comment half funny; it was also a little rude to be making fun of the people she was spending the night with.

"Time for me to call it a night," he announced.

"Will I see you again?"

Olivia hated herself for letting the question escape.

"Only if you're willing to pay to see the show again when we're next back."

His tone was matter of fact but not cruel.

"Do I get to know your name?" she asked awkwardly.

He considered her carefully.

"Best not to. If you know my name it makes this more than it was. If we leave it like this, you'll remember how it happened and that's what I want for you."

The reality of everything that happened, how it happened, why it happened and how it had now finished came crashing down on Olivia.

"Do you think losing your virginity for lust a lesser reason than losing it for love?"

"No," he replied. "But always remember this was lust. Maybe next time try love."

"Maybe." Olivia forced her tone to be steady. The trouble with lust was the intensity of the feeling could be fleeting. He'd gone from being perfection to behaving like a two-dimensional poster pin-up.

"I need to find that nightclub," declared Olivia, quickening her pace to keep her dignity intact and ensure it was the stripper who would be left alone in the theatre and not her.

145

Club Bangers

"I am horny AF," puffed Amber as she hefted two crates of soft drink behind the bar.

"What?"

"I SAID I'M HORNY AF!"

Her nearby colleagues heard her and smiled. There was every chance the drunken club goers heard her as well, but given they were all there to get themselves a little something something, any that did nodded their heads in agreement.

"How come?" asked Macy, crouching down to help Amber stack the small mixer bottles into the fridge.

"I was rostered on downstairs in the theatre bar. They had some male revue show on."

"Revue?"

"Fancy name for strippers but those boys were on another level. Plucking people out of the audience to bump and grind on. I thought I was going to rush to the stage."

"I need to get me a shift down there."

"You do. I had to mop the floor behind the bar twice because I was dripping, if you know what I mean," Amber gave an exaggerated wink.

"Damn! Don't make me jealous."

"How's it been up here?"

"Started off a bit quiet, but now the theatre and restaurant are closed people have been pouring in," said Macy.

"It was rammed downstairs. A ton of hen parties going crazy."

"I think most of them have come up here. I saw a troupe of middle-aged women come through. Living their best life. Thinking they're hell raisers but causing absolutely no trouble."

Amber stood up and scanned the nightclub.

"Yeah, they were with me downstairs, I think one of them was lucky enough to get onstage with one of the performers."

"We need to send a message downstairs to invite them up here to relax after the show. A little bit of eye candy. Maybe a lock-in afterwards," suggested Macy.

"I'm down for that. Let me send one of the boys down to bring up some more," she looked at the bar to see what needed refilling. "They can bring up light bottled beers."

Amber beckoned Levi over. She whispered some instructions in his ear. He winced but took the napkin she'd written her invitation to the performers on.

"I should trash this. I don't need the competition," said Levi wickedly as he lifted the bench to step out from the bar.

The team continued working as the nightclub filled and the lines of people keen for a beverage increased. Levi came back from glass collecting.

"DJ wants a drink," he shouted over to the girls.

"I'll do it!" chimed Amber and Macy simultaneously.

"Maybe I should. Don't want a cat fight to break out."

The girls looked at each other.

"Someone needs to keep an eye out for the strippers, and I wasn't down there to see them. I won't know them if they come in."

Macy put a strong case forward.

"You go!" Amber conceded to Macy.

"I owe you!"

Macy grabbed a cold bottle of beer and made up a double rum and coke. Ducking under the bar, she bobbed and weaved her way through the crowd to the DJ booth. And there he was – superstar DJ Marco Rossi. All the way over from Italy to perform a one-month residency at the launch of the New Victorian hotel. It was the perfect way for the nightclub to attract any party goer in the vicinity. In fact, his name would draw people from afar. He normally spent his year playing festivals round the globe, but clearly the hotel had deep pockets to secure him for a four-week stint. His black hair was curly. Sweat dripped from his handsome face as he tweaked knobs while pushing a headphone close to one ear. His blue eyes caught sight of Macy. He grinned – happy to see it was a friendly staff member and not another DJ groupie bombarding him with requests in a bid to get his attention. He dropped the headphone and held a hand out for her to climb the two steps past security and into his booth.

She offered him the drinks.

"Sit down with me," he said.

She crouched down behind the decks out of the glare of the envious fans. He sat next to her.

"Set's good for 20 minutes. Join me."

Marco was used to the insane sound of the crowd so knew the correct pitch to speak at to not have to repeat himself.

"I didn't bring a beer," said Macy regretfully.

"Share mine."

He took a swig between his cupid bow shaped lips and handed her the bottle. Macy let the cool beer run down her throat. She was glad to have five minutes off her feet, but even gladder to be next to the sexiest man in the city.

"I'm glad they sent you. I've had my eye on you."

Macy's face flushed.

"Really?"

"Yeah. You seem like you run this scene. You have your finger on the pulse of this place."

"Looks can be deceiving?"

"You looked like an angel coming over with that rum and coke," he said, taking the glass from her. "That must mean you have the devil inside you."

Macy was stumped for words.

"Naughty and nice. Sugar and spice?" teased Marco.

"I can be whoever you want me to be."

She hoped she sounded flirtatious and not like the awkward idiot she felt like.

"I would like to hold you to your word on that one."

"You better," she countered, taking another swig of beer.

"Party in my suite tonight. Can you make sure the prettiest people in the building attend?"

Macy felt like a pimp. She also realized he wanted to make sure he had a huge selection of girls to choose from before he selected the special one for tonight. All the same, a party in Marco Rossi's suite was something that needed to be checked off her bucket list. If she got a little alone time with him, she might be able to win him over before he laid eyes on Amber and the other stunning bar staff.

Returning to the bar, she sent the word out to all the staff that fitted the bill of Marco's appeal for pretty little things -which was anyone public facing who worked at the hotel. The atmosphere became more manic in the club because of the buzz regarding the party. It was already on the socials, so security had been alerted. The remainder of the shift flew by due to catering to the demands of the sheer number of people partying the night away as the club reached capacity. Macy and Amber couldn't have been happier when 5am finally came.

For once it wasn't too hard to get the party goers to leave. They were all keen for the after-party. A significant number were hoping to slip into Marco's private party. Once the club emptied it was only the last few staff cleaning and restocking the bar.

"Let's just go to the party and leave this till tomorrow," suggested Amber.

"The party's not going anywhere. In fact, it'll only just be in full swing by the time we clean up and get up there."

"Yeah, but I want to change and make myself look gorgeous for Marco!"

"Hands off he's with me," warned Macy.

"All's fair in love and war. Seeing as I let you provide Marco's refreshment tonight, the least you can do is let me have a head start to the party."

"Be off with you," laughed Macy in good humor.

She didn't own Marco anyway, although a little girl code might not go amiss when it came to Amber chasing anything with a dick and a pulse.

Macy finished cleaning the bar then went out the back to the club where the main storeroom was. The corridor was dark but there was a light coming from the room which was being used as Marco's personal lounge (a fancy name for dressing room). She knocked on the door. One of his security guards opened it.

"Macy, come inside," welcomed Marco.

He appeared to have his own little bar set up.

"You do realise there's a massive party happening in your suite?"

"Sure, but I can't be on time. I need to make a grand entrance and I need to warm up a little before I go. Get in the right headspace. Want to help?"

"Of course."

Macy sipped the vodka, lime and lemonade a security guard passed her.

"Come sit on my sofa."

The sofa was heart shaped. It could fit maybe two people at best. She sat next to Marco. He put an arm round her shoulders and nuzzled her neck playfully.

"Sure you want to play?" he asked again.

"I'm sure."

"And my boys, can they watch?"

If having two security guards watch her was the only way she was going to make out with Marco, Macy felt she could handle that.

"Absolutely."

Marco kissed her passionately as she imagined only an Italian man could. He was already tugging at her t-shirt and jeans. She knew Marco had pulled her t-shirt over her head and unbuttoned her jeans but wasn't sure who pulled the t-shirt from her arms and yanked her jeans off her legs. Her body quivered. She sat up to look round. The security guards were opposite ends of the heart couch, each holding an item of her clothing.

"Don't be shy," said Marco comfortingly. "You're so pretty. Let my boys look."

He pushed her from him. The two security guards gazed approvingly at her.

Marco jumped up from the couch leaving Macy solo. She curled into a ball.

"Don't be silly. We want to admire you. You're so feminine, so pure."

Macy forced herself to uncurl.

"Lay on your back," directed Marco.

She did as she was told.

"I'm honored to have a girl this beautiful in front of me. Can my boys touch you? I want them to feel how soft you are. Is that okay?"

The two security guards flanked Marco. They were both broad and muscular, but Macy couldn't make out their faces in the dimmed mood lighting Marco insisted on having in his dressing room.

"Okay."
She felt hands on her knees, spreading her legs and exposing her pubis.

"It'd be great to get those panties off now."

Marco's voice remained kind but firm.

She didn't know whose hands were unsuccessfully tearing at the material of her underwear. She wasn't sure whose hands were caressing her peachy inner thighs and whose fingers were playing with her pussy lips. Frankly speaking, she didn't care. One man alone could never lavish this much attention on her body. She delighted in grinding down, so the fingers went deeper.

She could hear mutterings of "feel how wet she is", "so soft", "must want more".

Rather than risk saying the wrong thing, Macy undid her own bra and sat up slightly. Two different hands from two different guys landed on her breasts and squeezed them as though testing to see if some fruit was ripe or not. One hand went back to cupping her mound and idly flicking her labia. She was relaxed and in heaven.

The door of the room swung open. She was mortified. There was nothing to cover her. Stuck in only skewed panties, Marco and his security guards didn't seem too interested in protecting her modesty.

"Sorry mate," said an amused voice. "We're in the show downstairs. We got an invite to come party. Are we in the wrong place or have we struck fucking gold?"

"Macy? These guys have come all the way from the theatre to party with us. You don't mind do you?"

Macy looked up at the Greek Adonis filling the doorway.

"The more the merrier!"
"Did I say that out loud? The pheromones are going to my head," she thought.

The three boys walked over.

"Can I have a feel?" asked one voice.

"Share the hole with me."

Marco's was the only voice she knew.

Various shaped fingers were going in and out of her pussy. They all felt different, but they all felt right as they dipped in and out of her slit.

"Hey, can you get on all fours so we can inspect your arse?" prompted a young voice – one of the strippers Macy guessed. Turning onto all fours, she was able to see the six figures ranging in height and weight surrounding the couch.

"Anything you want from us?" asked a stripper with brown, floppy hair and green eyes.

She swallowed to stare up to six topless men. Their faces were indiscernible, but there was enough light for her to enjoy the muscular torsos surrounding her.

"He wants to know if you want to see our cocks?" clarified Marco.

She was wet and wanting.

"I'm game," she consented.

All men unbuttoned their jeans or chinos, pulling them low enough for their dicks to spring out. Macy licked her lips at the variety in front of her. Marco stepped forward. His thick, seven inches sprung out of a bush, as dark and curly as that on his head. She opened her mouth to invite him in. From her peripheral visual she was aware that the security guards were either side of Marco. Her hands reached. One shaft she was barely able to close her grip round, the other one pretty average. She moved her hands and realized they were dry. Releasing Marco from her mouth, she licked each palm. Gripping the guards' dick, she worked up a rhythm that had them both groaning. Opening wide, she stuck her tongue out to entice Marco to let her mouth work his hard-on. Marco slapped the head of his prick on her tongue to lube it to his liking. Stepping forward, he allowed Macy to swallow as much of him as she wanted to or was able to.

The strippers watched for a while then decided to tend to Macy. She felt her underwear being bunched and hauled upward, the seam rubbing her clit each time it was yanked. Hands and fingertips of varying texture roamed her buttocks and thighs. She was rolling her hips to encourage the boys at the back.

"Let's get them off," she heard.

The panties were being ripped down her thighs. She lifted each knee one by one so they could be removed completely. Fingers were pinching her labia and a thumb was pressed on her arse hole. Two fingers wormed into her slit. All the while it seemed her buttocks and thighs were trapped in a never-ending caress.

"Shall we fuck her?"

"No, no," said Marco, thrusting his hips violently.

Macy gagged; her throat muscles forced Marco's length out. Spit fell from the side of her mouth.

"I want to try at every hole first," said Marco. "Then you're all welcome to have a turn."

Macy felt tears streaming down her cheeks from ejecting Marco's needy cock. Bodies seemed to be moving. She could tell from the fragrance of aftershave the strippers were at the head of the sofa where she was facing. Stretching her neck, she licked the furthest cock and had a suck. He was a good size for oral. Moving across the row she lapped the shaft of the next dick – slightly longer and slimmer. Swallowing him down, she sucked up and down his length. Releasing him she went to the prick at the end of the row – thicker but not ridiculous. Her tongue teased the under rim of the head of his rod. She opened her mouth wide to take in the dome. Once in, she held the base of the cock so she could control how much of him went down her raw throat. Her hands moved between stroking the rock-hard physiques of the strippers to grabbing the available erections to select which one she would taste next.

"Boys, start getting her ready."

Macy could hear Marco priming his security guards to prepare her body for him.

She felt fingers on her pussy again. One finger slipped in, then two.
"She'll need three for it to be as thick as my dick."

Three fingers rammed in – twisting left and then right.

"Stretch her nice and wide. I want her loose."

The roughness of the invasion of the fingers had her gushing.

"She's good to go."

A cock slid in her cunt. She immediately stopped tending the strippers realizing that Marco was inside her. She bounced up and down his length.

"Don't be rude and forget my friends."

Macy realized that the strippers were rubbing her neck and reaching down to cup her breasts. Forcing herself away from the feel of Marco's perfect penis penetrating her, Macy returned to the cocks. Marco fucked her a little longer before pulling out. Immediately another rod slid into her. It felt different but the same. A different size, a different shape, a different pace, but essentially just another dick thrusting inside her. Again, she felt a withdrawal and another prick plunged in. Macy realized it was the security guards being given Marco's leftovers. Because she had no real attraction to the guards, she let them get on with it and continued performing oral on the strippers as they rearranged themselves to get sucked and licked. The pace of the pumping increased, and Macy stopped – concerned about protection.

"No coming till my say."

Macy could sense the other participants nodding in agreement at Marco's command.

"Are we using con-" she asked, coming to a halt.

"Everyone is wrapped and ready," promised Marco.
"They don't taste it," said Macy boldly.

There was a break which allowed the boys to sheath themselves with latex, permitting Macy to take account of everything. Six guys wanting to fuck her – three were gorgeous strippers, one was a supremely cute superstar DJ. Everything was consensual. She was being taken good care of. Macy locked eyes with the tall blonde stripper.

"When's it your turn."

"Let's get the other hole ready," said Marco, clearly not liking the idea of Macy preferring any of the other guys to him.

A face dove into the crevice between her buttocks. The face sniffed and licked. Hands held her hips firmly. She felt a tongue pressing into her arsehole. She was already relaxed and into proceedings so pushed back hard on the tongue so it could get deep into her.
"She likes it."

A thumb pressed into her pink ring. Again, Macy responded by circling her hips and working her rim down the thumb.

"Maybe she won't need too much work," laughed Marco

"She'll still need to be stretched though," said a voice she didn't recognize.

Another thumb, thicker and longer, jammed into the entrance. Macy slowed her circling of her hips. It wasn't quite as easy to take two thumbs. The longer thumb jiggled its way down.

"Pull her apart so I can see inside," demanded Marco.

The thumbs tugged firmly at the entrance. It wasn't rough but it was testing. Macy gritted her teeth as she felt her arsehole widen.

"That'll do.'

She felt Marco's hands on her buttocks; his index and middle finger tapping on her rim.

"You feeling okay?" he checked in.

"Yes," she answered honestly.

"Let me sit."

Macy stood to allow Marco to sit on the sofa. Hands on her hips he pulled her between his legs. She went to kneel down to return her mouth to his cock. He shook his head to indicate she should turn to face away from him.

"Sit on my cock," he instructed.

She started to move to a sitting position. Assisted by the security guards she rested her rim on his dick. Marco held his cock firm in place and watched her arsehole spread as the head slowly eased in. Relieved the guards had taken the time to work her arse, Macy was able to ease herself onto the shaft. Marco let her stay seated on his rod and drew her close to his body – arms like a seatbelt, hands covering her melon shaped breasts. He moved his hips in the tiniest of thrusts and began laying back. Half propped by pillows, Marco took his weight on his elbows to plough her slowly but deeply.

The security guards lifted her legs and put them over Marco's. The strippers could see the dark purple flesh of Marco's hard-on moving in and out of her arsehole. The tall blonde stripper stepped between the spread legs. Stabilizing himself with one hand on the arm rest he directed his cock into her pussy.

Macy squealed. A security guard covered her mouth.

"She's alright," said Marco sharpish. "We can't be heard."

The stripper's eyes rolled back as he lost himself in her tight slit.

"Feels different, babe, doesn't it?" cooed Marco. "I can feel his cock inside you. Bet you've never been stretched this wide."

Macy hadn't. She hadn't had a three-some, let alone a gang bang. Hands were all over her again. Fingertips crawling over her mound to play with her clit, breasts being squeezed and stroked, her toned stomach being caressed. She closed her eyes to try and memorize the feeling of the two thick dicks working in and out of her. Trying to decide if she hated it or loved it and found herself leaning to the latter.

"Let's give the other guys a go. They've been very patient."

The blonde stripper withdrew and offered a hand to help Macy stand. As Marco stood up, a stripper with close-cropped jet-black hair and dark stubble immediately took his place – laying back on the sofa. The security guards helped her straddle and climb on the stripper's picturesque prick. She began riding him cowgirl style – fast and furious. The security guards held her steady, taking the opportunity to squeeze and pinch the nipples of her bouncing breasts.

"Lay closer to him," suggested Marco. "Open up your ass for his friend."

The stripper put an arm up and placed it behind her neck to help lower her to him. She nuzzled into his neck and felt the hard smooth skin of his pecs on her breasts as she slowed her pace on his cock. Buttocks helpfully being spread by security, the stripper with the floppy brown hair groaned as he dipped his dick into her arsehole. He plunged the full length in, then yanked it out completely. She thought Marco's smooth fucking had been the pinnacle of the encounter, but Macy decided this method, while unexpected, was definitely bringing her to erotic heights she'd never previously experienced.

"Everyone's had their go and we have another party to go to," announced Marco. "Macy, off the sofa and kneel down."

Macy knew what was coming. She'd watched these types of porn clips and the thought had made her want to vomit. Now all she wanted was each guy jerking off all over her face. She put some space between her and the sofa. As the boys removed their latex protection, they were able to form a circle around her. She licked her lips at the sweet shop of cocks masturbating in front of her.

Marco was the first to seize her hair to yank her head back.

"Open up," he encouraged.

As soon as the words were out of his mouth, ejaculate shot into her mouth and across her face. Another hand was grabbing her hair. More white fluid streamed across her face. And again. And again. And again.

Macy was literally wiping the semen from her eyes, trying to see whose cock was slapping on her face before shooting. A hand reached out with a cloth to clear away the mixed fluids. Raising her eyes, it was the stripper with green eyes and brown hair – he wasn't the most handsome or best looking, but he had the cute, boy-next-door looks that Macy liked. He offered his dick to her. She let her hand work it. Catching her breath, she took him in her mouth. The gang watched as she began to deep throat the young man. He lent back so she could swallow down his complete length. Reaching up she grabbed his buttocks and drew him in as deeply as she could. Her fingernails dug in his buttocks and he came hard. She could feel cock and cum filling her mouth. He wasn't budging so she swallowed the cum down. He dislodged from her throat.

"Wish I'd thought of that," whined Marco.

The men helped Macy to her feet, waiting patiently as she got dressed.

"I should be going," she said shyly.

"Noooo," said Marco. 'You should be coming. All. Night. Long."

She looked away, the reality of the embarrassing aftermath crawling into her consciousness.

"You should at least be coming to the party. You helped organize."

"Honestly, I've got to go," she insisted.

"Absolutely not," Marco took her hand and led the entire room to the private lift that went to the penthouse suites.

Exhausted, Macy made a mental note to leave the party the second Marco was distracted by new flesh.

"The party is here," he announced as the double doors to the suite were simultaneously opened by his security guards.

The suite was rammed. The crowd roared at his appearance. - evidently not too peeved by his incredibly late entrance. Marco held her hand tightly.

"Let's get a drink," he said.

Macy smiled. She wasn't sure a beer would do much, but a few shots might give her a little more energy and a little less self-awareness. A group of squealing fans rushed toward Marco. Macy let her hand slip from his and backed away into the dancing throng.

"You're here!"

Macy turned to see Amber. She kissed her friend's cheek, forgetting she'd serviced six cocks with her lips earlier.

"I've never been so glad to see you."

"I'm so sorry. I feel awful leaving you to clean up. I didn't realise how bad it would be. You've been ages," gushed Amber. "On a positive note, apparently Marco's only just arrived."

"Yeah, I know."

"You couldn't have missed it. Groupies galore, huh?"

"Yeah."

"Are you alright Macy?" asked Amber concerned.

"I'm super tired."

She wanted to tell Amber everything, but shame was creeping in and she had a feeling her antics could be as easily shunned as admired.

"I just popped in to find you and say hi and bye," explained Macy.

It wasn't untrue.

"But you can't go. The strippers have finally arrived."

"Then you can enjoy all three of them."

"I'm not greedy, one or two will do." laughed Amber. "Besides I wanted to show you something."

"Show me tomorrow."

"The party won't be here tomorrow."
"You sure? It looks like a rave."

"Honestly, you have to see it. If you see it and you want no part in the celebrations you can go, but at least have an open mind."

Macy assessed her friend. It wasn't Amber's fault Macy had decided to be a slut and needed to go home to rest and recuperate and reevaluate her life choices.

"Fine, I'll come," she agreed.

Amber took her hand. Dragging her through the crowd, they reached a corridor.

"This will seriously blow your mind," promised Amber.

She took her to the first door on her left. Pushing open the door and slipping in, Macy took in the magnificent long dining table. There was certainly room for formal dining entertainment in these suites. "Well?" hissed Amber.

Macy let her eyes focus. There were people scattered everywhere. And they were fucking everywhere and on everything. She could feel her nipples hardening. One girl was on her back on the floor, another girl eating between her legs, a boy on top dunking his balls in her mouth. A young boy was bent over a dining room chair as another man serviced him. A girl was pushed against a wall with a man sliding in and out of her. Another girl was on all fours being taken from behind as she sucked another man's cock with her mouth. Small groups of same sexes and mixed genders grouped together kissing and idly playing with each other's genitals. Everywhere her eyes went she saw snippets of different sexual acts and scenes.

"Sexy, hey?"

Macy nodded.

"Haven't you ever thought about participating?"

Macy considered Amber carefully. She wasn't sure what response she was seeking but Macy decided to be guarded after her antics downstairs.

"It's hot, but not really my scene. Definitely worth seeing so thanks for the tour. You enjoy it though."

Amber's eyes were cast downward. Her coffee-colored skin had a dark red tinge to it. Macy realized she was embarrassed.

"I'm not judging," said Macy in her ear.

"Feels like you are."

Macy felt awful. She was tired and needed to process her own evening. Her intention hadn't been to ruin Amber's evening – let alone make her feel anything less than the queen she was. Amber was standing there like a deflated balloon. Macy was kicking herself for killing her buzz – especially when Amber had been so keen to party with her. The door opened and the three strippers walked in. The change in atmosphere was palpable. Whether they were engaged in some form of sexual conduct or seeking out opportunity, all the women in the room slowed down or halted to look over at the boys in a bid to gain their attention.

"The strippers are here," cheered Macy lowly trying to engage Amber.

Amber smiled weakly.

"Hey Amber, pick yourself up. You were right and I was wrong. This is hot and being sexually liberated is hot."

Amber's smile widened.

"And if you're up for sharing, I guarantee you, I can get those strippers over there to free our sexual shackles."

"You're very confident," giggled Amber nervously.

"Are you in?" asked Macy.

"I'm in!"

Macy downed four shots from a tray on the table. She shook her head to shake off her weariness. Walking over to her favorite boy-next-door stripper, she tapped his shoulder. All three men grinned at her.

"Don't suppose I can convince you to go for another round with me and my friend," she enquired cheekily. "She saw your show earlier and said she was horny AF, hence your invitation."

The strippers smiled between themselves.

"Let's do this," they agreed as they headed toward Amber.

Forbidden & Taboo Explicit Sex Stories

Adult Erotica Collection - BDSM, Virgins, Gangbangs, 69, Lesbian, First Time, Anal, Threesomes, MILFs, Spanking, Creampies (Orgasmic Collection)

Written By:
G.G. Goode

- Goode Publications -

The Meadows High School gym was packed nearly elbow-to-elbow with well-dressed men and women in their late twenties. They were all well-dressed in formal, and business attire. A sparkling banner advertising the class of 2009's ten-year reunion was stretched across the school gym's entrance, and balloons bounced against the tall ceiling, as if they were trying to escape. People bustled and moved through the bunched-up lines, seemingly eager to get inside. The room was loud with various conversations and pop music from ten years ago playing in the background. All the former classmates curiously inspected each other's lives to see how accurate the yearbook's "most likely to" predictions turned out to be. They all sized each other up, hoping that they could appear more successful than the next. Groups of former friends began to form into cliques just like it had been when they attended the school. It was all very nostalgic for many, and terrifying for others.

At the edge of the room stood the smallest of all the groups, just two women that not many of the other reunion-goers could remember. Dayna and Ella were not popular back then by any means, so it did not surprise them that most of the other alumni could not recall them at all. For the first time, everyone in the room seemed almost obsessively interested in who they were. Their former classmates finally started taking interest in them, probably because they noticed their striking appearances, high-dollar clothes, perfect bodies, and Hollywood style. These ladies had clearly risen above the housewife status that most of the women in this room had achieved. Other women speculated and gossiped about who they must be, spreading rumors just to make themselves appear relevant. Several men had tried to offer the ladies a drink, as they flirted and gawked at them relentlessly. The two women had been close friends in school, and they seemed to be reconnecting seamlessly, ignoring everyone's attempts at making conversation, in the same way they had once been ignored.

Dayna and Ella chatted briefly before both grew tired of the class reunion. After all, they only came to see each other, and they had no interest in being gawked at or even spoken to by anyone else in this room. They both got in their cars and drove to the closest open bar they could find. It was a little sleazy, but they had agreed that it would be better than spending the whole night searching for something more suitable. The only alternative was driving hours to get to some place decent, so they settled on Mike's Hole-in-the-Wall, which had bar food that was far greater than what you would usually expect from a place like this. They sat at a high-top table near the bar and they each ordered their favorite martinis. The conversation began with polite chatter, and typical niceties, but that did not last exceedingly long. They learned the basics of each other's lives. Dayna shared photos of her only son, and Ella complained about her competitive career. With each drink they grew more and more comfortable and the conversation became increasingly personal. They began guiltlessly prodding one another for the most exciting and personal details of their lives. Just like they had when they met the first time, they became fast friends.

Dayna giggled uncontrollably as a bit of her drink sloshed over the rim of her martini glass and fell onto the table. She was having a great time catching up with Ella, her best friend from high school. It felt good because it had been a long time since she had had someone who she considered to be a real friend. They both used to be the outcasts in school. Both made good grades and always had a book in their hands, they went through a gothic phase together which did not do much for their social status. Other than by each other, and maybe a few teachers, they were hardly ever noticed when they walked through the halls. They both dressed dark and mostly plain back then. Dayna had an acne problem, long dirty blonde hair, and always kept her hair tied back. Ella was a tall brunette who hid behind thick-rimmed glasses. Their old selves probably would not recognize the people they were now. Now Dayna's hair was bleached and cut in a short choppy cut which accentuated her jaw line, and tattoos decorated much of her exposed skin. The red heels she wore highlighted her long legs, and her voluptuous lips were painted a matching red as well. Ella's hair was pinned into a fancy updo. Her low-cut top boasted her recently acquired fake boobs, which accentuated her hourglass figure perfectly.

"Oh my god! I can't believe it finally happened, I thought you were never going to give up your virginity!", Dayna exclaimed excitedly.

Ella scoffed as she noticed heads turning from almost every seat in the low-key bar. "Yeah, I know", she rolled her eyes and smirked in a way that indicated she was proud of the feat. "College definitely helped me grow up a lot!", she declared after gulping down the last of her drink. She waved at the bartender for another.

"Oh, come on spill it, Ella", Dayna pushed. "I told you how it happened for me already, so I want to hear your story".

"Alright, I'll tell it", Ella said. "But you gotta tell me a juicy one in return", She bartered.

"Deal", Dayna said firmly and without a second thought.
Ella's lips formed a mischievous grin as she remembered her deflowering. She squirmed a little in her seat and felt her pussy get a bit wet from thinking about it. She began telling Dayna every detail of how it happened.

Ella's First Steamy College Lesson (virginity)

She stumbled through the huge double doors relieved that she had made it just in time. Ella looked around the huge auditorium-like classroom. Hoping to avoid being noticed or called on, she chose a seat that seemed inconspicuous a few rows back from the front of the room and towards the middle of the row. After taking her seat, she clumsily rummaged through her brown shoulder bag, and got out her English textbook, and a purple spiral notebook labeled *English Notes*. She scooped up a handful of ballpoint pens, highlighters, and mechanical pencils before dropping her bag to the floor and used the sides of her sneakers to push the bag completely under the padded metal chair she sat on. She suddenly felt a light tap on her shoulder which made her jump a little.

"Did you sign in?", a deep smooth voice had asked.

Ella turned and looked towards the voice. There stood an extremely attractive guy. He could not be much older than she was. She could see his muscular form through the light blue button up he wore, pieces of his light brown hair fell into his face slightly covering one of his eyes. He pushed the hair out of his huge brown eyes and smiled softly at her. She stuttered a little, feeling embarrassed by her attraction to him as if it were something visible and obvious. She followed his gesture near the room's entrance and took notice of a notebook sitting on a desk to the left of the doors. A few of the other students were gathered around waiting to sign their names in the notebook. The sign above the table said *please sign in.*

"Sorry, I didn't see that. I'm going to get in line right now", she said as she stood and rushed off to join the group of her peers. As she waited to sign her name on the sheet, she wondered if the guy she had just spoken to was the professor. After pondering the thought for a moment, she decided that it was probably very unlikely because of how young he appeared to be. As soon as she had settled back into her seat and got ready for class to begin, a balding man with a beard in his late-forties, or early-fifties walked to the front of the room and to a podium. This guy looked much more like what she imagined her professor would. He introduced himself as Professor Wilson and started straight into the lecture after asking his assistant, Brennon, who had reminded Ella to sign in earlier, to pass out the class syllabus. Ella watched Brennon closely as he walked from table to table, sitting a small stack of papers on each one and telling the student on the end to take one and pass the rest down the row. Brennon smiled at her again as he walked by and her heart pounded in her chest with excitement. It seemed like it could have been a flirty smile. After that she was unable to get him out of her mind. A warm tingle and the wetness in her panties became an all-day distraction for her. The unwelcome distraction would continue returning every time she saw or even thought of him over the next few days. This guy had Ella more worked up than she had ever felt before.

She was laying on her twin-sized bed, with purple comforters in the mostly empty, and unusually undecorated dorm room that she shared with a girl named Fallon. Fallon was out, as she often was, so Ella was using the private time to do the only thing she could think to do to get the thoughts of Brennon to stop being so obtrusive and terribly distracting. Hopefully this release would make it so that she could focus on completing the introduction essay for her English class, which was due soon. She fantasized of him kissing her and touching her all over her body. Her thoughts were racing through her mind as she fiercely rubbed her wet pussy. She focused on trying to pretend it was his hand in her panties instead of her own. She began growing frustrated, as the rush did not come as fast as it once had, that was probably due to the change in how often she had been needing to do this. She rubbed faster, keeping the usually effective circular motion, circling around her clit. Finally, her body tensed up and she moaned in unbelievable pleasure, finally relieving her pent-up sexual frustrations.

Her body went limp for just a moment, and she took a deep breath before reaching over to the table beside her bed and grabbing her laptop from it. She put her hand into her panties to see how much cum was there. She pulled her hand up to her face to look. When she did, she licked her finger, tasting her own sweet nectar. Suddenly the door swung open. Ella opened the laptop quickly and sat it on her lap in a single motion and got back to working on her essay. Her roommate, Fallon, had just walked in and immediately began undressing herself in front of Ella. Ella noticed her perfect body; her dark hair fell back down to her hips as she pulled her top over her head. Ella looked away quickly so her roommate would not catch her looking at her. Fallon glanced over at Ella, with a curious expression while Ella pretended to be captivated with typing on her laptop.

"I know we haven't hung out much yet, but do you want to come out to a party with me tonight?", Fallon asked unexpectedly. She eyed Ella with a look of sympathy. It was probably due to the fact that Ella had barely left this room since her arrival to college, other than to go to her classes of course, and she had been thinking about how badly she needed some time out. So, she agreed to go out despite how nervous she felt about the idea. Just moments later, when Ella announced that she was ready, Fallon looked her over and crossed her arms with a thinking expression on her face. Ella looked down at herself questioningly after noticing the stunning blue shimmering dress Fallon was wearing. It was accompanied by an adorable white half jacket and black pumps. Fallon looked stunning, and Ella felt out of place next to her.

"You can borrow something of mine", Fallon said suggestively as she turned towards her closet. She glanced through her clothes for a minute or two and then pulled out a short maroon dress and tossed it at Ella with a smile. "Can you wear a size four?", she asked.

"Yes", Ella answered as she eyed the dress in her hands. She obediently stepped out of the comfort of her blue jeans and floral cowl-neck blouse, which was probably the most party-appropriate thing she currently owned, and she stepped into the dress. The thick knitted material clung tightly to her body as she pulled it up. She was surprised to see it looked great and accentuated her curves quite nicely. The sleeves wrapped around her arms hanging over her shoulders leaving her neck and the top of her chest exposed. After asking her shoe-size, Fallon handed Ella some black boots with short heels. Ella slipped those on as well and was surprised by how comfortable they were.

"One last thing", Fallon said, slowly dragging out the words as she rooted around in her bag. Her hand emerged with a tube of lipstick. She uncapped it and carefully applied it to Ella's full lips, then she looked at Ella with a smile, clearly satisfied with her work.

"Am I ready?", Ella asked eagerly. Fallon nodded with a grin. Ella looked back at herself in the full-length mirror that hung on the inside of their dorm room's door and her big brown eyes widened in surprise. She could not believe she was looking at herself right now, she felt a wave of new confidence as she took in her much-changed reflection. The dress's off the shoulder sleeves made her small bust appear to be much larger, the dress highlighted her thin waist and showed off her thick butt and thighs. Even she could not deny that she looked stunning, but it still did not stop her from feeling incredibly nervous about going to her first college party. When they walked into the party, Ella had her arms crossed tightly over her chest and holding each other as if she were cold, but it was not the September chill that was making her cross her arms. She felt very exposed in front of all these people with this tiny dress on. Fallon apparently saw what was going on, she leaned over close to Ella and told her to relax and breathe. She promised Ella that there was nothing to worry about.

"Why don't you have a drink", she suggested. Ella looked back at her and nodded.

"Yeah, that will help", Ella decided.

So, Ella forced her arms down to her sides, stood up straight, and walked over to the drink table as confidently as she could. There was a mountain of solo cups and a few coolers with spouts on the table where people lined up to fill their cups with whatever was in those coolers. Before she could even make her way through the dense crowd to get a solo cup, one was already being passed in her direction. She knew better than to accept a drink from just anyone. She had heard about the dangers of accepting drinks from strangers her entire life.

"No tha- ", she started to say but she stopped without even finishing her word, once she looked up at the person who was passing the cup to her, which was full of some blue drink. She smiled, took it from his hand and took a big gulp of the sugary blue liquid. The innocent-looking drink was burning as it made its way down her throat.

"Thank you", she managed to say through the fire in her chest. Brennon smiled at her knowingly, but he was polite enough to not mention her obvious unfamiliarity with her surroundings.

"I never imagined that college parties would be your thing", he said with a slight slur in his deep sexy voice.

"Well, I don't really know if it is my 'thing' or not yet", she said truthfully, but with as much confidence as she could muster up, "It's my first time attending one", she finished.

"Well, I think a tour is in order m'lady", he said gesturing dramatically past the crowded table that held the coolers and mountain of solo cups. She giggled at his silliness and walked ahead of him. They made their way down a hallway and they talked as he showed her each room of the house, which she learned was a historic building. He informed her that the house was owned by the school. He said students often used it for parties, even though it was not technically allowed, but most of the school's staff was well-aware of the shenanigans that went on here. They ignored it because they had done the same when they were young and in college. As Ella listened, she was starting to feel the warm and tingly effects of the alcohol just a few minutes after finishing her drink. She liked how good it made her feel. She had sipped her parents wine a few times on special occasions, but she had never felt what it was like to be drunk before.

She was enjoying the boost of confidence and the much-needed courage it was kindly lending her. The pair sat down beside one another on a bench, in a seemingly unused office that was on the far end of the hallway, and away from the crowd. It was either the alcohol, or just being alone with him that immediately got her pussy wetter than she had ever been before. She decided it was probably a mix of the two. While he was telling a story about his own first time at a college party, she was staring at him thinking about the naughty things she wanted him to do to her. She had hardly been paying attention to what he was saying because she was too busy imagining his hands exploring her body.

He glanced in her direction, and she looked back at him dreamily wondering if he could see it in her eyes how badly she was wanting him right now. She suddenly wondered why he continued looking at her expectantly, she had not heard much of what he was saying through her fantasizing about him. She began to hope he had not asked a question and was now waiting for her response, but then he put his hand on her thigh. She held her breath, and her chest pounded in anticipation as he slowly trailed his fingers lightly up her thigh, and closer to the place that was now tingling so intensely she had to fight the urge to squirm beside him. Then in one swift motion he moved his hands and firmly gripped the backs of her thighs, and lifted her up with ease, holding her against himself. He carried her forward until her back was pressed against the wall with his weight pressed against her. She could feel his hard cock pressed against her as well, which made her head begin to swim, and earned him a moan.

She noticed how dizzy she was feeling and wondered how much of it was the alcohol she had drank and how much of it was his intoxicating presence. She began to consider the possibility that they might end up having sex if things continued on their current trajectory. For the moment, she was still a virgin, which she felt immensely embarrassed about considering she was in college, her nerves began to take hold, making her doubtful that she was making the right choice. She wanted him badly though, and it wasn't even just her that wanted him, her body wanted him, every cell was pushing her to give in to her desires. She could taste the sweet drink he had just been sipping on as they kissed. He squeezed her ass, and trailed kisses up to her ear. He pulled her earlobe into his mouth nibbling on it gently. She felt his breath on her ear.

"Tell me how badly you want my hard cock", he whispered into her ear. Her heart began to race as she tried to make the words come out. At first, she only let out a moan but then as if it were a miracle, the words came out of her mouth naturally and seductively.

"Oh Brennon, I want your cock so bad", she cried out. "My pussy is wet and ready for it", She said breathlessly. She wondered where that had come from. She felt surprisingly proud of herself for sounding so seductive and sexy.

"Mmmm, yeah baby", Brennon said back to her, letting her know that she had given him exactly what he had asked for. He lightly bit and sucked on her neck for a moment and she moaned in response. It was clear what was about to happen. Ella pondered whether she should tell him about her being a virgin, or if it would just ruin the moment. Before, she could process her thoughts or come to any conclusions, the door swung open and they both startled a little at the sound.

"Well, that did not take long!", Fallon exclaimed, rushing heatedly into the room.

Ella straightened her legs, and her feet touched the floor as Brennon released his grip on her thighs with a confused look that quickly turned to guilt when he saw and recognized Fallon. Fallon grabbed Ella by the arm. Ella was stunned into silence, so she let Fallon guide her from the room feeling conflicted and confused. When Brennon was out of sight Ella's heart dropped into her stomach. She felt painful disappointment and unfulfilled desire. As they walked back to their dorm room Fallon apologized for her intrusion. She explained that she had only been trying to look out for Ella.

"It's just, you seem like you're way too sweet a person to be taken advantage of the way he does with girls", she started. "I mean, from what I hear around campus, he does this all the time."

"Really?", Ella said looking confused.

Fallon told Ella of her own experience with Brennon she had over the summer, when she had been here for her orientation, which was just a few weeks before school had started. She decided to go check out one of the parties because that is the part of college everyone talks the most about, so she snuck out of the hotel she was staying at and crashed a party. Brennon was the first person she met who had spoken to her while she was at the wild event. They started talking and she got the impression that he was really into her, and she liked him too. So, when he made a move, she did not object to it.

Ella felt a pang of jealousy when Fallon revealed that she had let Brennon fuck her, but apparently, the next day Fallon had looked around hoping to exchange phone numbers with Brennon, and she did not see him anywhere. Fallon had been disappointed, but she figured she would catch up with him when school started. On her first day she talked to some people about him and apparently, he got around like that quite a bit. When she finally saw him again, on the first day of English class, he acted as if he had never seen her before.

"He's hardly made eye contact with me since then", she told Ella, "I feel really used", she finished.

After she was done telling her story, Ella comforted Fallon. As she hugged Fallon, she felt a sore spot on her neck. Ella rubbed the spot for a moment trying to figure out what it was until it caught Fallon's attention.

"Did he leave a hickey on your neck?" Fallon asked with an offended look.

"I…I guess so", Ella said remembering how amazing his mouth felt against her neck. Ella could not help it, she honestly still wanted Brennon just as badly as she had before. The desire she had for him remained completely unaffected by the knowledge gained from Fallon's story. It was not that Ella did not believe Fallon; it was just that she was perfectly willing to accept the risk. She tried, for the sake of Fallon's feelings to convince herself that it was inevitably a bad idea to get involved with someone who had a reputation like that. Ella desperately wanted to put a stop to whatever was going on between them. Ella really did not want to betray Fallon's friendship, especially after she had been so nice. Fallon told Ella that she would not be upset with her if she still wanted to see where it goes with him, but Ella could hear the hurt in Fallon's voice as she said it. Ella felt nearly obligated to not get intimate with him. Unfortunately, her mind kept almost involuntarily trying to think of ways that she could get alone with him again so they could finish what they had started in that office. It left a raging war between hormones and wanting to be a loyal friend to Fallon. Ella knew the temptation could easily become too much, especially if Brennon were to actively pursue her.

Ella walked into the English classroom with her head down as her heart pounded in her chest. She immediately saw Brennon standing at the front of the room sorting through some papers at the professor's podium, looking as sexy as ever. She noticed how cute the jeans he had on made his butt look. When he was finished with the papers, he set them aside in a neat stack further down on the nearby desk. He briefly looked up from what he was doing and gazed directly at the place where Ella sat each day. They made brief eye contact before they both looked away nervous and wondering what the other was thinking. Ella tried to keep her eyes down and away from him during class and to pay him no attention. After class she quickly tucked her book under her arm and began to make her escape from the class, with her heart still thumping hard in her chest. She made it about halfway down the hall that turned towards her next class when she heard his voice calling her name loudly behind her.

"Hey, I was hoping to talk to you", he smiled nervously as he fiddled with some keys in his hands, "sorry about the other night", he added. Ella quickly assured him that he had done nothing that she did not want him to do. He looked relieved and he asked when her next class was beginning, he glanced over her body and silently wondered why she hid her stunning figure behind the baggy clothes she usually wore. She glanced up at the clock that was hanging on the wall above a classroom door. She felt disappointment when she had to tell him she only had 20 minutes to spare before she had a lab.

"Would you mind if I walked with you?", he asked hopefully.

"No, of course not", Ella said smiling. She noticed some people staring at them as they walked down the hall, and she wondered if it was a normal thing for him to be walking through the halls with a girl by his side. After walking down, a flight of stairs and a long hallway, they stopped in front of Ella's biology lab and she suddenly decided that now was as good a time as any to tell him about her still in-tact virginity. She wanted to go ahead and rip off the Band-Aid and get it over with.

"So, I probably need to tell you something.", Ella began, "I only have a few minutes, but I want to go ahead and get this out in the open".

"Okay", Brennon said with an apprehensive smile. She blurted it out plainly, and without any further explanations. He immediately looked downward and she could tell he felt bad about being so forward with her the other night.

"I'm sorry I had no idea", he said. Ella was quick to remind him that she wanted what had happened at the party and she assured him that it was nothing he should feel bad about. She said she had wished Fallon had not stormed in like that and dragged her away.
"Yeah, I may have upset her a little", he started to explain. Ella stopped him and told him she was already made aware of what happened between the two of them, and she told him that it had no effect on her feelings towards him. He looked relieved again and she wondered if he might actually want to fuck her as badly as she had been wanting him. Brennon broke the silence that had settled between them to ask Ella if she wanted to hang out with him again soon, he had a suggestive look on his face, and she knew right away what he meant.

"Of course, I would", Ella said as she leaned in to hug him tight. He ran his hand over her ass as he hugged her back and she giggled. After that they said bye to each other for now and Ella walked reluctantly into her lab and took her seat.

Once Ella's lab was finished, she went and got something quick to eat from the dining hall, and then she walked back to her dorm room. By the time she made it back, she felt completely exhausted by the day's exciting events and she plopped down onto her bed adjusting her pillow behind the arch of her back. She wanted to be upfront and honest, and tell Fallon about what happened today, but she had not made it back to the dorm yet, so Ella got out her laptop to bide the time. She decided to sign into the online portal for her English class so she could submit the assignment she had finished last night. When she tried to log in, a box popped up, *Login attempt failed*, it said. She tried again using the exact same password she had been given by Professor Wilson and it failed again. This time she slowed herself down and carefully typed the password, paying attention to the paper that she received with the class syllabus. It had her login information on it, so she was certain it was entered correctly this time. She hit enter again and right as she did, it dawned on her that she had already changed it to a more personal password. She tried to log in again with her own password, but unfortunately, she had already made too many login attempts and was now locked out of the account.

She cussed under her breath, and she came to the conclusion that there probably was nothing she could do until tomorrow, so Ella finished other class work and when Fallon still had not shown up, she gave up and pulled her comforter over her shoulders and went to sleep. Ella woke up earlier than usual and used the extra time to take a long shower and do a little bit of her seemingly endless schoolwork. Fallon invited Ella to have breakfast with some of her friends, but she needed some time to herself, so she politely declined the offer, and soon after, Fallon rushed out of the dorm complaining about being late. Ella noticed she had left her lipstick on her side table along with a few other things she usually took along with her. Ella thought about the other night, and how nice the lipstick had looked on her. She did not think that Fallon would mind too much if she used it, so she took it off the table, put some on, and put it back where it had been found. Ella smiled into the mirror and studied the effect it had on her pale complexion. After looking herself up and down once more Ella put her books in her bag and left the dorm feeling antsy and excited because she knew she had English today, meaning she would get to see him again.

Ella got to her class, and they jumped right into the lecture as usual. Halfway through the class professor Wilson finished the lesson they had been working on and called for the class to take a short recess so he could get himself prepared for his next lecture. Ella took the opportunity to request help with her account. She quietly approached his desk and when he glanced at her, she asked him what she should do about her account being locked. Without ever looking up from his computer, he told her that Brennon would have to help get it sorted out because his day was fully booked. Then he asked if she was available after class to meet with Brennon so he could get her logged into her account. Luckily, she had over two hours before her next class began because there was no biology lab today, so she happily told him that she had time.

"I will talk to Brennon and see if he has time after class as well", he said hurriedly. She thanked Professor Wilson and went back to her desk and sat down. She flipped through her book as she waited for class to resume. Not long after the professor resumed his lecture on how to correctly format citations for different writing styles, Brennon walked over to Ella's desk, and stuck a blue sticky note on it. As he walked away, she quickly grabbed it before anyone else could see what it said just in case it was personal. She held it under the desk and looked at it in secret. There were just four words, *see you after class* it simply stated in his neat, curvy handwriting. It had a little winking smiley face at the bottom. Ella looked up and smiled at Brennon to let him know that she was excited to see him. The remaining forty-five minutes of the class, Ella was very distracted by an intense giddy feeling in her stomach as several scenarios played out in her head that almost always ended in the two of them completely naked and exploring each other's bodies.

She knew that this was very unlikely to happen after class today, especially considering the professor would probably still be here to supervise them. After class, Ella stayed behind as the other students rushed on to their next class. Brennon came over and sat at the desk beside her and opened his laptop appearing to be all-business today. He said nothing about the sexual tension that lingered thick in the air between them. He quickly got Ella a new temporary password, and he asked her to sign in just to make sure it worked. While she was signing in, she noticed Mr. Wilson leaving the room with his bag over his shoulder. Ella successfully signed into the English portal.

"Thank you", she said smiling at him expectantly.

"How much more time do you have?", he asked plainly with a serious look on his face.

When she told him she still had over an hour to spare, he got up, without uttering a word, and locked the classroom doors. He turned and looked at her hungrily. He smiled mischievously at her and winked. Her body responded to the gesture immediately. He walked over to her looking confident and sexy. She was nervous about being caught until he assured her it was okay which made her immediately relax. He told her that Mr. Wilson would be gone the rest of the day, and other than the dean, who was too busy to worry about two students being alone in a classroom, no one else had a key. Ella bit her bottom lip feeling excited and ready. Brennon leaned in close to kiss her. Their lips met as he lifted her up the same way he had at the party, except this time he laid her across the professor's desk. Ella held her breath and her chest pounded with excitement as he slowly unbuttoned her shirt, each button exposing more of her bare skin when released. When he made it to the last one, he started leaving a trail of kisses up her stomach until he reached the band of her purple bra.

She arched her back instinctively as he reached under her and swiftly unclasped the bra. She slipped it over her arms and dropped it to the floor. She trembled as Brennon cupped her little breasts with his hands and he leaned in to take one of her nipples into his mouth. He sucked hard on the tiny nipple, and it perked up immediately in response. Ella moaned in anticipation as his hands reached down to the button of her jeans. He quickly unbuttoned them and pulled the tight material down her hips, kissing her trembling skin all the way down. She watched him as he methodically removed her shoes and socks, one at a time, and then pulled her jeans over her ankles and completely off. Then he pushed her panties to the side and stuck his fingers into her tight, wet pussy.

"Ready?", He asked, looking at her sweetly.

"Yes", she breathed, it was hardly even a sound, just her mouth making the shape of the word she meant to say.

He took his thick, hard cock out of his pants and held it in his hand. He grabbed her hand and put it on his boner. As she touched it, she felt intimidated by its size. The intimidating feelings were forgotten when he started rubbing her clit with the head of his big cock. She felt like she could cum for him at any moment, but she held it back, wanting to take it slow and enjoy every moment and store it into her memory forever. He grabbed her hips and easily turned her over onto her hands and knees, so she was facing away from him. He rubbed his cock in the wetness from her excitement, and then she felt the pressure of it trying to enter her tight pussy. She gasped and squealed as he pushed into her pussy.

"Fucking hell, it's so tight", he grunted, trying to find a good position. She felt a dull pain in her lower stomach that lasted only a moment, but it did not matter to her because the pleasure of feeling his cock inside of her greatly outweighed the momentary pain by a long shot. He thrust gently and slowly into her at first. He noticed his cock tinged with the blood from breaking her hymen. She pushed her hips back against his cock, so he started increasing the speed and began to thrust into her with more voice. Her tight pussy felt so good as it squeezed his cock. He took her by her hips and started fucking her hard, making sure he hit her cervix. He did this three times in a row before he found a way into her that made her gasp for breath. He pulled her head back by her hair, so she was staring straight up at the ceiling and he put his cock deep into her pussy. He fucked her hard as her tits bounced, he stroked her cunt with his cock and she almost came again when he pulled her down on her knees.

She started stroking his cock with her hand. He pulled her lips down onto his cock, and he groaned as he came inside her mouth. It was even more intense than he had imagined. It seemed like he was coming every time he pulled her head closer to his cock. He grabbed her head, and he made her lick his cock clean. She sucked hard on his cock and she felt it swell and he groaned loudly, pushing her head down. Her tongue was covered in his cum as she stroked his cock with her hand. She licked and sucked, every last drop of cum she could get. He pulled her up and held her. Her body was covered in sweat, but she felt exhilarated. She knew she could get used to this.

They created a makeshift bed with some things lying around in the classroom and they lay there relaxing, Ella was stroking his cock, trying not to let it go limp. She looked into his eyes and they both had a silent conversation between them. They both knew what they wanted to do to each other, but neither one wanted to push the other one into doing it. They knew the other would probably back out. They talked about their past relationships and other things as they both worked their fingers slowly in and out of each other's mouth.

They both knew what was going to happen next and they both wanted it. They opened their eyes and saw that the time had come to share. They looked at each other in amazement. "Are you sure about this?", he asked, still holding her hand.

"Yes, but what about you?", she asked, also still holding his hand.

"I am sure. I want this too."

Ella lifted her leg and slipped off the desk. She got on all fours and let him slide his cock inside her. She wrapped her arms around his back and buried her head in his shoulder. He grabbed her ass cheeks and slid his cock in and out of her pussy.

"Fuck, your pussy feels incredible.", he groaned

"I want you inside me," Ella whispered in his ear. She got on all fours again. He slid his cock in slowly at first, until he was deep inside her. He started fucking her slow, making sure he felt every inch of her tight pussy. He pulled her hair as he fucked her slowly, then started fucking her faster. He grabbed her hips and started to slam his cock in her with a force she didn't think she could take. Ella could not believe the way his cock was fucking her. He kept fucking her harder and faster, as her ass was bouncing up and down. He suddenly realized he was about to come, so he pulled out, not wanting to risk getting her pregnant. He groaned as he watched his cum shoot out all over her lower back and on her beautiful ass. Ella rolled to her side, looking up at him. Brennon told her to stay still, and that he would be right back as he stepped into the professor's office and wet some tissue with a water bottle. She remained laying on her side until he returned and cleaned the mess of cum and blood off her. She turned and hopped off the desk as he wiped himself off. She smiled shyly and hoped they would be able to do that again.

Dayna listened quietly to Ella's entire story intently and wished her first time had been as steamy as Ella's had been.

"That was really hot", Dayna said as she dramatically fanned her face with her hand. Ella was feeling pretty buzzed from the martinis, and she realized she had not eaten much that day, so she placed an order for a few appetizers for them to share. "I honestly always figured you'd be pretty basic as an adult", Dayna told her,

"My parents tried to raise me to be conservative, but I had to learn to have fun at some point" Ella responded with a thoughtful expression, "Brennon definitely helped me start to do that". She explained that she and Brennon had dated for a couple months after that, they got along well together, but neither of them was ready to be in a serious relationship, they were far too busy enjoying college, so they decided to go their separate ways, and remain on good terms, although after leaving the school, they only contacted one another every now and then. "He gave me a great first sexual experience though," Ella said, smirking.

"I can only think of one thing that could possibly have made it better", Dayna teased. Her short hair bounced around as she bawled her hand into a fist and moved it side by side near her cheek as she pushed her other cheek out with her tongue, a gesture that indicated she meant a blowjob. Both women laughed loudly, and several people turned to give them an annoyed glance, but the ladies hardly noticed.

Ella rolled her eyes, "Sure that's fun but I much prefer being on the receiving end of that".

"Why choose when you can do both?", Dayna asked jokingly and they both burst into a fit of laughter. "That reminds me of something fun I did once", Dayna remarked.

"Well, it is your turn to be the storyteller", Ella leaned forward patiently waiting for Dayna to start telling her story.

Dayna's Satisfying Deal (69)

Dayna had not really been paying attention as Jean, the property manager who was an older red-haired woman, and spoke in an obnoxiously loud voice, gave her a tour of the small, basic two-bedroom house. Dayna was already on borrowed time living with her mom and her mom's boyfriend, her boyfriend was a pervert and she managed to make him angry every time he made a pass at her. Her mom would ask her to keep the peace, but she could not. So even her mom was a little ready for her to get her own place, and she knew this place was it unless she wanted to experience what being homeless is like. The thought made her shudder, so she pretended to be interested and after the showing she indicated that she was happy with everything and ready to sign the lease and pay the deposit. The maintenance man walked in the house right as Jean had pulled the lease from the back of her stack of papers. The maintenance man eyed Dayna as he began doing a final check of the house. He was in his late twenties, maybe early thirties. He was surprisingly good looking, very fit from his physically demanding job, he looked a little rough around the edges in a way which Dayna could not decide if she found sexy or not.

She straightened her legs and bent over the counter to sign the lease; she took special care to arch her ass out as far as possible just to see if the maintenance man took notice of her. He took the bait, Dayna watched him almost run smack into the wall as he tried to gawk at her perky ass as she bent seductively over the kitchen counter.

"Are you about done in here Greg?", Jean yelled, also taking notice of the maintenance man, whose name was apparently Greg, and his less than focused work ethic. Jean made her way up the hill to get a camera and a few other things she needed. Greg angrily muttered something under his breath before he disappeared to the back of the house. Dayna held in a giggle as she watched the scene play out. Once Jean was gone, she continued signing the last pages when suddenly she felt something behind her. She jumped and turned to see Gregg.

"You shouldn't fuck with people like that, little slut", he said. Dayna just laughed as he pressed his weight against her body, pinning her to the counter. He backs up and returns to work without another word as Jean walks back inside. Dayna gave the papers back to Jean along with Jean's pen and all the cash for the deposit and first month's rent. Jean counted the money once out loud so Dayna could hear and a second time to herself. Then she shoved it all into a large black zipper pouch greedily. She tucked the pouch protectively in a fanny pack she had been wearing, which was buckled firmly around her wide hips.

"When can I start moving in?", Dayna asked, trying to avoid showing how desperate and eager she was. After talking to Greg for a moment, Jean informed Dayna that she would have to wait until Monday to move in because the air conditioner needed a replacement part that could not be bought until the heat and air store opens on Monday.

Dayna got in her car and drove home as she chanted "just 2 more days", over and over in her head. She hated it there, her mom's boyfriend was an ass, and he was constantly trying to hit on Dayna. He was a creep, and she could not wait to get out of that disgusting broken down hellhole she called home, although she felt terrible about leaving her mom alone with him. After pulling into her mom's driveway, she sat in the car for a while, listening to the radio and thinking about the furniture she wants to get for her new place. She looked at the clock on her car radio and realized it was almost eleven, "Hopefully Danny will be passed out drunk by now", she thought as she gathered her things to go inside.

She opened the car door and got out, carefully closing it behind her. She crept slowly up the steps skipping the ones she knew were loud. She carefully unlocked the door and turned the doorknob slowly. She crept inside quietly. Danny appeared to be asleep on the couch, she breathed a sigh of relief and began to tiptoe past him to get to her room.

"You find a place yet?", he suddenly said.

Dayna jumped at the abrupt disruption and sighed loudly. "I will be out of here Monday, Danny now leaves me alone please, I'm going to my room.", she barked angrily.

"Sure, you don't want daddy to come tuck you in and kiss you goodnight?", Danny said, showing off his rotting teeth as he smiled.

"Ew, no thanks", she responded feeling disgusted.

"Stupid bitch", she heard him say as she made her way quickly to her room and shut the door.

She locked the door behind her and got straight into bed, her insomnia kept her up for a few hours as she stared at the alarm clock on her nightstand beside her bed. She woke up around ten in the morning and began packing her things into boxes, while she remained locked in her room. Her mom always worked long hours on weekends, so she avoided leaving her room because she did not like being around Danny when her mom was not there. She carefully and neatly packed everything over the next couple days, staying in her room, only coming out to jot to the bathroom across the hall. By Monday she had her whole room cleaned spotless too. She felt her stomach growl. She had gone two days surviving off a box of Fig Newtons, a Moon Pie, and a couple bottles of Gatorade she had stashed in her room. She decided her mom was probably home by now, so she left her room to find herself something to eat for breakfast.

When she opened her bedroom door, she immediately smelled a delicious and unfamiliar smell that made her stomach growl and lurch even more than it already had been. She walked into the kitchen and was shocked to see her mom making a big breakfast. There was fried bologna, pancakes, and potatoes, which sat on separate plates beside the stove as her mom scrambled eggs in a buttered pan and biscuits baked in the oven.

"Hey baby girl", her mom said as Dayna sat down at the table, "Danny said you're leaving today, and I thought I'd make you a farewell breakfast".

"Thanks mom", Dayna said looking around "Where is Danny anyway?", she asked.

"Oh, he went to help his brother with something.", she replied. Dayna was glad to get to spend some alone time with her mom before she had to leave. They sat at the table and ate breakfast together for the first time in forever and Dayna told her mom all about her new place. After they had eaten her mom pulled out an envelope from her purse and held it out to Dayna. "I got you a housewarming gift", she said, giving her the envelope, "Please don't tell Danny", she said putting her finger over her lips, to signal that it was a secret.

Dayna carefully opened the envelope and took out a card decorated with a floral pattern. Something fell out of the envelope and into her lap as she opened it. She saw that "I love you, from mom" was written on the inside of the card as she picked up the thing that fell from the inside. After examining it she realized it was a furniture gift card for one hundred dollars. She thanked her mom and hugged her tight, before tucking the gift card into her pocket. Her mom had also packed a few boxes with some of the extra dishes and towels she had. Afterwards, Dayna packed as much as she could into her car and headed to her new place.

When she pulled into the gravel driveway, Greg, the maintenance man, had just been locking the door and leaving her house. He most likely just finished fixing the air conditioner. He handed her the keys, as he looked her up and down. She took the keys from his hand and thanked him before heading inside. She opened the door and brought the things she had packed in her car into the house and sat them on the floor. As she did, Greg stared intently, enjoying the view of her ass each time she bent over. She turned to shut the door and caught Greg once again eying her and she smiled and waved as he got into his old truck. As she looked at the way he carried himself as if he did not have a care in the world, she decided that she did find him quite attractive. He may not be the best-looking guy she had ever been into, but he had a way about him that made her think he would be good in bed. She wondered what fucking him would be like. She imagined his cock was probably big just based on the size and shape of his body.

She still had a bunch of stuff she needed to get from her room, and she wanted to get it done before Danny got the chance to go through it and confiscate anything he might want. She shivered at the thought of him going through and touching all her things. She pulled her phone out of her back pocket and began scrolling through her contacts trying to think of who might have a truck. After calling 8 people, only half of whom had a truck, she was still no closer to getting her things from her mom's house. Her uncle Rich was currently out of town for a job and everyone else was busy with work or family or had already left for college. Despite getting accepted into a decent school, Dayna decided to skip college. It is so expensive, and she would prefer to go ahead and enter the workforce, because she knew she would have to keep at least 2 jobs to afford school and trying to juggle that with going to school seemed like too much. She also really needed the break from school honestly.

Her mind went back to thinking about Greg, she thought about how sexy he looked getting into that old truck, his muscles expanding anytime he would tense up his body, which happened quite a bit when he was working. She looked up and her eyes widened as an idea came to mind. She remembered that Jean had said his phone number had been written on the lease just in case emergency maintenance is ever needed. She pulled out her copy of the lease and began flipping through the pages, scanning them fiercely. Once she found the number she was looking for, she punched it into her phone. She hesitated for just a moment and then dialed it and listened as it began to ring.

"Who's this?" He said with a clipped tone that indicated he was annoyed by the call.

"Hi, this is Dayna, from the house on...", she began.

"I know which one", he said, cutting her words short as his tone went from annoyed to amused.

"Sorry to bother you", she began, "But I noticed you have a truck, and see, I'm trying to figure out a way to get the rest of my stuff from my old place." Greg listened patiently on the other end as Dayna rambled on about how far it was and that it would only take a single trip, and that she was willing to pay him, and how she could not afford much and that she could not think of anyone else to ask.
Dayna was not great at asking for help, she liked to see herself as an independent person and often refused to ask for help because most of the few people she has accepted help from have tried to hold it over her head or use it against her in some way, but she really wanted her belongings safely here with her, so she was willing to accept the risk. So many of those things are special to her, they remind her of the good memories she had of her childhood. All the notes she and Ella used to write to each other and pass in between classes, what she had left of her grandmother's jewelry, and the only photo she has of her dad is all packed up in those boxes. Greg did not give her an answer, all he would say was that he would come by to see if they could work out a deal. Dayna was determined that she would work out a deal with him.

"Luckily mom has the day off work, so that should keep him out of my stuff for now", she thought feeling a little relieved by the realization, "but I've got to be there to get everything first thing in the morning because once she leaves for work, it probably won't take him long to start going through it all, especially since it's all packed up in one place and not hidden all over the room like I had it when that was my room".

Dayna had begun unpacking the little bit of stuff she did have here in her house. She blew up a twin-size air mattress with the little electric pump it came with and placed it on the floor of the biggest of the two bedrooms. She threw a sheet over the air mattress and topped that with her pillow and a fleece blanket with a blue snowflake pattern that she had got for Christmas last year. In the kitchen, she organized the cabinets and refrigerator with the dishes and a few days' worth of groceries that her mom had packed. and she stacked the towels and washcloths in the bathroom closet after placing her toothbrush and other toiletries on the sink. She looked around her empty place and she decided she would try to go to the furniture store tomorrow and see if they delivered, the place being so empty made her feel even more lonely than she already did. Then she heard a low rumble that kept getting closer coming from outside her place.

"That's probably Greg pulling up in the driveway", she thought excitedly, ready to get away from the nagging feeling of worry and loneliness that plagued her every moment she spent in this barren house. She met him at the door, already holding it open gesturing for him to come inside. He smiled at her flirtatiously as he walked in, he looked around at the place and asked her what she had in mind. She told him again that she did not think it would take more than a single load because she only had one small bedroom to get stuff from. She pulled a small wad of money from her pocket and he smiled, looking at her with an amused expression that was almost condescending. She counted out twenty-seven dollars and smiled at him as she told him that was all she had.

"Where's your folk's place?", he asked, putting his hands in the pockets of his ragged and stained blue jeans. She told them it was about 35 minutes East and he burst out laughing in response, "Do you know how much it costs in gas alone to run that beast out there?". She nodded her head as a look of disappointment crossed her face. "I will make you a deal though. Anyway, I don't really want your money", he added. She had a feeling that she was not going to like the deal he was about to offer, but curiosity and sheer determination made her ask regardless.

"What do you want?", she said quietly as her shoulders slumped.

"I want that thing you were trying to show off to me the other day", he plainly stated with a devilish smile. She looked back at him unsure of exactly what he was referring to, and too nervous to say anything. "I want that ass", he said more directly this time.

"I'm not going to fuck you for a ride to get my stuff", she said looking very offended. "I'm not a hooker!", she exclaimed as her face began to flush with a mix of anger and embarrassment.

He started waving his hands around, "woah, woah, woah, slow down their girl", he said authoritatively, "First off I did not say anything about fucking you", he clarified, "and I have friends who are working girls, and I have incredible respect for them, so don't you be insulting them".

Dayna instinctively apologized for offending Greg although she could not tell how serious he was. She asked him to clarify exactly what it is that he was wanting from her if he did not want to fuck her. He explained that he loved eating pussy, and ass too, and he might like to get a little bit of head as well.

"And you should watch how you judge them girls, they aren't doing anything besides being strong enough to take control of their lives and being quite resourceful too", he suggested. Dayna saw his point when he explained it that way. She carefully considered his offer and the fact that she had already been thinking about fucking Greg, and she felt a little less ashamed to accept his offer after hearing what he had to say on the matter which she also considered may have been his motive. Dayna hesitated for a moment before determination pushed her into accepting his offer. Then she asked him if he was able to be here tomorrow morning to go get her stuff from her parents before she completed her end of the deal, she told him it was because she wanted to have someplace comfortable to complete her end of the agreement.

"Alright, that's fine with me, but you better make good on your end of the bargain because I can make your life very difficult here if you don't, I could probably even get you tossed out of here if I wanted", he gave her a look that indicated that he was serious about the matter. She assured him that she would hold up her end of the bargain. She asked if he could come around six in the morning and he said that was fine. He was normally up at five anyway. Before heading out the door and to his truck, he politely wished her a good night.

Her thoughts raced through her mind as she pondered what had just happened between her and Greg and how apprehensive and confused, she felt about the agreement as she began getting herself ready for bed. She thought about when she was younger, in the weeks right before her mom had met Danny, and how they stayed in different hotel rooms, moving every few days, sometimes only staying in a place for a single night. She remembered frequently seeing women of all ages, mostly dressed in short dresses, and skirts all around the hotels, her mom had once referred to them as hookers, it was years before she understood what that meant. She thought about what Greg said, and it made sense. She went to bed thinking about those women and the new-found respect she had for them.

She was startled awake to a bang on her front door. She looked around confused momentarily and almost immediately realized what was going on. She could not believe she had forgot to set an alarm. "Fuck", she said as she jumped up and ran to the door to meet Greg.

"Good morning sunshine", he said sarcastically, "you ready?". She asked him to wait just a moment and assured him it would not take her long to get ready. She ran straight to the restroom without waiting for an answer, and then she brushed her teeth, quickly applied some deodorant, and threw her hair up in a ponytail. She ran back to the door, stopping to grab her purse along the way. She slammed the door and locked it behind her. Greg was already sitting in the truck waiting patiently, and typing on his phone, he kept looking down at her shirt with a smile on his face. She followed his gaze and realized she had been in such a rush she had forgot to put a bra on. Her puckered nipples poked through her shirt and it was clearly visible. She smiled back at Greg and shrugged nonchalantly. The ride was mostly spent quietly listening to music. Every now and then Greg would light a cigarette, and puff hard on it until it was gone, then flick it out his window which was just barely cracked open. Dayna made a couple attempts at striking up a conversation, but Greg did not seem like much of a talker, so she quickly gave up and sat quietly and stared out the window or at her phone for the entire ride. They pulled into the driveway in front of Dayna's old home, a tattered old trailer that was clearly in desperate need of some major repairs.

"Do you need help carrying your things out of there and packing them into the truck?", he asked her thoughtfully. She graciously accepted the help. When they walked in Danny was reclining in his chair in front of the television which was playing a NASCAR race. She knew he was sleeping heavily when she heard his deep rumbling snore. As she expected, her mom was nowhere to be seen either. Dayna figured she was probably already at work, given she did not get very many days off. Dayna put her finger over her lips and pointed over at the sleeping Danny, signaling for Greg to be quiet as they walked past him, being careful to make as little noise as possible. They carefully carried the boxes and furniture out to the truck, making a surprisingly small amount of noise despite the trailer's old creaky floors and the clutter that lay everywhere. After three trips in and out of the trailer, they had completely emptied Dayna's old room and packed everything neatly into the bed of Greg's red truck. Dayna was relieved that they had been able to get it all done without rousing Danny, who likely would have only gotten in the way and made the process take much longer by trying to make conversation with Greg. Greg secured her things with a few tow straps he had conveniently laying around in the truck and they made the return trip, again without much conversation taking place between the two.

When they pulled back into the gravelly driveway of her new place, Greg helped Dayna unload her stuff into the house, setting everything down on the floor of the living room. Then Greg asked her to let him know when she would be ready for company. Dayna thanked him and told him she was just going to get everything set up and take a shower and get ready and then she would text him to tell him he can come back over. He eyed her petite body and long legs once again before turning to leave to get some work done. Dayna heard his truck start with a loud growl and then rumble loudly out of her driveway. She felt overwhelmed as she looked at the pile of stuff on her living room floor. She deflated the air mattress, putting it away on the top shelf of the closet in the bathroom to use if she ever had company staying over and then she replaced it with her bed. She dragged her small white dresser into her room and sat her little twenty-eight-inch flatscreen television she had got for Christmas a couple years ago on top of it, then she unpacked each box finding a place for everything in her new home. She hung any pictures she had on the wall with a few nails she kept in a jar and straightened her rug neatly out on her bedroom floor securing it in place by using the weight of her furniture. She still needed so much furniture, especially for the living room, which was still bare, but the place felt much less empty now that she had all her stuff unpacked and set up. She looked around her place one last time feeling proud. Once she was showered and fresh, Dayna texted Greg to let him know she was ready for him to come back. He showed up about ten minutes later and she let him inside and closed and locked the door behind him.

"Ready?" Greg said, being all business as usual, and he wasted no time with small talk and walked straight back to the room. Dayna completely undressed herself except for her sexy black thong and then leaned back on her bed feeling both nervous and excited. He sat on the end of the bed and removed his work boots carefully as he eyed her naked body with what was clearly a look of satisfaction on his face. First, he pinched her nipple and pulled it lightly. He then trailed his fingertips up her legs, and to that hot spot between her thighs.

"mmm", she moaned, her pussy was already wet and throbbing with anticipation. He pulled her panties down around her ankles leaving her completely exposed and planted a wet kiss right on her pussy. She moaned and thrusted her hips forward as he gently flicked her clit with his tongue. He parted her lips and shoved his tongue inside the tight little hole not far beneath her clit which he was now slowly working open gently with his fingers. She felt another finger press firmly against her asshole using the wetness from his mouth and her pussy as lubricant so he could slip the finger inside. Once he did, his tongue began prodding her asshole as he guided her hand to the bulge that was threatening to burst through the zipper of his pants at any moment.

She undid his jeans obediently and a large fat cock eagerly popped out. He grabbed her hips and guided her on top of him as he flipped her over, placing her pussy on his face with her face in the direction of his cock. She took the whole thing into her mouth and it gagged her as it pushed its way into the back of her throat. He groaned in satisfaction and buried his face deep in her pussy. She began to move her hips, pushing her clit against his tongue as she sucked hard on his cock, repeatedly pushing it into the back of her throat occasionally gagging. Every now and then she momentarily had to come up to catch her breath. He grabbed her ass and used it to guide her tight little asshole to his mouth and she moaned in pleasure as he continued to work her clit with his thumb. She had no idea having her ass eaten could feel this good when she had tried it before. She had never been this dirty before with someone she barely knew.

This was also the first time she had been fingered in the ass so deeply, so she was going to enjoy the hell out of every second of it. He pulled his finger back slowly and then dove back in hard and fast, fucking her ass like a madman, faster and faster until he pulled his cock from her mouth and shot his cum all over her face and lips. As he continued to come, she put her lips around the head of his cock and sucked some of his cum into her mouth as it dripped from his cock. She quickly licked it off her lips before pulling her mouth back to his cock and sucking it back in.

"Mmmm", she moaned once again as he reached up to her ass with his tongue and began to fuck her mouth like he was fucking her pussy. It was ecstasy. He grabbed her hands and pulled her down flat on top of him and switched to fuck her pussy with his tongue while he pulled on her tits. She squeezed his cock and rubbed her pussy against his face as hard as she could until it suddenly began to tingle and heat up, and she moaned again in ecstasy as she felt herself getting wetter and wetter and had to slow down as she could feel herself coming all over his face. She pulled her pussy away from his mouth and finished her orgasm, as she was overwhelmed with pleasure. She lay on top of him panting, his cock slowly sliding from her mouth.

She felt him rubbing her ass, rubbing her pussy and clit until she finally felt it break through again and that same warm sensation kept coming as it spread over her entire body. She felt her tight pussy spasm again as she licked his balls and moaned in appreciation. He slowly worked her clit in circles with his tongue.

She once again began feeling the same tingle that meant she was close to yet another climax. She moaned and pushed herself hard against his face once more as she came. He tasted as much of the sweet juices as he could, feeling her legs trembling with pleasure. She pulled away unable to take the feeling of growing intensity. He used her hips to lift her off his face and stood up beside the bed and grabbed her hair. He pushed his cock forcefully into her mouth and thrust it in and out until he started to come one more time. He pulled his cock from her mouth and watched as she held her tongue out, lapping up as much of the cum as she could reach with her tongue. He breathed a sigh of satisfaction and looked at her with a pleased expression. When he turned to pull his pants on, she wiped all the remaining cum off her face with a hand towel she had sat on the table near the bed and smiled at him. He was amazed by the fantastic time she gave him, thanked her politely and left. Leaving her feeling satisfied and tired, she put on the television and fell fast asleep within minutes.

Dayna looked at Ella in anticipation wondering if Ella would think badly of her because she used sexual favors to barter a way to get her stuff. Dayna had not had anyone to confide in in the last six years when she broke down and told her close friend Jessica all about her wild lifestyle. In the end that did not turn out well at all, and she nearly lost custody of her son. As a result, Dayna remains tight-lipped about certain parts of her life to everyone, and that often made her feel isolated. She studied Ella's expression actively trying to spot any signs of disapproval. Ella did not seem at all phased by the story.

"Wow! So, he did you have any more bedroom encounters with him?", Ella asked.
"Just the one", Dayna responded, "he never made another move, and I think he did stuff like that a lot, because after that I was always seeing him with different women".

"So, after that y'all's relationship remained strictly business, about the apartment I mean", Ella said as she stacked their empty plates neatly on the table. Dayna nodded. "I had a sugar daddy in college for a while", Ella laughed at the memory fondly. She told Dayna how easy he made things for her financially, and about the social perks it had as well. He gave her a lot of his connections too, which have proven to be infinitely valuable. She had been strapped for cash at the time because a year or so prior Ella's dad got sick.

"I'm sorry to hear that", Dayna said sadly. Ella told her that soon after her mom had stopped paying for college because her dad's medical expenses were piling up, so she got a job. Juggling work and school proved to be more than she could handle, so when her friend told her about her own success with a sugar daddy website, she signed up immediately. It did not take long for her to meet someone too. By this point Dayna had relaxed and decided that she could trust Ella completely. She did not feel like Ella was the type to judge others too harshly.

"I'm not going to lie, I really got into the whole being a sugar baby thing right away. He was older but not so older that it was gross or anything", she explained. "In fact, he was really in shape and fun, and there's something about being with an older man that I really enjoyed", she said as she dove straight into her next story.

Ella Gets Punished (spanking)

"Yeah?", Ella groggily murmured, lifting her head from the table. She had her arms shielded around her to block out the light that shone through the window. When she saw where she was, she quickly sat upright and looked around to see if anyone, besides the person who woke her up, had been paying attention. Luckily, the library was mostly empty.

"Are you okay?", Fallon asked looking concerned.

"Yeah, I worked late last night, so I hardly got any sleep", Ella explained groggily as she wiped the crust from her eyes.

Fallon nodded at her with a look of concern still on her face and suggested Ella take a break from studying and go with her to meet a couple friends at the cafe for something caffeinated. Ella agreed and started slowly stacking the books on the corner of the table and packed her notebook and pens into her bag. The whole way to the cafe Ella complained to Fallon about the waitressing job she took on to pay for her tuition. Fallon looked at her sympathetically for a moment before her eyes widened.

"I have an idea", Fallon said excitedly. "Maybe you should talk to Hannah, she told me something about getting help from some website to pay for tuition, and she said she doesn't have to pay it back either", she suggested. Ella knew she needed something like that badly, so she decided she would approach Hannah about it as soon as she got a chance. She did not know how she could possibly make it like this till the end of the semester, let alone to the completion of her degree. Working long hours at a physically demanding job, and then going to school to pursue a degree program that is also demanding was really an impossibly heavy load. Luckily, her chance to speak with Hannah came almost immediately, Ella saw her sitting at the cafe in the group's regular spot, her laptop was opened in front of her as she typed ferociously on the keyboard. Ella sat in the seat right across from her and Fallon took the seat beside her.

Before Ella could even think of what to say, Fallon blurted, "Hey Hannah, I was just telling Ella how you were getting help with your tuition on that website you mentioned earlier. She could probably use something like that herself". Ella's cheeks turned slightly red with embarrassment. Hannah looked up from her computer and smiled a tight sympathetic smile at Ella. She asked Ella if she had time to talk about it a little later. She said she was working on something that was due later today, so she did not have time to tell her about it at this moment. Ella told her that would be fine and asked her to let her know whenever she had a chance. Fallon started telling everyone bye as soon as she got her coffee, she had a class starting soon, so she left Ella at the cafe to hurry off to get to her class. Ella sat and sipped on the latte she ordered as she read over the notes, she had taken in the library in preparation for a test she had the next day. Even though she had finished most of the latte already, Ella was struggling to keep her eyes open. Hannah noticed Ella opening and closing her eyes.

"Here", Hannah said, handing her a bottle of pills. Ella looked at the bottle suspiciously, when she saw they said caffeine on the bottle she opened it and took one. She thanked Hannah and tried to give them back, but Hannah refused. She asked Ella if she wanted to walk with her back to the main building, and Ella agreed. Both girls began shoving things into their bags. Ella had made up her mind to head back to the dorm and get a power nap in before her psychology class anyway. She knew if she did not, she would most likely fall asleep during class and she preferred to not embarrass herself anymore by falling asleep in random places. Both girls finished gathering their stuff and stood to leave. Ella thanked Hannah for taking the time to help her. Hannah said she did not mind at all and they started towards the main building.

"I'd really appreciate it if you don't tell anyone that I told you about this", Hannah said quietly. Ella was confused and curious so she promised Hannah that she would not tell anyone. Hannah explained that she had been getting help with her tuition from a sugar daddy she met online. She told Ella that there were tons of local men on this site looking for young, beautiful girls to spoil. As Ella listened her jaw nearly dropped. This was not at all the kind of help Ella had been expecting, but she needed it badly, so she took the scrap of paper Hannah gave her with the website on it. When Ella made it back to the dorm, she set her alarm and crawled straight into bed falling immediately asleep.

The alarm clock abruptly jarred Ella awake, she sat up in bed and immediately started getting herself ready for class. After brushing her hair and touching up her makeup, she thought about the website Hannah had given her and realized she was a bit excited about the prospect of having a sugar daddy. She made her way to psychology class in a hurry, barely making it on time, and when class was over, she was eager to get started with making her profile. She meticulously filled everything out. She took her time deciding on the right username and bio for her profile. She used a photo she took for Brennon last semester as her profile picture. It was one of her favorite pictures of herself. In it she had on a black Lace crop top that exposed her flat stomach, and tight jeans that made her ass look perfectly round. Then she selected a few other sexy pics to use on her profile. Once she finished setting it up, she turned over and closed her eyes to finish catching up on some much-needed rest.

When she awoke, she was surprised to see that she already had four messages from potential sugar daddies. She checked them one by one, she read the messages in the order she had received them. Two of them were from the same sender, he seemed a little creepy and desperate. His first message asking if she wanted to fuck, and the second was an unwelcome dick pic. She frowned at her computer screen and quickly blocked the sender. Then there was one from a man who looked old enough to be her grandfather. She shuddered a little, and decided she just could not do that, so she blocked that sender as well. She moved on to the next message already feeling a little discouraged. This guy was older too, but still extremely attractive. He wore an expensive suite in his profile photo, he looked like he was in good shape, and he also had a wonderful smile. His message was written in a very formal tone. In it he invited her to have dinner with him at a nice restaurant. His message said his name was Shaun. She typed a message back accepting Shaun's invitation, and they set up a time to meet. It was just three days away, which gave her mixed feelings of anxiousness and exhilaration.

Over the next three days she continued checking her messages on the site for potential sugar daddies, but none seemed as interesting as her Friday night date seemed. She responded to a few guys, just in case this one did not work out for whatever reason, but she avoided making any other plans just yet. She did not tell Fallon or anyone else what she was planning to do. She kept it to herself as Hannah had asked her to do, also because she was a little worried about what the others might think of her. She did have another conversation with Hannah about it though. Hannah told her that each man would have different expectations, but most would expect some form of sexual favor. She said that she often got expensive gifts and was taken out on fancy dates and even an occasional trip, that all came on top of having her tuition completely covered. Later, Ella logged onto the site to check her messages again. Shaun had sent her a message to confirm their date the following day, he included his cell phone number and asked her to text him her response when she could. Ella saved Shaun's number in her phone and sent a text that said, "I can't wait to meet you tomorrow. Ella". She had trouble sleeping that night because she was so excited about the upcoming date. Ella got out of bed still feeling exhausted from working and attending school. She could hardly pay attention in any of her classes due to the exhaustion and excitement. She bolted out of her last class, speed-walking to her dorm as quickly as possible to ensure she had ample time to get herself ready for the upcoming date. Upon making it to her dorm, she picked up a dress she had laid across her bed that morning. It was red and trimmed with lace, the heart shaped top was classy and sexy, it was tight around her waist and the skirt flowed off her waist stopping at her thighs. She happily noticed how smooth and tanned her legs were. She put on some music and got to work on her hair. She moved her hips to the music as she applied her makeup. Before leaving the bathroom, she spritzed herself with her favorite perfume. Shortly after she finished getting ready her phone dinged. It was her date letting her know he was about to come pick her up. She had told him that she could meet him at the restaurant, but he insisted on picking her up. She figured his age was the cause of his insistence on picking her up. She was already waiting outside when she saw the deep red Lexus LC pull up in front of her dorm building. She looked around to see what attention the genuinely nice, and expensive car had attracted. All over the parking lot and in front of the building people looked up to notice the striking car, and to see who was getting into it.

Excitement bubbled up as she walked towards the door. A handsome older gentleman quickly got out of the car and ran around the car to open her door. He took her hand and gestured her into the car. She slid into the leather seat and marveled at its perfectly shiny interior. Shaun got back into the driver seat and looked at her and smiled with the whitest teeth she had ever seen.

"Your photos don't do you justice"' he said to her politely. He held out his hand and when she went to take it, he lifted her hand to his lips and softly kissed it. She returned his smile and thanked him. She buckled her seatbelt securely around her hips as he returned his attention to the road. They made small talk on the short drive to the restaurant. She talked about her classes and friends. He told her about his job as the COO of a major home security company. They pulled up to a contemporary looking restaurant called Aria. She had heard a few people talk about it at school, but she had never been. It was much too expensive for her. Shaun exited the car and made his way to open the door for her again. She took the hand he offered and got out of the car and walked inside with her arm looped into his. She noticed how great it felt to be treated this way. He seemed like such a gentleman, and it made him very charming.

The hostess took their jackets before seating them at a private table in the corner of the restaurant. She asked them each if they prefer sparkling water or still water. Shaun asked for still. Ella was not sure what that meant at first, so she asked for still as well. When the waitress got to their table, he ordered a bottle of wine. They sat sipping wine and looking over the menu. He ordered a prime rib, and she had the Chilean Sea Bass. They were having a great time eating, drinking, talking, and laughing. The food was delicious, and Shaun was funny, and down-to-earth. She started feeling the effects of the wine shortly after the second bottle was opened. Her glances at him became more and more flirty as she started to feel a warmth in her stomach and her pussy. That warmth turned to heat when she felt Shaun's hand lightly touching her thigh under the table. She opened her legs slightly and he eyed her with hungry eyes. He ran his hand up the inside of her thigh until it reached her panties. He rubbed the top of her panties, feeling the warmth and wetness. As he explored her pussy with his fingers, he asked if she wanted dessert, as if nothing were happening under the table, and she politely declined saying she was far too full.

Shaun requested the check, and when the waitress returned, he handed her his card without looking at the bill. Before standing to leave he threw a bunch of twenties down on the table. Ella was impressed by the tip he had left. When they returned to his car, he asked Ella if she would like to take a detour to go by his place to have one more drink before he returned her to her dorm. She smiled at him knowingly before happily accepting his offer and after a twenty-minute ride of more polite conversation, they pulled into a genuinely nice upscale neighborhood of huge houses and then up to a large 2-story house on a very private lot towards the back of the neighborhood. Shaun helped her out of the car and walked her to the front door and then inside. The inside of the house was as beautiful as it was on the outside, and it was exceptionally large, and very well decorated. He immediately walked over to a wooden liquor cabinet and asked her if she drank brandy. She never had, but she said yes so, he poured her some over a glass of ice. She took a big drink and then sipped it carefully after realizing how strong it was. Shaun watched her looking amused.

"You're a very bad girl", he remarked plainly.

"Excuse me?", Ella responded, not sure if she had heard him correctly.

"You let a stranger touch your pretty little pussy in the middle of an upscale restaurant.
That makes you an unbelievably bad girl", he repeated to her. She did not know what to say. Her words were caught in her throat. Her pussy got wetter, even though she became suddenly nervous.

"I..uh…" She stuttered unsure of what to say.

"I'm going to punish you", He stated, cutting her off without much emotion. He walked over to her and grabbed her firmly by the wrist. She did not object or pull away as he led her into a bedroom with a perfectly made bed. He walked her over to the side of a made-up bed with a deep red comforter. "Bend over", he said looking at her authoritatively.

"But- "she started to object.

"Do as you're told", he interjected in a demanding tone. She looked at him and obediently bent over the side of the bed as she felt a dizzying feeling of excitement, fear, and pleasure. She felt a stinging feeling and heard a loud pop as his hand met her ass. "A sexy little bad girl", he remarked as he rubbed her beautiful plump ass with the hand he had just smacked her with. She moaned a little in anticipation of more. He ordered her to pull the skirt of her dress around her waist, and she did as she was told. He smacked her again, hard, she whimpered a little as he pulled her panties off her hips and let them fall around her ankles. He smacked her ass once again. Her face was now flushed and hot and she felt that her pussy was so wet it might start dripping at any moment. She felt his hand slide between her legs. He used his hand to pry her legs further apart before smacking her again, hard on her supple ass. His hand reached up and pinched her nipple through her dress and he softly chuckled.

"I guess I like my girls a little bad", he said. He smacked her bare ass again. It was on fire at this point. His hand felt warm as he rubbed away the sting. "Are you my girl? he asked, putting emphasis on 'my'.

"Yes", she muttered breathlessly. He smacked her again. The pain was terrific. It was beginning to feel like fire every time his hand hit her smooth flesh.

"Yes what?", he asked.

"Yes sir", she said more loudly this time. She felt exposed as he paused a moment. She heard him rummaging around for something before it went quiet again. He struck her again but this time it was not his hand that hit her ass. It was hard and flat and rough. He struck her again and again. Each blow made her pussy wetter and her ass sting more. She wanted to scream but it was caught in her throat. She wondered if her ass was blistered. She felt it must be. She was not sure how many blows she had endured. It stopped again and he plunged his fingers deep into her pussy. She came almost right away. Squirming against the bed as he pounded his fingers deep inside her. When her orgasm stopped, so did he. He walked across the room and she saw him wipe his hands on a hand towel from the corner of her eye. Moments later, he came back and pulled his pants and underwear down to the floor and pulled a red blindfold out of a drawer and held it in front of her face.

"Your naughtiness, little girl, is cause for some punishment", he said, pulling the blindfold over her eyes. She felt the cold wood of what she now recognized as a paddle as he slowly smacked her bare ass over and over. The sting was unreal, the sting was everywhere, and it was painful, yet for a reason unbeknown to her, she enjoyed each second of it. He slapped her ass as hard as he could, and she flinched from the intense, powerful stings and the windiness that hit her pussy and spread up into her chest. He slapped her ass for a long time, and then he ordered her to kneel on the floor, where he began to slap her tits with a flogger he had tucked under his bed. He felt her spasm from the biting pain and her pussy get wetter. She moaned and whimpered at the terrible, painful stings on her body, and he knew she was enjoying it, even though she did not admit it to him, yet.

"Harder daddy", she begged. He grabbed her pussy and stuck two fingers deep inside her pussy. The feeling was incredible as he flicked his finger over her clit, catching it with his hand. The initial pain of the paddle on her ass and her pussy had made her so wet that she needed a lot more pressure on her clit before she could cum. The delicious pleasure of his finger rubbing over her clit was almost more than she could stand, yet he would not let her cum yet, as he knew she would be spanked again at a later time. "You are my good girl. Your safe place is with me, and I am going to keep it that way", he said.

"Faster daddy, faster", she begged as he slapped her ass again. The paddle landed hard against the wooden floor and the sound of it made her wetter. The pain was intense but now that it was coming, it made her forget everything else. She felt such a sweet release as he slapped her again with his bare hand and she came again as he rubbed his fingers deep inside her pussy, then he tenderly rubbed her ass, she could not take any more thankfully he was satisfied as well. She lay naked on the bed crying, her ass, much like her eyes, was red and puffy from the paddling.

"You can get up now sweetheart", he urged with a cool tone. Ella stood wiping her eyes and bent to grab her panties. She balled them into her fist and pulled her dress back down over her stinging ass. "The restroom is over there if you'd like to freshen up", he said as he gestured to a door on the other side of the room. She sheepishly walked over to it. She immediately examined her bottom in the mirror above the double vanity. She gasped at the sight, her skin was a deep red, almost purple color, and there were welts all across her swollen cheeks. It stung and was hot to the touch. She noticed a clean hand towel folded neatly on the corner of the vanity. She picked it up and wet it with soapy water and wiped her own cum off her pussy with it. She grabbed another towel she found in the drawer and used it to wipe up the eyeliner and tears that ran down her puffy face. When she was done her heart began to pound as she went to leave the restroom. She was not sure what she would say or how she would act when she saw him. When she opened the door, the room was empty.

"I'm in here", Shaun's voice called from the main room. She followed his voice into the foyer where they had come in. He already had his jacket on and was holding hers out politely offering to help her put it on. Without saying anything. she turned around and slipped her arms into the sleeves. He opened the door and she quietly followed him out to the car. She was completely exhausted when she made it back to her dorm. She had plans to go out with a few of her friends, but she called and canceled explaining that she was just too tired to go out. She slept great that night. She dreamed about her encounter with Shaun except in her dream he fucked her with his hard cock. When she awoke, she was still in a daze and trying to process yesterday's events. Her ass still had a slight redness to it. She was not sure why, but she had really enjoyed getting spanked by Shaun. She could not wait to see him again. Ella checked her student email as she did every morning. There was a message from the school's financial department. It notified her that her semester's tuition had been paid in full. She held her hand over her mouth to try to contain the excited squeal that she let slip out.

"I cannot wait to quit that miserable job I have", she thought with satisfaction. She felt relieved and renewed knowing she no longer had to worry about how she was going to cover her tuition. She was surprised by the fact that she did not feel the least bit guilty for accepting payment in exchange for sexual favors. She genuinely liked Shaun and the spanking he gave her had made a switch flip inside of her as she realized that she loved being dominated. She was excited to move forward with this endeavor and wondered what other treats this arrangement might include, or if he would take her on vacations to places she had never been. She had seen these types of arrangements on television, and it felt incredibly exciting to now be a part of one herself now.

Dayna felt so relieved that Ella had an experience that opened her mind to that sort of thing. At this point they were both catching a buzz and being a lot more forthcoming about their lives to one another. They were having a great time sharing their stories and learning more about the other's experiences.

"So that was your first time with an older man?", Dayna asked.

Ella nodded and said that it was. Ella was surprised by how much she was comfortable sharing with Dayna. Normally Ella was diligent about keeping up her appearances. For her mom, for her coworkers, and all her so-called friends who really knew nothing about who she was. Ella realized that since Dayna and she had graduated, she had not had a single real friend, no one to confide in. Ella looked across the table at Dayna and smiled. "I hope this friendship lasts", Ella thought. As she reminisced with Dayna about their innocent, and conservative ways as teenagers. She found it so funny how they both blossomed into adults with some wild and crazy sexual experiences. Dayna asked the bartender to get them another round. She checked her phone to make sure she had no messages from the babysitter.

"What do you have there?", Ella asked, glancing over, "texting a boyfriend?".

"No, I'm currently single", Dayna said, shaking her head. She told Ella she was making sure her son was okay with the sitter. She had paid the babysitter for the full night just in case but told her she might be home early depending on how things go. In light of how well things were going, Dayna decided to send her a text to let her know not to expect her home till late tonight or early morning. Once she got a response, she returned her phone to her purse, and her attention to Ella. Ella asked so she told her all about Brady, her son.

"I don't have any kids, and I don't really plan to", Ella said as if she were imagining what it would be like, "my job is way too demanding".

Dayna explained that she had not really planned it either, "It just happened", she shrugged.

"Is the dad around?", Ella asked.

Dayna shook her head, "I let him know I was pregnant, but I never heard from him after that". Ella continued prodding for information about Brady's father. Dayna did not mind because they were never really in a relationship. In fact, they were only in contact for a very brief time. So, Dayna decided to use her turn as storyteller to tell Ella the story about how she had ended up pregnant at such a young age and without the father's help.

Dayna Is Sweet as Pie (cream pie)

It was a beautiful day outside; Dayna had just finished cleaning up her house. She recently rented out a room to her friend, Tori. Dayna could hear Tori in the other room just waking up. She was in her room loudly getting ready as she did every morning, sometimes at oddly early hours due to her job. She turned the music up to drown Tori's noise out and sat on the couch as she carefully sipped her coffee and packed the bong full of weed. She mindlessly flipped through a book she had been intending to read for a while now. She propped her feet up on the coffee table, put the bong to her mouth, and began to light the weed on fire. Suddenly, as if she could already smell it burning, Tori burst through her bedroom door and into the hallway.

"Hey bitch", Tori greeted her in the usual way.

"What's up slut", Dayna replied.

"Have you packed the bowl yet?", Tori asked but before Dayna could even respond she started again, "Oh and I have a few new friends coming by in a bit. They said they had some good shit".

Dayna held her hand out with the loaded bong and told Tori to come smoke with her. They sat on the couch together and smoked. Tori asked Dayna if she wanted to come to a party and bonfire by the creek with her tomorrow. They had these things often and Dayna seldom went. As usual, Dayna politely declined because she really did not enjoy those things. People get drunk and fight and everyone is always acting ridiculous. Dayna worried about stuff like that getting her into trouble she did not need to be in. Both girls got startled when they heard a knock on the door. They looked at each other and laughed as Tori yelled for her visitors to come inside. The door opened and three people noisily entered their house. The first was a guy with a couple missing teeth that looked to be in his thirties wearing a Marlboro shirt, a woman who also appeared to be in her thirties and appeared to be strung out on drugs. She had brown frizzy hair and was very thin. Her arm was looped into the arm of the guy with the Marlboro shirt, as she possessively eyed Dayna and Tori. Behind them, a very good-looking guy that appeared to be in his early twenties. Tori invited them all to sit down. The couple sat in the recliner together and Tori and Dayna scooted down the couch to make room for the younger guy, who sat down on the end beside Dayna. Tori introduced the couple as Scott, and Renee.

"I haven't met this one", Tori said, eyeing the younger guy.

"That's my brother Jesse", Scott said dismissively as he held out his hand to Renee. She immediately dug into her black purse and revealed a gallon sized Ziplock bag of marijuana.

"Whew!", Tori exclaimed loudly, "I can smell it from here".

Dayna had not even paid much attention to the bud. She was somewhat distracted by the younger guy, Jesse. She had complimented the tribal tattoo on his arm. He thanked her and they immediately began telling one another all about their tattoos. Dayna was brought back to reality when Tori tapped on her arm to get her attention and immediately shoved the newly packed bong in her direction. Dayna hit it and blew out a huge cloud of smoke, then passed it over to Jesse, who hit it once and passed it along. Tori handed Scott a wad of cash, who then pulled out some scales and weighed some of the weed out onto the tray and poured it into a small bag. He passed it to Tori, and immediately said he had somewhere to be, so he stood up to leave.

"C'mon Jesse", Scott said. Dayna reluctantly said bye to Jesse and all three left without saying much more. As soon as they walked out the door Dayna turned to Tori with excited wide eyes.

"Omg! I call dibs on that hottie Jesse", she said quickly.

"Does this mean you're going to the bonfire tomorrow?", Tori asked teasingly.

Dayna asked if he would be there and Tori told Dayna that she had invited Scott and Renee, and they said they would come, so there was a good chance he would be there as well. Dayna sighed and reluctantly agreed to go, "but if he's not there, I'm probably going to come back here", she said, "you know I hate going to those things". Tori rolled her eyes at Dayna as she grabbed the remote and put on a movie for them. They sat quietly on the couch watching television together with their legs tangled together as they smoked some of the green Tori just bought. The day was quiet and lazy because it was one of the rare occasions neither of them had to work. Dayna could not help but feel giddy over Jesse. She really hoped he would be at the bonfire tomorrow. She sat and planned her approach in her mind as the movie played in the background. She thought about what she would say to him and imagined how he would respond. Jesse was the first person in a while that she felt this attracted to. Dayna and Tori hung out the rest of the day just watching movies, relaxing, and getting high.

The next morning Dayna hopped out of bed with more energy than normal and made herself some coffee. She called her mom and talked to her for over an hour as she slowly sipped on her coffee. Tori had left for work super early that morning so Dayna hoped she would get home early too. She walked into the house around two in the afternoon, and immediately sat on the couch by Dayna as she usually did. Dayna packed the bowl completely full and passed it over to Tori. Tori was more excited than she usually was about these parties, because this time, Dayna would be coming along with her, and lately that was exceptionally rare. The two girls got ready together, helping one another with makeup and critiquing each other's outfits. Dayna and Tori both decided on bikini tops and jean shorts. It was summer and they both wanted to turn heads. When they were both ready, they sat down and smoked some more till it was time to leave. Dayna decided to have a few pre-game drinks to build up her courage as well. They got in Tori's truck and left. Both were feeling excited about the upcoming evening. When they pulled up to the party, they saw a bunch of coolers littering the bank of the creek, in which each group had their preference of beer and maybe a few bottles of liquor too. Tori also brought a cooler for herself and Dayna, which remained in the bed of her truck.

Tori looked at Dayna and smiled, "Ready?", she asked.

"I guess", Dayna replied with an exasperated sigh.
Both girls got out of the truck and Tori grabbed them each a beer out of the cooler. Dayna popped hers open the second Tori passed it to her. She chugged nearly half of it down right away. Dayna quietly followed Tori around and they mingled with everyone at the party. There was a whole pig cooking in a smoker a group of guys made in the ground. The smell made Dayna's stomach growl. She kept searching for Jesse as they made their way down the creek. She was talking to an acquaintance when Tori grabbed and shook her arm. She pointed in the direction they had walked from and there was a truck parking right beside Tori's. Tori mouthed Scott's name as she pointed at the truck. So, Dayna watched hoping Jesse would get out of it. When she saw him, she thought of the ways he would be touching her by the end of the night. Her pussy got a little wet and her nipples perked up beneath her bikini top. She made her way back towards Tori's truck to meet Jesse. He looked her up and down and flirtatiously smiled when he saw Dayna walk up. She returned his smile as she approached him.

"Hey", she said with her hand held over her eyes to shield them from the bright sun, "what's up?". He examined the tattoo on her ribs,

"I can actually see it now, I really like it", he said of the floral tattoo on her rib cage as he trailed his fingers along the morning glories and vines that went down to her hip. His touch made her body react immediately. She looked at him wondering if he had noticed, he looked back at her with that same seductive smile. He offered her a shot from a flask he had in his pocket. She took a swig without asking what it was. Her face scrunched up when the taste of whiskey hit her. He laughed at the face she made.

"Sorry, I guess I should've warned you", he said, "that's some strong shit".

"That's okay", she said through a cough. They walked around together talking and drinking. There were a couple times when she thought he might have been flirting with her, but she was unsure. She wondered if he noticed her attempts at flirting with him. They mostly hung out amongst themselves until the sun started going down. They saw that a crowd was beginning to form around where the pig had been cooking, and they figured it might be ready. They made their way towards the crowd to get a plate of food.

As everyone finished eating, the party's energy seemed to be hyping up tremendously. The sun began to disappear behind the tops of the trees and all the parents began dutifully loading their children up to head home for the night. A single huge speaker appeared near the bonfire and began filling the air with intoxicating beats. A crowd of dancing people began to form around the speaker. They moved to the rhythm of the music with their bodies pressed against one another. Everyone appeared to be having a great time. Even Dayna was feeling the vibe as Jesse began to lead her toward the crowd. They got close enough to the speaker that they could feel the vibrations. Jesse pulled Dayna close, she felt the alcohol making her head buzz and her body warm. She moved her body against his seductively. She felt his hard cock as she rubbed her ass against it. His hands began exploring her body. They danced and laughed among the crowd of people for what felt like eternity. When they stopped, they were sweaty and completely out of breath. They decided to walk back to the trucks to get a drink.

Jessie retrieved two beers from the cooler and handed one of them to Dayna. He pulled the tailgate down on his brother's truck and they both sat on it. Jesse felt more confident thanks to the buzz he now had, so he reached his hand around Dayna's waist to pull her closer to him. She looked up at him with a huge grin and he leaned in to kiss Dayna's lips. The second their lips met they both dove into their desires. The chemistry between them that had been building up was enhanced by the alcoholic stupor they both found themselves in. He parted her lips with his thumb and pushed his tongue inside her mouth. Dayna responded with a moan as she arched her back to get her body closer to his. He began to use his hands to feel all over her body. She grabbed his hand to put it under the shirt that the night's chill made her put on not long ago. This was her way of letting him know that he could explore beneath her clothes as well. Dayna could feel that her pussy was very wet now, and it tingled in anticipation. She put her hand where Jesse's cock was. She felt that it was hard for her and it pressed tight against his pants, threatening to bust free. As Dayna rubbed his cock through Jesse's jeans he grabbed and played with her tits.

Seemingly at the same time they both stopped and looked around suddenly remembering where they were. They smiled at each other looking both guilty and disappointed. "We can leave if you want", Dayna suggested looking at Jesse seductively, "I can take Tori's truck and come back and pick her up or your brother can drop her at my place and pick you up". Jesse texted his brother to let him know where he was going and asked him if he could bring Tori home and pick him up there. As he did that Dayna ran to find Tori and get the keys to her truck. Scott agreed to bring Tori home and Dayna successfully got the keys from a very drunk Tori who was grinding on some random guys. She got in and began grabbing stuff from the passenger seat and setting it on the floor. Jesse opened the passenger door just as she had finished clearing the seat and she started the truck. The engine roared to life causing the entire truck to shake and vibrate. It felt good against her wet and already tingly pussy.

They talked and flirted relentlessly with each other as Dayna drove them back to the house. Every now and then she would cuss at the truck for making a questionable noise or jerking unexpectedly. She hated driving Tori's truck, because she was always afraid it would quit on her, but she supposed it was worth it this time. Jesse eyed her the whole way, and Dayna glanced over at him as much as she could. When their eyes met, they would grin at one another as if they were sharing an inside joke. They were both anticipating the sex that would surely take place once they got to Dayna and Tori's place. Dayna pulled into the driveway and parked the car as close to the house as she could. She unlocked the front door and threw her keys on the table as she let Jesse in the door. Before making their way into Dayna's room, both Dayna and Jesse needed to use the restroom. Dayna fixed them both a drink while she waited for Jesse to come out, and once he did, she ushered him into her room and closed the door. Jesse immediately resumed kissing Dayna. She moaned and pressed her body against him. She pushed him backwards onto her bed as their lips remained locked and their tongues swirled around each other.

Jesse grabbed the bottom of her t-shirt and pulled it over her head. She did the same pulling his shirt off and exposing his bare chest which was beautifully defined. She noticed that he was perfectly sculpted and tanned. He cupped her boobs in his hand through the bikini top she was still wearing. Jesse reached behind Dayna and pulled the string on her bikini top. It untied easily and it fell straight to the floor, exposing Dayna's chest. He cupped both of her boobs in his hands again but this time he leaned in and pulled one of her nipples into his mouth. Dayna eagerly began to undo the button of Jesse's pants. She had only gotten the button unclasped before he began kissing his way down her flat stomach, which made it impossible to remove his pants. He grabbed the top of her pants instead, after getting the button undone, he pulled her pants off, and threw them to the bedroom floor with her panties still on, he kissed her where her sex was, she arched her back readily.

Jesse slowly ran his tongue across her clit in a circular motion. Dayna let a sigh of pleasure escape from her lips. Her pussy was slick with a mixture of her juices, and his spit. It felt hot and ready for Jesse's cock. He stood and removed his jeans gazing intently at a naked Dayna lying on the bed. Her pussy wanted his cock so bad, but she wanted to feel it in her mouth too. She sat up on the bed and took his rigid cock first in her hand and then she brought it to her mouth. She heaved a little when he thrusted his hips forward, forcing it completely into her mouth. He groaned and ran his fingers through her hair. For a moment, he watched Dayna's head undulate as she sucked and licked him vicariously. When he was ready to bury himself in her pussy, he told her to lie back. She obeyed him without a word and looked up at him. He positioned himself between her legs and rubbed his cock against her pussy. He groaned when he felt that it was wet and ready for him. He could not help but to thrust himself deep inside of her tight little pussy. Dayna felt a dizzying pleasure as he repeatedly slammed his dick into her. She wrapped her legs tight around his and cried out in pleasure. Her pussy squeezed his cock as he pushed himself deeper. It felt better than anything he had ever experienced.

They were both completely captivated by one another and the pleasure they were giving and receiving. Dayna's moans, and squeals got more and more intense as she got closer to her climax. She began squirming beneath him and trembling as a feeling of ecstasy swept over her body. His thrusts were getting faster, harder, and deeper. Her mind exploded with pleasure and just seconds later so did his. She felt his cum rush into her, filling her pussy. He relaxed and began panting in exhaustion. He began to realize what he had done as he pulled his cock out and saw some of his cum dripping from her pussy. Dayna sat up and looked down at the cum leaking out in between her legs.

"Shit! I'm not on birth control", she said looking nervous. Jesse felt guilty, knowing what a slut he was being. He knew that he had come in her, and that he had fucked her in her pussy while she was not on any form of birth control. He thought to himself that he would rather have done that with some little slut than with the married woman.

"I can't believe I just did that!" Dayna exclaimed.

"I can't believe it, either," Jesse replied laughing nervously.

Jesse stood up and ran his hand over his cock and it was still rock hard. He walked up to Dayna and kissed her passionately. She opened her mouth, allowing him to take the kiss deeper. They both knelt and kissed each other and touched their tongues together. They laid down in the bed holding each other for a while. Jesse noticed Dayna's breasts rising and falling rapidly. She placed her hands on his chest and then pulled him down to her mouth. She kissed him deeply and lovingly. After a few minutes of passionate kissing, Jesse sat up. He made a deal with himself, he thought, that he would not sleep with Dayna again. He would let her think about it and enjoy it as much as she could, and then move on to her next lover. Jesse got up and went to the bathroom and brushed his teeth. He washed his face and combed his hair. He grabbed a couple of towels and wrapped them around his waist and headed back to the bed. As he got up on the bed, he noticed that Dayna was lying in the bed naked. Jesse lay down beside her and wrapped his arms around her. He kissed the top of her head.

"Jesse?", Dayna whispered in an anxious voice.

"Yeah."

"You are amazing", she whispered lustfully.

"You might be the only person who thinks so, and I doubt you'll think that for very long" Jesse said with a soft chuckle.

Dayna frowned and thought to herself about what Jesse had just said to her. She wondered what would happen if she turned out to be pregnant. She wondered if Jesse would stick around. What was she going to do? "What if I end up pregnant?", she asked.

"I don't know, Dayna. I suppose I would prefer you get it aborted. I am not ready for a kid", Jesse replied in a soft voice.

"Oh", she replied unsure of how she felt about that.

"It is kind of weird, but I know that you are a good girl, and that you will do what is right", Jesse said softly. She pondered the though in her mind. "Don't worry anymore. It will work out", Jesse whispered in her ear. Dayna began to kiss Jesse's neck. She pulled his head back and looked deeply into his eyes. She felt Jesse's cock getting hard against her thigh. She leaned down and began to kiss his chest. Jesse felt Dayna's lips move over the top of his chest and then lower to his belly button. She kissed the bottom of his belly and her tongue gently began to move along the inside of his belly button. She pulled her tongue out and started to lick down his pelvic bone. Jesse felt her tongue sliding across his skin. Jesse could not control himself any longer, and he began to lean over to grab her by her hips.

As Dayna felt Jesse lean over, she felt the warmth of his breath against her pussy. She inhaled deeply and the smell of his cologne was suddenly overwhelming. It was so strong that it made her feel warm all over. Jesse's breath felt like a cool breeze against her pussy and she felt her pussy begin to moisten again. She quickly reached down and grabbed his cock, massaging it in her hand. His cock was fully erect. He noticed how huge it looked in her tiny hands. Dayna grabbed Jesse's cock with her other hand as well and then spread her legs and rubbed her pussy across Jesse's cock. Jesse looked down at her beautiful naked body. He loved the way her long legs felt against him when they wrapped around his waist as he began to fuck her again deeply. He leaned back and lifted her on top of him. He watched, admiring her beauty as she rode him as hard and fast as she could manage. He came in her again as he thrusted his hips forward to get deeper inside of her.

"I'm so sorry", he apologized again looking ashamed. Dayna just shrugged. They talked and after discussing it they both decided that everything should be fine. If she did end up pregnant, they decided that Dayna would just abort it. Dayna tried not to think about it as she packed a bowl. They smoked until Scott showed up to get Jesse, leaving a very drunk Tori in exchange.

"That's how I ended up pregnant with Brady", Dayna said, "I went to the clinic, but I couldn't go through with it. I told Jesse, but he wanted no part of it. I haven't heard from him since".

Ella had seen things like this happen before. That is another reason she did not want to be a mom, so many women end up raising kids alone. Ella liked her freedom and the ability to make decisions without considering anyone else. Dayna clarified that although she may not have planned her son, he was the light of her life and she could not imagine life without him. Both girls jotted to the bathroom to relieve their full bladders after all those drinks. They chirped and chatted and took turns in the single stall and then washed their hands. Dayna showed Ella her stretch marks, which Ella could hardly see. They returned to the table and resumed talking with each other. Dayna asked Ella if she had ever had anal sex.

Ella nodded firmly. "It took me a while to actually try it because I heard it was painful, but once I did, I started to like it. You just get used to it", she explained. For me it enhances sex.

"Yeah, I didn't like it the first time, but once I got used to it, I couldn't get enough", Dayna said in agreement. They both admitted to being terrified the first time trying it, but within a year of their first experience, both had become total butt sluts. They laughed about each other's embarrassing moments and mishaps that happened while they discovered anal sex.

"I really only tried it because I wanted to get back at one of the worst bosses I've ever had", Ella said as she sipped on her drink some more, "It was the first internship I had out of college".

"This sounds like it's going to be a very interesting story", Dayna said as she rested her hands on her arms and looked at Ella to show she was listening intently.

Ella's Backdoor Gets Opened (First Time Anal)

Ella walked into the office for her first day of her internship as a design manager for an engineering company. She was almost an hour early because Shaun had pulled strings to get her this internship, and she did not want to disappoint him. She wore a flowing gray cardigan, over a black tank top with some silky black slacks. Her chunky gray necklace and black pumps perfected the look. She was dressed very business-appropriately yet her outfit was still somehow sexy. Every piece of it was form-fitting and showed off her beautiful curvy body. Her hair fell neatly over her shoulders without a single flyaway, or a bit of frizz. She approached the receptionist confidently. She stood tall and gave a friendly smile.

"I'm the new intern for Grace Patterson", Ella stated matter-of-factly. The receptionist pointed to a nearby seat and told her to wait till Grace came down to get her. Ella sat down and began flipping through a design book she had tucked neatly into her purse. Ella had been told to be here at eight in the morning, but it was almost nine before Grace made an appearance. She talked to the receptionist who gestured to Ella. Grace looked back at Ella with a displeased expression. She waved for Ella to follow her. Ella jumped up from the chair, remembering to maintain good posture as they walked down a long hallway, then up three flights of stairs, then halfway down the fourth-floor hallway and into a small office that opened to a larger one. Grace held her arms up when they entered the smaller office.

"This is your office, keep it tidy at all times, and no peanuts ever because I'm allergic", Miss Patterson demanded.

Ella peeked into Grace's office before sitting in her rolling computer chair in front of a desk that held a large Mac desktop computer. Moments later Grace had returned with a sheet of paper placing it on Ella's desk.

"These are your responsibilities for the day. Please try to get them all done", Grace said with a clipped tone.

Ella glanced over the list and it included creating some hard copy files, a few mailing and stuffing tasks, and a large report that she knew would take at least all day. She breathed a sigh of relief when Grace said she could take the report home. So, Ella got straight to work, and within twenty minutes she had the files printed and was organizing and stapling them as instructed. She then jotted down to the mailroom and it took her an hour to send out the items Grace needed sent. Once that was done Ella grabbed her lunch and returned to her desk. After she finished eating and cleaning up, she began the last, and most difficult task on the list. Which was typing out the report Grace had requested. By the end of the day, she was barely more than halfway through the report, so she gathered it together, put it neatly into her bag, and headed home to get it done.

The next day Ella dragged herself to work despite having been up all night finishing the report. Grace looked at her in disappointment without having so much as glanced at her work. The days were long and boring. She got similar lists each day and scrambled to get them done on time. As Ella walked across the hall and to the mail room she spotted a very handsome man and immediately wanted him. Suddenly Grace walked over and kissed the attractive man on his lips. Ella could not help but roll her eyes at the couples show of affection and sulk away to the mailroom. Before she closed the door behind her she looked back, and she swore she saw him staring at her as he remained in an embrace with her boss. He quickly moved his gaze, so it was difficult to tell whether he had been staring at her or not. Ella sat at her desk as Grace walked into the office with the man, who she introduced as her fiancé. She asked Ella to go get them both coffee from next door, so she did in a hurry so she could get back to working on the list. She brought the coffee back to the office, gave it to each of them and resumed her work. Ella had nearly passed right by the coffee shop as she walked home from work. When he waved at her, she stopped dead in her tracks. She was surprised to see that Grace's very handsome fiancé was waving her inside the coffee shop. She smiled at him and wondered what he needed from her as she walked inside the shop.

"What luck!", he exclaimed excitedly, "I'm Dimitri, you're my fiancée's assistant right?".

Ella silently nodded back at him with a curious expression.

"You somehow got my coffee order wrong. Do you remember exactly what you ordered?", he asked kindly.

Ella started to apologize but he cut her off. He said he liked it way better than how he normally ordered it and he and the barista had been trying to figure out what the difference was. Ella told him she got heavy cream instead of milk, and she explained that it was her usual drink, so she probably ordered it like that for him out of habit. Dimitri ordered two of them and invited Ella to sit down with him to drink her coffee. She knew she should not because of her unfinished work, but she took a seat across from him regardless. Ella took a sip of her drink and watched as Dimitri did the same. She sighed pleasantly and told Ella that he was glad she had messed his order up. He asked how long she had been interning for Grace. When Ella told him just a few days, he warned her that she could be difficult to work with. He just nodded as Ella assured him that she could handle it. She wondered what made Grace so bad when she saw the disbelief on his face. She thanked him for the coffee, and he offered her his business card.

"If you have any questions or need some advice", he offered kindly. She smiled and took the card from him. She tried to say thank you to him, but he insisted that it was him who should thank her.

When she resumed walking, she examined the business card. She gasped when she realized that he was a doctor. She decided that based on how successful he seemed, she was not incredibly surprised by that fact, as she tucked the card safely into her wallet. After walking only a block further, she was at her beautiful and historic, downtown apartment building. Ella went inside and worked until she fell fast asleep. She woke up to her alarm screaming at her. She jumped up and began quickly getting ready, trying to avoid being late. She cussed herself for falling asleep when she realized that she had not yet finished her report. When she made it to work, she already had coffee hoping it would cushion the blow Grace would almost certainly deal when she saw the unfinished report. Despite the coffee her heart still pounded when Grace finally made an appearance. Ella's gut feeling was right, Grace lost it, and for the rest of the day it seemed to be her mission to make Ella's life more difficult. She was constantly sending her to do gopher tasks, which halted her ability to complete her work. Ella held her frustrations inside as she endured the awful attitude Grace had towards her all day. The next couple days were no different either. So, on the fourth day she dialed Dimitri's number and asked if they could meet. He met her at the coffee shop an hour later and she immediately told him everything as tears welled up in her eyes.

He comforted her and told her he would meet with her later in the week with some completed reports he already had on hand that Ella could take the credit for. He also offered to walk her back to her apartment since it was dark outside. Ella graciously accepted both of his offers. They made small talk on the way back to her apartment. Ella wondered why Dimitri was being so kind to her, but she thought it might be rude to ask that question, so she did not. When they stood in front of her building, he offered her some comforting words and went in for a hug. Although it made her uncomfortable, because he was engaged to her boss, Ella did not want to appear rude, especially to someone who was trying to help her, so she returned his hug. When she did, he leaned in and kissed her on the lips. She looked at him stunned and tried to hide how pleased she was by it. As politely as she could, she asked Dimitri not to do that again. She explained that she did not want to risk her internship. Dimitri profusely apologized to Ella and said that he understood her situation. He asked if she would be kind enough to not say anything about it to Grace. Ella assured him that she had no plans to do that and then she turned and walked into her building without another word.

The next few days were more of the same. Grace piled on impossible workloads and every interaction between them was more unpleasant than the last. She sighed a huge sigh of relief when Dimitri texted her three days later. They agreed to meet again at the coffee shop. He handed her the reports and offered to buy her a coffee. She apologized and declined, saying that she had too much to do to be sitting in a coffee shop. She tucked the reports under her arm and excitedly made her way back to her apartment. Dimitri offered to walk her again, but she declined, simply stating that she did not want things with her boss to get any worse. So, Ella walked home alone and breathed a sigh of relief when she arrived safely home. Ella opened the door and immediately started to finish the necessary tasks. When she was done, she stacked the papers on the table where she would see them in the morning. She then went to bed and had vivid nightmares about losing her internship.

Ella woke up before her alarm began to buzz at her. She went ahead and set it off and started a pot of coffee. She took a shower and got herself ready for work. When the time came, she grabbed her bags and picked the stack of papers up off the table and made her way to work. Grace was fashionably late as usual.

She walked in and glared at Ella, "I hope you have your report done today", the snippiness in her voice infuriated Ella.

Regardless, Ella managed to plaster a fake smile on as she handed the stack of papers to Grace. She looked them over with a surprised expression but did not make any comments on them. Ella was fuming, but she kept her focus on her work and that helped her to refrain from reacting. Grace eased up on berating her for the day, but it almost infuriated her even more that Grace refused her any credit for handing in her report, plus two additional reports. She packed her stuff up and was getting ready to leave when Grace walked up with a page in her hand.

She laid the paper on her desk, "since I know you can handle the workload, I'd like this report handed in tomorrow as well", Grace's voice sounded cold and calculated.

Ella felt something in her snap, but she did not react in front of Grace. She waited until she had left the office and begun walking home. She pulled her phone out and dialed Dimitri's number. He answered on the second ring. She put on some tears that were only half-fake and told him all about how the mean bitch Grace had treated her at work today. He said he wanted to meet up with her, but this time they are going to get something a little stronger than coffee. When she walked up to the bar, he was already sitting at a table in the corner of the room.

She walked in and sat down next to Dimitri and looked at him with sad eyes. He placed his muscular arm around her shoulders and comforted her. She snuggled into the embrace secretly feeling delighted by what was happening. After a couple drinks, he predictably offered to escort her home, and she accepted his offer. When they got to the front of her apartment building, she noticed that he was shivering a little.

"Would you like to come up for a drink and to warm up? He said that he would be delighted to. She led him to the elevator and up to her apartment. Once they were both inside, she made a couple drinks. She sat on the couch next to him and he put his hand on her leg. She looked up at him and he made a second attempt at kissing her. This time she welcomed his kiss. She pressed her lips against his hard and they began to explore each other's bodies.

"Could I perhaps ask for a favor Ella?", he asked.

She said he could, so he explained that Grace flat out refuses to fulfill a long-time fantasy of his. He asked Ella if she might be willing to do it. She looked up at him curiously and asked what it was that he wanted. He told her he wanted to stick his cock in her ass. Anytime this had come up in the past it terrified her, but this time it turned her on. She agreed to do this for him, and they began removing each other's clothes. Once they both were naked, he grabbed Ella by the hips and bent her over the back to the couch. Her pussy got so wet he was able to use the juices as a lubricant for her tight little asshole. Ella remained perfectly still as Dimitri slowly worked his hard cock against her asshole until it began to let him in. She felt a searching pain as his cock stretched her virgin asshole. Once his cock was fully inside her, the pain began to slowly subside, and pleasure took its place. She moaned as his cock began to pound into that tight hole relentlessly. She moaned and wriggled against him as he thrusted into her. He had begun to groan. Sweat began dripping down their bodies and onto the couch and Dimitri's body began to clench up with pleasure. She felt him shake and strain as he began to speed up. He grabbed her hips and held on tight as he began to thrust and move his cock in and out of her ass. He stopped and let out a loud moan. His body clenched for a moment, but after a minute it was gone.

"Damn, I feel like I'm going to cum," he said. He pulled out of her ass and sat down on the couch. Ella slowly stood up, turned around, bent over and spread her ass cheeks. She pulled her ass cheeks apart and allowed Dimitri to slip his fingers in between her butt cheeks. His fingers slowly began to explore her ass hole as she continued to allow her ass to be fucked by his finger. He pushed his cock into her pussy as he played with her ass until she moaned loudly and pleaded with him to fuck her ass. He slowly put another finger in her ass and pushed it in farther.

His fingers felt so good Ella begged him to put his cock in her ass. Dimitri smiled and nodded. She nodded back and began to get nervous again. He pulled his cock out of her pussy and her asshole juices began to pulsate in anticipation. She gave a little cry as he started to slowly push in and out of her ass again. As his cock began to move back and forth in her ass, Ella moaned loudly and squeezed her butt cheeks. The pain was intense at first, but the more he moved it, the less it hurt. Once he was all the way inside her ass, she moaned loudly and pulled her ass cheeks apart. She was so turned on she began to push back against him.

"Oh god, it feels so good," she said. She began to rock back and forth slowly. Her fingers ran along her pussy as she pushed back at him. She wanted him to come soon so she could cum with him. He was shaking and holding on tight to her hips as he continued to slowly fuck her ass. He leaned back against the back of the couch and leaned his head against the cushions. Ella continued to push back against him as his cock moved in and out of her ass. Her whole body was shaking. She was so horny, her pussy was flooding with cum. Dimitri seemed close to coming too. Then just as she had anticipated she felt his body go tense again. His cock began to slowly pump his cum into her ass. She squeezed her ass cheeks together hard against him, trying to force as much as she could inside her.

She pulled away and grabbed his cock and started to give him a blowjob. She sucked him hard, pulling his cock all the way to the back of her mouth. She slowly let her lips wrap around the head of his cock, and slowly wrapped her mouth around his shaft. Her mouth was so hot and wet he was almost ready to explode. "Oh god," he said, as Ella sucked him hard. Ella pulled his cock out of her mouth and put her hand on his dick again. She stroked him slowly, pulling on his dick with her hand as she squeezed and pushed his cock back into her already jizz filled ass. He fucked her a moment longer before his alarm began buzzing. Alerting him that he had to get home. Dimitri gathered his stuff, put his clothes back on, and thanked Ella before saying goodbye to her. Ella felt satisfied by the night's events. She readied herself for bed not bothering to work on her reports. She wanted so bad to make sure that Grace would become aware of what happened between Dimitri and her. She wanted to gloat and make Grace feel as shitty as Grace had been causing her to feel at work, but she doubted she would go through with telling Grace anything about tonight for Dimitri's sake.

Ella pondered this before going to bed. The idea of quitting her internship also occurred to her. It was a very enticing idea because she did not know how much more of Grace's rude and demeaning behavior she could endure before she snapped. All that night, Ella dreamed of Dimitri and how sexy he was when he was fucking her asshole, and how good it felt to have her asshole fucked for the first time.

Ella finished her story by telling Dayna how she had quit the internship without explanation. Dayna looked at Ella nearly in shock. She was impressed by the actions Ella took in the story. She liked that Ella had refused to put up with Grace's bullshit.

"After knowing you in high school, I never would've guessed you would do something like that. I would expect something like that from me, but you? No way". Ella smiled and shrugged. They laughed for a moment about Ella's ballsy way of standing up to her tyrant of a boss. Ella's boob job was still relatively new, and her bra was getting increasingly uncomfortable as the night went on. She tried to adjust it so that it sat more comfortably but no matter what she did the wires pressed against her incisions causing her discomfort.

"I've got to go to the restroom and lose this thing", she said to Dayna as she pinched the top of her bra to show Dayna what she was talking about.

"I'll come with you if you don't mind", Dayna said as she stood up and walked across the bar and to the restroom with Ella. Once inside Ella stripped off her shirt and Dayna helped her undo the clasp that sat against her back. Ella slid the bra off her arms, dropped it into her purse, and began to massage the soreness out of her tender, swollen boobs.

"I wish I had some like that", Dayna said as she admired Ella's upgrade.

"Yours are perfect", Ella exclaimed. Dayna asked if she could feel Ella's boobs, just for research purposes of course. Ella said she could so Dayna cupped one in her hand and looked at Ella.

"Wow, they feel great", Dayna exclaimed.

Ella smiled, "I do love them. Do I get to feel yours now?", she joked.

"I guess so, if you want to", Dayna responded.

"Beautiful", Ella said as she cupped Dayna's boob in her hand," Your tits really do fit your body perfectly".

"Thanks", Dayna said. She was a little surprised when Ella actually reached over and grabbed her boob.

"You should go without a bra too, so I'm not the only one", Ella suggested. Dayna shrugged and removed her bra and put it into her purse. Both girls put their shirts back on and examined themselves in the mirror before returning to their table. The bartender brought them each a drink and said it was from the guy across the bar. The girls looked over and saw an older gentleman waving at them. Both girls waved back and yelled a thank you across the bar. They turned their attention back to one another. The man across the bar continued watching them as Dayna began her next story.

Three Is Better Than Two (Threesome)

Dayna had just woken up and looked at her clock. Still four hours till she had to be at the Cranmer's to watch their son Garret. The Cranmer's were a beautiful and wealthy couple. Arlene was tall and thin. She had long auburn hair that fell to the middle of her back. She looked ten years younger than she was. George was in shape and had a kind face. His salt and pepper hair gives it away that he is in his forties, but not much else about him does. They were heavily involved in the community and had college educations, and well-paying jobs. Their two-year-old son, Garret, was a bit rambunctious, but she did not complain. This job was a godsend. It came at a time when Dayna was on the verge of losing her home. Then she would have to move back in with her mom and Danny, and she did not want to do that with Brady. She got up and began pouring a bowl of cereal for her son. As she sat the bowl in front of him, she grabbed the toy truck he had carried to the table.

"You can have it back when you're finished with your breakfast", Dayna told him firmly.

"Awe, mommy", he whined as his shoulders slumped and he began to pout. Moments later he picked up his spoon and began eating anyway. Dayna watched him in adoration as he ate. His chubby little cheeks moved in and out as he chewed his cereal. He pushed the bowl away when he had finished and pointed to the truck sitting on the counter.

"Please", he said sweetly. Dayna helped him down from his seat before handing him the truck.

"Here you go", she said as she planted a kiss on the top of his head. He ran off to his room to play with the rest of his toys and Dayna sipped her coffee in peace. She opened the refrigerator and gazed inside. She could not find anything she wanted so she closed it and returned to her coffee after jotting a few items on her grocery list.

Dayna began getting herself ready while Brady was in his room playing. He must have heard the water start running because she heard his little footsteps coming quickly down the hall. He told her he wanted to brush his teeth with her, so she squeezed a dot of bubblegum-flavored toothpaste onto his spider-man toothbrush and handed it to him. He vigorously scrubbed his teeth. She had to lift him up to the sink so that he could spit and rinse. She carefully selected an outfit for him. The Cranmer's son Garret was always so well-dressed. You would never see a single stain on his clothes, nor any worn knees. Dayna tried to ensure Brady was well-dressed when they went over there too, because she did not want the Cranmer's to think badly of her. Dayna cared very much about the impression she gave the Cranmer's. They were so well put together. She was careful to always be on time and to present herself well, especially since they had been helping her out so much.

She finished getting herself and her son ready and she began packing his diaper bag with all the necessities she thought she might need for him. She loaded everything into the car and stopped along the way to get the boys some bath paints to play with during their bath that evening. Dayna arrived at the Cranmer's house about thirty minutes early. She got out of the car and walked around to unbuckle Brady. He was already yelling Garret's name loudly and looking at the house impatiently waiting to see his best friend. Dayna smiled, thinking about how adorable their friendship is and how quickly they had formed such a strong bond. Brady was a shy kid, but he took to Garret right away, and they have been inseparable ever since. Dayna lifted Brady onto her hip as he tried to struggle out of her arms so that he could run to knock on the door himself. Dayna asked him to stop and assured him that he could play with his friend very soon. Brady took on an expression that indicated he was thinking about it before he decided to calm down.

Dayna lightly knocked at the door. She heard a shuffle from the inside of the house and then she heard Garrett yelling at the door before George opened the door. He had on his black slacks and no shirt or shoes. There was dew on his skin suggesting he had recently gotten out of the shower. Dayna could not help but notice how great his body was for an older man. His lower stomach had that sexy v shape right above where his pants sat on his hips. Dayna pulled her attention away from George's body. She did not want to be caught staring at him like that. The last thing she wanted to do was disrespect Arlene, who had been so kind to her. George smiled at her knowingly, which alarmed Dayna at first, but she convinced herself that he had not seen her gawking and tried to pretend nothing had happened.

"Hey babe, Dayna's here", he called up to Arlene. Moments later she came down the stairs as she was trying to put an earring in her ear. She finally got it through and put the clasp on the back, then she hugged Dayna tight. She wore a stunning full-length gown. Much of the back was cut out exposing her bare skin which was beautifully pale. Her red hair fell over her shoulders, complementing the green dress. Dayna caught herself gawking at Arlene too, but that was not nearly as offensive, she decided.

"You look stunning", Dayna said to her, sounding in awe. Arlene smiled and looked down at herself and then backed up to meet Dayna's eye.

"Do you think so?", she questioned. Dayna nodded in approval.

"That's my beautiful wife", George said as he walked up. Once he was close, he slipped his hand around her waist and pulled her in for a kiss. She put her hand on his chest and pushed him back as she looked him up and down.

"Go finish getting ready", she demanded pointing towards their room, "We don't have much time before the party starts". George frowned and began to make his way back up the stairs. Arlene turned to Dayna and pulled a necklace from a small box. "Could I get your help?", Arlene asked sweetly.

"Of course,", Dayna said as she carefully took the necklace from Arlene, who turned her back to Dayna. As Dayna looped the necklace around Arlene's throat, she noticed how beautiful the silver and shining red gems looked against her skin. "What kind of party are you attending?", Dayna asked curiously. Arlene lowered her voice to a whisper.

"Between you and me", she began, "George and I concluded that our life in the bedroom was going dull. So, a friend invited us to go to a swinger's ball". Dayna's mouth gaped open. She had never imagined that the Cranmer's would go to a swinger's ball. Arlene giggled at the expression on Dayna's face. Dayna fumbled for an apology, but Arlene shushed her.

"No big deal", she said waving her hand, "Truthfully I'm as shocked as you are". Arlene began telling Dayna that Garret had been very hyper over the past few days. Dayna tried to listen, but she could not get over what she had just heard, so she just nodded, only really hearing some of what Arlene was saying. Dayna snapped out of her daze when George reappeared beside them. He looked very handsome in his button up shirt and slacks. His tie lay around his neck waiting to be tied. Arlene took the two ends of the tie in her hands and gracefully tied it. They both looked flawless. You would think they were going to something much more official than a swinger's party. Dayna still could not wrap her mind around it, but she wished the Cranmer's a wonderful night, and said goodbye to them as they walked out to their car.

Dayna called out for the boys wondering where they were. She checked the living room to see if they were watching television, but they were not there. She made her way slowly up the stairs and to the playroom where all Garret's toys were. Then she heard squeals coming from across the hall where Garret's room was. The boys were jumping up and down on the bed. Dayna called out for them. They both stopped jumping and turned to look at her with curiosity on their faces. She politely asked them not to do that anymore. She warned them that one of them could get seriously hurt. Both boys got down from the bed without another word. Dayna sent them off to the playroom to play with Garrett's toys, and she went to the kitchen to figure out what she was going to make for dinner. She was rooting around in the kitchen when she heard a knock at the door. Dayna looked out the peephole and saw a bright red hat. She curiously opened the door and there stood a young man. He was wearing a uniform with a pizza shaped logo and holding a box. Dayna took the pizza figuring that the Cranmer's probably ordered it for her and the boys.

Arlene probably told her that she was going to order pizza, but Dayna had been so shocked by the bit of information she learned about the couple, that she probably did not hear it.

"Boys, Pizza!", she yelled up the stairway loudly hoping they would hear her over their playing. A few moments later she heard little footsteps thumping down the hallway and Garrett yelling about pizza enthusiastically. She grabbed two plates out of the cabinet and turned around to both boys staring at her expectantly wearing huge grins. Dayna smiled and put a piece of pepperoni pizza on each of their plates and sat both plates on the table. Garrett climbed into his chair with ease as she lifted Brady into his. They both finished their pieces leaving only the crust behind. Dayna offered them a second slice but both boys were ready to get back to playing. While they did Dayna sat down on the couch to check her phone and let the Cranmer's know how the evening was going so far. Arlene responded with a thumbs up. Dayna got lost in thought about what the ball must be like. Mostly naked people all over the place. People fucking in every corner of the room. On couches and beds, sex swings hanging from the ceilings. Arlene being fucked by a stranger, and George fucking a stranger.

Dayna noticed her pussy was getting wet. She felt the need to get off, badly. She did not much care for using just her fingers, so she snuck into the Cranmer's room promising herself she would leave no evidence of her intrusion. Once inside their room she searched under the bed, there was nothing there but some boxes full of old keepsakes. She then looked in the nightstand drawer and again found nothing of interest. She pressed down on the clothes in the dresser, feeling for anything that was not clothes. She felt something firm and long, so she carefully lifted the clothes and there lay a purple vibrator. She smiled and picked it up. Before laying down on their bed she twisted the bottom of the vibrator. It came to life, buzzing hard in her hand. She was surprised by how much power the thing had. Her pussy got even more wet as she anticipated feeling it on and in her eager pussy. Dayna removed her pants and carefully laid them on the dresser. Dayna laid back on their bed and spread her legs open readying herself.

Dayna pushed the lace of her thong to the side and touched her throbbing clit with the tip of her finger. She twirled her finger in a circular motion a few times before picking up the vibrator that lay buzzing on the bed beside her. She slowly brought it to her clit and touched it lightly. Her body jumped in response to the intense pleasure that immediately coursed through her. She took a deep breath and then slid the toy as far into her mouth as she could. When she pulled it out, she tried to leave ample spit to use as lubricant. She put the toy over her tight little hole and slowly pushed it inside. She pulled it in and back out a few times and then she swirled it around inside her pussy. As she slid it out this time, she pulled it up towards her stomach letting the tip stop on her clit. She began to move it in a slow circular motion. Her body began to shake, and she felt the orgasm welling up inside her. She willed it to come, and then it did. She arched her back and moaned as pleasure took over her mind, every part of her body tensed up and then fell limp when it was over. She lay there for a few moments longer to catch her breath. Then she got up from the bed and went to the bathroom to wash her juices off the toy. She returned the vibrator to its spot and looked over the room once more before walking out and closing the door behind her.

Dayna went upstairs and into the bathroom to fill the bathtub for the boys. When the tub was full, she opened the bath paint she had bought and yelled for the boys. They followed her voice to the bathroom and when they saw the full tub and the paints they were excited to get in. She washed them up and let them play for a short while before taking them out, drying them, and getting them into their pajamas. They were reluctant to lay down, so she bribed them with a story. Even after the story, they both had to be reminded multiple times that it was bedtime. Dayna had just got both boys to fall asleep. They had put up quite a fight this evening. As Arlene had warned, Garrett had been especially rambunctious today, but Dayna could not complain, Garret gave her little man a friend to play with, plus she was incredibly lucky to have gotten this job. Without it there is no way she would be able to get her bills paid. She sat on the couch and began mindlessly flipping through the channels.

Suddenly, Dayna heard the Cranmer's laughing outside the door as they came in. It sounded like they had a pleasant time. She greeted them when they walked in and then started gathering Brady's things and grabbed the car keys from her purse so she could unlock her car, set her things inside, and carry Brady out. She smiled and asked how their night had gone, they said it went well. Dayna noticed a slight slur in their voices which was likely due to alcohol. They had been drinking, which was generally good for Dayna because they tipped her more generously when they are intoxicated. Dayna told the couple about how the boys played together non-stop and that she did not have much of a problem out of them. The couple thanked her and as Dayna had predicted, they handed her an envelope with seventy-five dollars in it. Dayna thanked them and wished them a good night as she walked back to the room where the boys slept so she could grab Brady. She lifted him onto her hip with his head laying on her shoulder. She froze momentarily to let him drift back into a deep sleep. Then she carefully carried him out to her car. She secured her son into his car seat and walked around to the driver's side and got into the car. She let the defrost run for a moment before she pulled out of the driveway. A few minutes later she pulled into her driveway and carried Brady inside. She laid him in her bed and cuddled up next to him and went to sleep.

She felt her phone buzzing beneath her. When she cracked her eyes open, she saw the sun streaming in through the window and Brady staring down at her as he waited patiently beside her. He complained that he was hungry, so Dayna got up and fixed him a bowl of cereal. He sat and ate his food without a single complaint. As she drank her coffee Dayna checked her phone. There was a text from the Cranmer's. They wanted her to watch Garrett again tonight. Dayna figured something unexpected must have come up. They promised to pay her extra if she babysits tonight. She texted them back saying that she would be happy to, but she reminded them that her mom always got Brady on Saturday, so it would just be her coming this time. They said that was fine and asked her to be there at seven, which was much later than normal. Dayna spent the day hanging out and playing with Brady. Then at six she dropped him off to her mom and went straight to the Cranmer's house. She arrived about fifteen minutes early and tapped lightly on the door. Arlene answered the door wearing nothing but a robe. Dayna figured she was probably running behind on getting ready. She greeted Arlene quickly, and then tried to give her space to get ready. She looked around and did not see nor hear Garret, so she asked where he was.

"He's at my sister's house this evening actually", Arlene said coolly. Dayna looked at her quizzically. If Garrett is at Arlene's sisters, why on earth was she here? Just then George walked down the steps, and much like Arlene, he was wearing nothing but a gray pair of sweatpants. Dayna was getting increasingly confused by everything that was happening.

"Oh, hey Dayna, you made it!", George said casually as he walked past the ladies and into his room.

Once he was out of earshot, Arlene leaned in close to Dayna as if to tell her a secret, "I absolutely must tell you about how our evening went", her breath smelled of something sweet with a hint of booze. Arlene told Dayna that despite their efforts they did not make many friends at the swinger's ball it was not that people did not like them. Plenty of men and women made passes at the couple. Unfortunately, everyone there was older, and they were hoping to meet someone young, sweet, and ripe. Dayna listened intently as she tried to figure out why she was here. Just then George came in carrying three champagne flutes. Arlene took two from him and passed one over to Dayna as he sat down. She took a big gulp to quench her thirst.

George looked at her with a look of disapproval on his face. "You know, I'm very disappointed in you Dayna", he began.

Dayna was so confused. She fiddled her thumbs as she waited for an explanation. Suddenly the realization hit her. She decided that she would just deny any wrongdoing. There is no way they possibly could know about her sneaky trip into their room for certain. She must have left some evidence behind but as she thought it over, she became convinced that there was no way they could possibly know for certain what happened in that room. He looked at her suspiciously as if waiting for her to confess, she could feel the pressure, but she remained silent and took another gulp of her mimosa. Arlene chimed in without warning,

"We never would've noticed if it had not been for the cum you left behind on our bed", she said thoughtfully. She leaned over to put her hand on Dayna's thigh. She said she was not mad at all and told Dayna that it was okay. Dayna worried about losing her job babysitting for them. She needed the money so badly. Arlene sat back up and finished her mimosa.

"I mean, at least she cleaned my toy off afterwards, right honey?", she said turning to George.

Dayna wondered how in the world they knew that. George's expression hardened, "What pisses me off is that she did not include us, and she did it in our home".

Arlene touched his shoulder, "At least we got to enjoy the footage though, right babe?".

Dayna's heart nearly stopped, "footage?", she whimpered quietly. The reality struck her that they must have had hidden security cameras in their room. Tears welled up in her eyes.

"Don't fret dear", Arlene said compassionately, "It was really great footage", she suggested as if it were supposed to make Dayna feel better. George suggested that they let her watch it. They ushered her upstairs and into his office. He started up his computer and opened his files and clicked on one with yesterday's date on it. After fast forwarding for a moment Dayna came into the frame. They all sat and watched as she used Arlene's toy in their bed. When the footage was over George seemed to be fuming even more.

"You can make it up to us can't you sweety?" she said, turning to Dayna. Dayna was unsure exactly what she meant. How was she supposed to make it up to them? The realization suddenly hit her. She remembered George's comment earlier about not including them and everything clicked into place.

"It would save your job", Arlene suggested with a soft voice.

They wanted her to have sex with them. She thought about George's knowing expression after he caught her checking him out and Arlene saying that they did not have success at the swinger's ball because they wanted someone younger.

She looked at them both, and tried to choose her words carefully, "I just really don't want to cause any problems between the two of you, or have things be awkward".

Arlene busted out laughing. She insisted that their relationship was solid and could withstand this, and in fact needed it. "Besides", she chimed in with a seductive voice, "we are all adults here, there is no reason we should not be able to have a little fun without it becoming awkward or any jealous feelings, right?". Dayna pondered the idea in her mind. She thought about the job and how much she needed it. Arlene had said this would save her job, and she would do anything for her son. Not that she was not already attracted to both George and Arlene.

Just then as if Arlene had been reading her mind, she set an envelope on the table, "Plus there's this in it for you". Dayna eyed the envelope and Arlene gestured for her to pick it up. She carefully lifted it from the table and peered inside. She flipped through the bills inside counting it up. Her eyes widened when she counted the sum of the money in the envelope. A thousand dollars in hundred-dollar bills were contained in the envelope. She knew she had to do it. That was a lot of money and the alternative was losing her job.

She nodded at the couple and told them that she would like to make it up to them.

Arlene smiled as if she had known this would be the result, and George's expression softened, "Really?", he said in disbelief. When they first texted her asking her to work another evening, they had already informed Dayna that this noteworthy babysitting job would be an overnight one, and they intended to keep that promise. In addition, Arlene had already planned everything meticulously, and there were to be some surprises for Dayna throughout the evening. Arlene told Dayna that she would be receiving some instructions from her over the intercom system, which she had no idea they had. She was told to go to their bedroom, shower and ready herself for the evening as quickly as possible and wait for their instructions. She did as she was told and made her way to their bedroom. To Dayna's surprise, Arlene had the foresight to leave two gifts that were both thoughtful, and appropriate waiting for her on the bed. The first was a clearly expensive romper with a silky, purple fabric that was transparent, and was trimmed with intricate black lace.

Dayna put it on and marveled at the way she looked and felt in it. The fabric felt soft and silky against her skin. Her puckered nipples were clearly visible, in fact every part of her body was visible through the fabric. It looked great on her and she felt so luxurious in it. The second gift was a twin to Arlene's powerful purple vibrator she had used, she guessed the Cranmer's got it because they had been able to tell in the security footage exactly how much she had enjoyed it. Arlene's voice came through the intercom instructing her to use the gifts that she left. She told her to have the romper on and be in the bed using the vibrator that Arlene had gifted her. Not long after she heard the door open and the couple came into the room. Dayna was there, and in the four-poster bed, writhing with pleasure from the intense vibrations of her new toy. Without hesitation, they took the vibrator out of her hands right before she could reach her climax. They cuffed her hands together and then bound her cuffed hands to the bed. Then they restrained her legs and ankles to the bed as well, and she was lying flat on her back, but unable to move about freely. She was completely at their mercy.

"Oh, please put it back", she pleaded, "I was just about to come".

"I wanted to be the one to make you come. I am not going to let a vibrator do it", George declared.

"But…", Dayna whined.

"Honey if you beg, he's just going to make you wait longer", Arlene suggested with a sigh. Then Dayna clamped her mouth shut and tried to wait patiently. After getting so close, she had a tremendous desire to reach her climax and it was nearly driving her insane. The Cranmers started kissing and feeling against one another and ignoring her. Dayna could not help but to moan in frustration, wishing that they would caress her, touch her, feel her already wet pussy, and please her. Arlene walked over and eyed her for a moment with an expression of approval, then she rewarded Dayna by licking, sucking and nibbling her pussy. They both moaned with pleasure, and George walked over with his cock in hand, and stood at the head of the bed close to Dayna. She was just close enough to reach his cock, so she took it into her mouth and began to suck it. After a moment, his wife grabbed his arm and pulled him over where she was and he tasted Dayna's young wet pussy, and after just a few licks, Dayna's body tensed, and her pussy got even more wet as she came for him. His cock was throbbing, but he wanted to see his wife's face and tongue pleasing their babysitter's pussy and watch her taste the juices from the pleasure he had just given her. He pushed his wife's face hard into Dayna's pussy, getting even more turned on as they both moaned in response to the ecstasy they felt. He gave Dayna a slap on her thigh, remarkably close to her pussy, but without giving any direct stimulation. She begged him for more. He took a feather off a dream catcher that hung on the wall and trailed in up and down Dayna's body. He smacked her tits hard. He appreciated their perkiness, the benefit of having smaller boobs. The impact made her inhale in surprise at the first slap but soon she was enjoying the attention that her boobs were getting.

She began screaming and begging him for more. George lifted her ass up off the bed and signaled for Arlene to spank her ass. Arlene delivered blow after blow until Dayna's ass was warm and red. He asked his wife to sit on Dayna's face. Dayna tasted Arlene's sweet pussy. As George watched, he decided it was time to get his dick wet. He slid his rock-hard cock into her young, tight, pussy as she groaned and tried to thrust her pussy up into him. He moved his wife to the side to slap her in the face and told her that he would fuck her at his pace, not hers. She moaned and nodded in agreement. Then he told his wife to get on all fours so he could taste her pussy. Arlene's pussy was getting wetter. He could not remember ever feeling his wife's pussy so wet and she was getting ready to cum. Her juices rushed out of her pussy with a gush. She leaned over Dayna so she could taste her cum. She moaned loudly in appreciation and swallowed as much of it as she could . He placed a strap-on around Arlene's waist so he could watch her fuck Dayna. As the dildo entered their babysitter, she squirmed in pleasure. He liked the sight of his wife fucking her. He put his hands around Dayna's neck and lightly choked her to quiet her down. She enjoyed the punishment and groaned and smiled up at him as he varied the pressure on her throat.

He leaned down to taste her little pussy. His lips trailed kisses across her body, from her neck down her chest he was giving each nipple some attention and continued kissing her till he reached her stomach. His wife stopped fucking her so he could place his tongue on Dayna's wet, waiting pussy, and instantly she came, splashing his face with her sweet juice. He licked up all the cum he could as she squirmed against his tongue. He began to feel an intense need to fuck them both. He placed his wife on all fours directly over Dayna so that their holes are both within his cock's reach. He began fucking them both alternating from one to the other at his will. He spread his wife's lips and thrust himself inside fast and hard. She was unbelievably wet, and he slid in and out of her with ease. He looked up to see the women kissing each other intimately and went at his wife harder and faster. Dayna began begging to be fucked. He pulled out of Arlene, and spread Dayna's ass to force his thick, rock hard cock into her tight little asshole. He thrusted hard and fast into her as both his wife and Dayna moaned in pleasure. Dayna began to beg for his cum. He hesitated for a moment until Arlene told him to cum inside her ass. Then he lost all the control he had left and spurted his cum deep inside of her and kept thrusting until every drop was inside her. As he pulled out his cock the cum came dripping out of her ass. Arlene put her mouth underneath and began to catch the cum with her mouth. Dayna lay there panting as they untied her. She felt so satisfied that she made sure to inform them that she would be more than happy to do this again whenever they wanted.

Ella fought the urge to start rubbing her pussy right there in the bar. Dayna's story had her so worked up that she was dying for some cock right about now.

"You got to live one of those fantasies that everyone wishes they could", she looked at Dayna and smiled, "You don't happen to still have their contact information, do you?", she said jokingly. Both girls broke into a fit of laughter.

Dayna told Ella it had been years since she had heard from them, "but I bet they're still freaks", she said with a huge grin. She told Ella how they had helped her discover her fetish for authority figures. She had many more similar rendezvous with them afterwards. It became a routine up until she had saved up the money and bought a house. Her new home unfortunately was too far away for her to continue babysitting for them, and then they just lost contact with each other. Afterwards she craved and sought out similar experiences. She liked being roughed up like that. The loss of control was such a big turn on. Ella nodded in agreement. She herself had experienced a lot of that, and it seems to never lose its appeal.

By this point both girls had consumed more drinks than they probably should've, and they were quite intoxicated. The slurs in their voices were becoming increasingly noticeable and they were now telling their stories without any hesitations. They openly shared all the freakiest details of their sex lives. They considered the fact that they both had far drives to get home, or in Ella's case, to her hotel. They decided to quit drinking and place an order for some food. They agreed they did not want to spend a night in jail or worse, so they began to try to sober up to safely get themselves where they needed to go. They looked over the menu again before ordering sandwiches, because they figured the bread might help soak up some of the alcohol. Dayna suggested Ella tell another story as they wait for their food to arrive. Ella already had the perfect story in mind. This one happened sometime after she had finished her internship, which she ended up not doing with Grace of course. In fact, after sleeping with Dimitri, Ella did not return to her internship with Grace. She had gotten fed up with being treated that way. Before Ella began her story, she checked her phone and gasped. To her surprise, her hotel reservation had been canceled earlier in the evening. Dayna mentioned that there was a decent hotel nearby, so Ella quickly placed a reservation before jumping into her story.

Ella's Master (BDSM)

Ella was having a calm evening at home alone. She was watching Netflix on her couch with a bowl of popcorn in her lap, a glass of wine in her hand, and a throw blanket laying across her bare legs. She was home alone so she had on just a t-shirt, and a thong. It had been an incredibly long week. Ella had just finished her internship and was about to begin searching for a full-time position on a good design team. She had a few places in mind that she knew had positions available, but she still needed to update her resume before she could submit it, and first she just wanted to take a few days to relax and celebrate. She felt she deserved it after a full academic year spent as an intern, being underpaid and overworked. She lifted her glass to her wine-stained lips and took a slow sip. The horror movie she was watching had her full attention. When the possessed doll popped out of the darkness she jumped and let out a small squeal. When she heard a clang, her attention turned curiously to the door that led to the basement in her adorable, historic, downtown home. Her heartbeat sped up, and she paused the movie and listened intently. After a few moments of complete silence, except the low hum of her air conditioning, she pressed play on the remote and began watching the movie again.

Ella supposed she was just a bit shook up. It should not come as a surprise considering everything that was going on in her life. She was asked to volunteer at a haunted house this year by helping design it. Also, she had just had to cut things off with the sugar daddy she has had since college because he was getting a little more serious than she wanted to be. At the haunted house, she was also playing a victim, who would be chained up to the ceiling by her arms, her white gown covered in blood, with fake intestines looking as if they were spilling out of her abdomen as she desperately screams for the spectators to help her. She had been at rehearsals all week. She met this hot guy there too. He was a little older, in his thirties, she assumed. He has asked her out and he is supposed to take her to a cool restaurant that is apparently doing a Halloween theme. He said it was supposed to be like eating in a haunted house. It sounded fun to Ella and she could not wait. They were even planning to wear their haunted house get up to dinner. By the time the movie had ended she had finished off five glasses of wine and was quite intoxicated. She made her way up the stairs and into her bedroom. She threw herself into bed and let the wine take her into a deep sleep.

Considering she had to get her costume for the haunted house on for the date, Ella began getting ready at around three in the afternoon. She got into the shower with the water running as hot as she could stand it. Her smooth skin began turning a bright red as the water ran down her body. She washed and rinsed her hair. She stepped out of the shower and onto the bathmat. Gathering all her hair up into her hands, she began to wring her hair out onto the bathmat, and then she wrapped a towel around her naked, red, and wet body. As she stood in front of the mirror, she used the towels to dry each part of her body before proceeding to blow dry her hair. When it was dry, she began to tease her hair and applied hairspray until it was a complete mess, like the hair of someone who had survived to the end of a horror movie should be. She sprayed even more hairspray until she was convinced that her hair would remain this way throughout the evening.

Next Ella began her makeup. She carefully placed various cuts and bruises at random places all over the parts of her body that would be visible in the thigh length white blood-stained gown. She paid special attention to the details in her face. She painted on dark sleepless eyes and some very convincing bloody wounds. She wondered if Evan was planning to go all out with it like she was doing. He seems enthusiastic about Halloween. Halloween was Ella's favorite holiday. She loved dressing up and scaring the shit out of people. After doing her makeup, she applied some finishing products to make her costume last. Once it dried, she carefully pulled her gown over her head. It fit snugly on her hips and chest, and the gown showed most of her legs as it barely covered her ass. She loved how sexy she looked in it even though she appeared to be nearly dead. She affixed her fake intestines to the front of her gown so that they appeared to be falling out of her with terrific gore.

When Ella finished getting ready, she poured herself a last-minute glass of wine and gulped it down and sprayed herself down with some perfume before doing one last costume check before she left. She smiled at her reflection in the mirror. She was thrilled with not only how terrifyingly realistic it all looked, but also how surprisingly sexy it was. The dress showed the perfect shape of her ass and left most of her legs exposed. She grabbed her purse off the back of a chair at her kitchen table, and then picked her keys up off the coffee table. She was careful to lock the doors before leaving. October always seemed to bring out people's crazy sides, especially in the city. She drove her car to a park near the restaurant where she had planned to meet up with Evan. She parked, got out of her car, and walked over to the restaurant to wait. Her date arrived looking dapper and terrifying. His costume makeup was every bit as good as hers.

They walked down the road in silence. Evan always seemed to have a quiet personality which made him mysterious. They walked up to an old and abandoned-looking building. It had a great ambiance thanks to great lighting and realistic decorations that convincingly made the place look and feel like a haunted house. Ella walked inside with her arm wrapped around Evan's. A creepy doorman with his head in the palm of his hand let them inside. A hostess who was decked out in gothic attire, complete with black nails and lips asked them if they have reservations. Evan pulled a card from his pocket and handed it to her. She glanced at it and nodded before leading them through the various terrifying scenes and to their table. Each table was sectioned off from the next for privacy. Every now and then, she would hear someone let out a blood curdling scream. On the walls next to them there were creepy animatronic hands everywhere. Occasionally, a few of them would move, scaring Ella and occasionally Evan. A zombie waitress came by to take their drink order.

She assured them she would be back with their beverages and disappeared back into the scene. A few minutes later she appeared with glasses full of a liquid that appeared to be blood but smelled like fruit punch and vodka. She ordered a mummified calzone and he asked for the monster BBQ chicken sliders. The food was simple but well prepared and arranged to look very suited for Halloween. More jump scares continued to surprise them all throughout the duration of dinner. Evan gave the waitress his card the moment she appeared with the bill. After they gulped down the last of their drink they stood to leave. Ella was grateful that Evan treated her to such a rare and cool experience. She was really enjoying herself. After leaving the restaurant the pair walked down the road together. The restaurant where they had eaten was not far from the location of the haunted house they were going to be volunteering at. When they approached it, Ella began to wonder how they were going to get it ready to open in time. The place was cluttered with various Halloween decorations. Evan wiggled the doorknob and the door easily came open. He looked back at Ella mischievously as he walked into the building. It was dark and cluttered inside. Evan turned his phone's flashlight on and shined it around the room. There were chains and hooks hanging from the ceiling and various decorations all over the floor.

Ella looked at Evan and had a very naughty thought. She walked over to him and dropped down to her knees. First Evan looked confused but as Ella began to unbutton his jeans, a look of realization crossed his face. Ella grabbed his cock and put it into her mouth. She sucked on it for a moment before the door busted open. Ella and Evan both nearly jumped out of their skin. A tall man with a mask came in.

"Ella, how could you do this to me?", he screamed. Ella was confused and shocked, so she just stood there wide-eyed. Evan looked at her in an accusatory way.

"You have a boyfriend?", he stated furiously. He left the building without another word. Once he was gone, the man laughed and walked over to her.

"Who are you?", Ella asked. He answered with a single word, Master. He grabbed her by the wrists and brought her to an area where chains were hanging from the ceiling. He chained her up by her wrists and lifted her dress. He ripped her panties off her. When he touched her pussy, he chuckled. She had not been able to help but get wet. She wished it did not but this whole scenario turned her on immensely. He heard him fumbling with his jeans for a moment before he began pounding into her pussy. As he did, he pinched her nipples so hard tears fell from her eyes. When he was finished, he declared himself her master, and informed her that her training was to begin soon. He left and she went to her car, looking over her shoulder the whole way. Part of her was excited about the upcoming "training", part of her was terrified.

Ella woke with a fear of Master and his punishment in the back of her mind, each morning she felt a mix of relief and disappointment that Master had not begun her training. Tonight, she hoped to put it out of her mind and relax with a bottle of bubbly in front of the giant 90-inch television she was gifted by her most recent sugar daddy. She wondered if she would ever be able to have another as the new man in her life had made it noticeably clear that he did not approve when he found her sucking Evan off in the haunted house. He ran Evan off and took her for himself, several times. He scared her, He had on that day told her that he claimed ownership over her, that he was her master now. He assured her that she should anticipate her forthcoming training. He would be in touch, he said. So, she waited.

"Why don't I go to the police?" she asked herself, many times these last few nights. He scared the shit out of her. But she was compelled to wait for him. Just as he commanded. Because he also created feelings which, as hard as she might try to put into words, she could not help but dream about. Not nightmares, no. These were a different kind of dreams. They were strangely realistic. She almost believed they had happened. Master stood over her as she woke, a sadistic grin on his face. She nearly screamed in horror.

"You start today, slut." Wordlessly, she nodded and got out of the bed. Master began to issue one-word utterances with slight motions of the wrist. "Strip." Briefly, the thought of an orchestrator directing his symphony passed through Ella's mind. When she would think back on it, he was more like a Necromancer. A ballet of pain and pleasure. A dance with the devil. "Now." And she did, all the way down to her underwear. He shook his head. With a sigh of reluctance, she took off the panties she wore during the night. He suddenly scooped her up in his arms around her waist and he began moving with haste. Before she knew it, she was thrown into the trunk of a car, her hands and feet were swiftly hogtied behind her back and the panties she had just dropped moments before, were shoved into her mouth. The Master stood there for a moment with a smug grin underneath the Halloween mask he wore. Then he slammed the trunk closed with Ella inside. A while later the trunk opened, and he untied her hands and feet. "Follow", he commanded. She followed him to the garage in his home. Yesterday, it had been filled with useless junk and odd broken Halloween props, today it was filled with Ella's nightmares. Rope, handcuffs, racks, gags, all types of machines and toys that half of which she did not even know what they could be for. Ella was terrified. Without a word, and with no compassion displayed, Master roughly grabbed Ella by the hair and pulled her over to an X-shaped cross. He pulled her legs apart, attaching them to the legs of the cross, and doing the same with her arms. Once Ella was sufficiently restrained, Master spoke.

"You know why you're here. You know what you have done. This is your punishment. Your training will turn you into my personal slave, my personal slut. Made to do exactly whatever I would have you do. Because after your little stunt, that is what you deserve my whore", he smiled at her as he spoke. Ella was stunned and bewildered. She could not believe the man had such disregard for the laws of man and god. She had no idea what he referred to. She had done lots of things but none that should have offended this stranger. "From this moment onwards, you will only refer to me as 'Master', and anyone else I decide to bring around you will be 'Master' or 'Mistress'. Am I understood?", he said expectantly.

Ella finally was able to break through her shock enough to speak. "Wait, who are you? What do you mean?! I did not do anything to you!", she screamed.

"You do not have a say in the matter. Everything you do now is to serve me. I will not hear another word out of you unless I ask for it. Am I understood?" Master viciously declared. Ella mutely nodded her head in defeat. He started preparing for the first task. He brought out a box of clothes pins. Ella looked at them with a mixture of fear and curiosity.

"I am going to attach 60 clothes pegs to various points on your body. Some painfully sensitive, some not so much. I am also going to attach a powerful vibrator to your leg and your cunt. For every minute you manage not to orgasm, that is another peg I will not pull off your little body. You last the whole hour, no pain. You last 15 minutes, that is 45 clothes pins that will get yanked from your body. Is the game understood?", as he spoke, he counted out the pins.

Ella responded with a simple, "Yes Master". She realized there was no way out of this situation except master's way. He just grinned, and she shivered at how evil he appeared. He pulled out the first pin, with a glint in his eye. He pinched some of the flesh around Ella's breast, pulled it taut and applied the peg. She yelped out in pain, "Ow!! That really hurts, stop!" Ella complained. He simply smiled at her pain.

"Good.", he said repeating the process, applying clothes pins to all her sensitive areas, her breasts, her abdominal area, her arms, and especially her pussy, each time eliciting a moan, a yelp, or a cry of pain from her. Once the process was completed, she was nearly on the verge of tears. Those tears brought her Master joy. He pulled out a vibrating wand which he was going to use on her. He tied it to her leg tightly and switched it on to its highest vibration setting. From the second Ella felt the sensations touch her pussy, she was moaning like a whore. Master was kind enough to remind her a couple times not to cum. She tried, desperately to hold her pleasure in, but eventually, around the 23-minute mark, she could not do it anymore, and she came with a lustful scream. A warm gush flowed down in between her legs.

"23 minutes. Not bad. You will have to improve of course. However, you still must deal with the penalty of disobedience", Master coldly remarked. Ella, with intense lust and fear in her eyes shook her head rapidly, begging him not to hurt her anymore.

She had tears streaming from her eyes as he continued to speak, "I know, my slave. I do not need to hurt you. I simply want to. And as I am your master, I reserve the right to do as I wish with you. You are now my property, and I will treat you as I wish", and with that, Master yanked off the first of the 37 pegs from her nipple. She screamed in pain, pleading with him to end her torment. He looked at her coldly and pulled them off one by one. He yanked them from her breasts, her nipples, her pussy, and everywhere else, until there were only 23 left on her body. These Masters took off very carefully, as promised to cause her minimal pain. Through the entire ordeal, he had very much enjoyed delivering her pain, so that by the end of it she was crying like a newborn child. Master took her down from the cross and asked her one simple question. "Who are you?", he said looking at her curiously.

"I am your slave, M-Master", she replied through sobs and tears.

"Brilliant. Now prove it. Suck me dry slave slut", he demanded. Ella dutifully took her master's trousers and underwear off, pulled out his cock and began to suck with a sense of duty greater than most soldiers might feel, giving her master what he thought would probably be, the best blowjob of his life. He felt her wet mouth glide up and down his shaft, and her tongue circling the head in synchrony. It was heavenly for her Master. It was a sensation that he had not felt for a long time. It was such a good blowjob, that he could not hold on much longer, and had to put both his hands on the back of Ella's head, holding her mouth balls deep on his cock while he came down her throat. She tried to pull her head away to breath while she gagged. She had never had a stranger come down her throat before, so she struggled not to swallow the cum that she held in her throat. He looked down at her wild eyes, and then he maliciously said, "Not until you swallow". Realizing again that he was essentially the ruler of her world, and there was no way out of this, she quickly gave in to his demands. "Good. You have learned", he remarked with an expressionless face.

"I know my place Master, it is below you, you don't need to hurt me anymore, I will be a good slut slave for you Master, please don't hurt me!" Ella begged. "Do you really think that I am going to be lenient with my 'slut', or 'submissive'? How little do you think I am Master?", he softly remarked. Ella started trembling in fear as she could see his erection in the distance. Master then continued, "If you try to escape me, I will punish you severely. Do you feel like you've suffered today? Disobey me and you will see what tomorrow brings" He started untying Ella, leading her to believe for a moment that the night was over. He brought her back to her terrifying new reality when he took out a whip and began viciously whipping her back. She screamed out in pain and writhed in pain.

"This is why you are in this situation.", he coldly commented. "You know how I punish my slaves? I make them suffer. I make them cry and I will make you cry. I will punish you for as long as it takes for you to admit to yourself that you are my slave." He brutally brought the whip down on her breasts.

She screeched in pain, and wailed, "I'm a worthless slut!"

"A worthless slut? No, you are a liar, you know very well that I own you." He continued to lash at her back. "And that you are going to be a very valuable slave to me."

"Really? So I am nothing more than your property?" she questioned in tears. "Please stop Master. I will do anything you want, I will do anything you want, I will do anything I can to please you. I want to please you. I CAN please you! Please!"

"Are you a whore?", Master coldly responded. "Are you not happy that you are in my harem? So, what is it that makes you happy? What are you going to do to please me? I can tell you what. You are going to masturbate, right now. You are going to masturbate for me, and I will tell you when you can stop. But you are going to cum. Now stand up", he ordered.

"Thank you Master", she happily responded with a smile. She rubbed her pussy almost forgetting the occasional lashes she received throughout. She became dizzy as she started to lose control of herself and started coming. She cried out as she gushed pussy juice, her squirt almost reaching her master as it arched through the air.

"Very good!" the strange man applauded. "Now, come to me." Ella dropped to her knees and began to crawl on all fours over to where Master was standing. She crawled right up to him and his cock immediately poked out at her. "Feel this slave." He ordered as he stroked himself. He stroked himself while she reached out and began licking the head of his cock. His cries and moans combined into the most ear-piercing sounds as she began to pleasure her new owner. He removed his hand and she stood and began to kiss and suck on his cock. His cock was very thick, and she had trouble getting it all in her mouth. She began to suck on him, and he reached down and began to play with her tits. He moaned as he felt her lips and tongue on his cock, running back and forth between his shaft and his balls. "I'm about to cum!", he told her.

He grabbed her hair and pushed her head down, so that she was literally eating his cock. He came, hard, in her mouth and she was so amazed that she gagged and choked as she began to swallow. The salty taste filled her mouth as she struggled to keep up. He pulled her up to her feet and closer to him, and kissed her passionately as his cock was left covered with his cum. He turned and walked back to his chair. Ella stared at her master in amazement, still not believing what had just happened. She kept her eyes on him as she walked towards the wall.

"There will be no limits on the work you do. You will be my pet, and my slave. You will do whatever I command. You will receive full training as a slave, including anal training. You will obey all orders that I give, and you will please me and satisfy me as I wish."

He then had his way with Ella, several more times. He had to make sure she was really his obedient slut now. He fucked each of her holes. First her pussy, He pounded into it as hard as he could while she moaned and squirmed. He had been surprised by how much she was able to take before he had her in tears. He relentlessly slammed his cock into her until he nearly came again. Then he noticed that it was swollen so he slid his rod from her pussy, and without missing a beat he thrust it into her ass hard. She screamed out with a mix of pain and pleasure as they both came in unison. Master looked down at her and smiled. He was clearly impressed.

The food had just arrived at the table and the ladies hungrily scarfed their food down. Like Ella, Dayna loved playing the submissive role. She had never experienced being the one in charge until recently. She thought of Ella's story and about her experience making someone else submit to her. She tried to decide which of the two made her pussy wetter. Dayna wondered if Ella had any similar experiences.

"Have you ever played the dominant role?", Dayna asked Ella. She shook her head as she imagined what that must be like. Ella had never really considered being the master. Being submissive came so naturally to her and she knew that would probably be out of her comfort zone. Ella was assertive in everyday life, but in bed she was always sweet and obedient.

"Have you?", Ella returned Dayna's question. Dayna blushed a little and nodded her head up and down. Ella tried to picture it but could not conjure up any images in her mind. She glanced at the time on her phone and asked the bartender what time they closed. The bartender informed them that they were closing in about an hour. They went ahead and announced the last call and offered the women another drink. Both shook their heads in refusal and paid their tab, so the bartender left them alone.

"Think you'll be able to drive soon?", Ella asked Dayna. Dayna shrugged looking a little worried. Ella assured her it would be alright. She said they would figure something out if she did not feel good about getting behind the wheel. To pass the time while they waited, Ella suggested Dayna tell the story they had just been talking about. The one about Dayna taking the dominant role. There was just enough time for one more story before the bar closed for the night. Dayna did not feel the alcohol as intensely as before and some of her courage was fleeting. She felt slightly embarrassed about this story but so far Ella had not judged her once, so Dayna decided to tell it anyway. Before beginning the story, Dayna told Ella that it was recent, and she explained that it had happened unexpectedly.

"Get on with the story", Ella said laughing, and knowing this one had to be juicy for Dayna to get so embarrassed suddenly.

"Alright", Dayna replied looking at Ella cautiously.

Dayna Robs the Cradle (MILF)

Dayna entered the principal's office looking clearly frazzled. The school had called and woke her up after she had been working all night. They told her she needed to come to the school but did not say why. She assumed Brady had gotten in trouble. Ever since he turned 8 and started hanging out with different friends he had been getting in tons of trouble. She was at her wits end, and despite many efforts she could not seem to get through to him. He was pulling away from her too. This was heartbreaking because they had always been so close. When all this started, she tried to talk reason into him but after many failed attempts she resorted to punishments, but that did not work either. She saw Brady sitting outside the office looking angry. She walked past him and into Mr. Grayson's office and sat down in the chair across from him. Her stomach sank when she saw the grave look on his face and the thought crossed her mind that Brady might have done it this time. He might be getting expelled.

Mr. Grayson tapped his knuckles lightly against his desk as he spoke, "Ms. Pascal, your son started a fight in the middle of class. Dayna buried her face in her hands and started to plead with Mr. Grayson. She told him getting expelled could really hurt his future and tried to explain that he was a good kid, and that he has just been having a rough time. Mr. Grayson paused to think for a moment. When he spoke again, he told Dayna that he would give Brady one more chance, but only under the condition that Brady join a community outreach program for troubled youth. He explained to Dayna that the program would assign her son a big brother to act as a positive role model. Brady would meet with this big brother and they would do activities together and volunteer in the community. Dayna agreed and even felt that it might benefit her son. She loved the suggestion and made a commitment to take him to the community center and sign Brady up tomorrow when they opened.

After the meeting Dayna walked over and looked at Brady. "Come on", she said to him looking tired and stressed. He got up and followed her to the car without a word. Once in the car, Dayna looked over at her son.

"You've been suspended for two weeks", she told him.

"That's it?" he asked, sounding surprised and a little disappointed. Dayna then began to explain to him that she bartered with the principal to avoid expulsion. She told Brady about the community program and he was immediately infuriated. She firmly told him that he was doing it and that was the end of the discussion. When they got home, Brady went straight to his room and slammed his door. Dayna opened her laptop and began doing research on this program. After seeing what it was about, she felt even more hopeful that maybe it could help her get through to her son. She had tried and every effort only seemed to make him angrier. Dayna enjoyed a long bath, and after setting her alarm, she put herself to bed.

Dayna got up and began making breakfast. She hoped it would improve Brady's mood when she woke him up this morning. She cooked him his favorite, blueberry waffles. She brought a plate to his room. First, she lightly knocked. When she did not get a response, she carefully opened the door. He was laying in such an awkward position that she did not see how it could possibly be comfortable enough to sleep in. She shook his shoulder, and gently called his name till he began to stir. He must have smelled the food because he woke up surprisingly easily. There was usually much more of a fight. When she asked him to get ready, he rolled his eyes but said he would. She felt particularly good because the waffles had paid off. Then she went to her bedroom and began getting herself ready. When she was finished and felt she had achieved the appropriate look for today's tasks, she went to check to see how Brady was getting along. When she knocked on his door, he yelled for her to come in. He was sitting on his bed playing video games as usual. Thankfully, he was dressed and seemed almost ready to go. She told him to come on and he did without a complaint.

They pulled up to the brick building that the brochure for the program had directed her to. She walked in and the waiting room was completely empty. There was a woman behind a window wearing glasses and doing crosswords. Dayna walked up and asked for an application for the program. The woman passed her one through the opening at

"

the bottom of the window and looked back down at her puzzle. Dayna and Brady both took a seat in the waiting room and Dayna began filling out the application, occasionally asking Brady a question that she was unsure how to answer. When she was done, she gave it back to the woman with the crossword, who told her that Dayna would get a call either today or Monday. Dayna nodded and thanked the woman. Then she took Brady back home. As expected, he immediately returned to his video games. Dayna loved that the morning had gone smoothly and without any drama, but she felt very frustrated at Brady's disinterest in hanging out with her. They once had spent time together every day. Now it was hard to get him to say goodnight to her.

Dayna was on the couch catching up on the last few seasons of Game of Thrones when she felt her phone vibrate beneath her. She fumbled for it and managed to hit the answer button just in time. It was someone from the community center who was calling to match Brady with a big brother. The man asked a few questions about the trouble Brady had been having. He asked about the influences in his life and things like his grades and what types of things he enjoyed. After he felt that he knew enough to make a good call, he told Dayna that he had the perfect big brother for Brady. He went on to tell her that he was an eighteen-year-old who enjoyed playing video games and playing drums. Dayna thought learning to play drums would be a great outlet for her son and she committed to buying him a drum set for his upcoming birthday. After hearing Dayna's satisfaction of the match, he asked when was a good time for Jonah to come over and get to know Brady. After the man had called and confirmed that Jonah was available, they had decided on the following day at three in the afternoon.

Dayna went directly to work on getting everything ready for Jonah's first visit to their house. She told Brady, who responded with an expected lack of enthusiasm. She asked her son to clean his room up. He had a bit of an attitude about it, but he said he would. She got started on the rest of the house. She went room by room and made everything spotless. Then Dayna went to the grocery store and grabbed what she needed to make her son's favorite dinner. On her way home she stopped by the local music store. After asking the sales associate a few questions she found a drum set she thought Brady would love. Dayna had not planned to do this, but they offered a fair payment plan, so she put a down payment on the drum set. She returned home exhausted but feeling prepared to make this thing go well. She checked Brady's room and had to give him specific instructions on a few more things he needed to do, but overall, he had everything clean. She went to bed early after a few glasses of wine in front of the television.

The next day she did one more check of the whole house to make sure it was up to her standards, then she began cooking her pizza casserole. It was getting close to three and she had the casserole in the oven baking. Brady miraculously emerged from his room to ask what smelled so good, and she told him she was making pizza casserole for dinner.

"Yum", he said, and for a moment Dayna felt as if she had her son back. She barely heard the knock at the door. She walked to it quickly yelling that she was coming. When she opened the door, Jonah politely held out his hand to her and introduced himself. Dayna shook his hand and welcomed him inside. He was tall and stocky; his brown hair fell in pieces in front of his strikingly green eyes. Brady was right inside, curious to meet the person that the community center had picked to be his role model.

"Hey man, I'm Jonah", he said to Brady who greeted him in return. Jonah asked what video games Brady liked to play and just like that they were off to his room to hang out. Dayna had imagined that her son would be much more reluctant to hang out with Jonah, but he seemed a little excited. When the timer began to beep, Dayna took the casserole out of the oven and sat it on a rack to cool.

She called both boys into the kitchen to eat as she finished putting three healthy-sized portions on three separate plates with a slice of garlic bread. She placed a can of soda beside each plate. They sat down and ate together, which is something her and Brady had not done in a while. Everyone seemed to be enjoying their food. When they finished Jonah thanked Dayna for the delicious meal, and her son surprisingly said thank you as well. Dayna was incredibly happy with how well everything seemed to be going. Before Jonah left, he stopped to speak to Dayna while Brady was in the restroom. He asked if they could set up a time to speak alone about her son. Dayna agreed and gave Jonah her phone number. Brady came out and said bye to Jonah before he left. They scheduled for them to hangout again and play some video games the very next day. After Jonah left, Brady excitedly told his mom all about Jonah.

The expression on his face when he told her that Jonah played drums let her know she had made the right call at the music store. She felt like for the first time in a while, she was on the right track with Brady again. Although she had to decide what to do about the one troubling thing she had heard come from her son's room during the visit.

Her and Brady had texted about meeting up and they had decided to meet the following day at a diner to discuss what Jonah is thinking that Brady might need from Dayna. Brady seemed excited about Jonah coming to hang out. Once Jonah arrived, they went straight to Brady's room to play some video games together. Jonah invited Brady to his studio where he practiced playing his drums. Brady asked his mom if she was okay with him coming and she agreed. She was excited that Brady was taking interest in Jonah and not rejecting him just because he was sent by the community center. They had planned to go to the music studio the following week. There were still two weeks left until Brady's birthday, but Dayna went and paid off the drums early and hid them in her walk-in closet, where Brady would not find them. At this point she was sure her son would love the drum set and was overly excited to see his face when she gave it to him.

The time that Jonah and Dayna had scheduled to meet up was only about an hour away. Brady had asked if he could go to a friend's house. She agreed because he had been on the right track since meeting Jonah, but she hoped that allowing him to go did not become a setback. After pondering it, she had decided that not letting him go would be much more likely to cause a setback, so she agreed to let him go. She also thought it might help keep him distracted so she had a chance to meet with Jonah without raising any suspicion. Brady left to go to his friend's house and Dayna got herself ready to meet with Jonah. She arrived at the diner just as Jonah was walking inside. They sat down and both ordered coffee.

Dayna asked Jonah if he was hungry, "My treat", she offered. He agreed after saying that she did not have to. Dayna ordered a breakfast scramble and Jonah got a blueberry waffle. Dayna laughed and told Jonah that was Brady's favorite as well. They talked for a while. Dayna told Jonah about the birthday gift, and Jonah told Dayna that he believes Brady just needs a positive male role model in his life. The diner was noisy as there was a birthday party going on. It had begun to make it difficult for Dayna and Jonah to have a conversation, so Dayna invited Jonah back to the house. When Jonah asked where Brady was, she assured him that he was visiting a friend, so Jonah agreed to go back to the house with Dayna.

On the way back to the house it had begun to rain and then Dayna's car broke down right at the driveway. She began to cuss unsure of what she was going to do to get her car out of the road. Jonah got behind the car and began pushing it into the driveway with seemingly little effort. She thanked him profusely and he told her it was no big deal. She noticed his clothes were wet from a mixture of rain and his sweat.

"I'm going to need you to take off those sweaty clothes you're wearing. I do not mind drying them off for you. You can use the bathroom". Dayna insisted. He went into the bathroom and began to get undressed. He started with his shoes. Then he took off his wet socks. As he was about to take off his jeans, he noticed her standing by the door, watching him intently. She was now not wearing any clothes from what he could tell, except for a short black robe and the latex thigh-highs which had showed off her very sexy, tattooed legs. He watched her as he removed his jeans, revealing his dark red boxers. He took off his black t-shirt and then turned to find the gaze of a beautiful tyrant. He saw her assessing his body and judging by the way she curled her lip; she was hardly impressed. Her eyes still turned lustful, however.

"Where should I put these clothes, ma'am?", He politely asked.

"Um, you can give those clothes to me, and please do not call me Ma'am, call me Dayna. Ma'am makes me feel old", she said as she gave him an awkward giggle.

He made his way to the couch and watched TV. Dayna made small talk with him every now and then. The storm looked like it was not going away anytime soon. It also made the house look darker than it was. Dayna must have noticed this and decided to switch on the lights and close the curtains. She made her way towards his direction. She placed her knees on the couch and tried to close the curtains behind him. She was right next to him, a small arm length away. He could not help but to stare at her ass. She may have been very petite, but her ass looked great. His dirty mind wanted to touch it. He wanted to feel what it was like. He may never get another opportunity. What was holding him back was the fear of how she would react to it. She was almost done closing the curtains. It was now or never. He placed his hand on her ass and slowly rubbed both cheeks. She immediately stopped what she was doing and looked at him. Simultaneously, her jaw dropped, and her eyes widened. He rubbed her ass for a good minute. Before she could even ask what he was doing, He told her the worst lie He could think of.

"You had something on your robe, and I was trying to remove it", he said.

"Really?" She asked, looking doubtful.

They both knew it was a lie. Neither of them removed their gaze on each other. He refused to back down an inch from his lie. The silence was brief but felt like a lifetime. Before anyone could speak, the power went off. The storm must have caused a blackout. Without saying a word, she removed herself from the couch and was on her way to her room. She turned and looked at him.

"Follow me. I don't want you to sit there in the dark, all alone.", she said. Jonah complied. They entered the master bedroom, with Jonah following her lead. He stood by the door awaiting further instructions. She opened her top drawer by the left counter looking for something. It was her tablet. She turned around and saw me standing awkwardly.

"It's okay Jonah, you can lay on the bed. Get comfortable", she said.

He could not help smiling. For some reason, He thought he must have been forgiven for what he had done earlier. Maybe she saw it as the perverted action of a young boy and decided to dismiss it. He laid on the bed and soon, Dayna followed suit. She slid herself right next to him. She unlocked her tablet and watched a video.

"What are you watching?", he asked her.

"It's a TV show about a young couple who fall in love. Nothing special really", she said.

She slightly turned the tablet to his direction, allowing her to watch with her. It took about 5 minutes for things to get stasis. A good sex scene was being shown. The couple was really going at it. Dayna showed no emotion at all. Jonah, on the other hand, was getting an erection. Without asking, He took his right hand and increased the volume on her tablet. Dayna, holding the tablet, said nothing. He then took his left hand and began massaging his dick underneath his boxers. He was so horny; he did not care that he was doing it in front of a grown woman. She raised her head slightly and saw him massage his dick. She then turned and looked at him. Her brown eyes revealed that she was slightly bothered, but more intrigued. He decided to try a bold move.

"Can you help me?" He whispered.

He removed his five-inch dick from his boxers, took her hand and placed it on his dick. He was hoping that she would do him justice... and she did. She began to massage it. she moved slowly. That was understandable given the fact she was still uncomfortable with what they were doing. But he had a sense that if he played his cards right, he might score a MILF. He placed his hand under her robe and began to massage her right breast. She had small tits. Not like the porn he had seen as he had stroked it many times before. Her nipple was hardening. He kissed her. it did not take long for them to be making out. They did that for about three minutes until he decided to move down her neck.

"Take off your boxers." she instructed. He complied. She rose from the bed and he reached for her skirt, but she stopped him.

"let me do that for you m-m-ma….." he tried. "Master,." she answered for him

She allowed him to pull the robe apart slowly and she revealed a garter belt connected to the thigh highs. She was clean shaven. He turned her around and slapped her ass. She made a soft moan. They then faced each other and shared a deep kiss. Dayna leaned back and opened her toned legs.

"Eat it," she said as if she was asking him to take out the trash for the tenth time. It was music to his ears. He dove in with as much composure as he could muster.
He could not believe he was fucking that dork's mom. He had jokingly threatened the boy with it earlier. Little did he know that Dayna had overheard him say this. She still did not quite trust the older boy completely with her much younger son and had followed them most of the first day. She was not angry at the boy's ego or the cruelty that he had been trying to use on her only son. No, boys will be boys. Dayna saw an opportunity to have her cake and get it eaten out too.
Jonah began to squirm between her thighs which were wrapped around his head like a vice by now. Dayna began to demand more cock. He jerked his head up gasping for air.

"Fuck me like a big boy." Dayna challenged. He quickly lifted his head and told her to give me a minute and went right back down there. A minute later, He let her have it. He slid in slowly, while looking deep into her eyes, deep into her soul. She was unbelievably tight which surprised him. He would have to pace himself or else he would cum too quick.

"Can you feel it?" Jonah asked. The older woman just looked at him with an arched eyebrow. His motions were slow. He wanted to savor everything.

"Good job." She said, "but I know you can do better than that!" Dayna laughed at the boy. He hastened his thrust. The moans were getting louder. "Faster, Harder!" She screamed.

After five minutes of pounding, the end was near for him. The first round of semen was at the tip of his dick. It was at this moment he realized he did not have a condom.

"Fuck. I am going to cum baby. Where do you want it... AH WHERE DO YOU..."? And he came.
It was all too much. His ejaculation made his legs feel weak and he fell on top of her. she spread her legs as wide as she could. He moaned like a dying animal in the Sahara.

"Wow, whoa", he said.

"I'm glad that you had fun but what about me baby?" she asked.

Dayna had yet to come. She stood up and grabbed him by the hair and forced him onto his knees. She then took his face with her other hand and squished it making the Big Brother's face scrunch up, her nails digging into his face.

She leaned forward and whispered, "Open your mouth, you dirty boy." Jonah complied with gusto. She took a breath in and on the exhale, spat into his mouth. She would be the mentor now.

"Down, now, lay down on the floor. Face up. Now!" Dayna yelled. The boy did as he was told. No matter what. She squatted over his face still on her heels, not yet her with her knees touching the floor and commanded him to feast. The boy did as he was told. Dayna cycled through feeding the boy her ass and her pussy, using his face as a tool for reaching climax. She feared she might have forgotten to let him breath on a few instances and would have to give him mouth to mouth. The boy always came back up gasping for air though. Dayna used him until she had come until she could come no more. Waterfall after gush after squirt drowned the boy but the boy did as he was told. He was hers now.

Dayna gave the boy the key to the back door, telling him that the neighbors watch the front and if they ever saw him, she would punish him but not like this afternoon. The cost for being found out by the neighbors was that he would no longer enjoy the subjugation of "Ms. Slut", as he had taken to calling her. If slave boy were to be seen, she would cut him loose. He could not live with the rejection of his new goddess. They both knew it. As she had commanded, neighbors would never see Jonah again. Nowhere, not even at the grocery store.

He asked if he could fuck her again before he had to leave. "Not yet," she said. "I want to play one more game first. You are going to suck my butt."

The boy stood up and walked over to her as she sat on the couch. "Now that's a good boy", Dayna smiled. He kneeled in front of her, spreading her legs wide and pulling them back. He began licking her and she smacked his cheeks. Jonah did not mind the smacks at all. She grabbed his head and pulled it into her cunt. She moved her pelvis, as she held his head in place, in a motion that rubbed her clit, full labia and finally to rest with his tongue rimming around her asshole before moving again in the opposite direction. She grabbed him by the throat now and forced him on his back again. This time she would use his cock. She had barely begun to grind her wet dripping cunt against him when the boy began to whimper and shudder. She felt as he lost control again. She looked at him and laughed.

"Brief" she said simply. She did not say another word as she moved herself from his cock and onto his face. She didn't get up again until the mess the boy had made was cleaned to her satisfaction.

Ella stared with wide-eyed fascination at Dayna's story. Dayna was still not comfortable driving after she finished telling her story, and the bar was about to close. Ella was happy to offer to let Dayna stay in her hotel room with her for the night. Ella felt she was sober enough to make the drive, especially since it would be a short one, so Dayna could ride with her, and they could come back the next day to pick up Dayna's car so she could get home. Dayna agreed but said she had to text the babysitter first, she still did not trust her son staying home by himself overnight after his shenanigans he pulled whenever he was acting out. She stared down at her phone as she carefully typed out the message informing her sitter that she had gotten too drunk to drive, and that she would be returning in the morning. She had apologized to the sitter and promised her some extra pay for having to stay longer than planned. The sitter texted her back saying that it would not be a problem. As the staff of the bar began to usher the drunks out of the bar, the ladies made their way to Ella's car.

They both got inside, and Ella told Dayna that after hearing her story, she now was interested in trying to be the dominant person, if she ever found the right situation, that is. Dayna looked at Ella and suggested that Ella tell one more story on the ride back to the hotel. They figured it would pass the time better than any radio station could.

"Have you ever been fucked by multiple men at once?", Ella asked Dayna. She shook her head no and told Ella that it had always been a fantasy of hers.

"Well,", Ella began, "your last story was pretty recent, so I think I will tell one of my more recent stories". Dayna nodded her head and adjusted herself in the seat so that she was turned somewhat towards Ella. The two seemed like best friends again at this point. Who knew exchanging sex stories could be such a bonding experience? In a mere twelve hours, it had brought these two ladies closer than they had ever been with anyone else since the time in high school, when they were best friends. In fact, they were probably closer now than they had been then. After a moment of thought, Ella began her story.

Ella Is Outnumbered (Gangbang)

Ella had just started a new job on a design team for a huge real estate developer. She was thrilled to have joined the team. She was nervous about coming in at the end of such a huge project though but from what her manager had said, her team was already ahead of the other design teams in the company. He also informed Ella that the company was offering a genuinely nice paid vacation for the team that won this year's competition. Ella was extremely excited about meeting her team. She understood that she was to be the only female member of this small design team. This made her feel a mixture of both excitement and nervousness. The excitement came from knowing that she could offer the team a more diverse perspective, but she was worried that they might feel superior to her and not accept her perspective. Ella pushed that thought from her mind. She knew she was smart and capable, and surely the other members of her team would be quick to see that, and therefore take her seriously.

Her team consisted of herself and three very accomplished men. Each of them, like her, had graduated from a university with high standards, completed internships at prestigious companies, and has had success in their careers ever since. She walked into the board room overly excited and nervous to meet her team. Ted was the team lead. He had been with the company for the longest out of all the members of her team. In fact, he had completed his internship with them and had been hired right in after his internship. Chang had lots of experience working with various companies in many different countries across the globe. This gave him a uniquely diverse perspective. Lastly there was Blake, who had graduated from an Ivy League College, his resume was fantastic except for a single black Mark that made him somewhat of a liability. Part of this company's culture is to take risks for a chance of big payoffs, they saw value in Blake's experiences that made him unemployable at many companies. Ella was to complete the team. She walked in and shook the hands of each of her new colleagues. She introduced herself and told them what her biggest strengths and weaknesses were. The team mostly seemed to accept her, except Blake who seemed to have some misogynistic tendencies. He was an asshole sometimes and could be hard to work with, but the rest of the team typically had her back when Blake was being disrespectful.

Since Ella had joined the team, they had strengthened and maintained their lead position in winning the paid vacation. She enjoyed working with the team most of the time, and the job paid well. It was demanding though. The men sometimes got a feeling of superiority over her because she was so outnumbered by them, but she was good at standing her ground. This infuriated them sometimes, especially Blake, who would eye her in a way that made her think that he wanted to put her in her place and teach her a lesson. In addition, there were lots of all-nighters, and the lack of sleep sometimes pushed Ella to her limits, but she managed to push through every setback and difficulty and come out on the other side much stronger than she had begun. When the team had received the announcement saying that they had been awarded the vacation, they were not particularly surprised. It was common knowledge that they were leading even before Ella's arrival, and they had only gotten stronger since.

It was their last day of work before their vacation. They had found out last week that they would be taking a trip to a resort in Cozumel that the company had designed the prior year. Ella and her entire team cleared out and cleaned their desks in preparation of their week-long absence. As they left for the day several coworkers extended their congratulations and wished them a fantastic time.

As they were leaving the area of the building where all the design team's offices were, someone yelled, "Bring me back a souvenir". Ella stopped a few times on her way out to say bye to a few friends of hers, including the receptionist who let it slip that she heard they would be staying in the executive suite together. She told Ella that the executive suite was a two thousand square-foot suite with two luxurious bedrooms and a loft featuring three full-sized bathrooms with jetted tubs and enclosed showers. It had a double door entrance and the foyer had Italian marble throughout, and a stunning view. Ella was wowed by Marcy's description of the place she would soon be visiting.

They were going by plane and leaving that same night, so the team met back up at the airport. They received their business-class tickets and were one of the first groups to be called to board the plane. They were seated at the front and as soon as they sat down, the stewardess offered them a pre-flight beverage. Ella noticed Blake eying the stewardess as if she were a meal, and it was obvious that she noticed as well because she avoided making eye contact with Blake for the duration of the flight. All four accepted the offer for beverages and soon the stewardess returned with two red wines, a mimosa, and a beer. They all reclined their seats into a comfortable position as they waited for the pre-flight safety instructions to begin. Soon they were in the air and bound for Mexico.

They landed in Mexico in the early hours of the morning. They all had slight hangovers as they disembarked the plane. A shuttle bus took them and their luggage straight to the hotel where the concierge took their bags and transported them up to their suite. When they entered the suite, they were in awe. Chang looked around the suite in awe with his mouth agape. Ted thanked the design company he worked for as he dove into a king-sized bed with a luscious feather pillow topper. Blake let out a loud whoop to express how pleased he was with their accommodation. Ella walked around the room taking pictures of the beauty and luxury before the guys turned it into a mess. It was not long before the excitement had worn off and they all began to crash. Ella, of course, being the only female, got one of the two private bedrooms. She took the smaller of the two, leaving the larger one for Ted, who was the team leader. Chang called dibs on the upstairs loft and Blake took the pull out which was surprisingly comfortable.

The following day had been planned by their company. They had three excursions to attend and then the remainder of the trip was unscheduled. They set off that morning after breakfast to meet their tour guide at the front of the resort. They first went to the Mayan ruins; they were beautiful, and everyone was in awe of the enormous structures. Next, they got to swim with dolphins in a huge saltwater pool that looked out into the open ocean. Ella loved dolphins so this was an amazing experience for her. She laughed when Blake was too scared of the creatures to even get into the water. The tour guide brought them to a small drive-through restaurant that sold just beans and rice. They did not expect much but they soon discovered that they were the best beans and rice any of them had ever tasted. The last activity that was scheduled was zip-lining. They had a great time, but the mosquitoes were terrible. Everyone in the group was thankful that Ella had the foresight to pack insect repellent to deter them. As per their request, the tour guide dropped them off at a bar just outside the resort. They each had a few drinks before deciding to head back to the resort. On the way back, Ella and Blake got into a heated argument about which way they should go to get back to the resort the fastest.

Ella and Blake tended to bicker quite often. When they were not around, Chang and Ted would joke about the sexual tension between the two. Unknowingly to Ted though, it was him that Ella had an eye for. She had made several attempts to flirt with him which had thus far gone unnoticed. The following day, all four of them began their day with a few mimosas. They walked from bar to bar, occasionally stopping at shops for souvenirs along the way. Once back at the hotel Ella got into the jetted tub to relax with a bottle of wine she had got from a shop while they had been out earlier. Unbeknownst to her, Blake was currently roping the other two men into a scheme he came up with. He figured he would best plant the idea while they were in a drunken stupor, and while Ella was intoxicated as well. Blake had suggested they just ravage Ella the moment she left the bathroom. Chang insisted that they get her approval first because he did not want to risk his job. All three men were very horny, so they agreed to at least try to get her to agree.

When Ella came out of the bathroom in nothing but a robe, she made her way straight to her room. She was surprised to find the rest of her team sitting in her bed waiting for her patiently with a nearly full bottle of tequila and a few souvenir shot glasses sitting between them. They first asked Ella to take a celebratory shot with them. She was already feeling quite buzzed, but she agreed. Ted poured them each a shot and passed them out. Their shot glasses made a pleasant clang as they all came together for a cheer. The shot went down smoothly. Authentic Mexican tequila was far better than the stuff they were accustomed to. Ella was enjoying the conversation they were having about what they wanted to do with the rest of their time here so much that she had forgotten that she was wearing only a towel. Blake was the only one who was brave enough to initiate the conversation that the guys had planned.

"I know something I'd love to do while we're here", Blake said as a naughty grin crossed his face, "Something us guys have decided we'd all like to do". Ella looked at him then at the other two with a quizzical expression.

Blake chimed in again, "We'd like to fuck you, Ella, would you let us fuck you?". Ella was shocked. She paused a moment to process what they were saying.

"You mean all three of you?", she asked, "at once?"

"Yes", Ted chimed in. Her pussy got soaked at the idea, and her face began to become flush. Part of her wanted to say no because she did not want to compromise her work relationships, but she knew she would not be able to do that, she could not resist the temptation. Ted had apparently sensed how nervous their proposal had made her, so he offered her another shot, and she took it gratefully. Out of nowhere Chang began to speak.

"If you don't want to, that's okay", he offered. Ella stopped him by placing her hand on his knee.

"I want to", she whispered breathlessly. She did not know if they heard her clearly, so she slowly nodded her head up and down to let them know that she was a willing participant. She watched as the realization hit all their faces one by one. First Chang looked bewildered. Ted looked excited and ready. Blake looked happy but in a way that made Ella's heart skip a beat.

Ella could not believe she was about to take three cocks in her tight little whore hole in a single fucking. She had dreamed of this day since she had first discovered how much she loved being a slut, while she was in college. Tonight, her filthy dreams get to come true. Her pussy had never been as swollen and dripping with anticipation as it was in this moment. She walked back into the room after going back into the restroom to get herself prepared for what was to come. She showered, and douched her ass, and put her hair into a ponytail. She wondered what plans the men had in store for her. Ella knew Ted had a hard on already. She could clearly see it through his jeans, and she could tell that he was well-endowed. Ella always got lost in his eyes, he was really a handsome man. She clearly recognized the look in Blake's eyes, and it made her shiver. He wanted to fuck Ella up, and he intended to do just that, and she intended to enjoy every bit of it. That lucky bastard Chang would probably cum five times tonight. He had certainly never experienced anything as hot as this. She was gagging at the thought. He certainly seemed happy enough. Her expectations were low as far as he went. She briefly considered the idea that he could surprise her.

Blake started by walking up to her and he glared into her eyes. She squirmed beneath his gaze in anticipation, she started begging him to hurry up and begin. He continued to stand there taking everything in and then a smile crossed his face. He dropped the robe from her shoulders, never breaking eye contact with her. She knew what was going to happen, and she wanted it to. This slut wanted to see her pussy stretched until it could not take any more. Blake pushed her back onto the bed and held her hands above her head, as he signaled for the others to move in. Ted pressed his body against Ella's. He began to kiss her hard, using his tongue to pry open her lips, and forcing it into her mouth as she started kissing him like she was starving for it.

"Fuck!", she thought, "Her nerves were making her tense". She felt so hot. Her nipples were aching. She was dizzy, fumbling with the cuffs Blake had just used to restrain her hands. She pushed her toes hard into the bedpost. Her legs spread wide open with Ted in between them beginning to thrust himself into her pussy.

She could hear metal handcuffs clinking against the top posts of the bed from the force of being fucked. Suddenly, Blake grabbed the back of her head, turning her face towards the side, and rammed his cock into her throat for a moment. Ella wanted to show off a little bit for them tonight, so she began sucking him off with every ounce of effort she had. She was feeling very warm, very wet as Ted buried his rock-hard cock deeper into her. She had always gotten this way around him. In this moment, he was like her sex god and they were his minions. All she ever really wanted was to have him. She groaned in frustration as his hot dick was pulled from her pussy.

"Please...", his lips parted to speak, "I want to hear you scream for me". She begged him not to stop, but he ignored her. Suddenly she was on her stomach with her arms crossed above her, still restrained. Chang was suddenly behind her with his cock out. He pressed his cock against her tight asshole with slowly increasing force until it opened to let him inside. She moaned and pressed back against him. She could hear him panting behind her. Both of her cuffed hands worked hard, massaging the cocks of the other two men who stood on either side of her. Ted shoved his cock into her mouth. She moaned loudly as she noticed the taste of her pussy juices that lingered on his cock. It did not take Chang long to release a gush of cum inside of her ass. The speed at which he was thrusting into her had increased. Both his breathing and his moans had gotten much louder. She heard him grunt and felt his load flow into her as he pressed hard against her. When it was completely done, she felt him relax and heard his breathing start again as he slowly slid his cock from her ass. Then Chang excused himself to the restroom so he could recuperate.

When Ted removed his dick from her mouth, Blake turned Ella's head in the other direction and began fucking Ella's throat again. He pounded his member into her mouth hard enough to make her gag. Meanwhile, Ted pushed his cock back into her still wet pussy. She moaned with her mouth still full of Blake's cock, and she began to squirm against Ted, trying to push him deeper inside of her. She could not believe how good he felt inside of her. She came faster than she knew she could. She felt as if her mind was exploding as Ted continued pushing his cock deeper in her cum-soaked pussy. She could tell Blake was about to come next by the way his boner felt like it was pulsating inside of her mouth. She wondered if he was going to make her taste the cum. She felt Ted's shaft slip out of her suddenly.

"Good girl", Ted cooed as he petted her head, "I want to see you taste Blake's cum". Blake came hard into her mouth, then she looked up at Blake and then at Ted awaiting his praise. She had Blake's cum running down her chin. She wiped her mouth with her arm as Blake undid her cuffs and positioned her in between the two men. In front of her Ted shoved himself back into her pussy, which he seems to have claimed as exclusively his. Blake had begun bucking himself up and down on her already exhausted ass. She screamed out as both cocks filled her holes. This was her first time experiencing real double penetration. It did not disappoint. She immediately felt another orgasm surfacing.

Suddenly, Chang appeared beside her, "show me how much you love my fat cock", he said as he pushed Ella's face down onto his cock. Blake stopped thrusting for a moment, to look at the fully stuffed whore, grinning in admiration of the sight. Ted began ramming himself harder into her and grunting madly. She moaned with orgasmic anticipation, knowing that he was about to fill her with his cum. She felt it gush into her pussy as his body repeatedly slammed into hers. She cried out in gratitude through the throbbing flesh in her mouth. She came again, but this time it gushed from her pussy and soaked the bed beneath her. She fell back onto the bed as they all finished with her and went on to clean themselves up, leaving her panting and whimpering on the bed. All her holes felt stretched to their limit, and she could feel the sticky cum all over her body. She could taste it in her mouth. She lay there panting as sleep overcame her.

Girl Time

Ella whispered the last part of her story so that no one could hear it as they walked across the parking lot and into the lobby of the hotel. The receptionist took Ella's identification and payment momentarily and then returned it with a key card. The receptionist told them where to go and they began walking in the direction as they had been instructed. The hotel was not as bad as Ella had anticipated. It was not what she had grown accustomed to, but it did not give off a trashy vibe, so she was satisfied with it. They came to the door of their room and Ella scanned the key card against the sensor. The light flashed green and they heard the faint click of the door unlocking. They walked inside and looked around taking the place in. Everything looked clean and smelled nice, so Ella plopped on the bed. Dayna plopped down beside Ella who already had the television remote and was putting on a movie. The two friends continued hanging out and chatting with each other, hardly paying attention to the movie.

Ella pulled a bottle of wine and a couple glasses from her bag. She proceeded to pour them each a full glass. They both began sipping the sparkling wine. The bubbles caused Dayna to make a high-pitch noise as she sneezed.

"You're so cute", said Ella, in an offhand manner that makes it sound like it was just an observation.

 Ella reached for the remote saying, "After all our exciting conversation, there is no way this movie could possibly hold my attention, so I'm picking something more interesting".

"Oooh, I'm intrigued", laughed Dayna.

Ella hesitated for a moment, gave Dayna a strange look, then took a deep breath. "Okay, then", She presses play on the remote.

They watch for a few minutes. After a while, Dayna felt compelled to mention, "Ella, is this one of those 'so bad it's funny' movies? Because these two chicks can't act for shit."

"It gets better, trust me", Ella stated.

"Okay, because I don't think I'm drunk enough to appreciate it yet", Dayna said laughing.

They kept watching. Then Dayna's eyes got wider and wider as realization dawned. "Ella, this is girl-on-girl porn?"

"Well, it's one of the few things I have yet to cross off my list", said Ella, looking up at the ceiling, "so I guess I have a fixation."

They watched for a little while longer in silence. Dayna became acutely aware of Ella's close proximity, as well as an excited little feeling in her tummy and a disconcerting wet feeling in her panties. She drew her knees together, concerned that the dampness might soak through to her leggings and become a visible wet patch. The silence started to become oppressive — she could even hear Ella breathing beside her — so she spoke up.

"I think I understand. That is one I have yet to mark off my list as well", Dayna said, "But I do have to be home in the morning. I mean I'd love to", Dayna's voice began to trail off as the scene playing out on the television caught her attention. Dayna tore her eyes away from the action on the screen, and briefly glanced at the hand that had started inching up from her knee to her thigh, then she locked eyes with Ella. She found herself unable to look away. Ella is so pretty, and smells so sweet, and she is warm, and she keeps getting closer to me, and I keep getting wetter. Dayna felt herself beginning to lose her resolve.

"I might be able to still make it home early if, if", she stammers as she loses her words, and Ella smiles a victorious smile, and suddenly that hand is alarmingly high on Anna's inner thigh and Dayna's legs are parting almost of their own accord, "Sorry I think watching this is, uh, affecting me", Dayna said.

"Is it having an effect… here?" asked Ella, and her hand was suddenly on that wet place. The place that she had just been worried about Ella noticing the wetness of. She could feel the heat and dampness, and that made her feel encouraged, which turned into desire. She began to lean close to Ella for a kiss. Dayna gasped when Ella's lips pressed lightly against hers, and then her mouth opened to allow Ella's probing tongue inside, exploring the insides of her cheeks. They suddenly fell into a steamy embrace, tasting the sweet wine in each other's mouths. Ella started rubbing Dayna's mound with her whole hand, then graduated to pressing her index finger into the enticing groove she could feel though the leggings Dayna had on.

"Oh fuck", moaned Dayna into Ella's mouth. It was an involuntary exclamation with a couple of meanings. The first meaning being, "this feels so good", and the second, "oh shit, I am about to have sex with my best friend from high school!"

"I have been wanting to do this so bad, all evening" whispered Ella, her soft lips kissing their way around Dayna's neck and ear as her constantly roaming hand sneaked down under the waistband of Dayna's panties.

Things began escalating more and more quickly. Dayna did not expect to feel Ella's finger go inside her pussy, so she gasped when she felt her soft fingers begin to slip inside her pussy. Dayna felt lightheaded. The look on Ella's face was one of control. Ella slid her fingers out of Dayna and walked across the room. She began digging through her larger suitcase, obviously searching for something. Ella emerged with a small pink backpack.

"I have some toys we can play with", Ella said as she began digging through the bag. She pulled out a strap-on, a leash and collar, a few butt plugs with cute tails attached to them and one that had the word slut on it, a vibrating wand, an odd-looking pink thing, as well as a few paddles and floggers. Dayna's mouth fell open as she looked at all the stuff Ella had brought. Ella insisted that Dayna select the first toy they play with. Ella picked up the odd pink thing, thinking it looked harmless. Ella smiled and asked Dayna to remove her pants. Dayna obediently took her pants off.

"Ready?", Ella asked as Dayna laid back on the bed. Dayna nodded.

Dayna pondered how Ella had suggested they discard their bras earlier in the night, so they could be more comfortable. She now considered, that might have been a clue as to her intentions.

Ella shifted closer, and gently placed the pink thing on Dayna's stiff nipple, then got a leg over so that she was half on top of her friend. She arched her back out as the toy pulled and released her nipple. They kept kissing and Ella started to get a little more passionate, grinding her crotch against Dayna's knee. Dayna's blood was racing, her head swimming, and her pussy creaming itself like crazy. All resistance faded away. Then she grabbed Ella's ass and squeezed it tight as Ella humped her leg. Ella slid the toy down Dayna's body. When she placed it onto her clit Dayna lost all control. Ella giggled as cum began to gush from Dayna's pussy almost instantly.

Dayna's hand slid into the back of Ella's pants, clutching at an exposed ass cheek bared by the skimpy G-string she was wearing underneath. Dayna notices Ella grabbing something from the pile of toys that lay near them on the bed. Dayna felt Ella place something into her hand. Dayna opened her palm and found the butt plug with slut written in red across it.

"I want to eat you," panted Ella, and then Ella slid Dayna's pants over her ankles and positioned herself in between Dayna's legs. Now she was staring down at the top of Ella's head, her bald pussy exposed to Ella's eager gaze, and before she knew it, she had her hand on the back of Ella's head, fingers in her soft hair, as Ella's tongue pressed into her groove. Ella arched her back and got on her knees to elevate her ass into the air and turned in towards Dayna. Dayna took this notion as an invitation and proceeded to wet the butt plug with her spit as Ella continued to eat her pussy. Ella explored deeper, her tongue probing between Dayna's inner lips, then stiffening and jabbing at her entrance, penetrating her and making her shiver. Her nose was pressed against Dayna's little clit, all erect and peeking out from its hood, and she slithered her tongue up to meet it. Dayna tensed, feeling jolts of electricity as Ella's tongue flicked over her bud. Dayna grabbed Ella's ass and slowly pushed the plug into the tight little hole. Dayna flipped Ella onto her back and began to eat Ella's pussy with enthusiasm. Ella loudly moaned in appreciation of the sweet taste. She wrapped her arms around Dayna's neck and her legs around Dayna's head. She wanted it.

"Oh God!" is all Ella could manage before she tensed again, and a wave of pleasure came as Dayna pulled the butt plug from her ass and pushed it back inside. Just as her pleasure was bubbling to the point of orgasm, everything seized suddenly.

"I was so ready to cum!" Ella spits. Dayna smirked playfully.

"And now you're not," she told her, running her fingers through Ella's hair and pinning her eyes with her gaze. "Don't worry, I'm going to fuck you up," Dayna said as she reached down to slip her finger into Ella's pussy. "But I'm not letting you cum without my permission, so be sure to ask". Suddenly Dayna planted her face back into Ella's pussy.

"Oh WOW!" cried Ella. Dayna sucked Ella's clit into her mouth and began to suck, and nibble, and pull. Then Dayna began pounding her fingers inside. An orgasm began to strike her completely unannounced.

"Quickly Ella blurted out, "Dayna can I come?"

"Use your manners", Dayna teases.

"Please?", Ella asked again. Dayna gave her permission to come before beginning to lick it up as Ella began to come. She kept her face pressed between Ella's twitching thighs until it was over, then pulled back and looked up with pussy juice and a grin plastered on her face.

Ella felt her face turning red and she quickly drew her legs up, curling into a ball. Dayna could still see the butt plug sticking out from Ella's ass. "Oh god, oh my god, I can't believe I just did that!" she giggled, hiding her face in her hands.

Dayna got up and hugged her friend, then whispered in her ear. "Do you want to go to bed?"

Ella bit her lip and nodded. "Yeah, I think I'd like to… um… do some other stuff…". Meanwhile, on the television screen, the blonde had tied her 'daughter' face-down on the bed, ball-gagged her and was busy plunging a massive strap-on dildo in and out of her ass.

"So, Ella… do you fancy doing that?" asked Dayna, and they both screamed with laughter.

I Cum When You Cum

Explicit Erotic Sex Stories MILFs, BDSM, Threesomes, Anal, Femdom, Tantric Sex, Wife Swapping, Roleplay, Forbidden Desires, 69, Orgies (Orgasmic Collection)

By G.G. Goode

The Casual Hookup

Lesbian, Femdom, Sex Story

Prostitutes have always intrigued me.

Maybe it was the fact that I was always curious as to why they chose that life, but that's how I ended up at the corner of Westmount and Chestnut, waiting for the mysterious "Ms. V."

Ms. V was advertised as some sort of hot femme fatale, and when I got to her, she looked me over, licking her lips.

"There you are, kitten. I take it you know the password?" she said.

"Spotted duck," I said out loud.

That was the code word that I was given, and Ms. V curled her lips into that of a smile.

"Good girl. So do you have the payment?"

"I do," I told her.

I gave her half of the payment, which was the upfront payment for this kind of thing. Half now and the other half after we're done.

Ms. V was one of the top lesbian femdom prostitutes in the area, and I was told by my friend Whitney that she would be perfect for me. She told me to give a nickname to myself, so Calico it was.

You know, like a cat.

"Very good, Calico. Come with me then. We'll begin," she said.

Suddenly, she moved behind me, grabbing my neck. I thought she would choke me, but a collar fitted nicely there, securing against my neck. The cold leather caused me to shiver.

"Ahh," I said, flushing as she looked at me with her red lips, a smile on her face.

"Does my little Calico like it? You're a good pet," she said to me.

I was a good pet. In fact, I was her pet. And tonight, she'd be all mine.

She put a leash on my neck, securing it right then and there, holding me secure as she walked me over to the hotel, or wherever it was that she did this. She then tugged on it a bit harder, goading me to go as I started to shiver, moaning with delight.

She put a blindfold on to prevent me from seeing where we were going, which was fine.

That's how I assumed this shit was done. We walked, her hand on the leash and the other on my neck, rubbing it slightly.
"Good girl," she said.

Hearing those words, the way that she uttered them, made me melt. I didn't know why, but it just...made me excited, a feeling that I hadn't truly felt in a long ass time.

She then pushed a door open, pressing me down so that I was on my hands and knees, a boot against my back, pressing there.

"Good girl. Now be a good pet and walk down the steps," she said.

So we were going down? I guess I'd do this. She undid the blindfold so that I wouldn't trip and fall, but I did so.

Each pat down the stairs was a little bit harder, simply because I had the leash there, right up next to me, and I shivered.

She then brought me all the way down, pressing me slightly with her boot.

"Good girl. Now get inside," she said.

I crawled on my hands and knees to the room. She closed the door, locking it.

"Good girl. Now down on the bed," she said.

I did as I was told, but then I saw her reach for the collar, taking the leash off, but keeping it on. She then grabbed my hands, pulling them slightly until of course, they were onto each side of the bed, holding me there.

"Ahh," I said to her.

"There we go. You're doing great," she told me.

The positive reassurance combined with her domineering personality made me start to sweat, excitement coursing through my body.

She soon took my knees next, too, pulling them outwards so that my feet were splayed out. I gasped as I felt her restrain my body there, leaving me like a fly in her trap.

She hovered over me, a smile present on her face. It told me everything that I needed to know.

"So my little pet, where would you like me to begin?" she asked me.

Where did I want her to begin? I mean, if she just took me and used me like the little fuck toy I wanted to be, that was fine. But of course, I was paying for her.

I didn't have a ton of time, but I knew that I'd milk this to every level that I could.

"Use me. Make me your pet," I said.

"Well, I'm already doing that. But is there anything you don't want?"

"No...blood or knives or anything that could actually hurt me. And...no scat obviously," I said.

"Alright, pet, well, that leaves us with a lot that we can do. But first, I think making sure that you can't see what's next is probably the best thing for you," she told me.

I shivered, realizing that she meant she'd take my vision away. What would happen next? I gasped as I felt the black blindfold move over my eyes, blinding me from the world around me. My head felt heavy, but the little hands that grazed down my body made me shiver with delight.

She got to my breasts, touching one of the nipples, watching me shiver with delight, moaning in pleasure as she laughed.

"Look at you! So turned on. The desire is obvious," she said.

That much was sure. I knew that she was making me into her little pet, and the only thing I could do was to sit there and take it.

I felt her hand move upwards towards my breasts, touching the very tips of them. Then, I felt two fingers against my nipple, pushing me there, holding me as I could feel her eyes boring into my own, even while blinded.

"So turned on....do you want a mistress to make you feel good? Or do you want a little bit of pain first?" she asked.

"Ahh, pain, please, mistress," I said.

The pain was such a pleasure for me. I was so turned on by the way that she took care of me, making me feel good, and the fact that I could feel her hands slowly skate over to my nipples again, touching them slightly, was enough to turn me on, to make me groan and shiver. She pressed two fingers there, holding the edge of my nipple, and that alone was enough to make me gasp out.

It was heavenly to feel her hands there, touching me, teasing me, and making me lose control. Her touches felt so rough, and when I felt a pair of clasps touch the tip of my breasts, I cried out.

"Quiet there, dearie. You need to be a good pet," she said.

She put the clamps on each of my nipples, but they were different from the ordinary pulling clamps that only involved two sides. No, this involved both sides, and when I felt her tug on this a little bit harder, I started to shiver, crying out, feeling it take hold of me. I grabbed the restraints, holding them there as she teased the tip of my nipple, which had become more sensitive due to the clasps, of course. I was at a loss for words, unsure of what to say, but of course, completely immobilized by the pleasures of the flesh, of the moment, and the ache and desire which flooded through me. I wanted nothing more than to relish in this pleasure, to enjoy everything, and to feel this as well.

She continued teasing me with her fingers, every slight touch dancing over the tip of my nipple and making me shudder and cry out. I was losing it, but I knew that she wouldn't stop at this. She would give me pleasure that I knew I'd remember and love forever. I was the dog, the pet that this mistress had, and I loved everything about it.

The mistress then stopped with the nipple teasing, but that didn't mean she got rid of them. She ended up moving her hands away, and I felt the rummaging of something. When it came back, I felt something soft and teasing right up against the tip of my armpits, tickling there. I started to giggle, squirming about as she continued tickling my armpits.

My armpits and sides were very ticklish, and, usually, I wouldn't say I liked this. But I did specifically ask for this in the planning with the mistress. Maybe it was the fact that she would treat me differently than anyone else. Still, there was a thrill in letting her masochistic tendencies out, teasing me, making me feel pleasure and awe, and enjoying everything she could give me. She soon moved her little feather tickler downwards, but she didn't move past the edge of my armpit. Instead, she teases the very edge of it, causing me to let out a small groan, teasing, feeling the pleasure, and enjoying everything that came out of this.

I felt her do this again, causing me to yelp, but not before moving downwards, moving her hands to one of my sides, lightly grazing her long, red fingernails against there. I wondered how those would feel inside me, and the thought of that made me want to just lose it right then and there.

She moved her hands towards one of the sides while she let the tickler move underneath my breasts, touching them there. I didn't expect such a feather-light sensation against there to make me cry out in pleasure, the feeling of this a massive turn-on for me. She soon moved her hands towards my stomach, teasing the edge of it with those same fingernails as she continued tickling my sides. She started tickling me a little bit harder, and that, of course, caused me to laugh my ass off, holding the restraints and giggling up a storm as she did this.

There was a thrill that came from being at the mercy of her, for being turned on by this, and this alone. The way she continued this, the passion and feeling that came over me was enough to drive me to the brink.

After a moment, though, she simply stopped, pulling away for a second.

"What's that, my pet?" she said as she heard me groan.

"It felt...so good," I said. The lack of ability to move made the tickling that much more prominent, and of course, I howled with laughter as I thrust my hips upwards, enjoying the feeling of this. She continued to smile, touching the very tip of my nipple once more, this time with the longest fingernail, grazing the edge of it there.

"Look at you, my little pet. You seem to enjoy the pain somewhat. If I'm hurting you, always say so, but I don't think I'll be doing anything you hate, though," she said.

"Not...at all," I said to her, barely able to make out the words that I wanted to say. It was hard to form coherent sounds when I felt her hands there, completely teasing me, making me shiver with delight, feel turned on, and enjoying all of this too.

She then slowly moved my restraints so that I was around on my tummy now. She leaned her body over mine, her voice right in my ear.

"Look at you pet. You're so turned on. I can't wait to see what you've got in you," she said, letting her tongue snake against my earlobe. The sensation of this sent a chill through my spine, the realization that I was hers, and hers alone, a totally rewarding and amazing experience.

I loved this, and I knew that she enjoyed this too. There was something nice about being taken like this and turned on at the same time. I rarely got to feel this level of pleasure as I started squirming about, enjoying the feeling of it all.

She smiled, chuckling as she did so. I knew that she was happy with the results of this, given how my body reacted, thrusting forward as I let out a small gasp. Her hands then slowly dragged down my back, moving downwards. It was so deep I wondered if she would draw blood.

But she didn't. Instead, she let her hands rest slightly against the very edge of my butt, moving her fingers up and down, slowly creating lines up and down my back. The little touch of it was enough to turn me on, driving me crazy and making me feel the rush of pleasure.

She dug her fingers in, pressing against there, making me suddenly cry out and feel the pleasure surge through my body. She let out a small hum, touching there, listening to the sounds that I uttered.

"There you go....good girl," she cooed in my ear.

She dug her nails a bit further until, of course, she got right towards the edge of my backside, touching there, tickling about. I shivered, crying out loud as I felt the hands just barely graze against me.

It was all so stimulating, so shocking to me, that I couldn't get enough of it. I wanted more, and before I knew it, her hands moved towards my ass, grasping it.

"Good girl. You have a wonderful ass," she said.

"Thank you, mistress. It's all yours," I said out loud.
She let out a small chuckle, and I felt my whole body stay on edge. That's when I felt it.

The smack of her hands, the echo of the feeling as it hit me, and the cry that came out of my mouth. She smacked me hard, hitting me there. I cried out once again after the third one, realizing that her hands were all on me, driving me insane, making me ache for her.

"There you go....I can see that you're slowly coming under my control and being a good little pet," she said.

"Yes, I am," I breathed out.

She smacked me once more, causing a guttural sound to emit from my mouth. The ache, the need, the desire for her, it was all stimulating me in ways I didn't expect to feel. I wanted this, though, and I knew that, with every single touch, it would set me on fire, making me hers.

She then whacked me once more with her hands before moving away. I felt like there was way too long of a pause for me, and I wanted to just….just accept the whole moment. I soon felt her hands move towards my ass, clutching it once more.

"I've got another special surprise for you," she told me.

What in the world was the special surprise, though? I shivered, imagining what it was that she had under all of this and the excitement she had next for me. She stimulated it, making me ache for her. The little touches were driving me insane.

Then, I felt something different against my ass. It was the feeling of stiff leather, touching and kissing right over the very edge of my body. I cried out, suddenly whimpering with delight as she grazed the little leather strip against my ass.

"Does my little pet like a bit of punishment?" she cooed.

"Yes, mistress," I said.

I liked it when she would tease me like this. She let out a small chuckle before she smacked me once more, causing me to react to her touches immediately. She used the leather flogger on me, every single touch of this making me scream out with delight.

She continued to tease me, and with every single touch, every single motion, I felt like I was losing all semblance of control. Something was thrilling about someone doing this to me. Maybe it's the masochist in me, but I really liked the way that this was happening and how everything was panning out.

She continued this for a bit until I let out a slight choked sound. She then stopped, moving away, looking me up and down with a smile.

"My little pet is alright?" she said.

"Yes, mistress. I love this. I want…I want more," I said to her.

She let out a small chuckle. "Then perhaps I can give you something that…you will surely remember. I'm going to make you squirm, and you have to beg for me to stop it," she said.

The way she said those words and the little smile that she had made me excited, albeit nervous. There was something almost nerve-wracking about all of this, but then, before I knew it, she moved her hands away from my body. I didn't feel any pressure or spankings, which was what made me wonder what was next.

Before I knew it, I felt a finger behind me, teasing my pussy, little circular motions. I let out a little whine, enjoying the feeling of this. But then, before I knew it, she pushed something into me.

It was big, and I let out a small groan as I felt it fill me up. I didn't mind big; it just surprised me, that's all. She then put it all the way in, letting it sit there for a bit.

"There we go," she said.

She turned it on, and soon, the little vibrator came to life. But what I didn't know was that it also had clitoral stimulation.
So not only was my pussy feeling this, but also my most sensitive parts! I clung to the bed, feeling the restraints there hold me entirely as I let out a low groan.

"You good there pet?"

"Yes, mistress. I want more," I told her.

I didn't expect to become this kind of person, but here I was. She let out a little chuckle before pressing the button, and soon, the vibrator roared to life.

I couldn't believe how good this felt. But also how different it was. It stimulated every single fiber of my being, every nerve ending that hit my core. It was hard not to hold back, to not just cum right then and there, especially given how this felt.

But I held back. I knew that if I gave in right away, the mistress wouldn't like it. And sure enough, she hummed in approval.

"You're persistent. I like that in a pet," she said.

"Thank you mistress," I told her.

"Now, let's see if you can handle more," she purred.

She pressed the button even higher, and the vibrator rumbled to life. I soon felt like it hit every part of me, every fiber of my being, and I shivered, crying out loud.

"Holy shit," I told her.

"There we go. Just take it easy. Be relaxed," she said, her voice soothing to me.

I tried just to feel this way, but it felt like the pleasure was hitting every part of me and that I was losing all semblance of control. After a few more moments, she pressed the button once more, and it was all I could do, not just to lose it right then and there, cumming hard against her.

She smiled, taking the vibrator out and sucking on it. I felt my body slowly fall to the ground, trying to give in, but I knew that this wouldn't be it.

"What's the matter, you want more?" she asked.
"Yes," I managed to breathe out.

"Yes, what?"

"Yes...mistress," I told her, struggling to form coherent words as I looked at her. She let out a small chuckle.

"Gosh, you're so easy to tease. You're already such a mess. There is something quite fun about all of this and about seeing you like this," she told me.

I loved it, too, even though I did feel slightly embarrassed by the way things were going. She did move slightly, moving away once more, but then she spread me apart, pressing her tongue towards my entrance, teasing me a little bit around before diving right in.

I suddenly felt the jerking sensation of this, the amazing feeling that came out of it, and in truth, I was in awe at how good this was. She soon began to move her tongue around in circles, touching and teasing before dipping herself into me, touching me deep within. I felt I was slowly crumbling, right then and there. There was something almost stimulating about all of this.

I enjoyed it, and everything about this was just damn perfcct. It drove me insane, and there was nothing more that I could do, other than, of course, to only accept the moment, enjoy the feeling, and just feel it all hit every single part of my fiber, my being, and the excitement that came out of this.

I ached for her. I knew that she enjoyed this, as well, given the way that she teased every part of me. As I sat there, feeling her hit every single piece of me, I tensed up, feeling the closeness of my body, and then, as it hit, I screamed out, feeling my back arch and my body suddenly held itself forward. I came hard, feeling my whole body whimper and my juices flow out. She licked me clean, and I laid there, struggling to remember how to think straight. Then, I felt her slap my butt one last time.

"Good pet. But I didn't want you to cum just yet," she said.

"Sorry, mistress, it was just...too damn good," I told her.

"It's alright pet, I'm going to make you feel even better," she said to me.

She moved her body and pushed mine down so that I was facing her once more. She moved the restraints a little bit so that my legs were up, but then I felt her hand lightly skirt against the edge of my pussy, teasing it slightly.

"You're so easy to tease pet. I love doing this," she said.

In a way, I enjoyed it too. But what I didn't see was the strapon that she had.

It was big, bigger than anything I've seen, in my entire life. And she was going to put this inside of me. Then again, I did ask for this. I wanted her to take me, to fuck me so hard I'd forget things, and soon, as she slid on in, I gasped as I fumbled with the restraints, holding her there, watching with widened eyes as I looked at her.
"There we go. Just relax. You'll be feeling pleasure soon," she said.

I already was, but I didn't know how to convey the feelings that I had adequately. I soon felt her push the dildo in further, and then it filled me up completely. I arched my back, letting out a guttural sound as she moved her body, thrusting deep into me, making me enjoy the feeling of this. I cried out, holding onto her as she did this, and every single touch, every single emotion, it was all just so damn perfect.

After a few more moments, she held me there, but then she moved her hands slightly, adjusting so that she could look at me. She soon moved towards me, kissing me passionately. I accepted the kiss, completely enamored by the feeling of her body against my own. And I couldn't get enough of this.

It was like she knew precisely just how to turn me on, and then, moments later, she moved her body slightly, pressing a switch.

That's when I felt it—the roar of the vibrations. The feeling of this just completely overtakes me. I clung to the straps, wishing I could hold her, but I noticed that she was enjoying this too. She pressed the vibration function, holding onto me, and then she cried out.

"There we go, babe," she said.

"Yes," I told her.

I knew that she was just a woman I'd get to experience for one night, but this night was magical. I loved being taken by the older woman. She started to increase her thrusts, pushing all the way inside of me, making me tense up, cry out loud, and ache for her. It was like a dream come true, and it was then when, after a few more thrusts, she moved her hands towards my clit, teasing it as I felt that, along with the vibrations that came from the toy she put inside of me too.

This was heaven, and I knew that it had to be. I was so enthralled by this, amazed by how just it hit all of the right places, that she simply chuckled.

"Very good pet. You're enjoying this, aren't you?" she said.

"Yes mistress! I love this," she told me.

I ached for more, and it was then when, after a few more thrusts, she pushed in, hitting that one spot, and that, combined with the vibrations, the stimulation, and everything in between, was enough for me.

I had the most powerful orgasm of my life. Before this, I always thought that this would be something that I would just accept for the moment, but she simply held me there, causing me to let out a series of small cries, feeling the orgasm as it didn't just hit my pussy, but it seemed to hit every single part of my body, and just made me feel like my core was practically fully stimulated as well.

I loved this, and I knew that she enjoyed this too. It was only then that, after a few mere moments, she slowly moved away from me, looking at my spent body, smiling at me.
"Looks like I was a bit too much for you pet," she said.

"No, you were fucking perfect," I told her.

"Very good. I'm glad that I could be perfect for you and show you an amazing time," she said.

She really did, and it was a feeling that I didn't even expect to understand or to feel. I looked at her, and then she took the restraints off, rubbing a bit of lotion on there to help with the burn from the restraints.

"There we go. How's your butt and body," she said.

"Good. A little sore, but I'll manage," I told her.

She nodded.

"Very well. I'm glad that you're okay, though. So you'll be alright," she said.

"Yeah I will be. And your money is...right there in the pocket of my pants. Take it," I said.
She looked at me with a bit of concern.,

"I'd prefer if my clients paid me. I don't take money without them giving it to me," she said.

I knew that made sense, but that made things so much fucking harder because I felt like I had significant weight on my body. With a sigh, I scrambled over to my feet, heading over to where my pants were, grabbing them and the wallet. I brought the bills out, giving them to her.

"But this is double what I asked for," she said.

"Take it. You deserve it," I said.

She really did. She was such a good call girl. I saw her smile.

"Thank you, pet. Just remember if you ever need someone to take care of you, I'm here for you. And maybe next time I can have it be my treat," she said.

"You don't mean...free do you?" I said.

I didn't want to cheat her out of her money, but she shrugged.

"I'm sure we can arrange something there. Now, let me lead you out of here," she told me.

I wanted to stick around, to get to know her, but I'm sure she probably had other clients— probably some men into being pegged by her, or maybe even more.

I didn't want to think too much about it, but also...I wished that I could stay here with her, for a long time. But I knew for one that it probably was for the best for her just to take care of her job, and work on it.

I'd meet up with her again; I was sure of it.

"Alright, let's make our way out of there," she said to me.

I finished getting dressed, and she goaded me out of the area. I didn't know why, but I felt like I was missing something. When we got to the corner where she met, she took the blindfold off, looking at me with a smile on her face.

“There we go,” she said.

“Yeah. That was amazing, by the way. Thank you very much,” I told her.

“Yeah, I’m pretty happy with the way things went. Don’t worry, I’ll be looking for you in the future. And next time…maybe we can go even harder,” she said to me.

Even harder? I was surprised that she even had a more complex function. I did enjoy the fact that she wasn’t the type to run away from a little bit of pain, though, and I nodded.

“Yeah, I wouldn’t mind that,” I told her.

She gave me a small kiss on the lips before heading off, walking down the alleyways and suddenly disappearing as she left the area.

I stood there, remembering the lingering soreness that was there and what she did to me. There was something just amazing. I didn’t know why, but there was definitely an exciting moment as I thought about this.

I didn’t mind the idea of seeing her again. I just was worried it was a bit much. But I knew that finding her was the right thing.

She knew how to make me feel things that I’d never experienced before, and I couldn’t help but want more of it. It was weird just how much I wanted it, but also, I couldn’t help but also wonder if this unlocked something within me, something new, exciting, and unlike anything I’d ever felt before.

The Hooded Man

Dark Romance, Restraint, BDSM

I didn't know why, but I was suddenly feeling like I was being watched. Maybe I shouldn't have gone to the park at night.

But perhaps that was the thrill. That was what I enjoyed about this. The fact that someone…somewhere could just come out at any time and do this to me was both scary as shit but also thrilling.

I walked through there, stepping into the forest. I was supposed to meet my friend Tanya out here. She told me she had a bag of weed for me with my name on it. And lord knows that I needed something to take the edge off.

And if I couldn't get dick, I guess I'll get the next best thing.

I walked a little bit around, seeing the shadows that were there. It made me nervous but also excited me.

"What if someone was out there, waiting to jump me? Would be scary as shit," I said to myself.

I uttered these words, but I couldn't help but wonder if I really wanted that to happen. I felt excited, but I was also a little bit nervous about what would happen next.
That's when I noticed it. The shadow of a person. Was I losing my mind? Maybe I was, and this was just life's way of telling me.

No….it couldn't be, could it?

That's when I whipped my head around. I heard the creaking of a branch, but when I got there, I didn't see anything. I pursed my lips, the revelation that I was being followed, watched, or something of the other hit me.

"This isn't good," I said to myself.

Though deep down, I kind of wanted something to happen. I didn't know; maybe it was that fucked up part of me that craved something like this. But perhaps it was also the part of me that wondered just what in the world would happen if I was attacked out here.

I kind of wanted this.

I started to move once again, seeing the shadows once more. This shit was eerie. I wanted to know if the rumors of someone living out here were true.

Then, I noticed it. The scurrying once more, the sound of the trees, and then, I noticed something getting closer and closer to me.

"W-whose there?" I asked.

I looked at the guy. He had a hood on so that I couldn't recognize his face. Was he some sort of stranger, or was he a friend? I didn't even know anymore. But I definitely was a little bit worried about what would happen next. I began to move away when I felt the force right behind me, holding their hands there, silencing me.

"Don't make a goddamn sound," he said to me.

I tried to say something, but I didn't want to. I figured that…whatever was about to happen definitely wasn't going to be some simple little thing. It would be something huge.

"O-okay," I said.

The voice let out a chuckle.

"I didn't know you'd be so easy to have here, my dear. You shouldn't be out here like this," the voice said.

"Maybe I want to be," I retorted as he moved his mouth. I licked his hand.

I don't know what came over me or if there was any reason for this. I don't know; maybe it was just the thrill of being taken like this.

"A feisty one, are you? Well, I guess that makes it more fun," he said.

His hands moved towards my hips, upwards. The idea of being fucked by a stranger was thrilling. I know that it's not for everyone, but I wanted this, and I craved the feeling.
And it made me wonder if, deep down, he wanted the same thing.

I heard the sound of shuffling, and soon I was up against the tree. I felt my hands tied there, and the hooded man came over, cupping my chin and looking into my eyes.

"What a cutie. You don't seem to be afraid of me either," he pointed out.

"Why would I be? I'm not going to run away," I said.

Running away was for babies, and I knew that he was not going to make me regret this.

"Very well. I guess I can show you just a peek of who I am," he said.

I was worried about this, and I wondered what the hell I was getting into as I stared into his eyes. He smiled, and for a second, I was transfixed by the way he looked.

He had beautiful blue eyes, soft, pale skin, with no hint of stubble. If this were anyone else, I

might be more hesitant, but there was something about this man, the way he looked at me, the smile that came upon his face made me feel excited and craved this much more.
"There we go," he purred into my ear.

"Yes," I said.

"You sure you want this? I can let you go, and we can pretend we've never met," he said to me.

I wanted this. I didn't want to leave. Even though I had no idea what this man had in store for me, or even if Tanya would come over to see me at this point, I felt excited as I looked at this.

"Yes," I said to him, my voice breathy and needy.

His lips curled into that of a smile, and soon, I felt his lips descend upon my own. He kissed me hard, holding me there. The touch of this man completely enveloped my quivering body. I didn't want to leave, even though I had a feeling that this may go differently than I thought.

I noticed his hands start to move around my body, touching me. Being restrained meant that I couldn't touch him back, but giving up that power, that need for control, I ached for this kind of thing, and I knew that he liked this too.

The hooded man was someone I'd never met before. Naturally, some people would probably shrink away at the opportunity for this, but there was something thrilling about a man that I barely knew, who would take me like this and make me feel things that I liked.

Was it wrong? Maybe, but also...I liked it. It helped stimulate something within me that I didn't really know that I needed, a want and desire that grew more and more as the night continued. His lips were amazing, and I felt like I was just drunk off of this. I wanted him, and I knew that this mysterious man, who was here in the forest with me, would give me just that.

His hands moved about, touching and teasing every part of my body that he could without taking off my clothes. I wondered if anyone would see us. I doubted it.

But then, he pushed his tongue in, which surprised me. Albeit I gratefully accepted it, kissing him back, our tongues intertwined, dancing together, and the pleasure was exciting and fun.
It fulfilled a fantasy of mine. A stranger, someone who could show me some amazing feelings, making me excited and ready for more.

He then moved his lips downwards, touching, teasing, and playing with them. I let out a small gasp, surprised by how amazing it felt. It was like he knew exactly where to touch me, which parts that I loved to have focused on, and I felt like I was relishing in everything that went on. His hands moved up towards my breasts, teasing them slightly, his lips hungrily moving downwards, kissing, nipping, and teasing them.

He bit down on my collarbone, hard enough to make me cry out, leaving a mark but not deep enough to draw blood. I shivered, realizing just how good this felt and how much I enjoyed it. I didn't want any of this to stop; something deep inside me was awakening, a feeling I couldn't get enough of. The desire for him...the desire for more...and the lust that seemed to drive me insane, practically crazy, and the lust that I ached for, on so many different levels.

His touch was like a drug, making me shiver, cry out, and indulge in the feeling of this, no matter what. I suddenly noticed that he had his hands right up against the hem of my shirt, pulling it upwards so that, of course, I was exposed partially. My bra was still on, but his hands moved towards my breasts, touching and squeezing the soft mounds, making me shiver.

"You're so easy to tease. I enjoy this. And nobody will hear your cute little sounds. Besides me," he said.

The way he uttered those words in my ear made me cry out suddenly, pressing upwards, understanding of course, that he was the one in control. He was the man behind it all, and I was just here, at the mercy of his touches, and enjoying the feeling of this every which way.

He then moved his hands to where my nipples were, teasing them through the confines of the bra. I suddenly cried out, realizing I could be as loud as possible. The idea behind that excited me because it's not every day I can make noises like this. Showing how much I genuinely enjoy being teased like this, my aching desire for him, the need for more driving me forward.

He soon moved his hands towards the bottom of my bra, pulling the cups down so that my large breasts tumbled out. They fell, being held up by the bottom part of the garment, and I shivered, realizing how cold it was out here. My nipples hardened, both from the weather and also because of how stimulating this was.

"Look at you, so turned on," he cooed.

He grabbed my nipples, pinching them, and I moved towards the touch, suddenly feeling the excitement of that and the thrill of the moment. He continued to lightly tap at them, teasing them so that they got harder, and soon, I cried out, the excitement and need growing within me.

He pressed and pulled on my nipples, tugging on them and making me shiver. I arched my body forward, realizing how much-limited motion I had due to my hands being tied up, and he smiled.

"Damn, your large cow tits are already so needy. It's clear you like this. You like being my little cow," he said, teasing them against his fingers. He rubbed his hands in circles, causing me to let out a series of guttural moans and sounds.

"Yes! Make me your little cow," I said.

He let out a chuckle, continuing to tease me, making me utter out the neediest sounds I think have ever come out of my mouth. I ached for this, I needed it, and he seemed to get it.

He understood how much I liked it, and I, for one, couldn't get enough of it. He continued to move his hands there, teasing my nipples until they were unbearably hard, and I felt like I was about to burst at the seams. He then pulled one into his mouth, flicking his tongue over the tip of it, making me shiver with delight, the ache for him growing.

I don't know what it is about this man, but there is just...something so amazing about the way that he touched me. He seemed to know exactly how to turn me on, where to tease me, and to let my body lose all semblance of control.

I knew that he enjoyed this too, and there was something just so utterly thrilling about this. He let out a chuckle as he pulled away with a pop, teasing it with the very tip of his tongue. "Look at you, taking this like a champ. I'm impressed there, cutie," he said.

"T-thanks," I said.

He then suckled on my other breast, teasing the nipple against his mouth before he moved his other hand towards my lonely nipple, teasing the very tip of it with little touches, pressing there and making me shiver with delight. I loved every moment of this, suddenly feeling like I was losing my mind with everything that was happening, the desire for him growing, and the need for his body making me feel even more in shock and awe.

He then moved his lips downwards, taking it fully into his mouth, flicking his tongue around. I was at the mercy of him. I didn't want him to stop, and I knew that I could feel the desire, the orgasm that I had, bubble deep within me.

I knew that I was close to my limit, and he seemed to get it. Well, at least the first limit that I had.

I knew that I wanted more, and I knew for a fact that this was something that excited me, turned me on, and made me shiver with delight, the desire growing within.

He then moved back, right as I was about to release, and I looked at him with slight annoyance on my face.

"Why did you stop?"

"Because I want to make you cum in other ways," he said.

He slid his hands downwards until he got to the edge of my thick thighs, pressing them apart, letting his hands skirt upwards. The way he said those words, the force that came with the way he uttered it, was enough to drive me utterly mad and made me ache for him.

He soon got between my legs, cupping the heat, and as he did so, he let out a small chuckle.

"So wet already. I can't believe you're such a little slut," he said.

He rubbed my clit, touching against there, and it was all I could do, not just let out small, guttural sounds of desire and need, the pleasure growing within me, making me lose everything. The control that I felt, the need for him that was there, all of it was overwhelming me, making me realize just how much desire I had within.

He moved his hands towards the sides of my panties, sliding them downwards with force. I gasped, surprised by the way that this felt. My naked pussy, along with my bare breasts, made me feel so exposed, despite wearing clothes. He smirked, but not before sliding his fingers between my legs. I started moving apart, realizing just how much I ached for him, and how much I wanted this man to explore me.

He rubbed against the tip, sliding his hands around my slippery folds, letting out small gasps as he teased me. I could see the noticeable bulge in his pants and the fact that he was....well, pretty fucking big for lack of a better word. He then slid his fingers around, touching the very tip of my clit, making me utter out small little gasps and moans of arousal. His hands then slid in, right near the entrance, and I braced myself, the need growing.

I was shocked by how easily he was able to tease me.

It wasn't just a tiny little thing either. He was so skillful, every single touch of this driving me closer and closer to the edge. This stranger knew just how to tease me, and I couldn't help but wonder if he knew me from somewhere.

Or maybe he was an ex. But I didn't have an ex who was…this good at this kind of thing. Usually, they'd just eat me out and call it a day. But not this guy.

No, he seemed to have this determined action in his arsenal, to make me lose it, and as his fingers slowly moved in and out, pumping me, moving the tip of his finger against my clit, rubbing it there, I felt my whole body start to slowly grow needy with pleasure. I could feel my legs buckling, but then, he slid another finger inside me, holding it there, teasing the very tip of this, pushing against that area. Suddenly, I felt two fingers in there, pushing against me, and I cried out, trying to move about, but I squirmed under his touch.

"There you go. Good girl," he said.

I loved the way that this felt. The fact that he did this and I was just accepting of it was so much fun. There was something thrilling about this, something that I so desperately enjoyed, and I wanted to just indulge in this moment, and I wanted to accept this from here on out.

He continued pumping his fingers into me, keeping me there as I continued to moan, holding the tree as he did this. Finally, he pushed there one last time, and I cried out, tensing up once more as I suddenly fell back, relieved and enjoying the orgasm that I just experienced.

But then, he pushed me down so that I was on my hands and knees, still bound to the tree. I looked up at him with curiosity. What was he going to do now? He then slowly undid his pants, and I watched with widened eyes as he slowly undid it, pulling his cock out, stroking it.

"How about this? You want it?" he said.

I wanted it inside of me in another way, but I guess I could take this. I slowly moved my lips forward, taking the tip of his cock into my mouth. I sucked on it slowly, hearing the delicious cries that came out of his mouth as I did this. I continued to suck for a little bit, watching him groan with pleasure as I continued to tease him.

"There we go," he said.

I took him further down against my mouth, feeling it slowly gag my throat. I didn't know why, but there was something nice about this. He reached out, grabbing my head, and soon he pushed me down further, holding me there as I cried out, garbled cries that made me shiver with delight.

He started to force my head further downwards, keeping me there and in place.

I started to feel it move closer and closer to my throat, causing me to gag slightly. He held my head there, continuing to jerk himself there. I felt the cock bulge slightly in my mouth, and I wondered what it would feel like deep inside of me.

He continued this for a little while until, of course, he pulled back, looking at me with a smile on his face.

"Look at you, enjoying all of this. You like it when strange men use you," he said.

"Yes," I spat out. I usually wouldn't be this upfront, but the feeling of this was perfect.

He then picked me up, holding my body like it was nothing right over his cock. I was glad that I was on the pill because it led to encounters like this, making things more fun.

He plunged himself into me, and I cling to him with my legs, feeling him pull my body closer.

"That's right, just lay there and take it," he said.

And take it I would. I enjoyed the feeling of this and how he simply knew just how to make me feel good. He started thrusting in deeper, holding me there, and I let out a series of garbled sounds. Being loud in the forest was a fun adventure because it meant that I could be as loud and as out there as I wanted to and that he would just simply take it all right then and there.

He pushed himself all the way into me, filling up my pussy with his fat cock. He held me there, stroking my hair and touching me slightly as he continued this.

"Such a good girl. Taking my cock like this like the little slut that you are," he said.

"Yes, I am a slut," I said.

I loved everything about this, completely enraptured in the pleasure of this and the moment that he shared with me. He continued this for a long ass time, holding me there for what felt like forever, and I could feel him angling his cock, hitting every part of my pussy. I let out a series of tiny cries, moans of pleasure, and he seemed unable to get enough of this. I was his toy, and he would take care of me.

It was rare for me to fall for someone like this when I barely knew who the fuck they were, but I had it bad for this man. With every thrust, every single touch, I was losing my goddamn mind, enjoying the feeling of this, feeling like I was slowly going mad with pleasure at the touches that he gave to me.

After a few more thrusts, he stopped, pulling out of me. I let out a frustrated groan as he laughed at my needy sounds.

"Look at you. So hot and bothered for this. I didn't know you were such a little slut," he said.

"Yes, I am. I need your fucking cock in me," I said.

"You're like a dog in heat. Maybe I should fuck you like one," he said.

I wanted that, and soon, he untied my hands, flipping me around so that I was facing the tree. He then held my hands there again, tying them the other way. But before I could process everything, I felt his cock fill me up once more.

I let out a small cry, feeling the pleasure of this hit every fiber of my being. He was thick, and his cock hit every fiber of my being, making me shiver with delight, crying out loud, enjoying the touch of his body.

Everything about this just felt so damn right. I loved it, and he pushed my head against the bark as his cock filled me up, thrusting into me like I was a dog in heat.

I let out a series of small cries, enjoying the touch of this, feeling like I was at the mercy of this man's touch, unable to get enough from him.

He continued to hold me there, fucking me deeper and deeper, and I simply enjoyed it, relishing in the feeling of his hands there, just taking me, using me like the little slut that I was, and he soon pushed in harder and harder.
His fingers moved to my clit, touching and teasing, rubbing me with subtle, gentle strokes as he pounded hard. The difference in touches, in pleasure, it was all just so raw, and there was something so thrilling about this. I didn't get it, but I knew that he couldn't get enough of it, and it was then when, after a few more thrusts, he let out a groan, pushing himself deep into me, filling me up with his seed completely.

I suddenly felt a hand press against the nub of my clit, teasing me there, tugging on my breasts hard, and as he did this, I suddenly arched my back upwards, crying out loud with a pleasure that I didn't expect, but there was something amazing about all of this.

He soon finished up, pulling out of me as I felt the trail of cum moving down my leg and the shivering sensation of this. I fell to the ground, completely enthralled and lost in the feeling of pleasure that came from this.

As I felt my hands get untied, I moved my body around, looking to see the hooded man there. But there was something different about him. Usually, after getting fucked in the woods by a stranger, normally you'd' feel the urge to run away, right?

Except I didn't want to.

I stared at this person, realizing something oddly familiar about them, but I couldn't pinpoint what that might be.
"You okay?" the voice said.
"Yeah. I'm good. Thank you," I said.

"You're very welcome. You're fun to mess around with," he said.

Something was interesting about his voice. I didn't know what it was. As he walked away, though, I suddenly spoke.

"Wait."

He whipped his head around, looking at me.

"Just who are you?" I asked him.

He simply chuckled, pulling the hood off his face. Who I saw was someone I didn't expect. My boss Lance. He simply smiled.

"Someone you very much know. But you never saw me here. It's best if I be going," he told me.

"Wait, don't go!" I said to Lance.

But before I could say another word, he was gone.

Weirdly, it was Lance of all people. Did this mean something more? Or did he just like to fuck random women in the forest because why not? It was all...so bizarre, that's for sure. And as I stood there, my pants and underwear still in the corner, and my top asunder too in the dark forest, I realized I was supposed to meet Tanya, and that was that.
But I guess I'd meet her eventually, right?

I got myself dressed, still trying to understand why in the world he came out here.

Lance was....well, he was one of the most prominent Executives at the company, and he was also someone who supposedly was dating this really hot woman. So why did he come to the forest and then do this? I didn't get it, and it seemed to make absolutely no sense.

I definitely wondered what would happen now, or even what would come of all of us, because of our encounter. It all seemed so different and not what I was expecting.

I did finally get dressed, looking around, finally figuring out where the pathway was, and then making my way over to where I was supposed to meet Tanya. Did I tell her about Lance, though? I didn't think that was the kind of conversation she wanted to have, of course.

Maybe it was my own personal worries about this, but I also was curious about what may happen now or even what may transpire because of this.

Well, I guess the only thing that I could do at this point was to just wait and see, and maybe, just maybe, Lance will say something.

I got to where Tanya wanted to meet up, and she was sitting there. But I saw the look of confusion on her face.

"Why did you come that way?" she asked.

Shit, I should've gone another way. She probably thinks it's weird that I came from within the forest rather than the parking lot like an average person.

"Sorry, you got here later than I thought, and I was early, so I took a little bit of a walk," I told her.

"Be careful. There are supposedly reports of a creepy ass person out there. They stalk women and will go after them when they are least expecting it," she said.

Was that supposed to be Lance? Did he do this to others? Well, I liked it. It finally fulfilled that role of being fucked in the forest by a random stranger, something that I so desperately desired.

"Well, I'm fine. I'm alive, aren't I?" I said.

"Are you sure you're okay? You seem off," she said.

"Yeah, I'm good," I told her.

We hung out, and Tanya showed me a few things, but they weren't really around here. She was too spooked to stick around this area.

And in a way, I didn't necessarily blame her.
I went back home; there was definitely a feeling of excitement and the desire for more.
I wondered what Lance was doing or if I should talk to him about this. I didn't really have evidence, so maybe he'd forget and just play it off.

Which would suck total ass, but I guess it is what it is, of course.

I wondered though, what would come about with this all. What does one do now after all of this was said and done. He did fulfill a fantasy of mine, and there was something nice about this, but I didn't know what to do next.
The Monday after, I went to work like it was nothing. I saw Lance there, but he didn't make a move or even acknowledge my existence. It was like nothing had happened.

But then, on lunch break, as I sat in the breakroom, I heard the door open. I turned, and there was Lance. There was tension there, making me wonder what he would do now.

"Lance," I said.

"Here. If you want to see me again, you know where to find me," he said.

He calmly gave me a card, showing me the times he'd be out there, in the forest.
"But what about...that girl you're seeing?" I asked.

I felt terrible that I was making him cheat on her, but his lips curled into that of a smile.
"Let's just say that won't be a very long-term affair," he said.

I looked at him, unsure of what he meant; he simply left the card, closed the door, and left.
He didn't say a word to me after that. But I didn't know what it meant. Did things with that new girl go downhill? Possibly, but the idea of this, the way that things were...it was just so shocking that I couldn't believe that this was happening.

And that, of course, also made me wonder what would come about next. What did he have planned for me? Would we just meet up like this? Or would there be more of a plan to it?

There was so much I didn't know, so much that seemed to be hidden away, obscured by the way things were. And of course, I enjoyed this too. It was the beginning of something. A secret kept between the two of us, never to see the light of day, and something that could change my life forever! If things end up panning out in certain ways. My mind goes wild with the thought of it all.

Of course, I'd just have to wait and see.

Miss Layla's Little Maid

Femdom, MILFs

"Hello there, Miss Layla," I said as I walked in.

Miss Layla, the mistress of this mansion and my boss, gave me a small little smile.

"Hello there, Freya. You're early, and you wore the dress too. Great job," she told me with a smile.

I flushed, realizing that this was happening like this. I realized that Miss Layla was always such a damn tease. Then again, I didn't mind it.

In truth, this was probably the best boss that I ever had. She was the one who helped me get the hell out of debt, for starters. When I was desperate and needed a job, I found the ad online, and I decided to scour it. I looked it over, realizing that she needed a full-time maid. So I signed the fucked up.

But what I didn't know was that she wanted…that kind of maid. Not just one to clean her house, but one that was a tease.

When I first joined on, I thought that this wouldn't work out, but Miss Layla definitely showed me that this could be fun. She put me in this tiny ass maid dress, had me clean floors while her hands would move against my body, touching my big butt and cupping it sometimes along the way. I would always gasp and be surprised, but also….I really liked it.

For starters, Miss Layla was older, but there was something about her that made me excited. I didn't know what it was. Maybe it was how she treated me, almost like her little pet, and how she always praised me.

I got off to that. I would be lying if I said that I didn't sometimes head to the bathroom, rub one out, and then go back to see her. She was incredibly attractive. Tall, with long brown hair, big green eyes, and a curvy body. She knew just how to make me a mess, and she was such a tease, which drove me crazy.

But what kind of sucks is that she never went further than that. She would just touch and tease and sometimes get close, almost like she was giving me a kiss. But she never did.

It was so damn frustrating that sometimes I just wanted to scream to her that I wanted her to fuck me already, to pin me down and use me like the little slut that I was. But I never dared tell her this because I feared what may happen.

She might fire me. Perhaps she liked the teasing, and this was her kind of thing. I didn't understand women, but maybe that's all it was.

No....I had a feeling there was something else here, something much, much more.
That day, when I walked in, I saw a look on her face, that of curiosity, like she wanted to say something.

"You alright there, Mistress?" I asked.

"Oh yes, thank you, Freya. Say, are you busy tonight? Do you have to head home early?" she asked me.

Sometimes I'd have to head home to take care of my family, but tonight they'd be fine.

"I don't have to. Why?"

"Because I'd like for you to meet in the master bedroom after your tasks," she said.
Was she...implying something else? I didn't even know, but I couldn't help but feel an excitement course through my body, making me ache for more.

I was worried about bothering her, though, or that I was getting too excited for something that wouldn't happen. She wouldn't choose me...would she?

No, I couldn't think that. That's way too damn good to be true. But the idea of Miss Layla....doing that to me was exciting, and it made me ache for her. It would be a dream come true.

But I didn't want to get my hopes up. However, I did do my work, cleaning up the front room and the kitchen. However, I'd notice her looking over my body, a small smile on her face. It was like she....she had plans, and the way her gaze just penetrated deep into me made me want her, need her, and I craved for her.

But I didn't want to move too fast. I decided the next best thing for me to do would be to wait and see and to hope for the best.

At the end of the day, I went up to the master bedroom. I noticed that the door was slightly ajar. Was Miss Layla in there? I started to wonder about these things, and as I opened the door, I saw her there.

But instead of her normal business attire, she was in lingerie. My eyes stayed focused on her, lingering against her body, and she smiled.

"There you are, Freya. You made it," she said.

"Miss Layla, what is this?" I asked her.

"Simple. I have a special...offer for you if that's what you'd like," she said to me.

"Alright," I told her. I felt my body grow excited as I looked into her eyes. She then beckoned me closer, holding my chin up, staring into my eyes.

"I've seen you," she said out loud.

"W-what do you mean?" I asked with a bit of a flush on my face.

"The way you look at me. You've wanted this, haven't you? For me to just...take you and use you in the ways that I know how to. That's what you desire, correct?" she purred into my ear.

I shuddered, realizing just how much I needed this. I felt my pussy start to moisten at the sound of her.

"Yes," I squeaked out.

"What was that kitten?" she asked.

"Yes. I want this Miss Layla," she said.

"Good girl. That's what I like to hear," she said.

She grabbed my head, pulling it upwards so that we locked eyes. The way she stared at me was just...so lovely. She seemed determined to make me feel good, and I felt so exposed here in this maid dress that I adored it. She pushed her lips to my own, and for a second, we simply kissed.

We stayed like this for a long ass time, both of us enjoying the touch and taste of one another. She was so soft, but also her kiss was forceful like she knew exactly how to make me slowly lose control, the ache and need driving me crazy, and I enjoyed everything about it.

She seemed to get it too, and that's what I liked about it. I felt...happy that she wanted this as much as I did and that there was clearly a need, a desire for her, and a raw emotion that only seemed to grow over time as we kissed then.

She pushed me down on the bed, her lips taking over my own. I was shocked by just how dominant she was, her hands moving against my body.

"You're fine with me taking control, right, Freya?" she asked.

"Yes, Miss Layla," I breathed out. Though deep down, I was about to lose it if she didn't. She let out a small chuckle, pressing her lips harder to me, dominating me.

I'd never been taken by a woman like this, and there was something so foreign about it, but at the same time, so damn perfect, that's for sure. We made out for a little bit, feeling her hips move closer to my own and the touch of her hands sending sparks through my body.

I gasped, feeling her touch and grab my sides, teasing me there. Just that touch alone was enough to drive me crazy, and feeling her hands there was enough for me.

"Good girl. You're already so eager and needy. Let me guess you've wanted this?" she asked.

"Yes," I breathed out finally, after remembering how to use words. I'd be lying if I didn't.

"Really now? Tell me how much you've wanted this," she said to me.

"I mean....I really wanted this a lot. I wanted...you for a while," I said.

"Tell me how much, though? Come on, don't be shy," she said.

Should I really tell her...that? Well, she seemed determined and eager to get an answer out of me, so I sighed.

"I really want you. I've thought about it and.... it's something I've desired for a long ass time," I told her.

"I see. Well, to tell you the truth, I've wanted this too. I just wasn't sure if you wanted it. But I guess since you said yes...I can make you feel things you've never experienced before. Especially with a woman," she said.

Just hearing those words was enough for me to lose all semblance of control, feel turned on, and enjoy the moment at hand.

I felt excited just kissing her, and it brought forth feelings that I couldn't get enough of. Her lips were so amazing, driving me crazy, and I ached for more from this. She soon pressed her body against my own, touching me slightly, and it was enough to make me lose control but just for a moment. I knew that she liked this as much as I did, and I frankly enjoyed the hell out of it so far.

Her lips began to trail downwards, touching the tip of my neck, enjoying the little sounds and moans that came out of there. She let little touches and brushes move downwards, until of course, she got to my collarbone, teasing and sucking on the flesh there. I shivered, excited by the way she moved her lips so skillfully. She then let her hands move upwards, dancing against my neck.

"Just look at you. So turned on. You have such a beautiful body," she said to me.

I cried out, enjoying the sensation of this, and I craved more from her. She then moved her lips towards the tip of my collarbone, sucking on the flesh there. As she did this, I let out a small cry, surprised by how good this felt and the need that came out of my mouth.

I could tell she enjoyed this as much as I did, letting her lips slowly trail towards the very top of my collar, and then, of course, her hands moving towards my maid dress.

"I love this little outfit for a variety of reasons," she said.

"W-what do you mean?" I asked.

"Because I can do this," she said.

She slowly undid the strings on the bodice of the dress, pulling it downwards, revealing my breasts. I didn't have nearly as much as she did, but when her eyes glazed over mine, I saw the haughty look there.

"Wow, very nice, my dear," she said.

I shivered, and then, of course, her hands moved towards my breasts, cupping the area there, touching them slightly. I let out a small cry of surprise, unsure of what to say to her, other than I enjoyed this. She moved her lips towards the tip of one of the nipples, touching it slightly, sucking on the flesh there, making me tense up, cry out, and feel turned on by the sensation of this. She continued to suckle on my breast, causing me to suddenly grab the sides of the bed, holding the covers there and crying out loud, in pleasure, and with an ache that was obvious. She smiled, looking into my eyes.

"Very good girl," she told me.

I cried out, surprised by how just the tiniest of touches was enough to make me like this. I knew that I was excited, but even I was surprised by the way this felt. She soon teased my body, pinching my nipples and moving her lips towards my other nipple, sucking on the flesh there. The touch alone was enough to drive me crazy, making me cry out with surprise, pleasure, and so much more.

I knew that she enjoyed this. There was some sort of thrill she got from teasing me to the point where I was a helpless mess on the bed. Her hands moved up to the tip of my nipple, rubbing there, and then her tongue moved around the sides and then the tip. She looked at me, the apparent need and excitement there, and I shivered. I could see the need in her eyes and just the way...she knew precisely how to make me feel like this. It was like she had this idea all along, and I was hers for the taking.

And yet, there was something nice about that. To be taken by her, worshipped by her hands and mouth, to cum by her touches...this was like a dream come true.

I never thought that I'd dominate her at all. I always felt that she'd be the one to exercise control and to make me become this aching, needy mess for her. And yet, I liked that.
The idea of that was a bit nerve-wracking to me, but I didn't mind it in the least.

She soon moved her lips towards the other nipple, letting her tongue circle and tease the very edge before flicking over, and the other hand moved and rubbed with her palm against my other nipple. I let out a small gasp, surprised by this.

"Good girl," she said.
She moved back, and I soon reached forward, grabbing her breasts, teasing and massaging them through the confines of her outfit. She looked at me with abject surprise, shocked by the way that I moved towards her immediately.

"What's this?" she said.
"I want...to make you feel good too," I said.

The truth was, I was so new to this whole thing. She was my first, and I felt slightly embarrassed by that, but I had a feeling that she would definitely be a fun first that I could enjoy.

She pursed her lips and chuckled.

"Very well, my dear," she said.

I moved towards the back of her lingerie, pulling off her bra and letting it fall to the sides. I quickly moved my lips towards the tip of one of the nipples, awkwardly moving my lips there. She chuckled as she saw the awkward struggle that I had.

"You're adorable but so damn inexperienced," she said to me.

"It's not like I have all that much experience, to begin with," I said, moving my tongue and flicking it in the same manner she did to me. Her breasts were so much bigger, and it felt nice just…being taken like this and being able to reciprocate everything. I watched as she smiled, touching my hips as I licked and teased her nipples.

"You don't have to do all of this, though. Tonight I wanted to make it about you," she purred. I shook my head.

"Maybe I want to," I told her.

I licked and teased her, exploring her breasts, letting my other hand move upwards. I touched against the very tip of her nipple, causing her to let out a small cry of surprise, and then, of course, I did what she did to me before, which was, of course, pinching and then rubbing my palm against the tip of her other nipple.

I noticed Miss Layla's composure start to crumble slightly. Perhaps she intended only to dominate, but I wanted to make her feel good too.

After a little bit, she pushed me back down on the bed, hiking up my skirt, her hands moving towards my thighs, touching them.

"You have the most divine thighs," she purred.

"Thank you," I said, shocked by the way her hands seemed to know exactly where to go. I felt slightly embarrassed by the way she looked at me, enjoying the way that her hands seemed to know exactly where to explore. I wanted her though, I craved her, and I knew that this was something she desired too.

She quickly moved her hands over towards the very edge of my inner thigh, touching the tip of it, moving her hands in a massaging manner towards my inner thigh. She was so dangerously close to my pussy, and in truth, I'd been wet since the moment she mentioned it. The sparks were there, flying, of course, and that made everything even better for me as well.

For a little bit, she simply touched and grazed over the edge of my pussy, causing me to let out a small cry of need, the ache of desire, and everything that seemed to fall through, making me excited for this. She soon moved her hands towards my clit, touching the very tip of it, rubbing there, and as she did so, I cried out, rubbing myself against her fingers.

"Look at you, slowly losing all semblance of control," she said.

"Yes," I said.

I'd be lying if I said I didn't want this, though. She knew just how to touch me, to make me feel amazing, and that, of course, made everything all the better as well. It was like I was experiencing the best thing ever, and she knew exactly how to touch me, to tease me, and to make me feel good.

After a little bit, she soon moved her fingers away, and soon, she pulled off my panties, revealing my shaven, aching pussy. I was dripping, the need increasing, and as she explored my insides, I let out a guttural sound.

"Needy already?"

"Yes," I muttered, still trying to keep myself together throughout all of this.

She let out a small chuckle, moving her hands there, touching the very edge of my clit, moving her fingers about, making me shiver with delight and cry out with pleasure. She soon dipped a finger against my entrance, and I tensed.

"First time?" she asked.

"Yes," I breathed out. I hoped that it wouldn't be too weird for her if she heard that. But instead, she chuckled, a cute little sound that echoed through the room.

"How cute. It's been such a long time since I've had a first, but I'm excited for this," she said. She moved a finger towards my entrance, sliding it in. At first, it felt a little bit full, but as she moved her digit around, I let out a small cry, holding onto her as she continued to move and tease. She pushed a second digit into the, making me shiver with delight, surprised by just...how good this felt.

She knew exactly how to turn me on, her dominating fingers making me become a puddle of goo in front of her. There was something just so nice about this, so damn thrilling, and I wanted her so damn badly.

She moved her fingers in and out, an undulating feeling, and as she did this, she pushed her tongue outwards, touching the very tip of my clit, flicking her tongue there, resting it, and moving it around. To the point where I suddenly felt a rush of pleasure as I felt the teasing grow even more so.

"Holy fuck," I said out loud, arching my back and moaning with delight as she continued the actions against me. Everything about this was such a damn turn-on that I didn't know what else I could do besides take this and roll with it.

She continued the motions for a bit, watching my eyes widen and my hips thrust upwards. She then hit against a spot that made me scream out, suddenly surprised by how turned on I felt, and then I felt my orgasm just hit me square in the face.

It was different than it was with myself. This felt far more powerful like she was a pro at this kind of thing. She continued to jerk her fingers, teasing them, and then moving away, looking at me with a smile.

"There you are. Good girl," she said.

I relished in those words, surprised by how much I desired this. She seemed to know exactly how to make me feel good and turned on by the sensation of this. She then moved her hands towards my clit, rubbing it once more and looking me in the eyes.

I was curious, but then she spoke.

"How about we try to 69?" she offered.

I mean, that could work...right? I'd never tried this before, so I was a bit nervous, but I certainly wasn't going to be against it in the least. I suddenly felt her body get over me, her wet, pink pussy there for me to see.

I tried to do like she did, shoving my tongue into there, exploring and teasing her body. As she did that, she spread me apart, her tongue diving in, exploring me.

I let out a muffled scream, surprised by this but more shocked at the sounds that I made her feel. She seemed to be enjoying this too, and I could tell from the little cries and such alone that she was getting into this. But then she pushed her tongue in deeper, pressing against that one spot, and when she did, I suddenly felt like time had stopped, and I tensed up.

I didn't want to cum yet. I wanted to make her feel amazing, and I wanted to see her lose control, creating a whole different person. But I knew that she wouldn't give in. I was so close, and with every single touch, every single movement of her fingers, the way she pushed her tongue and fingers into me was more than enough. I was drunk off the feeling of pleasure, completely amazed by how amazing this was, and then, shortly after, everything went white.

I cried out, arching my back as I came once more. She then let out a small moan, moving herself off of me. I wanted to bring her to orgasm, but then, she looked at me, a needy smile on her face.

"How are you holding up?" she asked me.

"Pretty...good actually," I told her.

"Very good. I guess I can ask if you want more. I have a special toy that I'm sure you'd love," she offered to me.
I realized what she meant by that. She wanted to top me, and she knew how to use a strap. I shivered, nodding.

"Please," I said.

It was weird to desire a woman so much. In the past, I had little crushes and the like, but they never amounted to...wanting someone so damn badly. She then gave me a small little grin, touching my hips, rubbing them there.

"I promise I'll be nice and slow. I can show you what real pleasure is," she said.

The way the words came off of her mouth made me suddenly feel heady. I wanted her to just take me and make me feel things that I otherwise wouldn't get to feel. She was so experienced, and I felt like this was one of the best moments of my life.

I quickly nodded, watching as she moved towards the drawer that was there. She got a strapon out, but it was double-ended. She grabbed some lube, shoving it into herself slowly, letting out a small gasp. When she was done, she spread me apart, looking me in the eyes.

"Everything okay?" she asked me.

I nodded, feeling her eyes glaze over my body, the need in her eyes obvious.

"Yes," I told her.
She beamed, sliding herself slowly into me.

This was different from just fingers, and when she fully breached me, I let out a small, guttural sound. She looked at me with slight concern on her face.

"I'm not hurting you, right?" she asked.

"No, it's just...different. That's all," I told her.

I'd be lying if I said this was a familiar sensation. It was not, but that didn't mean I disliked it in the least. Instead, I enjoyed the hell out of it. The fullness of my pussy with how she looked at me, I could just imagine this moment forever in my mind, and I'd love and cherish it forever.

There was always something truly exciting about this and something that I liked. She slowly began to move her hips a little bit into me, and as she did that, she looked me in the eyes, a smile on her face.

"Are you good?" she asked me.

I nodded, unable to perform words or sounds other than that of lust, desire, and pleasure. It was so obvious that she was enjoying this too, and of course, I was completely enamored by everything that she did to me that it was only a matter of time before she took this further.

And further, she did. She grabbed my legs, pulling them to her shoulders, bending them down. She then moved deep within once more, and then, shortly afterwards I let out a small cry, holding onto her as she pounded into me. She continued this, causing my eyes to widen in shock and surprise, and it was then when, after a few more thrusts, I felt something against my clit.

It was her finger, and I was utterly amazed by how good this was. But then, moments later, I moved my hands upwards, touching her clit too, rubbing it at the same time. She then looked at me with slight surprise, and I smiled.

"I want to make you feel good, too, mistress," I said.

And that was that. She pushed her finger into a certain position, hitting that one part inside of me, and as she did that, I rubbed her again too.

After a few more moments, the two of us looked into one another's eyes, crying out each other's names as we sat there, embracing one another as we felt the high of our orgasms and then slowly coming down, of course, of everything else.

I felt amazing after all of that, and when I came down from that high, I noticed that Miss Layla had pulled out, putting the toy away, and laying down on the bed next to me.

What do you do at this point? Do you...talk about it? I'm not really that good with this kind of thing, but when I looked into her eyes, I saw a slight smile.

"You did well," she said.

"Thank you. That was...amazing," I said. That really was the best way to describe it. I felt like I just got a chance to experience something novel, something amazing, and I loved every goddamn minute of it.

But what do you do next? What now? I kind of was curious. I looked at her, and she took a deep breath.

"You know, there's a lot that we can say here, and a lot of things that well...we could discuss, but I guess the best thing to say is that I had a wonderful time. And I knew that you wanted this for a little while. So I'm glad that I can make you feel good," she said.

I flushed crimson, nodding.

"Thank you. The same to you," I told her.

"With that being said, we have to keep this under wraps. I don't want anyone to find out about this. Not even those who are close to me. If the press discovered this...it wouldn't be good," she said.

That's right. Miss Layla was one of the strongest businesswomen in the world. If people found out about this, it would be a bit of a scandal, to say the least.

"Yeah, I get that," I told her.

"Anyway, I want to see you again Freya. You're such a good maid, and I wouldn't mind if you...stuck around a little bit. I enjoyed this, and I know that you seemed to like this too," she purred in my ear.
"Yeah, I did," I said.

I didn't know if this meant that she was going to hook up with me or not, but I liked the way that this sounded. She leaned in, giving me a kiss on the lips, and I kissed her back, enjoying this.

There was something special about kissing a woman like this, and there was something I so desperately enjoyed.

She then pulled away, looking into my eyes.

"Don't worry, you'll also be getting a nice little bonus from me for this," she said to me.
I flushed. A bonus sounded heavenly.

"Thank you," I said.

"You're very welcome. I'm really excited for you," she said to me.

I felt happy about this. I mean, there was something about the way that Miss Layla treated me that told me I was making the right decision, especially involving her. It was rare for me to feel this good about something, but knowing that I gave such a beautiful woman my virginity and also getting to experience a whole new world with her was just....I couldn't get enough of this.
I did put my clothes back on, but as I was about to leave, I felt her hand against my backside, cupping my ass. She touched me there, and I shivered.

"I can't wait to have you again," she purred.

"I can't wait too, Miss Layla," I said.

And I meant that. I didn't want to lose this chance. I walked on out of there, knowing that this sealed my fate and the future that I'd get to have.

I was excited, to say the least. I didn't know why, but the fact that she could make me feel these things was such a damn thrill. I was excited for more, excited to experience all of this, and I knew that she liked this too.

What did this mean for me, though? I honestly didn't know, but I was just about ready to relax and wait to see what the future has in store for me, both with this job and, of course, with Miss Layla too, and the future she wanted to bring to us as well. I figured it was the start of something new, something amazing, and I was already excited for what it brought.

College Witches

Orgies, Lesbian

I never believed in the paranormal.

At least…that's what I told myself.

I'd always say that it was some bullshit, some crap used to lure stupid women in. That is, until I met Aya.

Aya was…something else, that's for sure.

It all started when we were in class together. The professor told me that we'd be working on a group project. Naturally, I expected it to be some sort of stupid project that we'd have to word ourselves to work together.

But Aya was different. We clicked right away.

Almost too well if I do say so myself. She was super chill, very cute, and honestly….I couldn't get enough of her. At first, it was just a little bit of studying, and some playful flirting. But I always got the feeling that there was much more there, and that she wanted to say something else, but she never did.

That is until about a month after we started the project.

We went over to her dorm for the first time. She seemed nervous, but when I walked in, seeing all of the different spell books and interesting content in there, I was floored.

"Wow, this is all yours?" I asked her.

She nodded.

"Yeah, I'm curious about the occult. I've started talking to other girls who aren't in it, and I figured that maybe…it could be good for both of us," she offered.

She did say that before but I also felt like…it may not be the right thing to do.

"What do you do in those meetings? If you don't mind me asking," I said to her.

She turned to me, a small smile on her face.

"If you want, I can show you," she said.

Wait, she was getting me in the occult? I don't know if this was a good idea or a terrible one, but Aya was hot, and she was kind of weird, so maybe things would work out. She told me that the next meeting of course would be during the full moon.

I probably should've been more careful. I mean, isn't this how girls get sacrificed to Satan or other crap, was it? Maybe, I'm not totally sure. But I followed Aya over to a small, abandoned building that was on the edge of town. When we got there, she said some words, and with a flash, the door opened.

"Come on in," she told me.

I didn't know why, but the idea of this felt a bit nerve-wracking so to speak. I felt a bit scared, and I had no clue what would happen next. I walked on in, and there was a coven of four other girls.

"Hello ladies," she said.

"Hello Aya," the girl on the right said.

"That's Rachel. The one next to her is Elaine. The bigger girl is Shana, and the other one is Monica," she said.

I waved to all of them, and they all scoured me over, like they were looking for something.

"So you're the newbie, aren't you," she said.

"Yeah. This is...interesting," I said.

"You'll have fun," Rachel said.

I noticed Shana looking me over the longest, and Monica giving me a wry smile. Just what the hell were these ladies up to?

I had no clue, and I could feel the slight nervousness that flooded through my body as I thought about this. There was something about this which felt so damn off-putting, that I couldn't really pinpoint why I feel this way.

But, it's not like there was much that I could do. I plopped down at the chair that was empty next to Aya.

They began by saying some chants. They closed their eyes and held their hands out, which I followed suit with. For some reason though, I couldn't shake the fact that something about this was wrong.

"Alright, so we've said the spell for good luck. I guess the next order of business is the new recruit," Aya said.

The girl's eyes looked at my own. I then noticed Elaine smile.

"Alright, so do you know what goes...into this?" she asked me.

I shook my head.

"No." I said. " I just spent time with Aya, and she showed me things. She said this would be fun, so I decided to join in trusting her."

I didn't know why, but there was something about this which felt a bit off to say the least. Maybe it was my own personal worries about what may happen next, but then, I saw Monica smile.

"I guess you haven't been told of the initiation rite. Of course Aya would leave that out," Monica said.

"Hey, it was a lapse of judgement. Get off my fucking back," she said.

"What do you mean by...rite?" I asked.

I figured I'd at least ask. That way I kind of knew what the hell I was getting into.

They looked at me, laughing slightly. I was so confused, but then, I heard Aya speak.

"The initiation rites involve...an orgy with the other witches," she said.

An...orgy? Like all of us? I looked at her, my eyes wide with shock and surprise.

"You're not fucking around are you?" I asked her.

"I'm not. That's usually the rites that we use here. But if you don't want to do it we can—

"No....I want to," I said.

It wasn't just because of my crush on Aya, but also because well...everyone else was insanely attractive.

I was gay, and honestly...being taken by any of these women would be a treat for me, which made me flush just thinking about it. I didn't know why, but I liked the idea behind it.
"Are you sure?" Aya asked.

I nodded.

"Yeah, I'll do it," I told her.

She looked at me, smiling as she spoke.

"Good. Then get on the table. I'll start the rite," she said.

I looked at her, wondering what she was about to do, but then she pushed me onto the table, climbing up on top. We looked at one another, my face red as a tomato.

I'd be lying if I said I didn't have a crush on Aya. She was small, pretty, and she had a domineering energy right about now. I liked the idea behind it, even though I had no clue what this would mean for me. But then, moments later her mouth was on mine, kissing me passionately.

She was a forceful kisser, but I liked that about her. While she kissed me, I felt a pair of hands move towards my shirt, tugging it off. I gasped as it was pulled over my head, only for me to realize it was Elaine who was smiling as she did this.

She enjoyed the tease, and Rachel of course was right behind her, pulling off my bra with one motion.

I gasped as I realized just how quickly all of these women got me undressed. I was a bit impressed if I wasn't so damn turned on as I looked at them. Aya continued to seal my lips with a kiss, staying like this for what felt like forever. I enjoyed the touch, the tease, everything about this, and I ached for her. I wanted her so badly, and I knew that she enjoyed this too. Her hands moved around my body as each pair of the other hands were touching her. As she did this, she pulled back, saying something in Latin.

I had no fucking clue what she was talking about, but then her hands moved downwards, massaging my breasts. This felt different from a normal, massaging touch. The action felt almost exact, and I liked the way that this felt. It was...strange to say the least, but it was something that I relished in, enjoying, and desired from her. She seemed to like this too, judging from the small motions of her hips against me.

I felt the other hands against my body, realizing that all of the other women were against me, touching my body, exploring me. Monica was one of the handsier ones, touching me closer and closer towards my crotch. But Aya stopped, looking at them.

"Let me be first. Then you guys can," she said.

I flushed, wondering what exactly she meant by that. I wanted to ask, but she sealed my lips with a kiss before I could say much more.

She took my nipple in her mouth, lightly pressing and touching there, looking into my eyes as she did this. I shivered, moaning out loud, letting out a series of small cries as she continued to tease me there. Every single touch was enough to drive me mad, and I was slowly losing all semblance of control, enjoying the touch of her body, and the way she felt as I looked at her.

For a long time, she continued this, until she moved downwards, pressing her hands against my pussy. I shivered as I felt the hand against my heat, touching me, teasing me, playing with me as I looked into her eyes.

"Fuck," I said out loud.

"You good there?"

I didn't know what to say. Of course I felt good. But the fact that she seemed to know exactly where to touch me, where to make me feel good, and just how to make me lose control was hard to beat, that's for sure.

"I'm...amazing really. Just struggling to put words together," I said to her.

"Then don't worry about putting those damn words together, and just...enjoy the moment," she said.

The way she uttered those words was almost a demand, but I liked it a lot. There was a thrill that came from a woman telling me what to do.

She moved her hands downwards, between my legs, rubbing me through my pants. I let out a small moan, excitement flooding through my body as she continued to move her hands there, touching slightly.

I cried out, and soon I felt her hands move towards my pants, hooking onto them and pulling them downwards. I shivered, feeling the cold air hit there, causing me to cry out slightly. But then, before I knew it, she tossed off my pants, hiked up my legs, and I felt a tongue slither down between my legs.

I cried out, clinging to her. Her explorative tongue was so amazing, and I felt my toes curl together as I felt her tongue move towards my clit, teasing there. She explored, using her lips, mouth and hands to make me lose control. I cried out, holding onto her as she continued the onslaught of attention to me down there, making my head spin, and my body practically lose control.

I was losing my mind, excitement and need growing within me. I ached for her, and I knew that she enjoyed this as much as I did. Everything about this was just...it was so damn good, and I wanted her to continue.

She then pushed her tongue in, pressing against there, and then, moments later, I felt my body tense up, and I cried out, arching my back as I felt my orgasm hit me. I shivered, crying out with pleasure. But then, I felt something against my lips.
It was Rachel's ass, and her pussy was right there, waiting for me to take.

"Go ahead. We need to keep you quiet. Don't want you getting us in trouble and all," she said.

Fuck that's true. I knew that if I was too loud, I'd be in deep shit. I moved my tongue upwards, exploring her. The whimpering sound that she made was delightful.

I felt a hand move between my legs, teasing me there. I muffled my moans into her, holding onto her as she rides my face. I cried out between her legs, feeling the fingers touch and tease me, dragging against my folds.

I looked to see who it was, but I didn't think it was Aya. I didn't necessarily care though, because Rachel was right here, and I wanted to explore her.

She was the smallest of the group, and her pussy was tight. I pushed my tongue around, exploring every nook and cranny of her, hearing the delicious moans that came out of her as I was deep inside of her. I continued to move my lips around, exploring every part of her that I could, sliding my tongue in between her, into her, and doing what Aya did to me.

Meanwhile, the fingers that were on the outside, grazing against my clit and teasing my outer folds suddenly moved inwards. But it didn't hurt, nor was it too forceful.

Instead it felt…nice. It was relaxing to be taken like this, and I liked the feeling of this. The hand continued to lightly push into me, and I felt the thumb move against my clit.

As she did that, I started to cry out, but then Rachel's pussy was in my face.

"Keep quiet. You need to be careful," she said.

I knew I needed to be quieter, but that shit was hard. I wanted to just scream out how good this felt, but maybe that was the thrill of this. The fact that I couldn't be too loud, and that she would make me feel this way. I continued to tease and play with her pussy, pressing my tongue in, moving upwards, watching the sight in front of me.

Apparently I hit a spot, because as soon as I did that, I felt her suddenly tense up, crying out loud, holding onto me, but then her lips were silenced with a kiss. Then there was a finger that arched upwards, hitting my g spot, and as it did, I suddenly let out a shuddering moan, completely immersed in her pussy as I felt my second orgasm of the night. I was amazed, and when the finger pulled out, I moved my head around to see who it was.

It was Shana. She looked at me with a smile on her face.

"Not bad. Looks like Aya found a fun one," she said.

"Y-yeah," I said to her.

"Anyway, I have a date with a cutie," she said.

Rachel looked at her, and soon, the two of them were in the corner, making out. I laid there, completely amazed at how good I felt, when suddenly, I saw Monica there. She looked me over, licking her lips.

"You're looking delightful there," she purred.

"Really now?" I said to her with a laugh.

She came closer, holding her hands to the sides of my body, touching it slightly. I cried out, shivering as I felt her hands graze against my body, touching, teasing, and moving her longer fingernails against the side. I looked over at Shana and Rachel. Shana's hands were between Rachel's legs, touching and pressing into Rachel's tight pussy. Well maybe Rachel could take a bit more than I thought. I looked at Monica, who licked her lips.

"It's so hot watching those two get it on. It's been a while since we've done this. I know that Aya gets to take your virginity in the coven, but god it's so hard to resist. Especially with how pretty you are," she said.

My…virginity? But I wasn't a virgin. Hell I hadn't been for a long time.

She then shook her head.

"Don't matter if you are a virgin or not. With the coven…the leader takes the other woman," she said.

I was surprised by that, but it kind of made sense.
"I see."

"But…that doesn't mean I don't get to have a little bit of fun with you," she said.

She then slid herself against me, our pussies touching. She scissored herself so that our legs were together, and I simply sat there, taking all of the pleasure that I felt.

This was a first for me. I felt a little embarrassed by this, but she looked me in the eyes, shaking her head.

"Don't worry about it. I'm sure you'll be fine. And of course, Elaine can also tease you a bit too," she said.

Elaine moved her body so that the front of her pussy was right there in my face. I shivered, moving my tongue outwards, teasing her clit. But then she spread herself apart, rubbing herself there in front of me.

"Fuck you're so cute. I'm going to have a taste of you after Monica is done," she said.

I tried to reach forward, to tease her, but she simply wanted to give me a show, while Monica of course, rubbed our bodies together, both of us moaning with shock and amazement.

I didn't expect this to feel so good, but I was suddenly enveloped in pleasure, enjoying the feeling of this. I clung to Elaine, and as Monica danced her body on mine, she started rubbing herself while moving her fingers towards my clit, rubbing it too.

There was something different about the way that she touched me. She used her nail slightly, which offered a more penetrating feeling, like it was hitting me deep within my soul. I clung to her, holding her there as she started to move herself, our bodies enjoying the touch of one another, both of us excited and ready for more.

She looked me in the eyes, seeing the way I was turned on, and then, she moved herself forward, pressing against there, rubbing our clits together. As she did that, I held onto Elaine's thighs, crying out loud as I felt another orgasm.

But then Elaine silenced my sounds with a kiss, and I sat there making out with her as Monica finished, pulling away. I could see the glistening trail between the two of us, enjoying the feeling of our bodies together, both of us enjoying each other's touch.

Then, Elaine moved herself so that her fingers were right up against me. She pushed three in, dipping her tongue there, and I felt her curl them upwards, almost methodically touching me.
"Holy—"

"That's Elaine for you. She knows exactly where to make you feel good," I heard Monica say.

I didn't expect this. Her touches were on the ball, hitting every single part of me, and when she did that, I couldn't help but moan, excitement growing within me as I started to hold onto her, crying out loud and enjoying the feeling of this. I continued to move my hips, enjoying the touch, ravaging my own body, the hype and feeling of this becoming such a turn on that I didn't know how to stop.

After a few more thrusts, she angled her fingers upwards, her thumb pressing against my clit, almost pushing it in. I formed fists with my hands, feeling them ball together as I arched my back, moaning out loud as I felt the pleasure of my body as she took it and used it completely.

I ached for her, enjoying the sensation, the touch, and the feeling. But then she did it again, and I suddenly let out a guttural sound, holding back the screams that I felt.

This was just...amazing really, and I felt something shoot out as soon as I felt her touch me right then and there. She moved back, licking her dainty fingers, looking me in the eyes.

"You taste amazing," she said.

"Thanks," I said.

I felt completely spent, but I knew that it wasn't over yet. Not until the leader took me.

I looked over at Aya, who was naked now, her hand against her body, jerking off to the sight of me cumming. I looked over, and noticed that the other girls in this coven were already making out with one another. I was so hot and bothered, but also so spent, that it was a combination of both of these feelings that made me feel amazing.

Aya walked over, rubbing her clit against mine, and I let out a small cry. But before it could go anywhere, she looked at me.

"Are you ready for this?" she said.

She meant of course, the culmination of this. The sounds of moans and sex were what filled the room. I didn't expect for this to all happen, but I wasn't going to complain about it, that's for sure.

"You sure?" I asked her.

"It's not my call hun. It's yours," she insisted.

Of course it was my call. I felt a bit embarrassed, but I knew deep down that this was indeed what I wanted.

I simply nodded.

"Yes. I want this," I insisted. I knew what I wanted.

Her lips curled into that of a smile, giving me a small kiss.

"I knew you were the right one when I started talking to you in the lab that day. I just thought you were cute, but I didn't expect this much fun," she said.

I flushed, realizing she enjoyed this as much as I did. I quickly nodded, excited about what may happen next, and just what she had in store for me. There was so much excitement, so much feeling, that I knew that she was making this fun for me as well.

I didn't expect this much as well, but there was something exciting, almost thrilling, about being taken like this, used in this fashion, and enjoyed by all of these beautiful women.

I couldn't get enough.

I watched as they moved their bodies near my own, looking at me as one of them gave Aya a double sided strap on dildo. She fastened it onto her body, while sliding one side inside herself, letting out a small cry herself.

The other 2 women were in the throes of sex, and I could feel the heat rising in this place.

Maybe we were more hidden away than I thought.

Aya's hands dragged against my body, sliding downwards, massaging my hip bones, before she looked me in the eyes.

"You're beautiful. I can't wait to show you...true pleasure," she purred into my ear.
"Ahh, yes," I told her.

I wanted this as much as she did, and there was something exciting about this, something fun and extremely thrilling. She then moved her body so that she was right up against my entrance, sliding the other side of the dildo inside of me.

I grimaced slightly, surprised by how...full I felt as she did this. She pushed all the way in, looking me in the eyes as she slid herself further and further inside of me.

"There we go. Just relax," she cooed into my ear.

It was hard to truly relax, but I listened to her, completely immersed and mesmerized by the way she seemed to have complete, utter control over my body. I knew that she would take care of me, and she would make me feel good.

She soon slid herself fully into my opening, opening me up and holding me there. She then moved her body slightly, and while she filled me up completely, I let out a guttural sound of pleasure.

"You good?" she asked.

"Yea. Amazing," I said.

The way she had command over my body, combined with the sounds of the women in the background, it was all just...utterly amazing. I felt like I was under her spell, her control, and I ached for her.
She then started to move her hips, pressing in and out, in and out, and I relished in the feeling of this, enjoying the sensations that I felt as she leaned forward, grasping my breasts, teasing them from between her fingertips. I shivered, holding onto her as she continued this onslaught

against my body. She was moaning with me, feeling the pleasure she was giving herself at the same time.

I knew that she was good, but I didn't expect this good. But the way she touched me was enough to drive me crazy. I started holding onto her as she arched my body, keeping it there as she pushed herself deeper and deeper into me, keeping me in place while she was grinding herself out on the other end of the dildo that had filled her up.

"There we go. Good girl," she cooed into my ear.

She pulled my knees upwards, bringing them over her shoulders, keeping them there as she thrusted deep inside me. I sat there, taking this, enjoying the sensation of this, enjoying the fact that she was also receiving pleasure from all of this, feeling completely immersed in the experience, the pleasure of it all, and the absolute fun that came out of this.

After a few more thrusts, she reached forward, rubbing me. I wanted to touch her as well, to make her feel good in other ways, but she kept my hands downwards, holding me there.

"Yes, that's good. You're getting close aren't you?" she said.

I nodded, completely shocked and surprised by this.

"Yes," I said to her, completely shocked with need and desire. I was at my limit, and she was too.

But before she finished, she looked at me, saying a few words. I had no idea what they were, but I presume it was in Latin. She then grabbed me, angling her body so that she was right up against the very edge of me, and then pushed there, hitting that sweet spot inside of me.

I cried out, shivering with delight as I came hard, holding onto her as I felt the end, the pleasure, and the orgasm that I had just completely overtaken me while feeling her being overtaken by her own orgasm. Her body tensed up with mine and we both exploded together. The sensation was like shocking waves that we were both experiencing at the same time and it felt like they had brought us closer than ever before. It felt like a true initiation into something amazing. Something I couldn't quite put words to.

It was heavenly, the pleasure was not just all mine, which made it all so much better and it was then when, after a few more thrusts, she pulled out, giving me a kiss on the lips. I enjoyed the feeling of this, and the surprise that I felt definitely was driving me crazy.

She then sat back, looking at me with a small smile on her face. I had a feeling this had something to do of course, with what just transpired.
"You good there?" she asked.

"Amazing," I breathed out, still unable to really process everything.

She smiled.

"Good. It seems like everyone else is good too," I said.

The smell of sex, and the desires of all of these women permeated through the room. I looked at her, seeing the smile on her face as I tried to process everything that happened.

"So what does this mean?" I asked her.

"It means what you want it to mean my dear. We can....invite you to our coven fully, if that's what you want. I'm sure it would be quite the experience for everyone," she said.

"Do you do this a lot?" I asked her.

"Sometimes every full moon. It depends," she said.

I didn't know why, but there was something exciting about this, and I liked the prospect of this.

I started to pause, thinking about it all, when I nodded.

"Yeah, I want to be a part of this," I said.

"Good. And I like your attitude my dear," she said.

I flushed, but then nodded.

"Thank you. I'm excited to...to make this something special for all of us," I told her.

"Yeah, it is special, and I'm sure that it's an enjoyable experience for everyone," she purred in my ear.

I'd be lying if I said this wasn't. The fact that she made me feel this way and knew how to turn me the fuck on, and was just...perfect really, it was all so surreal, and I couldn't help but enjoy this.

"So what's next?" I asked her.

"Well, we can finish up the meeting now, but if you want...we can go get some food," she offered.

Was this a date? I had a feeling this had the vibe of a date, I just wasn't sure.

"You sure about that? Like a date?" I asked her.

Her lips curled into that of a smile.

"Of course. Like a date hun," she told me.
I beamed. I couldn't believe it! She was really asking me out like this. There was something special about this, and it definitely was something that I was happy about. I was just ecstatic to know that I could experience something this good, this much pleasure, and this much excitement from her.

"Anyway, I figure it's time for us to head back, we have to get some studying done, don't we?" she said.

"Yeah, let's get some food and then do that," I said.

The women all came back together, clothed this time, and they started to look at me. They started to say some words, and I joined in, even though I didn't really get what they were saying. All I knew was that it was in Latin, and I figured they weren't necessarily bad.

"What were you guys saying back there?" I asked her.

I didn't know what she could possibly be saying, but then she spoke.

"We were saying 'we thank you for this new addition to our coven, and we hope for a lot of moments together like this one, and a pleasurable experience for all'" she explained.

I blushed, realizing that I meant so much to them.

"You all mean this, right?" I said to her.

"Yeah, I'm really glad that we can have you here with us. It's an exciting feeling, and something that I can't help but love," she told me.
That was nice to hear. It was a pleasure to behold too. The sounds of sex, of pleasure, of excitement which came out of this....it was just amazing.

"I'm glad I can experience all of this with you," I told her.

"Well, you'll be experiencing a whole lot more too down the line," she told me.

I shivered, nodding.

"Yeah, I hope that I can," I told her.

She grabbed my hand, pulling me in, kissing me passionately.

"Now, let's go get some dinner together. I'm starving," she said. I quickly nodded, following suit, not letting go of her arm in the least., I loved being able to hold her hand.

And that's just how it all happened. I never really believed in witches or any of that, but I started to wonder if maybe this was a sign that something bigger was about to come for me. I was excited for whatever it was. It was new and exhilarating. And regardless, I would never forget the night I shared with these women, the orgy we had, and the fun that came out of this, and the excitement and need that I got to experience, not just with Aya, but with the other girls too, who taught me a whole new world of pleasure and seduction that I never experienced before.

Elena the Dom

A Femdom, Roleplay, 69 Story

Chapter 1

"Are you fucking shitting me?" I asked myself as I read the contents of the bill.
There was no way this was true. I can't believe I had a bill of this size. I clutched the paper, my red fingernails resting on it.

Another expensive electric bill. Well that, along with the student loan debts were only making things way worse. I looked at the options on how to pay this.

I could do it now and bite the bullet. However, by doing that, it meant that I'd be screwed on rent and god knows what else.

The other option was I could defer it. Again. They'd probably come after me this go around. I wondered what the best option would be here. Or even what I should do.

"Come on, think," I muttered to myself.

I needed something, anything to get out of this fucking rut. But that's easier said than done, especially when you're someone who can't even have a normal fucking paycheck. I was sick of never having enough money, always having to make sure that I could get to work and back, sacrificing food for all of this bullshit.

I was just so damn...sick of it you know?

There was a lot that was sitting in the back of my own head, a lot of problems that were only getting worse and worse for me. Should I just take the bullet for another month? Or should I look for another option.

Then, I remembered what Sadie said.

"You should join me at the dungeon. You can help Dom some of these guys. They 're such suckers, and you'll love it."

I thought about that offer. I mean, would domming a bunch of random ass dudes be worth it. I've never done it before. A lot of people always saw me as that sweet, little woman who could hold her ground of course. But being a dom? That sounded like so much work.

But maybe, that's the type of work I was looking for. Being a dom would mean of course that I'd get to have control over men, tease them, and have my way with them too. But I didn't know what guys would want.

How mean could I be? I tried to do a bit of research on this, scouring the internet and looking for something, anything that could give me more information on how to do this. But all that came up were trashy articles talking about shit that I already knew.

I wanted the real answers, and I wanted to find out about this too.

I looked at the options. It was kind of early, that's for sure, but I definitely wanted to see what was up.

I got my shit together, heading out to the dungeon, and I figured this could be something fun to do.

There was also the fact that it could help me get my mind of things. Maybe it was for me. Maybe it would be the worst thing that I'd get to do. But who knows, maybe things would work itself out.

I put on a pair of black heels, a short black skirt, and a black shirt that cut off at my midriff. I put my black hair in an updo, coating my face in makeup to make me look more seductive. I thought I looked hot at least.

I guess there's a first for everything, right?

I walked over to the car, getting to the club, enjoying the feeling of the night, the thrill of this, and the excitement that flowed through me.

When I got there, I saw Sadie at the entrance, looking around. When we locked eyes, her blue ones lit up.

"Yo! You're here," she said, surprise obvious in her voice.

"I told you I would come out eventually. And well...I need the help," I told her.

"What do you mean?"

"I have another one of those bills," I told her.

"Oh shit, I'm sorry Elena. Anything I can do to help?" she asked.

"Well, I think I just...need to have some fun tonight," I told her.

"There you go. It's not that hard. Plus, I'm guessing Christina is at her dad's?" she asked.

"Yah she's with him," I said.

And thank god she was. I did like Christina, but she definitely made things a lot harder. But maybe I can provide a better life for her down the road. She was my kid, and while she was of school age, it really didn't make things any easier for the both of us.

"Anyway, you want me to hook you up with someone tonight?" she asked.

I flushed, wondering what she meant by that.

"What do you mean?"

"I have a couple of regulars I haven't been able to say. They're cool with me having them go with other people, and I told them I had a really great one for them. Maybe you can show them a good time," she purred.

I couldn't believe this.

"How much?" I asked. I wasn't going to do this shit for free.

"Well, let me show you the going rate for what one of the guys was willing to pay," she offered.

She flipped through the little pocketbook that she had, showing me the numbers that were there.

I almost shat myself at the numbers. For one night, 500 bucks. That could get me out of a jam and then some. I couldn't believe this, and for a second, I didn't know what to say.

"You're...you're serious?" I said to her.

"This is what they normally pay, yeah. It's why I'm a stay-at-home mom you know. I do this to help pay for my daughter. And they know that I have kids. They love it," Sadie said.

So, it's okay to do this while having a kid. I'd never really gotten a chance to explore the dominating side of me. When I was married to Dave, he was anything but submissive. He always wanted to dominate, even when I tried to take control.

But now, I get to explore something more.

"You...sure about this one?" I asked her.

"What do you mean?' of course I'm sure," she said.

I started to put it all together, letting all of this seep on in. They would pay me this much.

"By the way, here's what they kind of like. Perhaps you could help them experience this," she said.

She gave me another piece of paper, with a couple of notes written down next to the client's name, who was called Brayden.

Feet, ball busting, nurses. I just need someone to dominate me while also caring for me.

I thought this guy was some sort of weirdo. Just reading the laundry list of fetishes made me nervous. I turned to her, and she smiled.

"Don't you worry. I'm sure this will be fine. If you do a good job, there's a lot more where that came from," she pointed out.

A lot more than this? Jesus, what kind of clients did she have?

I quickly nodded, heading on inside. I saw a series of costumes out, picking up the nurse uniform and tossing it on, keeping the black leather panties and heels. I knew it was door number two, so I went down there, knocking on the door.

"Come in mistress," the man said. His voice was hesitant, like he was scared of me coming in.

"I'm coming in no matter what," I said to him.

I opened the door, seeing him sitting there. He was in a pair of black boxer shorts, his hands already up on the nightstand, clinging to some cuffs. They were attached to the bed.

For the first time in a long time, I felt nervous. I'd never done something like this before. In fact, I had no idea what would come out of this.

"You're Brayden, aren't you?" I said.

"Yes. And what should I call you?"

I hesitated, almost saying my real name, when I shook my head.

"Mistress is fine. And you better not call me anything else. Or else—"

I grabbed my foot, putting it right up against his cock.

"I'll crush your fucking balls underneath my heels," I said to him. Hearing those words out of me felt so damn foreign, like I was doing something wrong. But then, I heard the moan as I dug into there slightly.

"O-okay mistress. I believe you will," he said.

"Good. So today you asked for a nurse, right?" I said to him.

"Yes, I need someone to take care of me. I'm tired of taking care of others and—"

I grabbed the thermometer, shoving it into his mouth hard. He shut up, and I checked it.

"Good, now that'll keep your mouth shut. You want this nurse to do her job, right? And she will, as long as you stay quiet, and you follow my instructions. I'll give you everything that you need to get nice and healthy," I purred.

He nodded, his eyes widening. For the first time in a while, I felt strong. I felt confident, and when I checked the temperature, I pulled it out.

"Looks healthy. But you said you had some pain. Where was it?" I asked him.

"My stomach and—"

I pushed my heel into his stomach, causing him to moan and cry out in pain.

"Ahh!" he said.

"I can help with that stomach pain. How about this?" I said, lightly moving about. I continued to press down there, watching his eyes widen, and a moan escape him.

I continued to touch, to tease him with my shoe, and I didn't expect him to enjoy this so much.

"So, I heard you like feet, right? Maybe you can take care of this mistress's feet. Since of course you're still a bit sick, aren't you? I said to him.

"Y-yes mistress," he said.

I dug the heel right into there and he extended his tongue, licking the tips of the shoe, then over to the heel.

I then pulled the heel off, and he began to service my toes, licking, teasing, and touching them. It was so weird, because I was never one to enjoy feet, but seeing this man become so enamored in this was fun.

But I wasn't going to let him feel satisfaction. In fact, I wanted to see him squirm a bit more. I looked at the obvious erection in his pants, standing at attention and waiting for me. I smiled as I enjoyed this man's reaction.

"Look at your pathetic cock, already getting hard for me. I see how it is," I said, stepping on his cock. He let out a low groan as I continued this. But then, I pulled away. I looked into his eyes, smiling.

"Now...what is it that you need?" he said.

"I need...medicine. I need your medicine," he said.

"Ohhh really now? You're going to need to beg for it," I told him.

I stepped down on him once again, hearing him groan in slight agony and pleasure, and then spoke.

"Please, give this to me now!" he said.

I laughed, watching his pathetic body squirm in response. I pulled back, looking into his eyes.

"Well now, maybe I could give you the medicine that you desire...for a price," I told him.

"Please, anything mistress," he said.

I looked at him, smiling in contentment.

"Turn around. Turn on the bed," I said to him.

He quickly did so, his ass in the air. He did have a nice butt, very spankable, and I saw the crop that was there.

I grabbed the crop, rubbing it against the tip of his backside. He let out a small moan, and I smiled. And then, I pulled back, pressing it there, slapping him slowly, and then a little bit harder.

"Come now, you need to beg for your medicine," I purred into his ear.

"Arrgh yes, please mistress give me this," he cried out.

There was a thrill that I enjoyed. I saw the flogger in the corner, grabbing it and placing it right over his backside.

"What was that I heard?"

"Yes mistress! Give me more!" he screamed out.

There was that excitement, that need, and that desire which came from all of this. I readied the flogger, hitting him straight on the backside, hearing the grunts that came from him. I looked at him, seeing his butt arch up slightly, and I couldn't help but laugh at him.

God, he looked so damn pathetic, but there was something fun about this man being on this level with me, so turned on and used like this. There was an excitement which came forth about it, and as I hit him once more, he let out a cry.

"Now...what was it that you wanted?" I said to him, rubbing my hand against his hard backside.

"Please mistress...I want you to...to take me," he said.

"Really now? What was that?" I said, rubbing a gloved hand against him. Just seeing him shiver like that was a thrill I couldn't get enough of.

"Please mistress. Just...take me please," he said.

I wanted to see him squirm. He'd be the first one.

"You want your medicine then?" I asked.

"Yes! I want the medicine. Please," he begged.

Seeing him come apart like this sent a thrill through me that I didn't even expect. I slapped his ass hard once more, hearing him shiver with delight.

"Well, I'm sure that you can get your medicine then...just give me a moment," I said.

I turned him around, seeing his hardened cock there. I touched it, grabbing it hard, watching him cry out. Having a man under my control like this felt so damn different. But man was it fun.

I rubbed him at first, hearing him let out a series of small cries as I did this, and there was something fun and thrilling about this, about watching him just completely lose all semblance of control like this. For a long time, I simply teased him around, watching him tense up, moaning.

"Please mistress, just one more," he said.

"Ah ah. You can't tell me what to do. Or else you'll get punished," I said, lightly grasping his cock again. He shivered, crying out in slight shock and surprise.

"Please mistress I need it! I need your medicine," he said.

Hearing the agonized cries of this man sent something through me. Was it...a feeling of excitement? Was it the fact that I had control over this man, and there was nothing that he could do to stop me?

Perhaps it was, and in truth, I liked hearing him lose control over every single touch, losing his mind at the sheer mention of my touches, the teases, the pleasure that this man had.

"Well since you asked nicely, I think I can give you your medicine. But only because you've been such a good boy," I teased, hearing the whimpering sound of approval from this man. I moved my panties off to the side, moving downwards until my pussy was right over his face.

"But you'll also need to take care of me too. That's how the medicine works," I teased him.

He groaned, pushing his cock upwards, and soon, I rested myself downwards, sitting on his face. He let out a small, muffled cry as I started grinding my hips there, watching him tense up. I took the tip of his cock into my mouth, sucking on it, moving down against it, hearing him groan out.

I smothered my pussy on his face, my juices coating his mouth and face. This was a thrill that I couldn't get enough of, and watching him groan and move around in agony was fun, and yet I could also see the nervousness that was there, and the way that he seemed to just completely lose it all as I did this.

I loved it. I knew that he liked it too, but there was also that feeling of desire and raw need, that seemed to only drive me closer and closer to the edge as well.

I continued to move my hips against him, hearing him groan with delight. I took him further down my mouth, finally getting it to the base of my throat. I moved my tongue, licking the shaft, hearing the sounds of desire that came out from this.

"Fuck," he muffled under me.

I pushed my hips downwards, letting out a series of small cries.

"I'll let you cum when you're done with me," I said to him.

He worked his magic, his tongue moving outwards, roving against my body, making me shiver with delight, moaning slightly in response to everything that was going on. This brought forth a feeling and thrill that I wasn't expecting. But I started grinding my hips, hearing him groan with pleasure at the sensation of this.

"Yes. That's a good boy! Continue," I cried out, enjoying this way more than I expected to. He worked his magic, still touching, teasing, and moving his lips around as much as he could, savoring me.

When he stuck his tongue in, pressing into me and upwards, I suddenly felt that sudden urge surge through me. I pressed my face down, rubbing it there, grinding against him as I took his cock in my mouth, moving my lips up and down.

"Yes," I said out loud. I was so damn close, and he knew this too. I knew he enjoyed this as much as I did, and with every little touch, every way his tongue poked into me, turning me on and touching me, I knew that I was near my limit.

After a few more moments, he pressed his tongue upwards, causing me to tense up, letting out a small cry as I pressed my hips there, coming hard as I suffocated him. In response, he let out a barely audible groan as he came against my lips. I quickly swallowed it all, moving off of him.

The man was spent, and my lips curled into that of a smile.

"There we go," I said out loud.

I moved my hand to his thighs, touching it slightly.

"That's a good boy. Now be good. I'll come back and give you the medicine you need anytime," I purred in his ear.

He let out a small cry before laying there, completely spent and amazed by this. I undid the restraints and slowly got the blindfold off. He looked at me, smiling.

"There we go," he told me.

"You're good. Do you need anything?" I asked.

That's part of the dom lifestyle. Making sure that every one of them was taken care of.

"Yeah, I'm good," he told me.

I beamed.

"Great. Well, you're free to leave whenever," I said.

After he was done, I cleaned up the room and then went outside. My friend looked at me with a smile.

"So, did you enjoy it Elena?" she asked.

I beamed.

"Did I? That shit was so much fun! And I mean...I liked that I got a little something out of it too," I told her.

"Yeah, that's the fun of being a professional dominatrix. So, if you want to, you're always welcome to come back," she offered.

Was this the big moment I'd been looking for? Was this the gig that would spur me to do something different with myself, with my life?

Perhaps it was.

My lips curled into that of a smile as I thought about Sadie's offer.

"You know, you might be onto something," I told her.

"Yeah, I know I am. Well, you're welcome to come back tomorrow. Oh, and here's the money from that guy. He's a pretty big businessman, which is why he wears the hood," she said.

A couple of hundreds were thrown into my hand. After counting it, it was nearly a grand! I got a grand just from being a bit of a bully to a random guy?

Something about this seemed almost too good to be true, and I felt that excitement and desire grow within me.

"You know, you may be onto something with this," I told her.

"I know that I am. I've been doing this long enough. I guess I'll see you tomorrow," she said.

And when I left, that's when I realized it. I enjoyed this, far more than I thought I'd enjoy something of this caliber. I mean, I did like teasing guys, but the fact that I could get paid for it, and it was good money was almost too good to be true. But here I was, thinking about all of this, and the realization of it all.

It awoke something within me, and I had a feeling this would drive me to make other decisions, ones that would be different from the life I led before.

Chapter 2

That's what began my descent into being a femdom.

At first it was just one situation where I ended up choosing to mess around with one guy for fun and giggles.

But now…it's something more.

It turned into something different, and when I walked in today, seeing that he wanted me to roleplay a cop, I certainly felt a whole burst of excitement there. The thrill of roleplaying different types of characters that would otherwise not happen….it was quite fun.

I walked over to the entrance, seeing Sadie there. This time she was in a leather dress that hugged her body, and straps that hugged her thighs, showing a teeny bit of the extra thickness that was there. She looked hot, but the smile that she had on her face said everything.

"So, ready to rock and roll tonight?" she teased.

"Born ready," I replied.

"Good. This is your next client. I guess he likes cops. Maybe he's wanted to be dominated by one," she said.

I looked at what he wanted. I flushed seeing the words that were there.

Pegging.

I'd never done this before. I thought about this, noticing that she was curious about my response.

"Something wrong?" she asked.

"I've never pegged someone before," I admitted with a reddened face.

"Oh, that's easy! Trust me on this, guys love this type of shit. It's clear that he's probably use to this too. So, don't worry," she replied.

I wasn't planning on worrying.

I liked this. It awoke a feeling of power within me, something I wasn't used to. Maybe it was the fact that I got to experience something so fun, so magical, and so different from the norm. but also…it was that feeling of power, something that I definitely enjoyed and craved.

"That sounds like fun," I told her.

"This guy loves that shit. He's so into women taking control of him, so I imagine he'll like what you have planned for him," she told me.

I hoped that he did.

I got into the cop uniform, a tight leather skirt, and a shirt that showcased my cleavage in an ample manner. There was something fun about dressing up, about letting go and experiencing the fun of this. I looked at the door, preparing myself for what I was about to see.

When I opened the door, I saw a man sitting there prone on the ground, his ass in the air. He shivered with delight.

"I'm sorry officer I—"

I took my heel, digging it into his back.

"You have the right to remain silent. So, what's it going to be? You're coming with me to jail? Or.... maybe you want me to treat you a little differently than the others that I nab," I said.

I dug the heel in, watching him grimace, but there was also that moan that escaped his voice as I continued this.

"Please mistress, I'll do anything," he said.

"Anything I say? Even of course...submitting to me?" I said with a laugh.

"Yes! I want that mistress," he told me.

"Well then aren't we the feisty one. Fine, I guess I can take you up on this offer," I pointed out.

I took the heel, walking on him. He let out a low, guttural sound that made me excited, shivering with delight, enjoying the feeling of this man against me. There was something fun about taking a man like this, making him mine, and watching him submit.

I certainly could see that he was enjoying this too. I looked down, seeing his cock standing at attention.

"Look at you, all turned on by my heels! I can't believe this. I'm surprised you can even say things. How are you feeling? Like you're under my control?" I said, grabbing the chains that he was in, pulling on them.

Ahh yes! I'm under your control," he replied.

"Heh, good. I'm glad we can see things like this. Because look at your pathetic ass. Such a poor soul, only here to be used as a cocksleeve and nothing more," I said.

I pressed my heel against him once again. But that's when I saw it.

His tight little hole. It twitched as I did this, making me chuckle.

"Just look at your pathetic ass. You're sitting here, ass in the air, turned on by the sheer mention of my foot against your hard cock. Wow, what a pathetic little bitch," I told him.

"Yes, I'm a pathetic bitch mistress. Please just—"

I stepped on him again, this time slapping his ass as well. He let out a small yelp, twitching in response to my motions.

"Silence! You have the right to remain silent. We're not done here," I told him.

I then moved over towards the array of toys, seeing a variety of different dildos. There were also ones specifically for the strap-on, which were quite bigger than I imagined.

Would he really enjoy this?

There was also a double-ended one. I considered that, but it was one of the bigger ones.

"Let's see how well you handle my treatment," I told him.

"Is this punishment?"

I gave him a long, hard slap on the ass, causing him to let out a yelping sound.

"You're goddamn right it is," I spat in his face.

He let out a whimper as I began to lube up the first dildo, something that's pretty small and tame. I figured this was something that most people could handle.

I spread his cheeks apart, sliding the toy inside. He let out a small, garbled sound, but then a moan as I began to press it in and out.

"Look at you, all turned on by this," I told him.

I continued to press in and out, watching his eyes widen, and the moans that he had escaped his mouth. It was hot to watch, that's for sure. I continued to tease him, but then I pulled it out slightly.

"You seem to be taking this very well. But this isn't something you should be enjoying you little worm," I told him, smacking him hard against the ass.

"No! I don't want to enjoy this! I want you to hurt me! make me pay for my crimes," he screamed out.

"You're goddamn right I'm going to make you pay," I said to him, spitting in his face.

Before I knew it, I had a bigger dildo in my hands, one that was about eight inches, but a bit girthier. I shoved it inside, at first slow and steady, but as he took it, I pressed it in a whole lot harder, watching him cry out with pleasure as I continued to move it deep within him.

"Look at this slutty little hole, taking this toy like this. My, I can't believe you haven't been taken sooner. I'm surprised, you may be liking this," I told him.

He grimaced, letting out a small cry of pleasure as I continued to move the toy in and out, watching him shiver with delight, and the sounds that it made turning me on immensely. I smirked, watching his eyes widen as I continued this, enjoying the sounds that he made, the squelching that was heard as I shoved the toy in and out, and the excitement that came out of his mouth.

He was turned on, but I also heard the slight grunts of pain. He enjoyed the torture though, given how hard his cock was, and how he didn't use the safe word that I'd been given by Sadie to continue this.

"You like that you little slut? Me just assailing your hole?" I told him.

"Yes! Give me more! I crave it," he screamed out.

"Heh, look at you. You're a fucking mess," I said.

I grabbed the whip that was in my belt, unclipping it and then hitting him directly with it. He let out a small, sensual cry as I did this, whipping him again and again.

"Yes! Give this to me! I'm bad and—"

I wrapped the gag around his mouth.

"Quiet down. I didn't tell you to speak," I said, whipping him hard one last time for good measure. The arch of his back, the cry that he uttered, it was driving me insane.

And that's when I decided to do it.

I took the dildo out, watching him whimper in response to this. I looked at him, seeing the way his body shook slightly, the little sound that came out of his lips, the ache that was clearly there.

He was enjoying this. Probably more than I should be letting him.

"I never told you that you could enjoy this!" I said to him, smacking him hard.

"Ahh! Yes, I'm not. You're using me like the bad boy that I am. Please, just use me," he said.

I looked at the way his hole stretched out, looking almost inviting to me. I never really thought about pegging a guy like this, but seeing how he just completely lost all semblance of control the moment I started to tease him was fun.

"Fine, because you're already so turned on, and you're asking nicely, I will," I told him.

I moved over to the cabinet, trying to figure out which toy I wanted to use. There were a variety, but the double-ended one was calling me. That way I could have my fun too while teasing this man.

"Please officer! Just use me. I promise I'll never do it again," he cried out.

I didn't expect this to be so hot to me. My tits were perked, my pussy wet, and soon, before I knew it, I could feel that ache growing within, that need growing as well.

I moved my body so that my back was right up against his. I lubed it up—I wasn't that mean of course. I wanted to make sure that this was something that he would enjoy too.

"Alright, ready? This is your punishment," I said.

"Please officer! Give me the punishment," he told me.

Such a pathetic man, looking all turned on. I slid myself slowly into him, feeling him twitch and quiver slightly, a little bit of resistance as I entered into his pucker.

"What's the matter? Can't handle it? I can always pull out, and then you'll have to get your punishment a different way," I teased.

"No! I need this. I want you to punish me. Please," he said, the cries of pleasure obvious in his voice.

"There we go," I said, feeling the resistance diminish slightly. This would be enough, right? I quickly moved myself so that I was deep inside, hearing him groan out loud.

In truth, this was turning me on too. The fact that I could feel him inside, and the way the toy moved against me was quite fun. I enjoyed this, feeling like I was in control, that I could take the lead, and that he was definitely at the mercy of my touches.

"There we go. So easy to work with. Such a good little bad boy," I told him, sliding myself in and out of him, listening to him cry out in response to me. The thrill of this was something that I enjoyed, and there was an excitement that grew within me as I started to feel him move against me, fucking the dildo as well. I tried to hold back my own moans, but the truth was, this was turning me on immensely too.

"You're so good at this, such a good pet. It surprises me," I told him.

"I'm only aiming to be the best that I can be for you mistress. I know that it's a lot, but I want to be the best that I can, to make you feel good too," he said.

"Good, as you should," I said.

I gripped his hips, moving them up and down, pushing them against me. as he did that, I angled the toy a little bit, feeling the moans escape my own mouth. I was aroused, enjoying all of this.

I moved the angle of this a little bit differently, feeling like I was on top of the world as I did this. It was then when, after a few more thrusts, I pressed deep within, watching him cry out, and the spurt of cum shoot out of him.

I felt my own orgasm hit me, feeling the toy press against my g-spot, causing me to cry out, feeling my hips move, pressing into his prostate, watching the cum fly out, hitting the floor there.

I pulled back, catching my breath.

"Good job. So good at being an obedient little slut," I told him.

"I-I try to be," he told me.

"Tell you what, clean that up, and maybe I'll let your pathetic ass go," I said.

I moved his face down, forcing the man to clean up his own seed, causing me to smile in excitement. There was something fun about this, about making him lose all semblance of control like this, that I couldn't get enough.

He cleaned it all up, and when he looked at me, a little bit nervous, I laughed.

"Look at you. Such a mess. Go ahead, you're free. You get off with a warning, but if I catch you doing this again...your punishment may not be as good as you think," I told him.

"Y-yes," he said.

I walked out, smiling as I pulled the double-ended dildo out of me, sighing.

"Damn that was fun," I said.

There was an excitement that came from this, a feeling of power that grew within me. I could definitely get used to this.

I felt like I was slowly becoming more and more of a degenerate when it came to turning on men and making them feel good. But who knows, maybe it's just the nice paycheck too.

When I got out, Sadie looked at me with a smile.

"There you are," she said to me.

"Yeah, sorry, it took a little longer than I expected. That guy was a bit of a tougher nut to crack," I told her.

"Well, whatever you did, he loved it. He gave you a bonus," she said.

She handed me a bunch of stacks.

"This is two grand," I told her.

"Yeah, because you gave him pleasure. Us doms can make a ton of money out of this, and the guys here are pathetic little worms, I'm sure they'll love it if someone took them and used them like this," she told me.

I didn't expect there to be such a market for this.

"I'll take on more clients," I finally decided.

"You sure? I know it's a lot, given your daughter and all and—"

"No, it's fine. This gives her a good life. Why would I deny my child that," I said.

I was a mother sure, but I also knew that if I continued this, I could be the best parent possible to my kid.

"Very well, I'll give you some more clients. I'm sure this will be fun," she said.

Chapter 3

"Come on you have to beg for it. Beg for me to sit on your cock," I said, rubbing the whip against the tip, coiling it there.

"Please mistress, do this. I've been a naughty boy. I ate the chocolate chip cookies," he said.

I whipped him again, watching him cry out in pleasure as I started to laugh.

"You are a little bit. You were a very naughty boy, eating your mistress's cookies like that. I thought you were the gardener, but here you are, thinking that you own the place or something," I told him.

"No mistress! I'm sorry," he cried out.

I smacked him again with the whip, hearing him shiver and cry out.

"Now, will you promise to never do it again?" I asked him.

I rested my fingers on his delicate chest, touching, teasing his nipples by pulling on the clamps. It's something special that he liked.

"Yes mistress! I promise ahh!" he said, crying out and arching his back as I continued to tease him with the chain.

I smiled, enjoying this as I watched him become a mess in front of me, completely turned on and enjoying the feeling of this.

"Good boy. I guess now that you've suffered enough, your mistress can give you what you want. But I'm going to put a condom on there, so you don't fill your mistress's pussy with your cum," I told him.

I grabbed his dick hard, watching him tense up, moaning out loud in response.

"T-that's fine mistress! Whatever you want," he said.

"Heh, good boy," I said.

I watched him whimper as I got off, grabbing a tight rubber as I started to move it over his cock. I started to see him shiver as I pushed it on there, letting the elastic of it bounce back, causing him to let out a small whimper of both pleasure and pain.

"Look at you. Such a goddamn pathetic mess," I told him.

"Yes, I am! I'm a pathetic mess mistress! Please just...just take me," he said.

"Wow, you really are over here begging for this. What a pathetic little bitch," I said.

This was one of my favorite clients, because no matter what I did, he always sounded like he was seconds away from orgasming all over the damn place. I moved my hips onto each side of him, sliding myself down on his shaft, letting out a small cry.

It was fun teasing guys like this. As they sat there, at my command, their cocks hard as I teased them and played with them. Dominating men was a whole lot of fun, and I slowly changed my career to doing this full-time.

I started shifting my hips, going slowly at first, watching him lose control as he started to tense up. I then stopped.

"I will tell you when you can cum," I snapped at him.

"O-okay mistress," he said.

I giggled, moving my hips, watching him tense up, crying out as I slowly, languidly let his cock sit deep within me. I watched him tense as I saw him cry out, trying his best to thrust his hips up, but I stopped him.

"I didn't tell you that you could do that," I said, slapping him.

"Ahh mistress!" he said.

I then started to move faster and faster. He struggled to hold back the delicious sounds that came from him, and I couldn't help but feel the surge of power, excitement, and fun that came out of this.

I continued to thrust my hips up and down, watching him tense up, screaming out.

"Please mistress I can't hold it back any longer! Please let me cum," he cried out. I watched him, smiling in excitement as I held onto his hips.

"Do you want to cum? Do you really want to cum?" I asked him.

"Yes," he breathed out.

'Really now? You've got to convince me better than that," I said with a giggle.

"Ahh mistress! Please let me cum!" he screamed out.

I looked into his eyes, seeing the need, the pleasure, the desire that came out of this.

"Well, I guess since you asked nicely and all, I'll let you cum," I said.

I then pushed my fingers away, watching him cry out, groaning as he moved his hips. He hit that one spot, which made me gasp, holding it for a second, and then I let out a small moan too, cumming there.

He then groaned, the cum spraying out, the warm sensation hitting me. This was nice, and I didn't have to worry about diseases or pregnancy of course. It was fun to just tease him like this, watching him lose all of the control that he struggled to hold onto as I thrust in deep.

"There you go," I said.

When he was done, I moved off of him, undoing the restraints.

"You good to go? Because if so, the mistress has another appointment right now," I told him.

"Yes mistress," he finally managed to breathe out.

I smirked, enjoying how much of a mess he was. I then watched him struggle as I left the room.

"There you are again? How was this customer?" Sadie asked.

"It was fun. He was easy to mess with," I told her.

"Good. He paid decently to. Check that out," she said.

Another couple grand.

"This is great. Definitely will help with my daughter," I told her.

"Well, that's what's so fun about this. You can do whatever you want, and you can have a bunch of fun while doing so," she said.

That's kind of what I enjoyed about this. It was the fact that I could be myself, and tease men. There was a thrill that came from that.

"Well, I think I'm going to head in, work with the next customer tonight," I told her.

"Good. I think they'll enjoy that," she replied.

And that was it. It was time for me to move onto the next one, the next customer, who would make things even more fun. I felt the excitement and need grow within me but I had no clue what would happen next.

All I did know was that I was ready to be a dom, ready to make men squirm, and I loved that I could make money doing just that, enjoying the aspects of this that I could enjoy too.

The Massage Therapist

A Tantric Sex, 69, BDSM, Wife Swapping Story

Chapter 1

"How was meeting up with Casey?" my husband Arnold asked.

"It was good. He helped me with that crick in my neck. Really did me some good," I told Arnold.

"Yeah, it was nice meeting up with Melonie too," he replied.

My husband and I were in a swinging "Wife swapping" sort of thing. He would go with Casey's wife Melonie, while I would go with Casey to explore some of the sexual aspects that Arnold normally didn't really like.

Arnold was a little bit older than I was, and a traditional man. He had short blonde hair, blue eyes, and was of average build. He was a man that I'd fallen for, and we've still been close to one another, I definitely felt like this whole wife swapping thing was good for both of us.

He was seeing Melonie, who was Casey's wife. Melonie was cute. Small, thick, and a redhead with green eyes. She kind of looked like me, albeit a little bit younger than myself. Which wasn't necessarily wrong or anything, but it's clear that Arnold did have a spot in his heart for the more traditional types, something that I couldn't totally fill.

Meanwhile, I'd been seeing Casey. Casey was much different. Between the array of tattoos on his arms, his long black hair, and his brown eyes, he was the antithesis of Arnold. However, he was muscular, and although he looked like a tough guy, he was definitely very sweet, and he was a massage therapist in town, one of the most popular out there.

This wife swapping thing began about a year ago, when he suggested it to me drunkenly regarding Melonie. We agreed, and I saw Casey. That's when things changed. We soon got to learn one another, and it was a different kind of game for us. Rather than it just being something vanilla, there was the fun of variety, something that I didn't necessarily get with Arnold, and something that, deep down I did utterly miss in a strange way.

It was odd, but our first-time swapping was...different; it awakened a whole new world for me.

Arnold just wanted the thrill of having someone who wasn't his wife. It was strange to me, but he was the one who asked about it. I, of course, was cool with just being with Casey.

Casey and I were old friends. In fact, we almost ended up together, but our differing interests pulled us apart. But that didn't stop me from feeling a surge of excitement as I thought about the fact that I'd get to see him again, his beautiful cock penetrating me and the fun that we'd get to have.

"So.... when are you two meeting up again?" Arnold asked, looking me over.

"This Friday. He told me to meet up at his office. Not sure why though," I told him.

I think it's because of what we discussed the week before after we had sex, lying in bed together. Sure, Arnold and I still had an awesome relationship, but the pillow talk with Casey was a bit different.

"So...is there anything you want to try?" Casey asked me, touching the tips of my thighs.

"I don't know. I've been reading a bit about tantra. I don't really know much about it, but I'm curious about it," I told him.

Tantric sex was something I tried to bring up to Arnold a couple of times, but he just thought it was some weird sort of sex thing and wasn't cool with it. I tried to explain to him that it was something that was a bit different, but I guess he just wasn't feeling it.

"I've been reading up on tantra too. And I can give you a tantric massage, and maybe we can try tantric sex too," he purred.

Would that even work? I flushed, thinking about this. I don't know what Arnold would say if I tried it without him, but we were in this wife swapping thing, and he was boning Melonie whenever I was with him. I figured it was something that we'd get to explore down the road.

"Do you think that you can teach me? Or at least show me?" I asked him.

"Sure! I've been doing some research on this. I offered Melonie a chance to try it, but she didn't seem all that interested in it either. It's weird, because we ended up marrying two people incredibly vanilla, when we're not," he told me.

That's what I always found strange too. It wasn't the fact that they were vanilla, but it was how it ended up like this.

Still, I sat there, my eyes on his.

"Yeah, I'd like that," I told him.

"Good. Then that settles it. Next Friday we'll meet up, and we can see what this tantra is all about," he said.

I beamed.

"I'd love that. But first...why don't we take care of that," I said, pointing to the obvious erection in his pants. He gave me a small smirk, his blue eyes looking into my green ones.

"Sure, I'd love that," he told me.

I soon moved so that my pussy was right in his face, covering him with my juices. He extended his tongue, the pink muscle moving out, exploring my folds, teasing the tip of my clit. I shivered, realizing he knew exactly where to go with this, and the pleasure that this was giving me.

"Fuck this is pretty good," I told him.

"I told you it'd be fun. Besides, what's the point of sex without a little bit of...exploration," he told me.

I smiled.

"Sure, you can definitely explore me all you like," I told him.

"And that's exactly what I plan to do," he purred.

I shivered, knowing this was exactly what he wanted. He continued to tease his tongue there, moving it around, and I soon pressed my lips to the tip of his cock, teasing the very edges of it, watching his eyes widen with rapt delight as I took him further and further down, feeling his shaft fill up my mouth.

That's also something that Casey had over Arnold. He was much thicker. While Arnold was a little bit longer, Casey made up for it in girth, so it was two different instances. I started to move my lips all the way to the base, feeling it graze against the back of my throat, enjoying the sensation of this as I continued to press against there, thrusting my lips all the way down, feeling him there.

"Fuck," he said, groaning as he thrust his hips upwards.

"You like that?" I said with a smile.

"I'm loving it," he told me.

I started to gasp against his cock, feeling it hit the back of my throat. I continued to move my lips against him, up and down, up and down, sucking him off without any reason to stop. He held my hips, exploring me, thrusting his tongue deep into me, pressing against me, hearing me cry out, tensing up and enjoying the sensation of this.

"Fuck," I said, tensing up, feeling the pleasure of my orgasm as it hit me.

He then pressed his hips upwards, hitting the back of my throat relentlessly. He then groaned, his cock tensing, and then the release hitting my mouth. I swallowed the salty mixture, enjoying the taste, looking at him as I moved off, a smile on my face.

"How was that?" I said.

"Amazing really," he said.

"As it should be," I replied.

We sat down, enjoying the warm touch of one another. While Arnold was a lot more vanilla, Casey was fun to get those kink tendencies out, and to try something a bit different. That of course, would involve tantric massage, and maybe tantric sex.

There was that feeling of desire, of excitement, of need that grew within me at the thought of this, and I couldn't help but feel excited for what was to come.

I thought about the conversation we had that night, remembering the fun we had, what we enjoyed, and what we planned to try out the next time we saw one another. I looked at Arnold, who seemed curious.

"Honey, I think I'm going to try something new with Casey. That's okay, right?"

"It's kink-related isn't it?" he asked.

"Yeah, it is," I said.

"That's fine. Just be safe. And maybe you can show me when you get back to me," he said.

"Of course. But only if you learn something new from Melonie and want to try it with me," I said.

He pulled me in, kissing me passionately and I hungrily took his lips against mine. Sure, he was vanilla, but there was something nice about having the stability of this relationship right here, waiting for me, and something I could never let go of, no matter what happened next.

Chapter 2

I felt a bit of nervousness as I started to realize the day was getting closer. I wondered what would transpire here between Casey and I.

When I left the house, saying goodbye to Arnold, he gave me a kiss. I felt an excitement grow. I wanted to feel the excitement with him too, but I figured this would be something that I'd learn from Casey first.

When I got to the massage parlor, he was already closed up for the day, which was good. I figured that he'd be busy till late, but I guess not, which made things a little bit easier for us. When I got to the doorway, seeing him there, he gave me a small smile.

"There you are Katie," he said to me.

I smiled, feeling his eyes glaze over my body. I wore a simple black skirt with a blue sweater, seeing his eyes dance over my curves. There was something fun about this, seeing the way his body, mind, and eyes continued to dance over me.

"Hey yourself. So, are you ready to begin?" I asked him.

"Course. I've been working on the technique. Hopefully, I can make you feel magical," he said to me.

I followed him to the room, and he soon looked at me.

"First thing that I want you to do, is to get naked, and wear only this robe. I'm going to give you a massage first. Just a general one, help with the nerves and such," he said.

"Alright," I replied.

He left the room, and I took off my clothes, putting the white cotton robe on. I looked around, flushing at the realization that this was how we were going to do this.

I laid down on the table, feeling him walk in, closing the door behind him.

"Now, let's start with a simple massage. That way you can relax, and I don't know, I just want to make sure that you feel good too," he told me.

"Thanks. I do appreciate that," I told him.

He looked into my eyes, and then I put my head down. His large hands started from the top of my back, near my shoulders, slowly massaging the muscle tissue there. It felt really good, and it was enjoyable to me. I shivered, letting out a small sigh of contentment as he continued this touch.

"You feel good?" he asked.

"Amazing really. It's nice to get a massage period. I've been meaning to work out the kinks in my neck and such," I told him.

"Well allow me to help with just that," he purred in my ear.

He pressed against that area of muscle tissue and I tensed up, letting out a small moan as he massaged that area. He then moved downwards, pressing his hands to my buttocks, teasing the flesh that was there. He then moved to my legs, massaging the back of them.

When I felt it press against that area between the thigh and the knee I tensed up, letting out a small cry of both pleasure and surprise, enjoying the feeling of this. I tensed up, watching him smile.

"There you go. You're doing so well," he said to me.

"Thank you," I said, letting out a small moan.

"Now, we can begin tantra," he said to me.

I felt a thrill grow within me as I started to look at him, seeing the way his eyes looked over mine.

The first thing that we must do is connect our breaths," he told me.

To connect our breaths? How does that work?

"How though?"

"We're going to use something called Bliss Breath. First thing you need to do is constrict your throat. Then take a breath in, and you'll hear a sound that's like whispering. Then, you want to exhale and make that sound once more," he explained to me.

I thought he was crazy, but I decided to try it. I took a moment to take a deep breath in, letting my breaths become slow, audible, and easy to use.

"There you go," he replied.

"What's the purpose of this?" I asked.

"It's to help with grounding you. It also will help with a full-body orgasm," he said.

"Full...body?" I said.

Was that even possible? This was something that I'd never heard of.

"Yes, full-body. It's a little different from what you're used to, but just trust me on this," he said.

I did trust him. even though I didn't expect this to feel well...so intimate, it was exciting for me to feel.

"Alright, I'll do that," I said.

"Good. Let's bring our breaths together," Casey said.

We did as he told me, and as we brought the breathing together, I felt that hint of arousal grow within me.

We locked into one another's eyes, and I stared at him.

"You ready?"

"Yes," I breathed out, flushing crimson.

"Alright, lay down on your back," he instructed.

I did as I was told, the robe spilling open and showing my breasts that are exposed for him to see. I looked at him, and he smiled.

"Alright, let's start with a simple breast massage," he said to me.

"Alright."

"Close your eyes," he instructed.

I trusted him. I knew he'd give me pleasure beyond my wildest expectations if he did this. I heard the sound of something being uncapped, and then the sound of something being squirted out. I imagined that it was massage oil, but wasn't sure.

"Alright, let's begin," he said to me.

He rubbed against the very sides of my breast. At first, I didn't really feel much from this. But then his hands moved downwards, the nerves of my body immediately reacting.

"Ahh," I said.

"Don't worry, this is a warmup. It's to help you feel relaxed, and also to help with building arousal," he explained to me.

"A-alright," I told him.

I believed that this would feel better once we continued to explore one another. His hands then moved against the edges of my breasts again, circling the outside. The little, slight touch was enough to make my body react, but then I remembered the breathing. Even though I didn't really see him, the connection that I felt was something different. It was an intimacy that even I didn't expect from this sort of thing.

I jolted slightly, letting out a soft little moan of appreciation and arousal as he continued to do this.

"Very good. Now just relax," he said.

"I'm relaxing as much as I can right now," I said with a laugh.

"I know that you are. But just…watch what happens," he said to me.

He then massaged down towards the ribcage, touching me with the slightest of touches. That was enough to set me on fire, making me suddenly lose my composure. Then, he moved towards the lower abdomen. I felt my body tingle, a rush of pleasure as I responded to his words. His touches also were different too. When it was on the ribcage, it would alternate between lighter touches, and stronger touches, making my body heat up with arousal, need, and something more.

"There we go," he said to me.

He moved his hands upwards, massaging around the areola that I had, teasing my nipples from the outside.

"Ahh," I cried out, feeling them harden against his fingers.

"Don't worry, it's okay for your nipples to get hard. Just relax," he explained to me.

That was definitely a bit easier said than done, but I tried my best to keep my wits about me, relaxing as I felt his hands continue to touch, decorate, and tease against me.

He then encircled his fingers against my nipples, pressing there with the tips of his fingers, and then, lightly pinching them slightly, enjoying the sounds that came out of my mouth.

"Fuck," I said, moving my hips forward.

"There you go, you're feeling good right?" he said.

I felt a feeling of heat as he did this, touching and pinching them lightly, letting his fingers roll against the tips of my nipples. I shivered, moaning.

"Y-yes," I said.

I felt like my body was already on fire, but I knew that this was merely the beginning of it, and I was in for quite the treat.

"Good, if you're ready…we can start with the next part of tantra. The yoni massage?" he asked me.

"What's that?" I asked. I didn't know the terms that were associated with this.

"It's a clitoral massage. And maybe I can teach you other forms of the massage too," he said.

He was such a good teacher that this was already better than I expected. I looked into his eyes, nodding.

"A-alright," I told him.

"There we go. Now sit back and just relax. You can watch my hands and such if you like. Just remember the breathing," he explained.

I'd remember that as best as I could. But my brain was already on edge, and there was definitely a feeling of nervousness that came from this.

He slid his fingers down towards the apex of my legs, but when he stopped near my pussy, his finger extended out. It was merely his pointer finger, but I felt it gently touch the tip of my clitoris.

As I felt that, I let out a small cry of surprise. It was just the tip of his finger! Why did it…feel this good?

"How?" I said.

"Just relax. I'm going to put a little bit of pressure on this. Just take a moment and relax into this," he said.

He started with the slightest of touches, moving from the tip of the clitoris from one side to another, moving from the tiniest of circles to a larger circle against the little nub. The pressure of course started out feather-light, but then became heavier.

I was already a sweating mess. I didn't expect it to feel well…this good.

"Holy shit," I said, the waves of pleasure hitting me hard.

"There we go," he said.

"What are you going to do now?" I asked him.

"Just relax. A bit more teasing. If you're too sensitive for one side, we can tease it," he said.

I knew that the clitoris had a ton of sensations, but I didn't expect this. He then pressed down and started to lightly move the finger against there, then sliding the finger against the edge of my clitoris. He continued to tease the sides, lightly pressing and then pulling on it slightly.

My body was already on edge. He grasped the sides of my clitoris, and then I felt a slight tugging sensation. My eyes widened, my hips moved upwards, and I cried out.

"H-holy shit," I said to him.

I could feel the pleasure, from the tip of my clitoris, all the way down. He then moved his fingers against there, rolling it slightly between the pointer finger, and the index finger, making me suddenly lose control, making me lose my mind, and I couldn't help but feel like I was so close.

But I didn't want to cum yet. This was too good to miss out on, and I loved every single touch this man bestowed onto me. He rolled it around, and my whole body felt the pleasure, surging through every fiber of my body, making me hold the sides of the bench as he did this.

It was then when he slowly tapped his fingers there, making my body respond. A low, guttural scream came from my throat, my whole body on the edge of orgasm. But I didn't feel like this was the end of this for some reason.

"Ahh," I said, feeling the heaviness of the touch, but then, he slowed down.

"Are you ready for more?" he asked me.

"Yes," I breathed out, slowly becoming like putty in this man's hands.

He then spread my lips apart, two fingers slightly curved and entering into me. I felt the fullness of this, but then I felt his hands move against a ridged area.

That set my body on fire. I cried out, feeling his hands lightly press against there, touching slightly.

"There we go. Now, I'm going to stimulate both your clit, but also your g-spot down here. Don't worry, if you orgasm, that's fine," he told me.

I shivered, feeling my body on edge, enjoying the tips of his fingers just barely grazing against there. Then, he slid his fingers forward, and for a moment, I forgot how to speak.

He continued this, his thumb right up against my clit, massaging the area. Making me lose my mind, completely enraptured by the sensation of this. He continued to move his hands there, making me feel the pleasure in every fiber of my being, causing me to hold onto the tip of the massage table, his other hand moving towards my nipples, feeling the sudden force of this making me tense up.

That's when it happened. The waves of pleasure hit me, and my orgasm suddenly made me lose all semblance of control. I cried out, moaning out loud as I continued to feel him do this. It was then when, after a brief second, he then moved his hands towards my nipples, teasing them while also pinching my clit between his thumb, and the feeling of my g-spot being stimulated once more.

This wasn't but one orgasm, nor was it just a series, but it felt like I hit the point of an orgasmic precipice, and I cried out, feeling my hips thrust forward, massaging against the tip of the g-spot, losing my mind, completely enjoying the feeling of this as I continued to feel him tease me, playing with every part of me, my whole being feeling the utter pleasure that came from this.

It was like I was having multiple orgasms, again and again, crying out and thrusting my body forward. I felt the orgasm not just against my pussy, not just from my clit, but from...all over.

The wave of pleasure was one that I enjoyed, one that I could get used to, and something that I couldn't get enough of.

I cried out, pressing my hips forward, losing all semblance of control.

"Holy shit," I screamed out, feeling the last of the orgasmic waves jolt me forward, and I couldn't help but feel like I was not only turned on, but...at peace. It made me feel really good, and then, he pulled his fingers out, teasing them against his lips and licking them.

"Wow," I told him. I didn't know what to say. It was like all of my thought processes were all gone. I never thought that a yoni massage would make me feel this way.

"You good?" he asked.

"Yeah. I'm feeling...amazing really" I told him. It was a form of an orgasm that I never thought I'd get to enjoy.

"This is a really powerful thing. In fact, it's one of the main components. It's a bit different for guys, but it definitely lets you feel that sexual energy that you want to have in your body. And of course, it shows you new sensations," he explained.

"Yeah, I certainly felt some new sensations," I replied.

They were sensations that I didn't really experience up until now.

"Is there...something I can do to you?" I asked him. I didn't want to just have an amazing orgasm and then say fuck it to everything.

"Well, that depends. Do you want to try a massage on me...or do you want to try sex?" he asked me.

I wanted to try both, but honestly, I needed a moment, and I knew that Casey had a pretty fast refractory period.

"Let's...try the massage next. I want to try this with you," I said with a flush.

"There we go. It doesn't have to be something long either. We can take this nice and slow, it's just a matter of connection, and bringing us closer together," he said.

I didn't expect to feel this when I thought of swapping. In truth, I always thought we'd just have sex, but the connection we had was...something more.

That's what I enjoyed about this. I liked the swapping because of how good it normally felt.

"Yes, and we can take this slow, explore the meditative aspects of this, so you can have fun with this too, and learn how to use it," he explained.

"Alright let's try that," I said.

We switched positions, with him in a robe this time.

"Okay, first you want me to lay down, with my legs apart," he said.

"Yeah," I said.

"Good. Now, let's breathe...together," he said.

We both breathed together, an energy and feeling that we felt as we both inhaled and exhaled making me feel a connection.

"Alright, first, I want you to grab the lube, and move it around down there. Don't forget the thighs, the pelvis and pubic bones, testicles, and perineum," he explained to me.

"So, all of those areas?"

"Yeah, just take it slowly. You can move your hands around there, and you should just use your own discretion with this," he said.

I flushed, realizing how he was letting me have this kind of control. I just hoped that I didn't fuck this one up.

"You're sure about this...right?" I said.

"Course I am. I wouldn't be letting you do this if I wasn't," he said.

There was definitely a deeper bond, a sort of trust that was there between both of us as I started to get the lubricant, moving it around there. I put the lubricant into the area, moving my hands first and foremost against the thighs.

I grabbed them, feeling the meaty muscle, with also a little bit of fat on there. I rubbed my hands there, grabbing it hard and softly, and he let out a small hum of approval as I did this, watching me with excitement in his eyes. I continued to watch him relax against my hands, and I did as he said, moving my hands against there, rubbing the edges of his thighs with the smallest of touches.

"There you go...good job," he said, his voice laced with lust and pleasure. I soon felt his hands move towards the sides, relaxing against him.

I then moved my hands upwards towards the pubic bone, lightly resting my hand against there. He reacted to the touch, so I figured a little bit of a massage may be good for him to experience. I started to rub against there, touching, teasing, playing with him as he started to let out a small groan of arousal, of need, and of desire as I continued to press against there, watching his responses.

Then, I moved to the perineum. I flushed realizing that we had this kind of connection there, but I soon moved my hand there, lightly touching it. It didn't take much for him to respond, a small groan of pleasure and need filling the air as I did this. I watched his hands grip the sides as I began to let my fingers stroke there.

Little gentle touches. I also pressed a little bit harder there, watching his eyes widen and his hips move upwards, touching the very edge of my fingers.

"Fuck," he said.

"You good?" I asked.

"Yeah, I just didn't think that this would feel so...good?. I wanted to try this with Melonie, but she thought that it'd be weird," he said.

"Well, she's clearly missing out," I said with a laugh.

I then moved my fingers against there once more, until I could see his cock slowly standing at attention.

"What about your...balls?" I asked, flushing with embarrassment at even asking about this. I didn't expect this to be so intimate, and feel so damn good.

"I want you to massage them. Don't be too rough obviously. But you can pull and fondle them for the most part. If you have fingernails...I can take a little bit of the touch from that, but nothing too crazy," he explained.

This felt way more intimate than I expected, but I took a deep breath, realizing the state of everything, and soon, before I knew it, I moved my hand towards there. At first, I grazed his balls, barely touching them, my face flush with arousal, enjoying the sensation of this. It felt weird touching the soft sacks like this. I thought that they'd be a little bit harder, but they weren't very malleable. I pressed there, slowly pulling on them, massaging them with my fingertips. I took each one in my hands, lightly rubbing my fingers against there, still keeping the same even breath.

He looked at me, his eyes widening as I did this. I didn't really move too hard. I simply just...touched them, teased them against my fingers, watching his body respond to the actions that I took. I continued to lightly fondle them, moving and thumbing over the very tips of his balls. I then moved my fingernails towards the tips of them, grazing there, enjoying the touch from his hands, loving the way that he immediately reacted as I pressed against the edge there.

"Holy fuck," he breathed out.

"Are you good?" I asked him.

"Yeah. Just feels good you know," he said.

"Alright, I'm moving upwards," I said.

I pressed my fingers towards the shaft, slowly moving my touches around. I moved from the base to the tip, using a soft grip at first, then moving the pressure a bit harder, touching against there, watching his eyes widen, and his breathing grow. I started to watch his eyes widen as I started to move my hands in different strokes, starting slowly with a lighter grip, a little faster with a lighter grip, and then harder and slower, feeling his body just become putty in my hands as I continued to move it around.

I then started to twist his cock around in different motions, using one hand at first, then using two, one on top of another as I moved it slowly, and then a little bit quicker in response to this.

I continued to press my hands there, exploring his cock, using different speeds of jerking, of touching, of teasing, and I enjoyed the way he simply let out a series of soft moans, and I couldn't help but feel his body just react.

I continued this for a bit, until I saw the look in his eyes.

I didn't want him to cum yet but he was close.

"Please...down here too," he said.

He lifted his legs up, exposing his prostate. I flushed, realizing what I was about to do.

"Are you sure? It's a little...different for us you know?" I said to him.

"Yes. If you're comfy with it, I'd love for you to do this," he said.

"Alright," I said, flushing crimson at the realization that he wanted me to tease his prostate.

I started to lube up my hands, slowly entering into him. I started to look at him, seeing his body just immediately react.

"Good. You want to…go for the prostate," he said.

"Alright," I said, flushing. I knew where it was. The truth was…Casey let me try different things on him, including femdom, so it didn't seem all that off for me to do this with him in a strange way. That's what I enjoyed about it.

I started to move my fingers inside, finding the little pea-shaped gland that was there, pressing against there. I slowly stimulated it, at first with little touches, and then made them a little bit faster, touching, pressing, teasing the flesh that was there. He let out a series of cries, pressing forward in response to the actions that I took.

And I loved it. I loved seeing him lose control, the slow touch of this making me excited about this. I continued to move my fingers there, doing a similar motion that he did to me down by my own spot.

I continued to massage, stimulating this, and slowly, he gripped the edge of the massage table.

"I'm going to cum," he said.

"Then do so. I know that you can," I told him.

He held the edge of the massage table, giving me a look, and then, he let out a small, low moan as he pushed his hips up, holding onto there, the sound of an orgasm reverberating through the room.

As he finished up, I looked at him, seeing the look of feeling spent, but also, he seemed…happy. I finished up, letting him sit there, taking a moment to process the orgasm that he had.

"Are you…. okay?" I asked.

"Yeah. Amazing," he said.

I flushed, realizing that he probably was in no position to have sex.

"You alright? Do you still…want to try tantric sex?" I asked him.

"I do. I just…need a moment okay? I'm pretty amazed at how good this feels," he told me.

I didn't expect it to feel this great if you want the truth of it. I just thought that it'd feel good, and would be like a massage, not feeling like the third eye I had was open, and feeling the slight overtaking of pleasure as it continued to hold me there.

He left the room, and I sat there, trying to figure out what to say next. He came back shortly after with two cups of tea.

"Here. Drink up," he said.

We drank this together, both of us not saying a damn thing as we looked at one another. He then gave me a beaming smile.

"That was…amazing really," he said.

"Are you sure though? I don't want to make you think I overstepped any boundaries and—"

"No, you didn't. I enjoyed the hell out of it. I just wanted to make sure that you were taken care of too. The next part involves a connection between two people. I know we're just swapping, but I feel like we do have a connection," he explained to me.

I nodded.

"Yeah, I think so too," I told him.

He smiled.

"Yeah, I can tell you feel the same way. The smile on your face. The way you look into my eyes. It's obvious," he added.

I did feel like we were connected. In our own weird way, we were definitely together, enjoying the feelings that we had for one another.

"Do you want to continue then?" I asked.

We finished the tea, and then he nodded.

"Yes, but let's do this at my place. It's a bit more...personal you know?" he said.

He was right. I quickly got dressed, and we took his car over to his place. I didn't know why, but there was something about trying this with him that excited me, that made me happy, and that made me realize that we were definitely learning more about one another as we continued to grow with each other, in a passionate way that we both weren't expecting.

Chapter 3

When we got there, he opened the door, bringing me upstairs. He took some time to light the candles, some incense in the air.

"Melonie hates the smell of this stuff, but I love it," he said.

"It's really not that bad. And it kind of helps set the scene you know?" I said to him.

"It sure does. So how are you feeling after...all of that," he said.

"In truth? Amazing. I feel like I've unlocked something that I didn't expect that I'd love so much," I told him.

I knew that tantric massage was some powerful shit, but I didn't expect this, nor did I expect to do this with someone, building this level of a connection with him. It was weird, I felt more connected with him than I'd felt with Arnold before.

"Alright, so first...we need to get our breathing together, and we can touch," he said.

"Alright," I said.

We slowly undid one another's clothes, breathing in the same way as we did before. The way we breathed was different. We were soon synchronized, touching one another with slow, sensitive strokes.

I moved my hand between his legs, massaging his cock in the same way that I did before. With a slight touch that would make him feel arousal, but nothing too hard. Soon, he was slowly starting to get hard, and I could feel the warm pleasure that came off this start to take over me.

"Are you...good?" he asked me.

"Yes. I'm good," I said, feeling a deep connection, and arousal with him that only made me ache for him more.

"Alright, so we're going to try the yam-yum position. It's based on the energies that involve male and female traits. It doesn't matter though, since we can work on...switching this, and see how it makes you feel," he explained.

"Okay.... what should I do then?" I asked.

I had no idea how this would go, but I was definitely a little bit worried about this too. I felt a little bit embarrassed, but I also wondered what would happen next between us. How could we build this connection even more?

Casey moved over to the pillow that was on the bed, sitting there cross-legged with his cock standing fully at attention.

"Alright, I want you to get on top. You can of course put your legs over my own or you can use a pillow to sit on in my lap. Whatever you want," he told me.

I nodded.

"I think I'm going to sit in your lap," I told him.

I moved towards him, but I didn't insert myself.

"There we go. You need to put your shoulders around me, and we need to be facing one another, touching either at the cheeks, or at the forehead," he said.

"Why is that?" I asked him.

"The energies. Remember the chakras that are a part of this?" he asked.

I didn't spend a bunch of time learning about this, but I did have a vague idea of what he meant.

"Yeah kind of," I said.

"Well, this helps with that sexual energy, moving it between us by going up, and between our bodies," he said.

I nodded. Moving my cheek next to his, feeling our breaths move closely.

"Then, we need to just breathe together," he said.

It was different. Instead of it being focused on massaging, it focused on the two of us bringing our breaths together. We soon synchronized our breaths in the same way that we'd been trying. Then, I started to feel him slowly enter me.

It was very slow at first, but the undulating feeling of his cock inside me made me shiver with delight.

"Holy shit," I said.

"You good? That's our bodies moving together as one. You can take control too. I don't mind letting you do this," he said to me.

"A-alright," I said, feeling a bit embarrassed. He was just letting me take control like this, and I didn't know why, but there was something almost embarrassing about this. But then, I began to dip myself against him, feeling the energy that flowed through me. I arched my body a little bit, feeling the way that it touched and tingled against my body driving me slightly mad.

"Wow," I said, feeling the heat grow through me.

"There you go. Now take it nice and easy. Let's do it together. Take it slow, and find that energy that works together," he said.

I felt his cock move around, slowly moving in circles, holding me a certain way. The connection between us as he did this was different from what I thought. I always thought that it was just sex, but this was something far deeper, more intimate, and more amazing than I expected.

We looked towards one another for a second, feeling our breaths connect as we did this. It tingled within me, making me feel it in every part of my body. From the top of my body over to the bottom of my toes, I could feel the energy, the force, and the connection that was there. The movements were slow, like an undulating wave, but that was perfect for me. It built a deeper pleasure that I thought that I would never get to experience.

He wasn't even getting deep either. But it hit differently. It hit in a way that made me shiver with delight, made me tense up, and made me cry out with complete and utter desire. It felt like I was feeling this all the way from where we connected, all the way up to the top of my body. The way our bodies touched, the connection between us, and the feeling of our bodies as we did this was so nice. It was fun, and it drove me crazy.

We felt our breathing connect, and then, as he pressed in, he touched my nipples, slowly massaging them. The moment he did that changed me. I felt my whole-body tense up, the surge of pleasure roam through me, and that's when I cried out, feeling like all parts of my body had suddenly gotten to the edge of nirvana, feeling the orgasm overtake my whole body, soul, and being.

I cried out, shivering as I looked at him, feeling my entire existence grow, every fiber of my being completely overwhelm me. I then tensed up, crying out, feeling my orgasm match with his, and he groaned.

The way we both orgasmed together was a little bit different from before. I felt a connection on both a spiritual level, and together as two people, two souls with hearts beating as one.

When he pulled away, he looked into my eyes, giving me a soft, subtle kiss, and we stayed there, kissing softly. Then, he pulled back, smiling.

"How was that? Did you enjoy tantra?" he asked me.

"I sure as fuck did. That was...different from what I expected," I said.

I felt like we connected on a physical level, and on a spiritual level, together. It helped fulfill something different. And I don't know, even though we were supposed to just be swapping, a part of me felt conflicted with how good that this felt.

"So, what do you think? Amazing isn't it?"

"Yeah. It's a different feeling. Probably unlike anything I've ever experienced," I told him.

It was a foreign feeling. But there was something exciting about this. He leaned in, grabbing my hand and smiling.

"Good. Because I like seeing you enjoy this. You seem happy. And maybe...we can do this again together," he said.

"Yeah. I want to try and show Arnold this, but I don't think he'll like it that much," I told him.

"Well, it could be our little secret. Maybe you can come over and we can explore tantra together?" he offered.

I didn't think it was necessarily cheating. It was fulfilling a kink, something that felt nice, amazing, and a whole lot different from what I imagined.

"Yeah, I think I could arrange that," I said with a beaming smile.

We got ourselves together and I went to get the car, moving back to where the house was. I saw Melonie leave as soon as I got there, both of us smiling towards one another as we looked into each other's eyes. Even though this wasn't conventional by any means, it was a whole lot of fun. When I got inside, Arnold was in there, sighing with contentment.

"Hey honey, how did it go?" I asked.

"Pretty good. Did you learn something fun with him?" he asked me.

"Yeah, I did. I'd love to show you it," I told him.

I didn't expect him to immediately smile.

"Sure, I'd love to see what he taught you. Perhaps you can help me...understand tantra as well," he said with a purr.

Even though I didn't think he'd be the biggest fan of this, I wanted to at least see where this would go. The two of us went back to the bedroom, kissing passionately together.

"Okay, so we first and foremost need to synchronize our breathing together. Try to breathe together at the same time," I explained to him.

"But why?" he asked.

"It's to help us connect, build trust and understanding, and to work together. It will benefit both of us," I told him.

He seemed a bit confused by this, but then nodded. We started to try to do this together, and then, when we looked at one another, we started to kiss slowly, breathing as well.

The first time with Arnold was awkward to say the least. He wasn't as into it as I was, and it was hard to truly match the connection. But he did like the touches, that much I was sure of, and I figured if nothing else, he'd enjoy that, and that alone.

While I thought we'd have something a little bit deeper than just an awkward connection, it was fine. I would continue to learn and master tantra with Casey, even if I felt that it would be hard for us to do.

The connection that we shared was something magical, something amazing, and for both of us, with the way that we shared the desire and connection with one another was something amazing, and I knew for a fact that no matter what, that time we share together would be something amazing, something different, and something that we both would be able to enjoy, no matter what.

Just One Night

A Forbidden Desires, Threesome Story

Chapter 1

I looked at Rocky and his girlfriend Celine. Both of them were attractive as hell. They were also way out of my league.

I clutched the textbooks that I had in my hands, seeing them walk by on campus.

"Hey there Marnie," Celine said, waving at me.

I waved back, trying to hide the flush that was there on my face. In truth, I always thought that both Rocky and Celine were attractive.

Rocky of course, was one of my best friends, a guy I'd known since I was in kindergarten. We kept in touch even after we changed schools, and we happened to end up at the same college together. To say that I had a crush on him was a bit of an understatement, given the fact that we still had that same connection after all this time.

But when I found out that Rocky was dating Celine, it made me jealous. When he brought it up to me, I remembered the clenching of my body, the anger that flowed through me, the fact that he did all of this, and it made me feel terrible.

"You're not mad, right? I mean Celine is a wonderful girl, and we're both in the same classes and stuff," he told me.

I didn't want to be mad. I was happy for him, since he finally found a girlfriend that made him happy.

But I couldn't help but feel the jealousy bubbling in my body when he sat down with me, senior year at the school, right before we were going to graduate and go to the same college together.

It sucked even more because I was going to ask him out to prom too, and I felt a bit like a moron as I realized this.

But, there couldn't be anything done. He chose her over me, so I guess I had to just...live with the consequences of this. It pissed me off, but I guess that's just...how it went so to speak.

When I met Celine though, that's when things suddenly changed. Celine was someone who was incredibly familiar, and for a moment, I wondered if I knew her from somewhere. She was pretty, I'll give her that, and I couldn't help but feel like I knew her from somewhere, wherever it might be.

"Who the hell was she?" I asked.

Besides being utterly gorgeous, I didn't know at all. I decided to do a bit of research on this, to see if I could find anything on Celine. I looked her up, trying to figure out who she was.

That's when I realized it.

It was her!

I thought she seemed familiar. But this only made things a little bit more awkward when I realized it. Celine was the daughter of my old babysitter as a kid, a friend that I had for a long time, but then one day, she vanished, along with the babysitter. I tried to ask my parents what happened, but they said that they had to move.

And now, she was dating my best friend.

It felt so wrong, but I felt a bit of jealousy not just for Rocko, but for her too. I realized when I figured it was her that she was definitely the first girl I had a crush on, the first time I had an inkling that I may be bisexual.

The realization made me flush. I mean, how do you explain this one? It made it awkward to say the least, simply because I knew that if I brought this up, shit would be weird between us. But maybe...Rocky would understand?

I don't know for sure. But Rocky seemed to be chill, and Celine seemed to be really nice still too.

When we met up, Celine looked me over, her face curling into that of confusion.

"Something the matter?" I asked. I wondered if she figured it out yet. The secret to who I was. I figured she didn't when she shook her head.

"No. I'm sorry, you just look familiar. Like someone that I knew back in the day, but I can't put a name on it," she said to me.

I didn't know what she meant by any of that, or if it was a good thing.

"Well, I'm happy for Rocky and you," I told her.

"Yeah, I am too. But I'm also glad Rocky has such a good friend like you," she said with a smile on her face.

Those words alone made me flush crimson. I didn't feel like I was a good friend because I had an unbridled crush on him that wouldn't be easily resolved. But maybe...just maybe, one day I'll be able to come forward with it.

About a month had passed since then, and whenever I spent time with Celine, she would look at me, giving me a wry little smile, that little flame of excitement growing within me. I didn't know why, but I felt like...there was something more there.

When we accidentally would brush hands, she'd look at me, red as a tomato. I'd play it off of course, telling her that I was a bit of a space case and forgot. She'd laugh it off too, saying that it was no big deal.

When in reality, it was obvious that the two of us were this close to just losing our cool right then and there. I didn't know why, but I felt like there was something bigger, something going on there, and I couldn't help but feel it grow closer and closer with each passing day.

"Say Marnie? I have a question for you," she said.

"A question about what?" I asked her. Usually, Celine would just make small talk, getting excited about little things until Rocky would show up.

"Oh, it's just...I don't know, you ever just sometimes feel those urges that grow within you that are hard to explain? Things that you want to tell the other person, but you fear what they may say?" she asked.

"Yeah, I get that," I told her.

"I know it's kind of dumb but...I definitely think about that. And I don't know, I feel like you and I knew one another from a long time ago. I wanted to tell Rocky, but he thinks that I'm joking and that I'm imagining things when I say this," she explained to me.

"I don't think you're joking at all," I told her.

"I'm not. But I feel something deeper with you Marnie. Like we had a connection between us that is not known, but it's right there," she said to me.

I didn't know what she was getting at. Maybe it had something to do with what she said, about her knowing me in the past.

Suddenly, before I knew it, her face was right up against mine, her eyes staring at me. Her lips were mere inches away, and she cupped my chin, looking at me.

"Very interesting," she said.

Her lips were so damn close. It took everything within me to bridge the gap, to kiss those lips. But I stopped myself.

I knew that if I did this, it would ruin things with Rocky. But ugh, just one kiss. That's all I wanted. I wasn't asking for some sort of large-scale thing. I just wanted to know what her lips on mine felt like.

She then smiled.

"It's all good. I'm sorry if I'm being weird. I just feel a deep connection with you. Maybe.... I don't know, it's stupid but I almost feel like kissing you would help. But I couldn't do that to Rocky. I feel like...if I do that, it will break his trust. He's already a little jealous of me and you, you know," Celine said.

I looked at Celine, taking in and drinking her beautiful face up. The long, flowy red hair, the blue eyes, her tall, thin frame with a bit of curve. She was beautiful, something I couldn't help but marvel at. And in truth, I felt like she was the pretty one, and I was just the goblin that tagged along with them.

"Yeah, I figured," I told her, feeling a bit disappointed that I couldn't kiss her.

"But maybe...down the road something can change. You never know what may happen," she pointed out.

I wanted to ask her about this, but then, before I knew it, she was gone, leaving me alone. I sat there, mulling on what the hell had just happened.

What did this mean for us? What could happen now? I had no fucking clue, and I felt like I was being tricked or something. Maybe this was all a figment of my imagination though, and he really didn't feel anything towards me, and neither did she.

I guess that settles it. I guess. I'll just.... see what will happens now.

I packed my bags and went to class, trying to figure out the cryptic meaning behind Celine's words, but still at a loss for what that meant.

Chapter 2

About three months had passed since that weird confession Celine gave to me, and they stuck together strongly. I was jealous about that. If I could have either of them for just one night, I'd be happy as a clam.

When I was alone in my own room at the dorms, I'd sit there, my hands down my pants, touching myself, teasing my clit with one finger, touching my right nipple with my other hand. I let out a series of small breaths, imagining both Celine and Rocky taking me.

First, I imagined Rocky. I wondered how good his cock felt, how big he was, or even how he'd taste. I wondered what it'd feel like if he took my virginity, if he finished within me, all of that. I wondered what would happen if this happened one time, and the future that this would mean for us.

But then my thoughts would shift to Celine. The feeling of her soft lips against my own, her hands against my breasts, touching the fingertips of my hands, moving her own fingertips down to my nipples, painting little touches against the edges, teasing the very tips with the pads of her fingers, causing little moans to come out of me.

Then I imagined her between my legs, eating me out, making me feel good. That alone was usually enough for me to orgasm, the tiniest, smallest of moans coming out of me.

"Celine...."

There was suddenly a knock at the door. I let out a small squeak as I quickly got dressed, hoping that it wasn't my roommate, or worse, Celine who would hear her name from my lips and wonder what the hell was going on.

I quickly made my way over to the doorway, opening it, coming face-to-face with Rocky, who was looking at me with a concerned glance.

"There you are. I didn't hear you come out right away, was a little bit worried for a second," he said.

"Sorry, I was getting ready," I lied. It was such a shit lie, but it had to be enough for him to believe it.

"Anyways, I wanted to talk to you about something. Is it cool if I come in?" he asked me.

I shrugged.

"Be my guest. I don't have classes for a little bit," I admitted.

I just hoped that it didn't smell like I had just masturbated in there. He then opened the door, closing it, sitting at the desk that I had. He paused, trying to figure out what to do, or even what to say.

"What's the matter?" I inquired.

"It's about Celine," he said to me.

"What about her?"

"I don't know, but she talks about you a lot. She keeps telling me how nice you are, how sweet. Your name gets brought up a lot by her, and whenever I look at her...I notice that she's got this little look of excitement on her face. I don't get it. Does she...like you? Have you done anything with her?" he asked me.

I shook my head.

"No. but I can see it too kind of. She seems very passionate about me. I don't want to make you feel bad or anything but—"

"No, it's not that at all Marnie! In fact, I'm sorry, I know that this is a bit embarrassing, but the truth is...I definitely wanted to see if there was something that...I don't know you could do about this," he asked me.

"What do you mean?"

He pursed his lips, trying to find the correct words for this. I could tell he was flustered, when he spoke.

"It's just...I don't know, I feel like...fuck this is embarrassing," he admitted.

"It doesn't have to be though. You can tell me Rocky—"

"Can we have a threesome? With you," he spat out, turning red as a tomato. Now it was my turn to feel a bit flabbergasted.

"With, you mean like...both of you with me?" I asked him.

He nodded.

"Yes. I'm sorry, this is embarrassing. I wanted to ask you if you wanted this. I know that it's probably rude, considering you're like...not with anyone and we're together, but I think it'd be good for her and all," he admitted, turning red in response.

I looked at him, trying to figure out what to say. This was definitely a bit different from what I thought would happen.

"Are you sure about this? I don't want you to find it weird or anything," I told him.

"Not at all! In fact, I think it'd be quite nice. Just the three of us," he offered to me.

I mean, this was what I thought about. I quickly nodded.

"Yeah, I could do that. But only if she's cool with it," I told him.

"She'd be very cool with it. And I know that you like me Marnie. That much is obvious. I figured...it could help her get it out of her system, and we could get to the bottom of this. And I know that you'd like that., I'm sure that one night together might be...just what you're looking for," he told me.

I thought about that. One night together. That was exciting, and while I did feel a flush of embarrassment as he said those words, I liked the sound of it.

"Sure. I'd love that," I told him.

"Oh, thank fuck you're not weirded out. I felt bad for kind of just admitting this to you like that, but I'm glad that you're cool with it," he said.

I flushed.

"Yeah, I've liked you. And the truth is…I remembered Celine. She was a girl I had a crush on. I wanted both of you, but I knew that it was wrong, especially since you were together and all," I said.

"Well, just for one night, you can tag along, and be included. Why don't you come over to my place this Friday? Not the dorm obviously, but you know, my house," he said.

"What about your mom?" I asked him.

"She'll be out, along with my dad. They left the house to Celine and I, but I'm sure a third would be a fun little thing for both of us," he told me with a wink.

I blushed, but nodded.

"Sure," I said to him.

He left the room, and I pursed my lips, thinking about this. He was my best friend, and Celine was an old friend. I didn't think I'd get a chance like this like…ever. But there was something about this that excited me, that made me feel like…deep down this would all work itself out, and things would soon be more different than I ever imagined. I guess I'd better get ready for Friday.

The excitement and desire that I felt in my body was only growing even more so, and there was definitely that feeling of lust, of need, and of excitement that came with the fact that one of the deepest, darkest secrets that I had was about to be fulfilled, and I'd be at the receiving end of it all.

Chapter 3

Friday couldn't come soon enough. I got my homework done a little bit earlier so that I didn't have to worry about this, but that didn't stop the excitement that I felt in my heart at the prospect of this.

When Friday rolled around, he told me seven would be the best time. At seven on the dot, I pulled up, and when I got there, Celine was at the front of the doorway, waving.

"There you are," she said.

"Hey," I replied. Did she know what was going to happen?

"Come on in," she said.

We walked inside, and things all seemed very…simple at this point. I looked at her, and then she motioned upstairs.

"By the way Rocky is up there. He told me to bring you up," she told me.

"Sure," I said.

We got up there, and Rocky seemed to be smiling.

"There you are," he said.

"Hey," I said to him.

"I was thinking we could play a little game first," he said.

What kind of game did he have planned? I flushed at this, realizing what was going on. I didn't know what would happen next, but then he got out a bottle.

"Spin the bottle," he said.

That sly ass bastard. He was totally planning this so he could get Celine to admit her feelings, but then he stopped.

"Or we could do truth or dare," he said.

"Let's try the latter," Celine said.

"Yeah," I replied.

We started playing, and soon, things seemed to be pretty normal. At first, it was a bit nerve-wracking, since I didn't know if he'd bring up some sort of dare between Celine and I but then, at the one-time Celine picked truth, Rocky spoke with a smile on his face.

"Alright Celine, this is for you, and for Marnie," he began.

"Sure," she said to us.

"Did you know Marnie before I got together with you?" he said to her.

She paused, flushing, and then, she nodded.

"Yeah. I didn't know if it was true or not. I thought that I was seeing things, but then, when we met up, I realized this wasn't just my brain fucking with me. You really were the girl that my mom babysat when I was younger," she said.

My eyes widened in surprise.

"You remembered that?" I asked her.

"Yeah, I did," she said with a beaming grin.

"Good," I told her with a small smile.

"Alright…your turn," Rocky said to Celine.

"I guess this one is for you then Marnie," she said.

"What do you mean?" I asked her.

"Truth or dare?" she asked me.

"Umm...truth?" I asked her. I felt my heart race as I said those words. Did I make the right choice?

Her lips curled into that of a smile. I think I started something.

"Did you ever have a crush on me back when we were younger?" she asked me.

I paused, feeling the embarrassment flush against my face.

"You mean like a...crush crush?" I asked her.

"Yeah, like you liked me," she teased, giving me a small grin.

Fuck this was embarrassing. I felt nervous, unsure about it, but I certainly was a little bit scared by this. I then started to look at her, feeling the excitement and worry cross my face.

"Alright fine, I guess I can tell you," I told her.

She looked at me, unsure of what was going to happen next.

"Well come on, spill," she said.

I felt the nervousness take over my body, feeling like I was about to make a mistake uttering these words. When I finally said it.

"Yeah, I had a big crush on you back then. I wanted to tell you, but I didn't know for sure. We were also kind of young and all," I said.

"Aww that's cute," she purred in my ear.

I immediately reddened, feeling a bit embarrassed by it all.

"Well...now what?" I asked them.

"It's your turn," Rocky said, a grin on his face.

"Fine. What about you Celine? Did you ever have a crush on me?" I asked her.

I realized this was supposed to be truth or dare, but I spat it out. I didn't even care at this point. She flushed, but then nodded.

"Yeah," she said.

I realized she felt the same way that I did. There was something almost...exciting about this, and it made me feel good about this.

"Alright then. Truth or dare Marnie," Rocky said.

"Umm...dare?" I asked him.

"I dare you to kiss Celine," he said, giving me a small, devilish smile on his face. I felt the sudden realization of what was about to happen hit me.

She liked me and well...I liked her. I knew that after tonight we wouldn't be able to explore this, but there was something almost fun about this.

I moved closer, feeling my heart skip a beat. I didn't know why, but there was something exciting about this. I wanted to know exactly what would transpire next. Then, our lips were right up against one another, the closeness of our breaths obvious, the realization that she was right there, kissable and within range, and that of course made me feel a rush of excitement.

"Are you...sure about this?" I asked her.

"Damn sure," she said to me with a surefire smile on her face.

Here goes nothing. I leaned in, pressing my lips to hers. We kissed for a second, and for a moment, I got lost in her lips, realizing how soft, sensual, and amazing they felt. I kissed her passionately, enjoying the feeling of this as the two of us simply just stayed there, enjoying the feeling of this.

For a long time, we simply just sat there, making out, enjoying the sensation of it all. We continued to touch, tease, and make out. She pressed her tongue to my own, and our tongues moved and mingled. We made out for what felt like forever, but was probably just a few minutes. I heard the sound of a throat being cleared, and then, I felt her pull back, looking at Rocky with a smile on her face.

"What's the matter Rocky? Jealous?" She asked him.

"Little bit. You two just look so fucking hot," he said, his voice filled with a haze of lust.

"Well, maybe we should take this over to the bed, so we can both explore and tease you appropriately," Celine said.

I realized that I was under her control, and I enjoyed every single moment of this.

"Yeah, I'd love that," I said.

She giggled, touching me, and then bringing me over to the bed. I felt Rocky move behind me, sharing a kiss with Celine before she moved back over to my lips, touching the tip of them and looking at me.

"Is this what you've wanted? Your best friend and your childhood crush to be here, taking care of you? Making you the star of the show tonight? Because that's the intent that I have with you," she purred.

Just hearing those words coming out her mouth was just so damn arousing. That's what turned me on when it came to this. I enjoyed the fact that she was just so nice to me, and how she teased me with just the utterance of a couple of words.

She moved her hands against my chin and neck, plunging downwards and touching my curves. I felt a pair of hands on my waist, and then I was turned back. Soon, my lips were against Rocky's.

His lips were a bit harder, and it surprised me at how good this felt. We kissed passionately together, enjoying the feeling of one another, the excitement and need only making me hunger for more from him. He continued to make out with me, our tongues touching, teasing, enjoying the sensation of one another.

He was a good kisser, a whole lot better than I thought, and I felt his hands move upwards, cupping my breasts through the confines of my clothing. I let out a small gasp, enjoying the touch of this.

"My you've grown Marnie," Rocky said in my ear, touching my breasts, feeling them up, and then letting his hands dance against my nipples.

"Not fair. I want to touch them too," Celine said.

"You'll get your chance babe. I want to tease them a little bit first," he said to me.

I flushed, feeling his hands move against my nipples, playing with them against the very tips of his fingers. I suddenly felt my whole body relax, immediately melting into his touch, loving every single moment of this.

I continued to feel like this was only driving me madder and madder. He knew exactly how to touch me, and then, I felt Celine's soft lips against my own, giving me deep kisses, and then peppering ones that went down my body, teasing my neck with the softest of touches.

In truth, I felt like I was in heaven, enjoying the feeling of two amazing people, just completely immersed in making me feel amazing, completely in awe at the sensation of what this meant for me, and completely enraptured in the feelings of pleasure that escaped from my mouth, enjoying the feeling of this too.

Suddenly, she got towards my collarbone, kissing the tip of it, and then sucking on the flesh there. She hit a spot that made me tense up, moaning out loud and in pleasure as I felt my hips arch, and my body suddenly change into that of complete lust, arousal, and pleasure as well.

She continued to tease me for a little bit, enjoying the sounds that I made, when I felt my sweater get pulled over my head. A pair of hands was on my back, no doubt Rocky's, and when he touched me there, I let out a small gasp of pleasure and arousal, enjoying the feeling of his hands there, touching, teasing, and making me feel amazing. He then moved to the back of my bra, undoing the clasp, and Celine quickly pawed it off, making me blush.

My breasts were out there, on full display for her. She moved her hands slightly, grasping them and touching them.

"So soft. They're bigger than mine too. I'm a little jealous," she said.

Rocky grabbed one of my breasts, teasing the tips of them with little touches and grazes.

"I'll be damned. They are," he told me.

I shivered, moaning slightly as I felt them both continue to touch my breasts. Rocky's touches were both against the nipple and I felt him grope and tease the breast itself.

He teased my nipples, causing me to let out a small cry, tensing up and moaning slightly as I felt the pleasure grow within me. This felt amazing, and he knew exactly how to tease me.

But that didn't compare to what Celine had in store for more. She moved towards my other breast, touching the very tip of it with her lips, looking at me with a wry smile.

"Look at you. You have the cutest breasts, and you make adorable sounds. I can't get enough of this," she purred.

I shivered, feeling the slightest bit of arousal as I began to watch her move towards the tip of my nipple. She breathed on it, smiling as she saw me squirm around.

"Look at you. All turned on. How cute," she said.

"Only because you keep doing this to me," I said with a flush.

"And I'll do so much more honey," she said.

I wanted her to do this. Especially since it... well...it felt really good. She moved towards the tip of my nipple, just over it, and she gave it a tentative lick.

That, combined with the little pinching that came from Rocky, was enough to make my head roll back, the pleasure seeped through me. I shivered, enjoying the little touch of her lips. It was the smallest of licks and little nips at my breasts, but that alone was enough to drive me crazy, turning me on, making me enjoy everything.

She smiled, moving towards the tip, touching the edge with her tongue, flicking it there. She then wrapped her lips around it, encircling against the nipple, watching my eyes widen in amazement as she began to suckle on it slowly but surely, holding my breasts there as she touched them. I let out a small hum, but then I let out another small little cry, enjoying the feeling of her hands against them, and Rocky's hands touching my nipples too.

The sensation of all of this was enough to drive me crazy, and I felt like I was moments away from losing it right then and there. I wanted more, my body and mind craving so much more from this. It made me hungry for them, aching for both of them, and it made me realize just how much I desired it all.

Then, that's when I felt Rocky move away from me. Celine pushed me down into the bed, smiling at me as she hovered over my body, touching the sides, letting her fingers skate over my breasts, lightly teasing, pinching, and playing with them as I looked at her.

"What's the matter? Enjoying this?" she said to me.

"Y-yes," I told her.

Realizing just how turned on I was by the mere mention of her voice. She teased my nipples, enjoying the sounds of pleasure that came out of my mouth. It was clear that she was enjoying this as much as I was, if not more for some reason. I guess there was the fact that she was of course, able to finally get what she wanted.

Which of course was to turn me on, make me feel good, and pleasure me like no other.

She then continued to press her fingers against the edge of my nipples, touching, teasing, playing with them for a little bit before letting her hands settle on downwards. She then got to where my skirt was, sliding that off of me. I shivered as she moved her hands against my thighs, touching them, squeezing them, the little touches of her hands against my thighs turning me on.

"Fuck," I said.

"Someone's a bit excited, aren't we?" she teased.

"Damn right...I am," I told her.

I was at a loss for words. I had no idea what else to say other than the fact that I was massively turned on and aroused by the fact that she was teasing me like this, making me the woman of her dreams, turning me on and enjoying every single aspect of this.

She continued to let her hands slither on upwards, until of course, she got between my legs. She cupped the heat there, making me shiver with delight, lightly gasping in surprise as I felt her hands right up against there, looking me in the eyes with smiles on her face.

She pressed against the heat, touching there slightly, the little touches were enough to make me shiver with delight, I let out a series of small gasps, and moved my hips slightly.

"Look at you. So turned on already," she purred, pressing her fingers against me.

"Please," I said, feeling my whole body at its limit. I needed them. I wanted her to touch me. I wanted to feel her against me.

She smiled, moving her hands towards the sides of my hips, pressing against there, looking at me and licking her lips. She slowly started to move my panties off, pushing them off to the side, looking at me with a grin on her face.

"There we go. That's better," she purred.

She moved her hands, exploring towards me, pressing against my folds. I let out a small cry, surprised by how good her hands felt. They were soft, sensual, and seductive. She looked me in the eyes, licking her lips as she pressed a finger into me.

"Ahh!" I cried out.

"Is this your first time?" she asked me.

I whimpered, nodding in response.

"Yes," I told her.

"Good. I'll take it nice and slow then," she said.

She began to press her fingers there, in and out, touching me and teasing me slightly. She then moved forward, touching the tip of my clit with her tongue, licking around, pressing against there.

I shivered, moaning out loud as I felt her lips and hands completely overtake me. This felt amazing, too fucking good, and I was losing all semblance of control right then and there. I looked over at Rocky, who was smiling.

"While she gets you ready, why don't I give you a taste," he said.

I realized what he meant. He undid his pants, pulling them down, tossing them along with the boxers off to the side. His large cock sprang out, and my eyes widened in surprise at this.

"Woah," I said, looking at the size of that thing. It was big, and the fact that he was going to put that inside of me both made me nervous, but also made me excited.

I leaned forward, licking the tip, and I felt the tongue that was right near my clit lick at the same time as well. I started to explore this, feeling him groan against me.

"Don't worry, it won't bite," he said with a laugh.

I knew that it wouldn't bite. I started to move my lips against his cock, bringing them down the length of it. And as I did that, another finger slipped into me, pressing in and out, teasing me.

I shivered. It both felt different, but also felt right as I felt these two just completely overtake me, making me enjoy the sensation of this far more than I cared to admit. I realized that they were enjoying this as much as I was, and it was then when, after a few more thrusts, I felt her fingers curl up slightly, hitting one spot, and as she did that, my hips bucked, and my pussy tightened. I then moved my lips against the very base of his cock, feeling it there, and he groaned, holding my head there as he fucked my throat. I suddenly felt completely aroused, turned on, and needing more from this man, completely excited about it all, and craving more.

I suddenly felt his cock thrust in and out of me, making me shiver with delight, enjoying the sensation of all of this. I craved more of this, desired so much more, and as I continued to move against there, thrusting in and out, suddenly feeling my whole-body tense up, I could feel the fingers curl up inside of me, breach me, and making my hips move against her, moaning around his cock.

"Fuck I'm already feeling it," he said.

He pulled me off of him, sitting down, sheathing his cock with a condom. He looked at me with an expectant glance, and in truth, I felt the excitement and desire that grew over me come to light.

I wanted this. I wanted him, and I wanted her as well. I slowly moved against him, feeling my whole body become tense with a bit of nervousness. Would this feel good? Or was I going to regret it.

I looked over at her, and then, moments later she smiled.

"There we go," she said to me.

I started to slide down on it, at first feeling a little bit nervous, but then, as it breached me, I let out a small groan of pain, and discomfort as well, only to suddenly feel him fill me the hell up.

"Fuck," I cried out, feeling like my whole body was on edge, completely amazed by how this felt. He held me there, looking at me.

"You good?" he said.

"Yeah," I told him.

I began to move and rock, only to see Celine move herself, pulling off her own clothes. I saw her small lithe body, but what interested me more was her wet pussy. I reached out, touching her there, slipping a finger in, my lips kissing the tips of her folds, my tongue reaching out and teasing her.

"There you go. Good job," she cooed into my ear.

There was something nice about hearing that praise that sent me to a whole new world. I quickly began to lick with excitement, looking at her as she smiled at me, holding my head there.

While she did that, I felt Rocky adjust the position, so that I was on my hands and knees, and soon, he began to thrust.

When he did that, I suddenly cried out around her, eating her out while also moaning into her muff. She held my head there, letting out a small cry.

"Yes. Good girl," she told me.

She held me there, and I felt his thrusts move deeper and deeper, making me shiver with delight, enjoying everything that was happening as well. As I started to feel him thrust deeper and deeper, and even faster as well, I licked that one spot on her, causing her to tense up, let out a small moan, holding me there as she thrust hard.

I stuck another finger in, pressing upwards, watching her tense, cry out, holding me there as she came against my face.

After a few more thrusts, I felt another hand move forward, pressing against my clit, holding it there as I started shivering. Everything was driving me crazy. I was already on the edge from this alone. After a few more thrusts, I began to tense up, holding onto the bed as I came hard, feeling my own desire drip out of me.

This was so good, but then, Rocky pulled out, motioning for Celine to come over. He quickly slipped it into her, fucking her hard.

Celine pushed me down again, going to town on my pussy, holding the tip of my clit, teasing it, letting her tongue snake out and move against there. I let out a series of small moans, completely enthralled. After a few brief moments, I saw Rocky's hands move down, rubbing against her.

"Fuck babe! I'm so close," she said.

"I am too. Want me to spray your faces," he said.

Celine looked at me, and I nodded.

"Yeah," she said.

He pulled out, tossing the condom to the side, and Celine grabbed me so that I was right in front of her, sitting there with her as we looked at him. I watched as Rocky jerked his cock, looking at me with a smile on his face.

"For both of you," he said.

That's when he released. His cum sprayed our faces, and I quickly licked it up. It tasted a whole hell of a lot better than I thought, and Celine savored the taste of it, smiling.

"There we go," she said.

He finished up, sitting back down and laying on the bed.

I quickly cleaned off my face, and Celine did the same thing. We didn't say a word to one another after all of that, completely amazed by how good this was, and how he made both of us feel.

In truth, for the first time, this shit felt really good. Even though I was in a little bit of pain because of what had happened.

We all sat on the bed together, none of us saying a damn thing for a bit. I mean, what would we say at this point? What do you say after you have sex with your best friend and his girlfriend who you had a crush on a long time ago?

"Well, that was great," Rocky finally said, breaking the awkward silence that was there.

"Well, it was more than just great Rocky. I had a wonderful time. And it did...help with a fantasy of mine," Celine said.

I looked to Celine, smiling.

"Same here. I'll be the first to admit that this is exactly what I wanted," I told them.

"Indeed. It was a lot of fun. And you're pretty cute," she replied with a smirk.

I flushed, feeling a little bit of embarrassment as I said those things. I turned to Rocky, feeling bad about this.

"I'm sorry for never telling you how I felt. I always...thought it was wrong to admit how I felt," I told him. I mean, I'd been harboring a stupid crush for a long time, but maybe he understood that.

"It's okay. I understand that Marnie. And in truth, I always thought you were kind of cute too, but I never wanted to date. It would impact the friendship that we already had. I didn't want that," he said.

It was kind of a silly reason to not want this, but I guess that's just the way that he did things.

"Well regardless, I'm just happy about what has happened," I told them.

"Indeed. If you want, you can stick around with us tonight. We were just going to chill once we were done with you," Celine said.

"Yeah. And don't think we don't want to include you Marnie. In fact, I think you awoke us to something that I didn't expect to enjoy," he told me.

I flushed, realizing that they did the same as well.

"You know, it's kind of the same way. And for someone to take my virginity, I'm sure as fuck glad it was both of you," I admitted.

I know that sounded pretty fucking stupid. I mean, I don't know if they felt the same way. But Rocky laughed, pushing his brown hair back, his blue eyes looking into my own.

"Well, I'm glad that I could make you happy Marnie," he said.

I pushed my black hair back, smiling at him.

"Yeah, I'm glad that we could do this too," I replied.

We spent the rest of the evening hanging out, having a good time together. The two of us did feel like our friendship was a little different now, and Celine was a part of our lives too.

But in truth, I didn't mind it. I was happy that I could have these two here with me, in my life, and they gave me a first time that I could enjoy. Even though I was short, thick with big breasts, and awkward, I felt like I really got to experience this with them, in a way that made me smile.

Forbidden & Taboo Erotic Sex Stories:

Erotica For Adults- First Time Lesbian, MILFs, BDSM, Bi-Sexual Threesomes, Hot Wives, Anal, Dirty Talk, Spanking (Orgasmic Collection)

Written By:
G.G. Goode

Goode Publications

Story 1 - Mother Lover (MILF)

Weddings were annoyingly tacky and bound to amount to nothing in the end. That was what Connor had always believed since he was eight years old. Few marriages survived these days and even fewer still lasted more than a decade—just like his parents' marriage hadn't. It wasn't like divorcing was in any way easy business, either. Everyone knew how messy it could be.

So why was it that so many people still went for the idea of marriage when even he could tell that they weren't going to make it? Was he the only one who could, or did no one have the balls to tell them? Or worse, simply didn't want to hurt their feelings? Connor was pretty sure divorce hurt everyone more. Did they choose to turn a blind eye and see everything through rose-tinted glasses instead?

Connor didn't understand. He could see it clear as day when two people wouldn't make it. Usually.

But these two… yes, these two were special. These two were different. They would succeed; Connor was sure of it. The love Rick and Jill shared was unlike anything he'd ever seen before. Genuine. Unconditional. Soul-transcending. It was so strong that Rick and Jill were sure to spend the rest of their lives together—no question about it.

It didn't matter that they were only twenty years old. They were one of the rare lucky couples meant to represent the true institution of marriage. It was intended for people like them.

Maybe it runs in the family, Connor mused, smiling as Rick and Jill kissed, sealing their married titles. The crowd erupted into cheers and whistles, clapping as the newlyweds began their descent down the gorgeous gazebo. Connor caught Rick's eyes and grinned, nodding his acknowledgment. Rick's eyes twinkled in return, their gleam so bright that Connor knew he had never before been happier.

Soon enough, their gazes broke; Rick continued to silently greet his guests and accept their congratulatory shouts, tightly holding hands with his young new wife. Jill did the same, grinning just as widely as he was.

When they were past Connor, his stare thoughtlessly went somewhere else. It followed the crowd and sought out the front rows, settling on a dark-haired middle-aged beauty hugging her husband's arms. Her eyes were full of unshed tears, ready to spill at any moment. Connor's heart skipped a beat.

Mrs. Harris was always a sight to behold. Any day at any time, she was a walking angel, blinding those around her with her grace. Her elegance. But today… Today, Mrs. Harris was something else entirely. Today, she was a vision of happiness; a perfect picture of breath-taking motherly pride.

Though every woman tended to be a mess when their son was getting married, Mrs. Harris was the best of them all. Connor had never before felt so strongly a parent's love of their child. But Mrs. Harris was portraying exactly that.

Somehow, that made Connor happier for his friend than watching him and his bride walk down the aisle.

He and Rick were good friends. Not close enough to warrant Connor a spot as one of his groomsmen, but Connor didn't mind. Even if they had lived together for the past two years—along with three other guys. Their schedules simply never matched up enough in those two years, so naturally, they never got many opportunities to get to know each other better.

Connor frankly wished that they had. If solely for selfish purposes: he could have seen Mrs. Harris more often. The most Connor had seen of her was at their apartment; at times, she would come over to bring Rick a few home-cooked meals—which she also always made big enough for all of them to share—but that was as far as their interactions had ever gone, really. It was a damn shame.

It still didn't stop her from entering his fantasies, however. A lot. As in a *lot*, a lot. It was a secret Connor made sure never to slip up on—Lord knows how Rick would react. Maybe he wouldn't be mad, but Connor was pretty sure no child ever wanted to hear their parent was the subject of their friend's dirty, dirty fantasies. No matter how hot the parent was.

Besides, it was already fucked up enough that Connor was picturing her covered in his cum when Mrs. Harris was such a happily married woman. Not that there was anything inherently wrong with that—but having witnessed first-hand the strong and genuine love that Mr. and Mrs. Harris shared, it was hard for him not to feel guilty about tainting the image of their perfect romance.

Especially when Mr. Harris was so nice and kind. And big. Connor was pretty sure the man could destroy him in a single punch.

But fucking hell, imagining Mrs. Harris on her knees in front of him, sucking him off with all her guaranteed expertise never failed to make Connor cum like a brazen Olympian masturbator—and that was only *one* of his many favored imaginations for every time he came to fap-town. And he went there *often*.

Not that he was obsessed with it. At least, he was pretty sure he wasn't.

As the crowd shuffled inside the nearby hotel lobby for the wedding reception, Connor lost sight of Mrs. Harris and knew it would be too obvious to try and relocate her. He followed the horde of wedding guests, straightening his shoulders as soon as they hunched, then noticed two of his and Rick's other roommates assembling with the bridal couple under a fairy light canopy. It seemed most of the guests were there in order to take pictures.

Connor smiled as many began to join in and photobomb and briefly considered jumping in on the fun, too, but he refrained. There would be time for pictures later when it was less busy. Going right now seemed like it would be a little crazy.

"Connor," someone greeted him.

Connor stiffened, his cheeks blooming red as he whipped around with embarrassing speed. He knew that voice. He'd recognize it anywhere—never needed more than a breath to realize who it was.

"Ah—Mrs. Harris."

Her answering smile was bright. Connor somehow managed to blush even further. He cursed himself in his head.

Only Mrs. Harris ever made him blush. He hated it. Anyone who knew him would immediately be suspicious of what was going on between them.

But she was way too lovely and kind for him to even begin thinking about holding it against her. It was impossible.

"I'm surprised you weren't up there with Aaron and Dmitry," she said. Her lips were so vibrantly red. Delectable. Connor wanted to taste them.

Bet they'd look even better on my coc—

Blushing further, Connor forced himself to snap out of the train of thought before it got anywhere too flustering.

"Oh. Yeah, I mean—Rick and I aren't—" He clammed up. *Aren't what? Close?* It would seem rude of him to say if he was at Rick's wedding in the first place.

Connor cleared his throat and rubbed the back of his neck. "We didn't spend as much time together as he did with them. Those three were always together. But Rick and I... You know. Work and all that." Offering her a small smile, he hoped that none of it would come off the wrong way. He was pretty sure it wouldn't, but one could never know. He had a record of unintentionally stepping on people's toes in his past.

Mrs. Harris smiled wider, and she put her hand up briefly, as if to halt the argument. She shook her head. Connor's shoulders sagged in relief. "Oh, I think it's just because he felt compelled to let Jill's brother be his third groomsman. He probably would have picked you otherwise."

Connor smiled back. Mrs. Harris was always so kind. He was sure she meant it, too, even if Connor was pretty sure that Rick still wouldn't have picked him. He was still closer to other guys. "Thanks. Congratulations, by the way. You must be so happy. I know your family is really close to Jill's. They grew up together, right?"

Mrs. Harris grinned. "Rick and Jill were practically in love since they could walk. You could never keep those two apart."

"Sounds like them alright." Connor's smile widened and he shook his head, thinking back of every moment he'd been a witness to their relationship. They were absolutely over the moon for each other; two soulmates lucky enough to have found one another. Early on, too. Who even met the love of their life back when they were in diapers anymore?

"And how is your family?" Mrs. Harris prodded, tilting her head in genuine interest. It made her look adorable. Not that she ever wasn't.

His eyes dipped to her red, delicious lips again. He swallowed and quickly met her gaze once more. "Oh... They're fine. Thank you. Just as boring as ever. Mom's been bragging about me to all her friends, though, so that's been amusing."

"Oh? What did you do?"

"Nothing," Connor said, his smile returning. "I'm just the first to graduate college in our family. With honors on top of that." His chest filled with pride, and he squared his shoulders. It still felt so good remembering the way his mom cried the day he got his Bachelor's in Health Sciences. "I'll be starting my Masters in PT in September."

Mrs. Harris gasped, and she clasped her hands in front of her mouth. Connor grinned in the same moment a squeal tumbled out of her. His neck turned bright red as Mrs. Harris threw her arms around his shoulders and crushed him with a hug.

"Connor! That's so wonderful!" she gushed, squeezing him tighter. For a moment, Connor thought he even felt her lips brushing against his ear, but he couldn't be sure.

It was probably his imagination. Right? There was no way Mrs. Harris was flirting with him right now.

So into his thoughts, he didn't even realize he never took his chance to hug her back before she already pulled away from him. His brain screamed a thousand curses at him, and it left Connor a little lost because wasn't it his fault in the first place?

"So distracted," Mrs. Harris said, her voice having never sounded so soft. Connor even dared to say she was *teasing*.

Mrs. Harris patted his cheek then carefully traced the line of his jaw. Connor's head clouded over entirely. Was he going crazy? This couldn't be happening. It couldn't. Could it?

"Come on, then," she whispered, her lips quivering up at one side. Her eyes gleamed with mischief. "Why don't you follow me, and I'll give you your graduating gift."

Holy shit. Holy *shit*. It was happening—He wasn't going crazy. Mrs. Harris was actually seducing him!

Connor's jaw slackened until his mouth actually dropped. Mrs. Harris grinned. She didn't waste a moment taking his wrist in her small hand. She started tugging him along down past the fairy light canopy and open bar where so many were gathered, shooting a shudder up his spine. His stomach tumbled when she threw him a hot, inviting look over her shoulder, heart thundering like a wild storm as they quietly slipped into the hotel lobby.

Connor couldn't think. Too stunned by the fact this was actually happening and very similar to some of his many wet dreams, too panicked about being caught and capture Mr. Harris' full enraged attention because he obviously loved his wife very much. It wasn't even fully about how the man could easily pummel him to death. Mr. Harris had always been so kind to both Connor and everyone around him. He was a loving father and adoring husband—the prospect of being the other guy to someone like him was simply appalling. Whoever tempted the wife of such a wonderful man surely had to be the lowest scum of the earth.

His thoughts must be showing on his face, Connor realized, because when Mrs. Harris next glanced at him over her shoulder with her mischievous eyes, the gleam in them faded with her surprise. Her smile waned and her thin brows rose. In the next breath, everything melted with sympathy.

"Don't worry. Fred knows," she said. Her smile was gentler. "We're in a… Hm. What do they call it now?" She put a finger to her lips and looked up pensively. "An open relationship? Polyamory? I'm not sure. Fred and I always knew these types of things as consensual non-monogamy. We've never thought we'd want to try it out. But we're both very happy with the freedom it has given us." She smiled, tugging more insistently on his hand. "I'll tell him about it tonight. He already gave me permission to sleep with anyone I wanted at the wedding. So don't feel bad."

Her gaze trailed over Connor, its burning desire igniting a fire in his bones as it went. Connor's guilt vanished. His breath caught in his lungs as Mrs. Harris sharply pulled him aside to a more secluded hall as they neared one. Her hand ran up his chest, warm even through his dress shirt—the touch so heightened by Connor's lack of his other senses that it sent a shiver up his spine.

Mrs. Harris giggled, seemingly able to feel it. She fisted both hands in his jacket and tugged him towards her in the darkness, their noses touching. "I've seen the way you look at me, Connor… It feels good to be this wanted by someone who is not my husband. Don't you want to have a good time together?"

A blush flared at the back of Connor's neck. His mouth dried, and his heart pounded. Silently, he nodded. He couldn't find the words to say anything as she led him further down the hall into a room, he was pretty sure was staff-only. It seemed to be some kind of storage closet of some sort, but he didn't have the time to inspect and confirm his guess as Mrs. Harris slanted her lips over his and rendered his brain to complete putty.

He was hard within an embarrassingly short time. All Connor wanted to do was touch her—anywhere, everywhere. So he did; slipping his hands over her silky dress to caress every curve of her body, take in every inch of softness she had to offer. It was downright nirvana.

In the past, Connor never understood why it was that he liked older women so much—but maybe it was because of this. Their confidence, the amazing plushness of most of their bodies. Mothers, especially, were particularly wonderful. With fuller hips, thicker thighs—and bigger breasts, too. All probably from the labors of birthing and nursing a child.

Not that Connor tried to think about that much. The last thing he wanted was to actually date a mother and become appointed their child's pseudo-dad. He wasn't anywhere near ready for *that*.

But fuck did he love fucking mothers. They were always less preoccupied about the imperfections of their bodies—the opposite to the many insecure girls Connor slept with through college. Connor loved that. There was something so sexy in the way they didn't squirm at half his touches, and how they didn't ever avert their gazes when his face was buried between their thighs.

And Caroline—Mrs. Harris—was already the very best of them all. There was nothing but encouragement from her. From the moment his hands found the perfection that was her ass, she was all delighted sighs and sweet moans. Cheeky grins and approving murmurs. She never even flinched as he roamed his hands over the thickness of her thighs, instead she leaned further into him, copping feels of her own.

When she expertly started undoing the buttons of his dress shirt and pushed his suit jacket off, Connor's heart skipped a few beats. It continued to do acrobatics as she smiled up at him, besotting him even more with every second. Mrs. Harris was a vision in all her gorgeous glory. And she was with him. Right now. Intending to have sex.

Holy shit.

"Is it just me or are you still all up in your head?" Mrs. Harris teased, smoothing her warm hands over his now-bared chest. Her eyes crinkled up at the corners.

Connor felt like he could barely swallow at all. "Still processing that this is actually happening, to be honest." He silently cursed himself for sounding so pathetic.

But at least Mrs. Harris found it charming. With a giggle, she grinned and gently pushed him back—just enough to be able to reach a hand out at the back of her dress. Connor heard a zip and instantly felt like his brain short-circuited. The next thing he knew, her dress was pooled around her feet…

And Caroline Harris stood in front of him, completely bare except for her pretty lace panties.

Connor's mouth dropped. He stared unblinkingly, void of any thought.

"Like what you see?" she prodded, her adorable smile shifting into a devious smirk. She tugged him forward, her sweet little hands guiding his hands on her body. One of them unabashedly presented him with her breast, nipple already peaked to perfection. Holy fucking *balls*, her tits were amazing.

Connor brushed his thumb over the dark nipple and Mrs. Harris hummed, arching into his hand. He wasn't prepared for the way she grinned at him after, or for her to grab his tie so assertively. He felt like prey—in the best way.

"Be a good boy and take off your pants, won't you?" she whispered.

Connor's control snapped. Mouth thinning, he aggressively pushed Mrs. Harris against the wall and slanted his lips on hers in a possessive, passionate kiss. Mrs. Harris had no complaints. Instead, as he started undoing his pants, her small fingers enthusiastically joined him in his task. Connor let his dress pants drop to his feet before proceeding to cup her jaw to angle her for a deeper kiss. It wasn't long before he hauled her up around his hips by her plush, round ass and instinctively grabbed for her breast again greedily.

His mouth soon followed the same path, leaving her reddened lips to make its way down with wet, sloppy kisses. The sound his sweet Mrs. Harris made when his lips closed around her nipple was so damn good it tore a groan out of him. He wanted to hear it again. Now.

Determined, he rolled his tongue over the stiff peak and ended with a hard suck, pride puffing out his chest as Caroline's breath hitched in return. Her fingers dove into his hair, raking through his locks. She hummed, then tried to tug him even closer.

"You sure are good with your tongue, Connor…" she murmured, scratching her nails across his scalp. It almost had him shuddering.

What was successful was her compliment, though. It was enough to have fire roaring in his veins, teeth-gritting with desire. He needed to give her more, give her something to *truly* merit the praise and—

A strangled laugh left his mouth, and Connor growled just as he dropped to his knees, quickly flipping Mrs. Harris around. He sank his teeth into one ass cheek far before she even had the chance to gasp, dick twitching in anticipation as her musky scent invaded his senses. He briefly glanced up to find Mrs. Harris leaning her forehead against her arms, those of which were now folded against the wall.

The sight had his mouth drier than a California summer.

Pulling away, Connor made quick work of her lacy thong and licked his lips, earning himself a breathless laugh. He frowned. Intent on killing off that sound, he spread her cheeks and dove straight for her rosy folds. Her laugh died instantly, replaced instead by a surprised moan. Connor groaned. He didn't waste time getting to work, slowly sucking and lapping at her nether lips while he reached one hand further up between her thighs.

Mrs. Harris was quick to catch on. Panting, she led him exactly where she needed him, whimpering approving sounds as he began to handle her clit with quick, firm strokes. His dick twitched again, begging for attention. He'd never been so hard before—so hard it physically ached him.

Fuck, he could cum just like this. Eating her out and hearing her moan, feeling her shift her thighs to open wider just for him. Most of the girls he'd been with had been embarrassed and self-conscious when he went down on them, which took out a lot of the fun—but not her. Not Caroline Harris. She was so fucking perfect.

Before long, Mrs. Harris started quivering, her panting breaking off into shorter staccatos of heat and pleasure. It surprised him; though Connor didn't have a porn star's equivalence in experience, he still possessed enough to know without any doubt what such tell-tales meant. Especially when his prime focus in any of his sexual encounters had always been trying to get his partner off—only it was hard to pull off the first time with basically anyone.

And yet here Caroline Harris was, ready to go off like a rocket any second now. With little more than brief guidance on her part.

Christ, that meant she was definitely having a *really* nice time with him. Because it sure as shit wasn't for his skills. He was good—but he wasn't *that* good.

Not enough to get her off this quickly anyway.

"Connor," she gasped, her voice hitching on a moan. Her hand reached back blindly to tangle in his hair. Her hold was a little rough, but fortunately, Connor liked it. He liked it even more when she pulled on his short, curly locks again, drawing a pleasure-pain hiss out of him. If he could speak, he probably would have asked her to do it again. Mrs. Harris whimpered. "Connor, get up. Please. I don't want to cum with your mouth on me. I want to cum around your cock. Now."

Holy fucking Christ on a cracker. She definitely didn't need to tell him twice.

Pulling himself up to his feet, Connor kicked his dress pants away and raced to push off his underwear, nearly making a fool of himself in the process as he tripped over them. Luckily, he managed to catch himself in time and Mrs. Harris didn't seem to notice his mishap—or at least, didn't seem to care enough to acknowledge it. His face sweltered red from both the embarrassment and his feverish desire, though it leaned more towards the latter as his gaze set back on Mrs. Harris' sweet cunt. He bit back a groan, unable to help himself from giving his cock a few solid pumps.

That Mrs. Harris noticed. She giggled and had his gaze shooting up at the sound, unprepared for the mischievousness swimming in her pretty eyes as she stared at him over her shoulder. The look was both seductive as it was devilish; Connor swallowed against his suddenly dry throat, hand still around his aching cock.

Mrs. Harris settled her palms flat on the wall before widening her legs and slipping a hand between them, her ensuing moan enough to make any teenage boy promptly cum in his pants. Connor was sure he would have if he'd heard it many years ago. The best porn couldn't even compare to the beauty of that sound. His brain melted so badly that he could barely process anything else.

"Are you even listening to me at all? Or does this wet pussy just take all your senses away? God, look at you. You're so hard just looking at me. I wonder how you'll feel inside me. Don't you wonder, too?"

Connor blinked and looked up at Mrs. Harris, the words leaving her mouth finally registering once more. He blushed harder and sought to distract them both by running both hands over her perfect ass.

It didn't work.

"Well hi there, welcome back," she murmured, giggling softly. "You sure know how to make a woman feel desirable, I'll tell you that…"

The fingers rubbing her clit moved down, sliding along her wet folds with a bite to her lip. She was tempting him—daring him to fill her. She smiled, gazing at him with what he could only call a challenge.

"Connor. Come here," she whispered, reaching back to spread herself for him. Connor's breath stopped. "I think I know a much better place to put that cock of yours in… Somewhere that'll make us both feel better."

Sweet Jesus' ballsack. Connor's thoughts slipped away from him, pre-cum dribbling from his slit as he stared at what her fingers presented him, wet and ready. He made some kind of strangled noise, both hands snatching out for her deliciously thick thighs. He wrapped his fingers around himself once more, holding his cock steady as he rubbed against the soaking wet cleft of her legs.

He didn't expect Mrs. Harris to reach down between them and position him at her opening, the move so hot and unforeseen that Connor swore it took him everything not to lose it and cum right there.

Shaking, he thanked every God out there for giving him the control. His heart pounded against his rib cage, mind spinning in a whirlwind of bliss as he began to push himself inside. He braced himself against the wall, eyes closing and a moan slipping from his parted mouth.

Until an epiphany struck him.

"Wait," he choked out, retreating and running a hand over his face. He gritted his teeth. "Fuck. Condom?"

Mrs. Harris looked back with another tempting smile, her gaze the perfect picture of seduction. She opened herself up again with one hand, wiggling her ass in invitation. "If you're clean, it's all good. I'm clean, too. And I've had my tubes tied a long time ago. So you can cum inside me as much as you like, honey."

The devilish smile she sent him right then burned away Connor's last thread of self-restraint. His chest rumbled with a guttural noise somewhere between a growl and a moan, bringing out an absolutely feral side of him that Connor never even knew he had. He positioned his cock at her entrance and this time, wasted no breath at all slipping inside her depths.

Mrs. Harris gasped, hips dipping towards him to take in more of what he had to offer. Connor bit his tongue, thrusting shallowly to coax her body to open up to him some more and squeezing her thighs so tight he was sure she would find them bruised later. They both moaned when his hips met her ass and a series of colorful swears danced on his tongue.

"Fuck, you make me want to cum already," he hissed, licking his lips. "You feel so good, Mrs. Harris."

"Caroline. Please—Call me Caroline," she replied, whimpering. She reached down to touch between them where they were joined, mouth parting with a soft moan. "Fuck me, Connor," she said. "Cum inside me. I know you want to. I know you've been dreaming about it. So fuck me until you do. Please."

Connor snarled and promptly heeded to her demands. Maintaining his death grip on her thighs, he started slowly thrusting and rolling his hips at first to test the waters of how wet and hot she was before steadily increasing his pace and the force of his movements. Soon, he was fucking her like a madman, bracing one hand against the wall to better leverage himself while she cried out and both uttered encouragements and praise.

It was unlike anything he ever imagined; feeling her squeeze around his cock, hearing the sweet sounds falling from her mouth, watching the way her ass rippled with his every thrust—it was a piece of fucking heaven. He wanted to be there every day, to never have to stop. And God, hearing the way his name fell from her lips… It had never sounded so good on anyone else. No other girl had made him feel like this, no other girl had ever riled him up so much he could barely hold himself back. Only Mrs. Harris—no, no. *Caroline.*

"Caroline," he panted, moving her in time with his thrusts, eyes squeezing shut at the blinding bliss coursing through him.

Caroline answered with a moan, rolling her hips into his on his next thrust, sending them both into a grinding mess desperately seeking friction. He groaned and bent down to rake his teeth over her neck, relishing the way her fingers slipped through his hair. He hoped she'd pull on it again—like she had earlier. Fuck, he really hoped she would.

"Just like that," she encouraged, her breaths choppy and hot. She ground back against him again and moaned, tugging at his locks to pull him even closer. Connor sucked in a breath, growling and grinding right back into her. Christ, her pussy felt so good. So, fucking good. "*Yes.* God, you're so good. Such a good boy. Such a great *cock.*"

A feral sound slipped from his throat. Connor sank his teeth into the tender flesh of her neck, seeing white. Shit, he was going to cum if she kept talking like that. He wouldn't be able to keep up—to make her fall apart, too. And there was no way he could let that happen now. Not when he'd been dreaming about having Caroline Harris like this for years. Not when she'd haunted his nights with seductive promises and mind-blowing orgasms that left his briefs a mess and left his sheets sweaty.

Every. Single. Time.

He couldn't let her down now that he finally, *finally* had her at his mercy.

But then Caroline squeezed her muscles down on him so deliciously that his knees nearly gave out and Connor's eyes snapped wide open, hips stuttering in their rhythm. This was it. His end was finally here. He could see it so clearly, just within reach. His thrusts turned from steady and rough to wild and frantic, desperate for release. His balls tightened. Caroline's pussy kept closing around him. Connor moaned freely, teetering on the edge. He swore under his breath, eyes slamming shut yet again.

"Fuck. *Fuck.* I'm so sorry, Caroline, I'm gonna—I'm gonna cum," he gasped. "You feel too good…"

God fucking damnit. He wouldn't be able to get her there. He wouldn't get to fulfill his dreams, and she'd be too disappointed to give him another chance. How laughable was it that on the brink of his greatest orgasm ever, Connor could feel like such a royal fucking failure? He wanted to cry. He wanted to moan. He wanted to cum so hard it hurt. He wanted to make *her* cum twice as bad.

But then Caroline turned to look at him over her shoulder and smiled, her cheeks so gorgeously flushed, and she slipped a hand between her legs. Her smile vanished, face twisted in bliss as she gasped and moaned instead. The sight sent Connor spiraling into bliss, brain exploding into nirvana as he spread her ass cheeks wide and ground out his milky release inside her, moaning unabashedly.

He was so loud he was sure someone had to have heard them, but he didn't care anymore. Not when he was having an orgasm this good. Not when he was with the actual woman of his dreams, spurting his cum deep inside her. Nothing else mattered.

He was still riding out the last waves when Caroline joined his high, crying out and milking every last drop from him with her sweet cunt as she ground out her release. Connor gasped and bit his tongue, groaning gravelly as he fought to keep them both upright. His knees shook, his breath stayed caught in his lungs, eyes wide.

Holy. Fucking. Shit. That was… He couldn't even manage to find the words. Fantastic? No. That couldn't even begin to describe what had just happened between them. *Jesus. Best sex of my fucking life.*

The only regret he had was that he hadn't gotten to actually watch her cum. He'd been in the throes of his own orgasm, too busy having his brain explode via his dick to be aware of anything else than how good he felt in the moment. It was a damn shame he couldn't hold out for her.

Still, the utterly sated smile on Caroline's lips was mostly enough to make up for it. So was her undeniable contentment, conveyed clearly in the way she sifted her fingers through his sweaty hair and hummed, sighing like she didn't have a care in the world.

"Did I leave you speechless?" she teased, when neither of them had spoken for a while.

How long had it been? Five minutes? Ten minutes? Less? The concept of time seemed so silly and inconsequential right now.

Caroline wiggled against him and giggled, the move pushing out his slowly softening dick. Connor swore he caught a pout before she turned her head away from him and bent down to pick her panties up. She slipped them on and went back down for her dress as well, beginning to make herself presentable again.

When she noticed him staring, dumbfounded, she grinned and offered him a wink. "You know, for someone still so young, you're definitely sprightly," she said, pulling out a hand mirror and wipe from her clutch. She moved on to fixing her make-up with such ease it was evident she had often fixed any post-sex smudges before.

Connor's heart did funny things in his chest. A blush rose from the back of his neck to the tips of his ears, intense in its heat. It was all frankly a little dizzying.

It must have been noticeable, because Caroline blinked and huffed the most adorable little laugh. She shook her head. "Keep that up and you'll have a bright future in your sex life. You'll make a lot of women happy."

"I don't think I can take all the credit. I almost didn't make you cum. You had to help yourself along, remember?" Connor didn't even know how he managed to string so many words together. Currently, his brain still felt like it was putty. Like he wouldn't even be able to count to ten. But his words were true, however.

Caroline smiled and patted his cheek. She shook her head and shrugged. "Sex is never entirely all about someone else's experience. I've learned a lot in almost thirty years. And as a mother of two. Mainly that no partner should leave the other to do all the work. You have to help each other out. Especially when it comes to orgasms."

She winked at him again, here, and Connor flushed even deeper. Jesus, it was ridiculous how much this woman could make him blush. Caroline thumbed the redness of his cheeks and grinned, her gaze briefly dipping down at his limp length. She licked her lips, and Connor swore he would have stirred to life again if his body didn't need time to recharge, still.

Jesus. Mrs. Harris was so fucking hot.

And tight, he mused with twitching lips, remembering the way her hot, wet walls clamped around him. Whoever said women who had given birth became loose and dry were deluded liars of enormous proportions. Caroline Harris was pure proof that they would be just as good as any other woman. Maybe even better. They could still be sexy as hell, even at forty or fifty years of age.

He must have looked deep in thought because the next thing he knew, Caroline laughed and called his name, seemingly amused or maybe even slightly confused. He blinked and shifted his attention on her once more, heart thudding loudly at her bright smile.

"Connor…? Hey, are you listening?"

In an instant, her smile was gone. Connor blinked and tilted his head, washed over with a sense of confusion. The sudden change was a little too odd, a little too abrupt. "Yeah? What is it?"

But Caroline's stare remained unchanged, unwavering. Her expression captured the same steadied level of confusion and… something else. Concern? But why?

"Connor!"

A hand waved in front of his face and Connor startled, jumping a little as he suddenly found himself back on the lawn near the fairy lights canopy, where so many were still huddling in order to snap some pictures with the bride and groom. Mrs. Harris was standing in front of him, brows knitted together and sporting a faint frown.

She'd been the one to wave her hand in front of his face.

Oh, God fucking damnit. Had it all just been a fucking fantasy?

"Connor, are you okay?" she asked, much like any worried parent would to their child.

So unbelievably sweet. So caring. So beautiful. Jesus Christ, she was so perfect. Of course he had to be daydreaming. There was no way in hell he could ever land a chance with her. Especially not with her husband in the picture.

Unless they would really have an open relationship—but they've never seemed the type. I don't think either of them like the idea of sharing each other.

His heart deflated in his chest, whizzing like a punctured balloon. Even if Mr. and Mrs. Harris *did* have an open relationship, Connor suspected she probably wouldn't be interested in guys around her son's age, anyway.

Damnit. His throat worked up a swallow. "Uh… Yeah. Sorry. I got a little... lost there. Caught up in some thoughts."

It wasn't exactly the whole truth, but at least it wasn't an outright lie. He couldn't very well tell Mrs. Harris that he'd been fantasizing just now about fucking her in a hotel storage closet. Especially when they'd barely spoken much before today.

Can't exactly bail and say it was a joke, either. I doubt she'd find that funny from an acquaintance—one of her son's friends, no less.

Thankfully. Mrs. Harris didn't press for more details. She merely nodded, concerned features giving way to relief.

"Oh. Good." She smiled; amiable but strictly platonic. His heart continued to deflate miserably. "Well, like I was saying… Your parents must have thrown quite a celebration for your success. I know I would if ever Rick graduates with honors, too. Fred would probably splurge the most. I wouldn't be surprised if he'd decide to surprise us overnight with cruise tickets." She chuckled fondly, shaking her head. "Now I have no other choice but to push him harder! We haven't had a family vacation in too long!"

Connor huffed. *As if there's a chance in hell that Rick wouldn't get honors,* he thought. But apparently Mrs. Harris misinterpreted his reaction, because she frowned deeply in return. His chest began to pound in a staccato of panic.

"Are you kidding? Rick is at least twice as smart as I am. He's the genius one out of our little circle. Always has been. You've got nothing to worry about—he's a wonder child. No doubt about it."

Mrs. Harris' eyes widened, then she laughed—the sound so melodious it took Connor right back to his fantasy. He had to shake the thoughts from his head so as not to lose himself from the moment again. But at least he could take some comfort in the fact he would never get her beautiful laugh wrong.

"Well," she said, sweeping her long dark hair back over her shoulder. "That's what you get when you get two brainiacs and put them together."

She grinned proudly, and the delight was so blinding that Connor couldn't help smiling back, even with all of his growing disappointment towards reality. Caroline Harris would never want him, and Connor would never know what it felt like to be with her, inside her. To hear her truly moaning his name. He'd never know what her wet cunt felt like—even what it tasted like.

"What's going on? What are you two so smiley about?" someone called from his right, happy and bemused.

Connor glanced at the newcomer to find Mr. Harris, faintly smiling and eyes crinkling as they always were. Especially when he was looking at his wife. Which he was, right now. Of course Connor couldn't blame him.

Mrs. Harris smiled at her husband, too, reaching to take his hand in hers. "Connor graduated with honors, honey. Isn't that wonderful? We were just talking about how proud you and I would be if Rick graduated with honors, too."

"You graduated with honors? Connor, that's great! Congratulations!" Mr. Harris clapped Connor's back and grinned, shaking his shoulder like all proud dads did. It reached something deep within Connor— though they barely knew each other, Mr. Harris was always so warm that he never came across as anything but genuine. As such, none of his compliments ever rang empty.

He's a good man. Good husband. Good father. He and Mrs. Harris are lucky to have each other.

Mr. Harris said something then, something about excusing him and his wife as they needed to get going—Jill's parents had been looking for them both in order to take official wedding pictures. Or something like that anyway. Connor had been too caught up in his thoughts.

As they walked away, he ran his hand through his hair—that of which was still perfectly coiffed and missing the wildness that fantasy-Caroline-Harris had made a mess of.

Jesus Christ, I'm so pathetic. Fantasizing while the hottest mother in the world was talking to me. Typical.

At least he'd been lucky enough not to soil his pants. He didn't know how he hadn't actually cum. Maybe because he hadn't been sleeping. But that fantasy-orgasm was definitely the best one he'd had yet—even counting the real ones.

So at least there was that.

Story 2 - Rosy Cheeks (Spanking)

This was probably the worst idea they'd ever had.

Any minute now, Dominic's parents could come home from the grocery store. Could walk in on the pair of them moaning up their house in a heated frenzy, their trip having panned short for the day. Dom found it terribly unlikely, but it wasn't exactly reassuring. For all they knew, maybe his parents would make a quick detour home after Mr. Reavers forgot his wallet again, in which case they might have even gotten caught already…

Still, Rosie couldn't bring herself to care. Not when Dominic was making her feel this good. This dizzy in the best way there was. Especially when they never had many chances to be like this in the first place. Not when Dom lived five hours away.

Stupid dream-colleges.

Dominic grunted. Digging his fingers into her hips, he leaned his weight on one elbow and rolled his hips against her ass in a slow circle, driving a shudder up her spine. Rosie whimpered, eyes squeezed shut tightly. She bit her lip as Dom mouthed the back of her neck, tasting the sweaty skin there.

Palming her side with his free hand, Dom groaned and rolled his hips harder. "Christ. You feel so good, Rosie," he whispered, burying his face in her hair. He resumed rocking, building up to his previous steady pace and sending her toes curling. Bracing himself against both the bed and her hip, he made sure each thrust buried him as deeply as he could go, as deeply as her body would allow him. Rosie gasped and spread her thighs wider, cheeks flushing hotly. She needed more.

Dom groaned, the hand at her hip running up her side again. A slow smile spread over his lips, which Rosie only knew was there because she'd felt it come to life against her shoulder. "God, I missed you. I missed the way you feel around me. I missed knowing how much you love having me inside you."

Flustered, Rosie's blush grew more feverish. She hid her face in his bedsheets, fingers curled around them for dear life. While Rosie had always cringed when Dom's talk got a little dirty in the bedroom, she still hadn't mustered up the courage to admit it to him despite the fact they'd been dating for the past six months. And despite the fact they'd actually known each other their whole lives. Dom was her first— everything about sex was still embarrassing to her. Though she *had* gotten a little better at not being so self-conscious of her naked body, lately…

It was hard to care when Dom was so clear about how much it always turned him on.

"You're so wet," he murmured, propping himself up from his elbow so he could palm her ass with his free hand. Humming, he grabbed one full cheek and held on to it possessively, picking up his pace until he settled into a beat of rough little pounds. A small cry left her lips and was promptly muffled against the sheets. Rosie moaned, spiraling in a mess of bliss.

"Oh God," she gasped, arching her back and trying her best to meet his thrusts. The grip she had on his sheets was death-like and her eyes remained clenched shut tightly. Rosie swore she could still feel his stare, though. Settled in the space where their bodies met, watching the way his cock pounded into her.

Dom always liked doing that.

Slowing down his pace, Dom sighed and ran his hand up from her ass to her side, then finally around to one of her full, peaked breasts. Rosie bit her lip when he played carefully with her nipple, recalling how different his touch was from three months ago when they'd only started getting sexual. He'd been too rough, back then—not from any lack of experience, but simply because none of any of the girls he'd been with had ever been as sensitive as Rosie. And it wasn't exactly like she had been much help letting him know as much, either; as her first real boyfriend and sexual partner at the tender age of twenty-two, she hadn't known much about herself in that department.

Even now, Rosie still wasn't used to how good Dom was when it came to sex. Jesus, he was good. *So* good. More than that, she was still trying to get used to how embarrassing some things were about sex. Awkward bodily noises, squelching bodies, communicating what humiliating things felt good—those were all part of a slow progress to accepting these things were normal.

She was just too shy. Too stuck on her innocent image, as Dom once said. There was nothing shameful about what they were doing or how good he was making her feel—no matter how differently her church-going parents might think.

Rosie was so glad to have Dom. He was a good partner—a good lover. She wasn't even sure sex would have been this good and comfortable if it wasn't for him. Even if they had his level of experience. Dom was a kind man—one who always sought to make sure she was comfortable with whatever they were doing. One who always went out of his way to make sure she liked what he was doing and who always sought to learn what she liked best—all for the sake of making her cum.

Jesus, he was good at making her cum.

She just wished they could do this more often than every few weeks. He left her wanting more each and every time.

Dom's hand left her breast. Peppering wet kisses over her shoulder, he halted his slow rocking for a moment to seemingly shift in a new position, yet Rosie was still helpless against stopping her whimpers from slipping out. She was barely aware of the soft, "Sorry baby, give me a second," that Dom murmured with a kiss to her lower back before both his hands found her hips again and pulled her snuggly against his lap, fully seating himself within again. Rosie let out another muffled cry, instinctively grinding back into him for some friction.

There was a beat of silence and then Dom chuckled warmly. He ran his hands from her hips to her ass, rubbing both cheeks with such heat and want, that it had her burning up from the inside. "Did that feel good, Rosie? Much better than a vibrator, huh?"

Her flushed cheeks returned with a vengeance and she buried her face deeper in his sheets, swallowing. "Dom… Stop it. You know I don't have one…" she whispered.

"You should," he replied, resuming moving and slowly building up a rhythm of steady, firm thrusts. He grunted and grabbed her hip in one hand, steadying her as he found a beat that pleased them both. "Then you'd miss having my cock inside you even more. Miss *me* more."

Rosie whimpered, her grip tightening around the sheets. She wanted to tell him how much she already missed him all the time, how much she touched herself thinking about him, but she couldn't. She met his thrusts eagerly instead, mouth parting as one of his hands slipped around and beneath her belly to play with her clit. She bit down on the blue fabric and cried out, fingers squeezing down on the soft sheets until all her knuckles were surely white.

God, his experience was so obvious in times like these. As his girlfriend, Rosie knew she should probably feel jealous towards the fact he so clearly knew his way around a woman's body—but she couldn't make herself care when it meant he could so easily draw out pleasure from hers.

"Dominic…" she moaned, begging him silently. She needed more, she could see her orgasm in the distance, getting closer and closer. She met his thrusts with more vigor, gripping his bedsheets even tighter.

A hand landed on her ass, swift and nearly painless. Rosie gasped, eyes snapping open wide as her pussy clamped down on him. Dom kept moving, grunting out his pleasure. He didn't seem to have caught on how much she'd liked the slap. He never seemed to notice anytime he smacked her ass and Rosie wanted to let him in on it—wanted him to do it more. Do it harder.

But she couldn't. She was too embarrassed to admit it. She only knew Dom spanked her on an instinctive level, loving the way her ass jiggled in return.

Dom's hand fell on her ass again, a little harder this time. Rosie gasped and whimpered, automatically bucking back against his cock and grinding. Dom groaned, thrusting harder. Faster. Rosie started trembling, breaths erratic as her mind spun out in bliss. Her path to orgasm was getting clearer, closer, steadily more inevitable with every—

Dominic smacked her ass again, and Rosie's eyes snapped open wide. A raw cry tumbled from her mouth, the pain stinging her so good this time that it sent her crumbling apart instantly. Distantly, she thought she might have heard Dom swear but Rosie was too caught up in the waves of her orgasm, too busy trembling like a leaf and grinding out her high against his cock that she couldn't be sure. She was pretty confident that Dom was helping her draw out each wave, though, vaguely aware of hips rolling back into hers and incoherent murmurs floating in the room.

And her stinging ass cheek. A delicious pain that only added to the glow of her release. One that she wanted to experience again and again. Every damn day they were like this.

God, she would love that.

Only when Rosie was coming down from her high did she become aware of Dominic lovingly kissing her shoulders and the back of her neck. The embarrassment rushed through her instantly, flushing her body head to toe with a dizzying blush. Jesus Christ. She'd just orgasmed the second he spanked her harder than usual. When she was close, but needed more effort, more friction. More *something*. She couldn't believe that all her buildup had ultimately been outgunned by a simple, rough slap to her ass.

Did that make her a pervert? Oh my *God*.

If she was lucky, Dominic wouldn't know any of that though. He'd have to take credit for making her cum—which he had—but he didn't have to catch on to all the details, right? Right?

God, Rosie hoped she was right. She couldn't bear the thought of Dom knowing she was so… so… *so damn far from the innocent girl he grew up with.*

"Fuck, Rosie… I missed feeling you cum. Squeezing all around me like that. And how you sound…" Dominic buried his face in her neck, sighing with complete contentment. He smiled against her skin and kissed her nape lovingly. "I was surprised, though. I knew you were close. I could feel it. The way your body was all tensed up and how you kept clamping down on me. Trembling and grinding against my cock like that. But… I didn't know you were *that* close. Hm? What's up with that, Rosie?"

Shit. Oh God, he totally knew. He totally knew that something was up and that it hadn't just been his usual skills. Damnit. *God freaking dammit.*

Silent, Rosie kept her face buried in the sheets, too flustered to even acknowledge the comment. She swallowed, fighting against her furious blush to at least try and not look so guilty of being coaxed to sudden orgasm by something so embarrassing.

Dominic chuckled and kissed her nape again, mouthing a path of slow, sweet kisses down her spine. Then he flattened himself against her back and buried his face into her neck once more. She couldn't help her gasp as the change nestled his cock deeper inside her, sending her squirming. Dom's lips quirked up against her skin in a clear grin, one that had her heart skipping a beat.

"You know… I notice that you seem to tense up and moan every time I spank your ass. I wasn't sure about it before, but I'm pretty positive that I'm right after today. You weren't there yet. I could feel that. Close, but you needed more to be able to cum. And I know you didn't just cum because I was fucking you good. Or because it's been three weeks since we last had sex. I spanked you hard and you instantly fell apart beneath me. That can't be a coincidence, can it Rosie?"

Rosie's throat worked in another swallow. Something about the way he was asking her was so sexy that it made her blood feel as though it had turned into hot lava. Her pussy throbbed, something had Dom's grin growing. Her face burned so hotly she grew dizzy.

Still, she didn't reply—she couldn't. She was completely mortified. What would people say if they knew she liked pain in the bedroom, however little? God, what would *Granny* say? Could she even look at her in the eye upon going home tonight?

Dominic's chuckle reverberated against her throat and he scraped his teeth against the skin there in a mock bite. Rosie shuddered, biting her lip as he left a trail of slow, wet kisses all the way up to her ear. He nipped the small lobe.

"What, did I leave you speechless, Rosie? Should I do it again just to confirm my suspicions?" he asked, tone dripping with equal amounts of teasing as it did temptation.

Rosie gripped his bedsheets tighter, swallowing down a moan of misery. She wanted to die. God, she was so embarrassed. And Dom knew it, but he still pushed her further, tried to get her to admit it. Or maybe even make fun of her.

Reaching for the closest pillow, Rosie whacked Dominic in the face as best and as hard as she could, quickly grabbing another to hide it in. Dominic laughed. She pouted. She clutched the pillow closer, whining. "Stop trying to embarrass me. You're being mean."

"I don't need to try," Dom gibed, grinning as he kissed her shoulder. He shifted off her back, presumably straightening himself up, then ran his hands over her sides, down her thighs, and over her plump ass. She glanced back just in time to see him licking his lips as he stared at the space they were joined. He slowly started moving again, setting up a languid pace. "You're already embarrassed."

Rosie went to protest, but Dominic's hand flew punishingly against her ass, tearing a moan from her lips. She clasped her hand over her mouth, her furious blush returning with a vengeance. Dom grinned, so cheekily proud that she needed to look away. She buried herself back in his pillow, praying his parents were still ways away from coming home because at this rate, Dom would have her moans ringing throughout their house.

"My oh my… You really *do* like it," Dom teased, running his hand up her back.

Rosie whimpered. Reaching back, she grabbed his arm, holding onto him firmly while he picked up his pace to something more patterned and rougher. It had both their breaths breaking into heavy staccatos of pleasure.

But then Dom chuckled, leaning down to kiss her wrist before pulling away from her grasp—seconds before spanking her ass again. Rosie muffled her moan into the pillow, evermore mortified by how much she loved it—though her back still arched and shuddered like a traitor to her own mind. Her pussy was, too.

"You're so impossible…" she mumbled, mind fogging more and more as she tried her best to match his thrusts. She could barely manage, though; even after a few months of sporadic but very enthusiastic and intense sex, it was hard to be able to keep up with him when Dom made her feel so damn good.

Dominic laughed affectionately and leaned down to kiss the back of her neck, all sweetness and silent love. He melded himself against her back so they could be close once again then braced himself against the bed with his elbow, thrusting harder. Rosie gasped and whimpered, attempting to muffle her moan in her pillow. Dom groaned and tugged it away before she properly could though, needing to hear her.

"You should be telling me these things, Rosie. I would have done it more often before if I knew. What else do you like, hm? What else have you been holding back from me all this time?"

I like when your cock is inside me. When you hold me down and fuck me, Rosie thought. Her cheeks flushed redder than the ripest tomato. God, she could never tell him that. She couldn't handle him knowing how dirty her mind could get. Not when she'd always been a little innocent Rosie, daughter of his mom's best friend and virgin until twenty-two years of age.

So she said nothing and stretched out a hand to his hip instead. She moaned and Dom swore under his breath, slipping a hand over her side and chest. He palmed her breast, taking care to remain gentle even in his fervor, and nipped her ear. His chest rumbled with a strange mix of a growl and a groan.

"What... nothing? You don't like me trying to figure out what gets you off? You don't want me to make you cum?"

Rosie smacked him firmly, frowning. She panted and dug her nails into his skin, loving the way he hissed. "Don't be ridiculous, Dom," she mumbled.

Dom chuckled and tugged on her lobe with his teeth, then pulled back to sit up on his knees like he had been moments before. Rosie's heart stuttered, knowing what was coming. He was going to fuck her good and proper, just like he had earlier.

Yet the words that left his mouth in the next breath told her he had other immediate plans. "So you won't mind if I do it again, will you? Heads up."

Rosie's eyes widened and her mouth dropped. She turned to look at him over her shoulder, face burning. "Wait, wha—"

Dominic's hand cracked across her ass and Rosie flinched, her elbows buckling underneath her weight. She bit back a heated moan, eyes squeezing shut and fingers twisting in his messy, sweaty blue sheets. Dom groaned his approval.

"Fuck. Yeah, you definitely like it…" he murmured, tenderly rubbing the sore cheek he just abused. "I can feel it. I can feel you squeezing around me. Like you're trying to milk me dry…"

Rosie barely had the time to process how hot his words were before he spanked her again, even harder than he just had. Her breath caught and a cry left her lips, her hips bucking instinctively against his cock. He cursed as she ground her ass on him, needing more.

He slammed his hand across her ass again, his chest rumbling. "God, I missed you, Rosie. You feel so fucking good." Another slap. Rosie gasped, eyes rolling at the back of her head. Stroking the sore ass cheek, he murmured, "Tell me if I do it too hard, okay?"

Rosie barely had the sense to nod, but she did. She knew she had to—he wouldn't go on without her explicit permission. If those past few months of sex had taught her anything, it was definitely that. Whether that was simply because that was how he had always been or if perhaps her lack of experience made him more careful, she didn't know. Maybe it was even a mix of both.

Dom delivered another slap then, and Rosie's mind promptly went blank. She whimpered and arched her back, biting her lip when he started picking up his pace. So badly, she wanted to push herself up on her hands to better meet his thrusts, but Rosie couldn't. She couldn't manage; her arms were trembling too bad, too weak from her recent orgasm and the onslaught of bliss coursing through her.

Slap. Her walls clamped down on him, a strangled moan spilling from her mouth. *Slap*. She gasped, her walls quivering around his cock. *Hard slap*. Rosie winced and whimpered. Her sore cheek throbbed in protest—but she loved it. Loved how much it hurt. It was the best pain she'd ever felt, the only pain she wanted again and again. God, why hadn't she told him earlier that she liked this so much?

"Rosie," Dominic panted. His voice was strained and full of bliss. "Rosie, I'm gonna cum. But I want you to cum too, baby. What—" He groaned. Slowed his pace to something languid, squeezing one tender ass cheek. "Tell me what you need. I know you're close… I can feel it. Tell me what you need, Rosie."

Rosie moaned, too flustered and full of bliss to be able to respond. God, he was so good. She was so close, needing just a little more. But then his hands wandered all over her back and sides, feverish and needier than they'd ever been—coaxing her—and Rosie whimpered, realizing his pace wasn't going to change until she let him. Until she told him what she needed.

She knew she couldn't cum at this rate.

Letting her desperation for release overwhelm her, Rosie whimpered and pushed herself up as much as she could manage. Trembling, she caught one of his wandering hands and guided it down between her legs, hoping with all her might that Dominic would understand. He did—barely even a breath later. She whimpered when he started stroking, just the way she liked.

Dom groaned gruffly and started moving faster, harder. He kept working her sensitive button, bracing himself with a single hand on her ass. Rosie moaned loudly, using all her energy to keep herself upright.

She wanted to rock back into him and meet his rough thrusts, but she was too weak, too zapped of strength to be able to manage. Dom didn't seem to mind, though, not once relenting his frenzied pace.

"Again?" he asked within a groan, his voice so incredibly strained.

Rosie could only frantically nod, moaning with abandon. She didn't care anymore whether or not his parents were home and could hear her. All she wanted was to cum. Touching herself by her lonesome never felt this good, this fulfilling. God, Dom was so good. So, so good. Only he could make her feel like this. Only he could ever let her innocent walls down. Only he could ever make her cum this hard and—

His hand left her clit to harshly smack across her ass and Rosie flinched, the most feverish moan spilling from her mouth. She crumbled in bliss, trembling like a leaf as she gripped his sweaty bedsheets like a lifeline, chanting Dom's name like a mantra. Dom followed closely after her, spilling himself inside with a series of curses and incoherent syllables.

At least, she was pretty sure they were incoherent. It was hard to tell when her brain wasn't exactly working right, at the moment.

As they both came down from their highs, Rosie lazily smiled as Dom bent down to plant soft, wet kisses along her back and shoulders, tenderly rubbing the abused ass cheeks. Now that the rush of sex was fading, Rosie was distinctly aware of how sensitive the skin was—and how even such a gentle touch was almost too much. Still, she let him; after all, since they'd had such an intense session, Rosie knew that there was no way Dom would even dare handle her roughly.

Dom pulled back and he sighed in pure, undeniable contentment. Rosie expected him to roll over on his side, finally spent. Instead, she startled when lips brushed her tender, aching flesh—causing her to blush all the way to her roots.

She gasped.

Before she could think of anything to say, though, Dom chuckled warmly and teased, "Rosie, your cheeks are all… *rosy*."

Eyes widening, Rosie erupted into bits of loud laughter, those of which were intense enough that she quickly struggled to gasp in breaths and soon felt her ribs start hurting. Jesus, Dom was so ridiculous. So, so ridiculous. A complete goofball and silly monkey.

But God, she loved him for it.

Rolling over on her back, Rosie spread her arms for him and continued to giggle as he obliged and hugged her, slanting his lips over hers. He kissed her deeply for a while, feeling up her side and cupping one breast tenderly. She shuddered as he played with her nipple, a sigh escaping her mouth. Dom smiled and rolled them over, so she lay on top of him; blissed-out, spent, and a little sore.

They stayed like that for a while, touching each other lovingly and sharing slow, lazy kisses.

"Think your parents are home?" Rosie murmured, her cheeks reddening. "Because I might need you to hide me forever if that's the case. I don't think I can look at either of them for the rest of my life knowing that they heard us…" She cleared her throat and buried her face in his neck, hiding herself. "Well… Heard *me*."

Dom puffed a laugh, the sound reverberating against her lips. It made her heart do all these funny things. Sometimes—usually in moments like now—Rosie dearly wished either of them would have admitted their feelings for each other a long time ago. They wouldn't have been pining for so long, wouldn't have been deprived of time and moments like these before he had to move out of town.

Then again, maybe it was best that they had so many years apart. Both of them had still been discovering who they were and what they liked, and Dom had always said that he learned so much about women in college. For all she knew, maybe Dom wouldn't have been such a wonderful lover and boyfriend if he never got to learn from those women.

Hm… No use dwelling on what-ifs now, she thought.

Dom turned to kiss the top of her head, smiling still. "Nah. Told you—Mom likes to go through every alley. We won't be seeing them back anytime soon. Plus, I think Dad wanted to stop by the hardware store after. Wants to replace some tools or whatever."

He attempted a shrug, but it was hard with Rosie lying on top of him, which made her smile. She kissed the line of his jaw and cuddled him closer, pleasantly exhausted and utterly satisfied. God, she missed moments like these. More than the sex, she missed the intimacy they shared afterward; missed the slow touches and sweet, drawn-out kisses. She missed being so… connected to him. Emotionally. Physically.

She wondered how he'd react if she suggested moving in together soon. She was still saving up money for college—maybe she could look into going to his. Or would that be too clingy? She just wished they didn't have to wait weeks to see each other. Wished she could wake up to his sweet, gorgeous face.

Familiar hands cupped her ass a little too enthusiastically and Rosie instantly winced and exhaled a sound of discomfort, one eye squeezing shut tight. Okay, so maybe he had spanked her a little too hard. Now the pain was too much to be pleasurable. Or was that normal as the glow of sex waned?

Fortunately, Dom seemed to notice that she was no longer comfortable.

"Shit. Sorry, I didn't mean to—Hang on, I'll go get you something."

Dom kissed her temple and gently let her slide to the mattress. Swiftly, he pushed himself off the bed and tugged on his briefs and pajama pants before hurrying out of his room and down the hall. Rosie held her breath and squeezed her eyes shut, begging every God out there that she wouldn't hear his parents. She sighed in relief when she only heard Dom rummaging around.

It was a few minutes before Dom came trotting back, holding a glass of water in one and in the other… a pack of frozen peas?

"Uh… What are those for?"

Dom offered her a cheeky smile, the one he so often gave when he would awkwardly scratch the back of his head—only his hands were full. He shrugged. "I couldn't find where they kept the cold compresses."

A second of stunned silence passed, and then another. Rosie's lips twitched and she started cracking up hard. "Dom! Seriously? Oh my God!" She continued to laugh and shook her head. God, her boyfriend was so silly. She loved him so much. "Put those back. I'm not putting frozen peas on my butt, thank you very much. Your parents are going to eat those someday."

"But—"

"Just bring me some gentle oil or something. Or cooling lotion. Anything that…" Her cheeks flushed, and she averted her gaze shyly. Rosie cleared her throat. "Anything that, you know… speeds up healing."

Silence was all that met her in return. Confused, Rosie's gaze flickered to Dom's once more to gauge his reaction, finding him smiling at her with awe. But there was something more to his expression. Something she couldn't quite pinpoint. Like amusement or a newly unveiled epiphany, or maybe—

Mischievousness, Rosie realized. Her face flushed. Whatever Dom was about to say next, she was pretty sure she wasn't going to like it.

"You read up on it," he said, his tone full of wonderment and playfulness. It wasn't a question.

Rosie blushed harder and groaned, grabbing a pillow to hide her face behind it. "N-No! I—I did not! It just happened to be on my dash. I was just—I was curious! I didn't do any research of my own!"

She peeked over her pillow to see Dom grinning in that way she so loved, and her heart skipped a beat. Had she not felt so flustered, she probably would have smiled back.

"Well, we should," he said, handing her the glass of water. She accepted it quietly. He sat at the edge of the bed, putting away her pillow and brushing a lock of hair away from her face. "Is this something you'd like to bring into our sex life… fairly regularly? Because I loved spanking you. And I loved how much *you* loved it."

Rosie bit the inside of her cheek and took a long sip of water, fighting hard against her blush trying to creep up all the way to her ears. Honestly, with how much Dom turned her into a tomato, she was surprised her face hadn't accommodated to being flushed all the time.

Still, she met his gaze shyly and nodded, covering his hand with her own. "…Yeah. That'd be nice. I'd like that."

Dom's eyes twinkled and his grin spread wider. He leaned in for a few quick pecks then pushed himself to his feet once more. He pointed behind him. "Awesome. I'll go get my laptop, too, then."

Rosie gaped. "What—Right now?! I didn't mean right *now*!"

Laughing, Dominic slipped out of his room, racing down the hall as he had earlier. "I did!"

Groaning, Rosie flopped on his bed and hid under his sweaty bedsheets. She buried her face in them, her blush forever present on her cheeks judging by the way they still burned. Still, she smiled thinking about how excited Dom was. All because he wanted to find out more about what she liked, start honing more skills to ensure he could make her cum.

Because Dominic was in love with her. Loved her just as much as she loved him. Would do anything for her, just as she'd do anything for him. No matter how embarrassing.

Snuggling up inside his warm sheets, Rosie sighed. She could only hope his parents wouldn't pick up on the fact that the two of them had been playing hooky while they were gone.

Story 3 - The Best of Both Worlds (Bisexual threesomes)

If anyone asked her, Sophie was sure that they wouldn't believe her if she said that Ezekiel was resistant to the idea of having a threesome with her and another girl. Because that was what men always dreamed about, right? Fucking two girls and getting to watch them kiss and fondle each other all in the same night. What guy in their right mind could refuse that?

But it *was* true, though. After Sophie had suggested the idea post-sex one night, he seemed into it. At first. But whether it was because of his mind-blowing orgasm or sleepiness, it was laughable how quickly he seemed to change his mind. How weary and not quite sold on it all he became. He would question her relentlessly, make sure she wasn't only wanting this for his sake. That made her laugh even more. Since when had she done anything sexual only for his sake? That's what she'd reminded him.

He was uncomfortable. That much was clear. But Ezekiel tried to play it cool, tried to shrug it off like he was just being the generous one who was only looking out for her. He wouldn't even take the out anytime she offered it to him. Probably because he was stubborn.

"You know, you don't have to do this. I can find someone else. Or just wait some other time. Whenever the opportunity presents itself—it's fine! Just don't feel pressured, Zeke."

"What? No. I want to," he'd argued, affronted. But his eyes were already shifty.

Sophie rolled her eyes.

Maybe Zeke was nervous that he wouldn't be able to perform. Or maybe he was just terrified that it would change the bond between them steeped in friendship and lust. They were best friends with benefits—there had to be a limit to what they could do before shit got complicated or something, right?

But he came through in the end, however hesitantly.

"Are you sure about this?"

"You're asking me if I'm sure? You're the guy who's about to sleep with two women at the same time. And get to watch them touch each other and make out. Shouldn't I be the one all antsy?" She laughed.

Of course, no one could ever know any of that now—not with the way Zeke was reacting. Sophie had never seen him like this. With such little composure and wild eyes, such hunger and fire in his touches. He was no longer too anxious or in his head. In fact, he probably wasn't even thinking at all—his mind too full of desire and wanton pleasure as he watched. Waited. Caressed.

"Oh, you're a lot of fun," Katarina murmured, sliding up Ezekiel's body with slow, wet kisses.

It was comical how much Zeke was turned on. His pupils were blown, blazing like tiny embers, his breaths so heavy and choppy you'd think he was having a panic attack. Sophie bit her lip to keep from laughing.

Katarina grinned once she'd made her way to his jaw, nipping along the line of it teasingly before pulling back to draw Zeke in a long, hot kiss. Zeke groaned, squeezing her waist.

Katarina smirked, pulling on his bottom lip. "Most guys I've been with have been so prissy when they didn't get any attention for long. They had other ideas in their head, you know? They wanted two women all over them. Didn't want to feel left out."

Zeke's chest rumbled but he didn't comment. Sophie suspected his brain still couldn't process much beyond the fact there were two naked women in bed with him. He dragged Katarina in his lap properly, winding his fingers into her long brown hair. Sophie's lips twitched as she watched, imagining the hands she was roaming over her body were his. *Theirs.*

"Some even thought they'd get to dictate everything that us girls should do. Wanted us to follow their every command," Katarina went on, chuckling. "That didn't sit too well with me. Because you see, I've always liked women better. If you gave me a choice, I'd choose to fuck women over men every single time. They're so much better… so much more attentive. So much more invested in every way. Wouldn't you agree?"

Zeke groaned in what could have been a yes or a no—or even an 'I don't care'. Katarina smiled. Sophie bit her lip and slipped her hand past her belly, curling against the aching wetness there. Slowly, she started to thumb her clit, sighing as the waves of pleasure lazily rolled over her. The sound instantly drew Katarina's attention; she peered back at Sophie, lips curling wider to form a grin. She coaxed Zeke to look at her, grabbing his chin.

"See? Sophie here only has to watch me kiss you and talk to you about how much I like women before she has to touch herself. Makes me wonder what she'd do if I'd touch you… Which we *can* find out. Because you don't mind when a woman's in charge. You don't mind whatever the fuck we do right now— something tells me you'd be happy just watching me finger-fucking her all night. But I'm not that mean… Don't you worry."

Sophie's breath caught as she watched Katarina's hand dip down between their bodies, feeling along Ezekiel's chest and his abdomen before curling around his cock. Zeke cursed and shuddered with a groan before she even started jerking him off, the image a strange mix of hilarious and hot. Sophie smiled and pulled her hand away from herself to crawl over to them, wanting in on the action.

Zeke was the first to take notice. As soon as Sophie was within reach, he broke from Katarina's kiss to grab her wrist, catching her lips with his. Sophie moaned. God, Zeke had always been such a good kisser. She never learned where he'd picked that up but whoever had taught him was a good teacher. The things he could do with his tongue… With one messy, passionate kiss, he could easily leave her wanting, throbbing, begging to be filled.

This kiss was no different.

The one Katarina dragged her into was somehow even better, though—maybe because her hand kept working Zeke's stiff cock, pulling tricks that had Zeke grunting and cursing. Sophie shuddered when she even managed to make Zeke moan, a string of vivid curses escaping him just before he muttered something like, "Christ, this is so fucking hot."

Sophie wholeheartedly agreed. Moaning in the kiss, she ran her palms over Katarina's breasts and circled her fingers around Katarina's dark nipples. She pinched both of them.

Katarina grabbed hold of her bottom lip with her teeth, a half-moan spilling from her throat. "God, I love girls."

"Shit. Me too, babe," Zeke concurred roughly, surging forward to close his mouth around one of Katarina's peaked nipples. Katarina inadvertently freed his cock and sighed, burying a hand in his unkempt hair to pull him closer.

Sophie laughed. She agreed with her own hum before dipping one hand between Katarina's legs. She started playing her cunt as she would play herself, pulling Katarina in another slow, heated kiss.

Katarina's breath hitched. She pulled away and tossed her head back, mouth parting with a soft, "Oh…"

Zeke let out another string of colorful curses, nipping her nipple before manhandling Katarina in his lap so she could better face Sophie instead. Sophie smirked, pride swelling inside her chest. Zeke smiled back, all mischievous eyes and devilish intentions. Katarina seemed to notice their exchange, smiling back at her and pushing her hand closer against her wet cunt.

Sophie's heart skipped a beat, pussy throbbing in response. God, being with a woman was so amazing. While she spent most of her life chasing after men and being ashamed of her attraction towards women, Sophie would always remember how liberated she first felt when she finally accepted and understood her sexuality for what it was—and allowed herself to act on her once-shameful feelings.

Being with a woman was nothing like being with a man. Their hands were nimbler, more experienced, kisses patient, more sensual. They knew how to handle women's bodies more accurately than any man could, aware of secrets most men could only learn with time—and sometimes even never would.

Katarina was reminding her of all of that, right now. How different she was from Zeke, how her reactions contrasted with a man's. There was no fighting with herself to sound manly and strong—no fear that her femininity would diminish in their eyes merely for being vocal. She was all shameless moans and beautiful, blissed-out smiles; all slow, burning kisses, and even hotter touches.

Fuck, Sophie loved women. And men. *Both*. She was totally one hundred percent—no, no, one *thousand* percent bisexual. Definitely. Truly, if tonight was showing her anything, it was how good she had it on that front.

She had the best of both worlds. Dick and pussy. An assertive mouth and a sensual one. A partner that could fuck her so good she could barely walk the next day, and another that could make her knees wobbly with only a single, very involved kiss and who never had to search for her most sensitive spots.

God, *damn* Sophie was lucky.

Katarina seemed to think so, too. She tipped her head back again and threw an arm around Zeke, smiling. "Mmm. Right there, baby," she whispered, closing her eyes. She opened her thighs wider for better access, moaning when Ezekiel started mouthing wet kisses to her shoulders and neck. Her ensuing moan was even louder when Sophie applied more pressure to her clit. She grinned and puffed a laugh. Fuck… So sexy.

"My God…. Mmmm can always count on a woman to find the sweet spot without any issue, huh?" she said breathlessly, her grin growing. She was so beautiful and radiant, Sophie was sure she easily outshined the sun.

Sophie grinned. She giggled when Zeke growled and bit Katarina's neck; he always could get so feral when he was exceptionally worked-up—which there was absolutely no doubt he was now. Sophie had never seen him like this before, never seen him so lacking in composure and downright frenzied. It was amazing.

Katarina seemed of similar mind, too, because the next thing she did was huff a small laugh and tug him forward for an awkwardly angled kiss. She moaned when Sophie slipped her fingers into her warmth, rocking against her fingers before Sophie even started circling her clit. A low hum fell from her mouth the moment after, pleased when Zeke cupped one of her breasts and wound his other arm around her stomach.

Sophie's breath hitched. In the process of grabbing Katarina's breast, his fingers had accidentally brushed against Sophie's own nipple, sending a shiver down her spine. The sound didn't seem to go unnoticed; breaking away from his and Katarina's kiss, Zeke looked at her with blazing eyes and grabbed the back of her head to slant his mouth over hers, too. Katarina didn't seem to mind, only giggling and turning her attention to Sophie's shoulders, lips tracing a sensual path of kisses.

Sophie moaned, winding her fingers through Katarina's gorgeous curly brown locks. This right here was absolute heaven.

"This is the best threesome I've had so far—and that's saying something," Katarina gibed, which had Sophie smiling into her kiss with Zeke. She started cracking up, and Zeke bit her lip hard as punishment. Sophie bit him back.

Ezekiel groaned. "This is the best sex I've had. Period," he muttered, drawing Sophie into another hot kiss.

Sophie complained and playfully protested the statement with a smack to his shoulder. Katarina laughed.

"Now don't be rude, Ezekiel," Katarina said. "I'm sure Sophie has given you the time of your life before."

Sophie grinned her appreciation. She pressed her thumb harder against Katarina's clit, drawing her in for a kiss as she gasped.

Katarina moaned. "God, yeah… I've never been so sure of anything in my life. I bet she's the best you've ever had."

"Sure you're not talking about me?" Zeke asked gruffly, his voice hoarse with desire. He went back to mouthing kisses on Katarina's neck… Then slipped his hand down with Sophie's, joining her in her task. "Sounds like you might be self-inserting."

Katarina laughed again, the sound a bit more strangled, this time. It was so oddly hot that it drove Sophie up the wall—and Zeke, too, judging by all the biting and growling he started doing. He started circling her clit more aggressively, urging Sophie to pull away and focus entirely on fingering Katarina's pussy.

The whole mood of the room escalated quickly, after that. So intense that Sophie could barely breathe, silence drowned them easily and filled the air with nothing but heat, drooping their eyes as she and Zeke continued to work in tandem on giving Katarina an orgasm. It wasn't long before she did; after only a few minutes of the three of them sharing passionate kisses and wanton touches, she keened a cry and crumbled apart in their arms, both of her own looped around their necks. She was blatantly drunk on pleasure as she came down from her high, proven by her slurred grin.

"Jesus… You're both really something," she murmured as Sophie pulled her fingers out of her sopping wet heat and Zeke retreated as well. Her smile still had yet to cease, though it waned to something softer. Lazier.

Sophie kissed her, dragging her hands up Katarina's sides all the way to the swell of her breasts. Squeezing one, she rubbed Katarina's own wetness over her peaked nipple, loving the way Katarina moaned and deepened the kiss. Zeke wasn't left unaffected either, muttering out another litany of colorful swears that his mother would surely kill him for before mumbling something like, "Jesus, you're both going to give me a heart attack."

Sophie giggled and smoothed that same wet hand down Katarina's side, up Zeke's strong thigh, and over his abdomen. She felt along the hot skin, the faint ridges that defined his abs. His chest rumbled with a deep growl and her hand continued to crawl up to feel his thundering heartbeat, a grin curling her lips.

It was such a thrill to know that Zeke was enjoying himself this much now. Given how reluctantly he came in about it all, nothing pleased her more. He'd probably forgotten all about wanting to get out of this. Whatever doubts he had, whatever it was that held him back—that was all gone now.

Katarina's hands delved into her hair and Sophie hummed, thoughts clouding. She moaned as Katarina deepened the kiss even more, touching her tongue to Sophie's with such exquisite finesse that Sophie's head got all hot and dizzy.

Her hand fell from Zeke's chest, then down into his lap, blindingly searching for his cock. It didn't take her a second more before she found it. She started pumping him the way he liked, goosebumps rising on her flesh as he started to grunt out his pleasure. Katarina kept kissing the life out of her, twining her fingers in Sophie's brown locks and tugging hard enough that the pleasure bordered on pain.

And then it was Katarina's turn to let her hand fall between Sophie's thighs, finding her clit with ease. She didn't waste a moment to start playing with it, her touch so light Sophie was sure she was teasing.

Sophie gasped, letting out a small cry. Her eyes squeezed shut, hand stuttering in their rhythmic beat against Zeke's cock, which had him covering her hand with his. He needed her to keep going.

"I'd finger you, but I haven't clipped my nails in a while," Katarina said, which frankly took a moment for Sophie to even process through all her blissful waves.

In fact, she took such a long moment that even worked-up-Zeke had the time to process the comment before she did.

"The fuck does that have to do with anything?" he mumbled, taking away the hand over her own to palm both of Katarina's breasts. He bit Katarina's shoulder hard enough to leave a mark.

Sophie didn't have a hard time processing that one. She and Katarina both burst into laughter.

"When it comes to lesbian sex? *Everything*," Sophie said, throwing her head back and rocking against Katarina's hand.

"Don't exactly want to finger-fuck somebody with scissors, do you? Same principle," Katarina added, dragging Zeke in a slow kiss.

Sophie opened her eyes when a hand joined her own, wrapping around her fingers as it gripped Ezekiel's cock, and she grinned when she found that it was Katarina's. Together, they started stroking him in rhythmic beats, tearing throaty groans out of Zeke and turning his face a rare, rare shade of scarlet red.

Sophie was amazed. "Zeke! You're blushing? It's so rare to see you blush for anything," she teased, drawing her hand away from his cock to brush the redness over his cheeks. "Wow. You really are so worked up, huh?"

"Shut up, Soph," Zeke bit out, blushing harder.

Katarina laughed, pulling away from their kiss and letting go of his cock, too. She winked when he groaned. "I think it's time you put a condom on that bad boy. Don't you?"

Zeke groaned again—this time, though, without any protest. "Yeah? Yeah, okay." He shifted her off his lap to reach for the condom on the nightstand, running one hand through his hair. "Just give me a second."

"Take two, take three. Take ten or even ninety," Katarina sang, pushing Sophie back on the bed and climbing over her. Sophie shuddered, gasping when Katarina's hand dove right between her legs, wasting no time to aim for her prized jewel. Sophie instantly wrapped her arms around her, shifting her legs open some more. "I've got something to keep me busy."

"Jesus fuck. That's so hot," Zeke choked out in the background. "Am I seriously not dreaming?"

Sophie wanted to giggle—truly, she did—but quicker than she could have ever anticipated, Katarina started working magic with her knowing fingers and rendered Sophie's mind to mush in seconds. Her moans swallowed any other sound she could make. God, Katarina was so right—women never fumbled around when they touched another woman. They knew which spot was the most important—which spot was the most sensitive and full of pleasurable nerves. Which spot would make them lose their minds the fastest.

And that's exactly what Katarina did to her. Made her lose her mind. Worked her clit in tight little circles that maybe weren't exactly the right pressure, but were still too damn good to make her care to correct her. She could definitely still cum at this rate. Jesus, she wasn't even sure who was swearing right now out of the three of them—was it her? Zeke? Were they all cursing?

Who the hell cares, she thought dazedly, writhing like a cat in heat. She ran her hands all over Katarina, focusing more on her perfect breasts as they kissed with abandon. Maybe the kiss was sloppy, too, with Sophie's desperation, but Katarina didn't seem to care.

"That's right," Katarina whispered. "Such a good girl. You're making me all wet just watching you…"

A low sound that could only come from Zeke rumbled through the room. "Need some help dealing with that?" he asked, his voice gruff with desire.

Katarina's fingers stopped moving and Sophie bit her lip to keep from whimpering. She opened her bleary eyes and struggled to become aware of her surroundings, mouth drying when she found Katarina looking over her shoulder and grinning. Katarina beckoned Zeke forward with a finger. "Mm. If you wouldn't mind…"

Zeke laughed and the sound was so strangled and thick with desire that goosebumps rose on Sophie's flesh. Still, the absurdity of the question wasn't at all lost on her and she giggled along even though her body felt like it was on fire. Never in a million years would Zeke refuse to fuck a willing woman in the state that he was in—and yet here Katarina was, asking him like he would be doing *her* a favor?

Absolutely hilarious.

Surging forward, Ezekiel joined them, slipping his hand between Katarina's legs just as Katarina resumed working her magic fingers on Sophie. She and Katarina moaned in tandem, drawing each other in for a hot, wet kiss.

Belatedly, Sophie realized that Zeke was probably too worked up to finger Katarina properly after everything tonight. Touching her right now—he was likely only testing how wet Katarina was, gauging whether or not she was ready to receive him. Just like he always did with Sophie. Once satisfied and confident, he would slip his cock in and set up a delicious rhythm, fuck Katarina good—

But not me. Not this time, Sophie realized, blinking twice. She began growing envious. More than that, Katarina hadn't even gotten her nails clipped either, so she wouldn't get to experience being filled another way. *Damnit.*

Sophie didn't realize the thought had her pouting until Katarina broke away from their kiss, curious as she met Sophie's gaze. She erupted into giggles—the sounds cut short when Zeke pushed himself inside. They both moaned and Sophie's envy grew, simmering like the sullenest green-eyed monster.

But it wasn't left unaddressed for long. "Don't worry, baby. You won't be left wanting," Katarina said, tracing her bottom lip. "You think I didn't prepare to fill the one between us that wouldn't get to have Zeke's cock?"

Sophie's mouth dried, belly burning with want. She just about quivered with anticipation.

In the background, Zeke groaned. He palmed Katarina's ass and hissed, seemingly acquainting himself with her delicious warmth, but refused to move. Sophie wasn't sure why; either he was exercising patience for her sake or he was simply trying to regain his control.

Whichever reason it was, Sophie giggled. She peeked further around Katarina's shoulder—enough to see his face—and asked, "You okay there, bud?"

"Just struggling not to bust a nut," Zeke returned, squinting one eye open and throwing her a feral grin.

Sophie laughed. The sound turned into a hum when Katarina started mouthing kisses on her throat. Katarina took both her hands and pinned them above her head, kissing a path up to her lips before breaking away and reaching further than Sophie's hands for something. Sophie took the opportunity to push up and capture one perfect dark nipple with her mouth, relishing in Katarina's hitched breath.

"Fuck, your pussy feels so good, Katarina," Zeke groaned, which had Sophie smiling. She giggled more, leaning over to glance at him again and find him with his head tossed back, eyes closed as he set up a steady rhythm. His breath was choppy, chest heaving rapidly.

He wasn't the only one feeling good, either. Above her, Katarina moaned lowly, tilting her head down enough that Sophie could see her eyes were shut, too. She opened them a moment later and smiled seductively at Sophie. Mischief reigned in her gaze as she brought down her hand and revealed what she had been reaching for earlier—a realistic, flesh-colored dildo.

Sophie's heart raced. She held her breath in anticipation.

Katarina moaned, eyes closing once more as Zeke started pounding into her. "Yeah, you don't feel so bad yourself," she breathed back to him with soft, high-pitched whines.

They made Sophie so needy that she pushed up to kiss Katarina again, pouring out all her impatience and sexual tensions. "Don't forget me. Please," she begged, grabbing Katarina's hand—more specifically, the one with the dildo.

Katarina moaned a laugh and kissed her harder, scraping her teeth against Sophie's bottom lip. "Wouldn't dream about it, baby," she whispered.

With joined hands, she and Sophie both brought down the toy to Sophie's wet, throbbing core, rubbing it all up with her wetness. Then, they slowly pushed it inside, Katarina catching Sophie's moan with her mouth. Finally, Sophie was filled; her envy was gone.

If what they were doing before was heavenly, it was nothing compared to them fucking and moving in tandem as they did now. They were a euphoric mess of sweat, moans, and groans—not overly loud like most porn portrayed threesomes but infinitely sexier in their relative quietness. Katarina even matched the pace of her dildo with Zeke's thrusts, setting a strangely more intimate, connected vibe to their encounter. One that Sophie absolutely *loved*.

But something was missing, that much was becoming clear. As good as it all felt, as much as she could see her climax in sight and writhed desperately to achieve it—she was also slowly coming to understand that she likely wouldn't get there unless she got a little more. She needed more… *something*. But she didn't know what.

The realization made her hopeless; made her even more frantic to achieve her end. Sophie wanted so badly to be wrong. She bucked up towards the toy between her thighs, clinging fiercely to Katarina. She whimpered, helpless to the pleasure while she left red marks on Katarina's skin—but none of it seemed to change anything. Even when Katarina dropped down and started sucking on her nipples, bringing shudder-inducing waves…

"Soph—Fuck," Zeke said, something like frustration seeped into his tone. Sophie opened her eyes, hoping to be able to distinguish the features of his face and tell what he was thinking, but she couldn't. Everything was too blurry, tears having long welled up in her dark eyes in the face of all the bliss coursing through her.

But at the next words that fell from her best friend's mouth, Sophie's heart skipped a beat.

"Katarina—Sophie's struggling. I can see it—she wants to cum so bad, but she can't get there. Can you go down on her like this?"

Holy shit, yes. Please. Please, Katarina—Yes. I want that—Need that. So much. Please—

Her lips moved in a desperate plea, but Sophie didn't know that until Katarina let out a breathless laugh and traced her lips, murmuring, "Looks like she loves your idea, Ezekiel."

Sophie's heart thundered, her cheeks heating up. Her stomach raced with wild butterflies, thighs quivering when Katarina pulled the toy out of her. Zeke stilled his movements, likely to give Katarina some space to place herself how she needed to. He still slapped her ass just because he could, though, and Katarina briefly bit her lip.

She drew Sophie in for a short, heated kiss before pulling away and clapping her thigh. "Come on, babe. Scootch back. Let me taste your sweet cunt—I'll make you cum so hard you see stars," she said, smirking. She had all the confidence in the world.

Sophie's mouth watered and she scrambled into position as fast as she could. She barely caught the way Zeke groaned, more aware of his short-winded laugh. "Fucking hell. You'll make us both cum if you keep talking like that, Katarina."

Katarina grinned, throwing Zeke a look over her shoulder that made him shake his head. But when Sophie was done settling, she didn't waste time diving down between Sophie's thighs, throwing her legs over her shoulders.

Sophie gasped and instantly grabbed Katarina's hair, trembling with need. Zeke muttered something she didn't have the mind to hear anymore. Her world was lost. She spun out in her storm of bliss and nirvana as she had just moments earlier, shuddering more and more with every passing breath. Her relief built back up, swirling tighter and tighter in her belly like it never waned, edging closer… closer…

Sophie's eyes snapped open. She moaned sharply, twisting her fingers in Katarina's hair. She threw her head back, spots dancing across her vision. "Fu—Gonna cum," she gasped out, whimpering helplessly.

Her world exploded into stars.

Crying out, Sophie held on tighter than she ever had in her life and rode out her high through all its powerful waves. Incoherent words fell upon her ears, but she couldn't focus, couldn't take in anything else than her glorious pleasure and how Katarina's tongue helped her extend her orgasm for all of its worth. *Holy fucking shit* it was good.

There was no question that Katarina knew what she was doing with her mouth—that perhaps she had given Sophie the best oral she'd ever had in her life. It had been so long since she'd cum this hard—even Zeke was never this good.

When Sophie came down from her high, a sated smile spread to her lips, body utterly spent, and tingling everywhere. Gradually, though, Katarina's moans took her out of her daze; moans which, Sophie realized, were quickly escalating in intensity. Katarina was close.

She tilted her head down to catch up on what she'd missed, belly churning as she finally became aware of the sound of wet, slapping skin. Her cheeks flushed as she glanced at Katarina, blissfully close and moaning, and then Zeke, grunting savagely and face tightened up in concentration. Sophie watched as they fucked frenziedly, Katarina crying out praises and encouragements while she stayed wrapped around Sophie's thigh. Zeke started becoming more and more vocal, grunts turning into groans and growls as he teetered closer and closer—

"*Fuck!*" he bit out, growing tense before he ground himself against her ass stiffly, his mouth parting with an angry moan.

There was a flash of disappointment on Katarina's face—but it didn't last more than a brief moment before Zeke growled and scrambled underneath Katarina's thighs to aggressively eat her out.

The sound Katarina made as his mouth met her cunt was so beautiful and sexy that Sophie moaned as well, reaching down to gently thumb her own clit. It was still almost too sensitive to be played with, but Sophie bore through it, the sight simply too much of a turn-on not to. Katarina grabbed Zeke's hair, pulling roughly. She moaned time and time again as she rocked her face against his mouth and rode it unabashedly.

With a final cry of, "Yes!", she succumbed to the throes of her climax and broke apart. She grounded the waves against Zeke's mouth, her moans vibrating directly on Sophie's thigh as her free arm wound tight around her other. She was a trembling, shuddering mess—so much that Zeke growled, proudly spanking her ass.

He didn't relent his oral assault until Katarina slumped, spent, and boneless. She looked absolutely stunning, bearing a grin so sated that Sophie wanted to kiss her for it—only Katarina was too far down to be able to manage. Still, the gentle nipping she did on her thigh and up along her stomach was enough for now. Sophie sifted her hands through her sweaty hair, exhausted, and content.

Zeke joined them in the next breath, sinking by Sophie's side with the most worn-out groan. But on his lips was still that same satisfied grin.

Gently, he nipped Sophie's nipple. He laved it up with his tongue, sucked the peaked tip carefully, then rose up further and captured Sophie's mouth, kissing her deeply, slowly. The affection coaxed a content sigh out of her. She wrapped one arm around his neck, burying a hand in his damp hair.

It wasn't all innocent, though. However sensual and amazing the kiss was, an odd, earthy tang still lingered on his lips—one that Sophie knew had to belong to Katarina. It made her moan.

A slap cracked through the room and Zeke flinched. Sophie erupted into tired giggles; clearly, the slap had come from Katarina—perhaps in revenge for how he slapped her ass moments earlier. She'd wager a guess that she'd more than likely aimed for his cute tush, too.

Sophie and Ezekiel both looked down, finding Katarina grinning at them both, happy and a little drowsy. They grinned back and let out a blissfully content sigh before Zeke buried his face in Sophie's neck. Katarina was apparently perfectly content to stay down between Sophie's legs, one arm curled around her thigh while the other affectionately traced patterns on Zeke's calf.

"I gotta say, Zeke… That was pretty freaking good oral—from a guy," Katarina said, breaking the comfortable silence.

Sophie felt Zeke grin against her breast. He laughed, the sound reverberating against Sophie's chest. She smiled, too.

"Mm. Can't take the credit. Greatest teacher right here," he said, wrapping an arm around Sophie's waist. "This one wanted to make sure I knew how to go down on a woman."

"Thank fucking God. Best decision ever," Katarina concurred, snorting.

It was Sophie's turn to laugh. She sifted her hand through Katarina's hair, her feelings all kinds of mushy right now. It was probably all the post-orgasm oxytocin. "I don't know, guys. You know what would top that right now?"

"What?" Katarina and Zeke chorused.

"Deciding to order us all some pizza."

There was a collective groan of approval and Sophie grinned widely—more than she had all night. Katarina threw her arm up in a victory air pump and Zeke snickered before doing the same. He then proceeded to kiss her shoulder, already starting to doze off.

"Extra-large, please," he mumbled.

"With extra cheese," Katarina piped in.

Sophie laughed again, humming her approval to both suggestions. Her grin stayed on her lips, the purest content sigh spilling from her mouth. Maybe she was exaggerating, but right now it felt like she had never been happier in her life.

Seriously. A hot as fuck threesome and post-sex pizza with two of the hottest people on earth?

Best. Night. Ever.

Story 4 - Filthy Mouth (Dirty Talk)

Seventy-one days. That was how long it had been. Seventy-one freaking days since he and his wife last had sex.

Andy was at his wits' end.

While this wasn't the first time they'd had such a dry spell, the last had been easily excused to their need to adapt their lives to the arrival of their baby boy, Flynn. They had been tired, but blissfully so, too preoccupied with providing for their child to even think about sex. It had been understandable. Predictable. Easy to overlook.

But this dry spell? It was another thing entirely. Andy couldn't understand it. Couldn't excuse it. Couldn't accept that it was happening for the reason that it was. Flynn was five now, energetic as ever but not as demanding and helpless as he was as a newborn. He and Maryssa had adapted to life as parents, experts in finding and making time to have sex to sate their needs. They were almost, if not just as active as they were before Flynn.

This is why Andy found this complete no-sex-interim totally unacceptable. Christ, they were usually so regular! Four days a week, on average—never less than two! How could anyone blame him for getting antsy about not having sex for *seventy-one* days with his insanely hot wife?

But this had to end. He would let it go on no longer. Their ongoing streak for the lack of intimacy would end today. Andy would make sure of it.

He couldn't let their incredibly busy work schedules be an excuse anymore. He would make time to make love to his wife and remind them exactly why they always set aside opportunities for this. Especially with how stressed Maryssa was with the new store launches from her highly successful meal-prepping company.

This was the first time they were opening several branches across the country for better service, quicker shipping times, and an extended reach for customers, and Maryssa was overwhelmed by it all. She had been so anxious every day simply making sure everything was going along smoothly—a mood that persisted when she got home. She was always too tired at the end of the day to do much more than their responsibilities as parents, but Andy knew she needed to let out all her pent-up stress one day or another.

And what better way than with an orgasm?

Preferably, one he would give to her—and not one she'd give herself all alone.

I wonder if she's been touching herself already? Maybe when I was at work doing some overtime? he mused. *Or maybe in her office bathroom… Maybe anytime she was on a break. Maybe Maryssa thought the same thing I did. Maybe she figured she had to let all that stress out somehow…*

The thought had him growing hard already. Fucking hell, he'd definitely been jerking off too much without her. The worst part was that it was never even *that* satisfying without her. He wanted to be inside Maryssa's tight pussy, feel her walls quivering around him as she came. He wanted to taste her sweet cunt, make her whimper his name helplessly like he always did.

Oh, God, damnit. He *really* was getting too hard now. At home, he probably wouldn't mind but as he needed to actually pay attention to the road and get out in roughly five minutes, it wasn't the smartest thing to let himself get a hard-on. It was bad enough to go out and try to hide a boner in public, but then at his wife's workplace, too? That was insane. Inconsiderate. Beyond stupid and risky.

Andy couldn't allow for her image as the CEO to be damaged by his feral lust. He loved Maryssa too much for that.

But behind the closed doors of her office, however…

Andy shook his head, smacking his own cheek. Silently cursing himself for getting so carried away with his thoughts, he focused on the road ahead instead. For anything to happen in the first place, he figured, he first of all had to succeed in getting there without drawing attention to himself. Or else the dry spell would most definitely go on.

Andy couldn't let *that* happen.

So calm down, Jr. Help a brother out. You're not getting any relief if you can't keep your chill.

Talking to his dick. Jesus. How much more desperate could he get?

Andy shook his head, sighing. He should really just focus on getting to Maryssa's building first. *And* picking up some flowers. The latter wasn't something he needed to do but Andy figured it would be a good, innocuous excuse to come see his wife at the office and he'd been feeling like giving her flowers lately, anyway.

Plus, Andy noticed that it always seemed to put Maryssa in a good mood when employees complimented her on the cuteness of their marriage. With him passing by to hand her flowers just because he felt like it, how would this not warrant Maryssa some of those compliments?

Rounding the corner of Maryssa's street, Andy spotted *Jill's Flower Shop* and was pleased to notice that it wasn't busy. He parked directly in front of the shop. For a minute, he remained inside and made sure he was presentable; triple-checking from different angles that his previously stirred friend wasn't making him spring a third leg through his pants, however faint. Once he was confident, Andy stepped out of his car and headed inside.

He didn't dawdle around in the shop. Knowing what he wanted already, he headed straight for the florist counter and requested a bouquet of white lilies (Maryssa's favorite), holding back his wince as the florist fetched the flowers and then summed up his total. He headed back into his car with a huge grin, already imagining Maryssa's awed response.

Once back, Andy put the lilies in the passenger seat then drove on to Maryssa's building just half a minute down the road. He pulled into his usual reserved parking space which Maryssa had secured for him long ago. He grabbed the flowers and swiftly trotted inside the lobby.

Kimmy, the receptionist, was surprised to see him. "Oh, hey Andy!" she greeted, smiling brightly. Kimmy was always so peppy. Her gaze dipped briefly to the lilies and mischievousness crawled amidst her features. She grinned. "Did you get in trouble with the missus last night?"

"Nope," Andy replied, grinning back. "Just felt like dropping by to tell my wife how much I love her. Maybe grab some lunch, too. Has she eaten yet?" Maryssa always ordered out when she didn't have her lunch, which Andy knew she hadn't brought today.

Kimmy shook her head. "Should I order the usual for you two?"

"That'd be great! Thanks, Kimmy!" Andy said. He hurried off towards the elevator. "Better make the most of the time before she gets busy again, right?"

"Maryssa knows how to take a lunch break, Andy."

"Not before she has food, she doesn't!" Andy piped back.

Kimmy laughed. The elevator closed and started riding up. Andy smiled.

It was true that sometimes Maryssa didn't know how to take a break unless she had food accessible at her hands, but today, Andy was going to make sure that her reason to be busy would be for something that had entirely nothing to do with work. With only about twenty-seven minutes free of interruptions as the rest of her staff also embarked on their lunch, Andy intended to make full use of them to be discreet and sate this unresolved sexual tension from the past seventy-one days. She needed it as badly as he did, he was sure.

When the elevator took him to the top floor and *dinged,* Andy's heart began to pound. He made a beeline straight for Maryssa's office, barely having enough sense to smile and greet back staff members as they noticed him. He could only hope he didn't seem rude to any of them he might not have greeted back.

Maryssa was on the phone when he knocked at her door and peeked in. She looked up, her face brightening like the sun at the sight of him, and smiled so happily his heart melted. She beckoned him inside wordlessly, eyes crinkling as they dipped to the bouquet of lilies. But she didn't stop talking on the phone, her gaze drawing back to a bunch of papers on her desk.

Andy closed the door behind him, quietly making his way around her office to shut her blinds, then grabbed the opportunity to transfer the flowers to a vase. She always kept one on the small desk by the door for presumably occasions like these. Making a quick trip to the bathroom to fill the vase with water, he carefully arranged the flowers and waited for her to be done with her conversation. He pretended not to be listening much, though it was hard to ignore.

She was talking with one of the new stores' directors, he was pretty sure.

"Those boxes need to be shipped out on time from now on. I won't tolerate any more lateness on behalf of your lack of hindsight. I hired you because you were spectacular on your last job and your references all said you were always timely, Mr. Korvick. Don't go proving me wrong now. Prove to me that I haven't made a mistake. Okay?" Her frown persisted, brows deeply knitted together until her shoulders relaxed at last. Andy smiled. Good—so her message was understood. She smiled back at him and winked. "Alright. Good. I have faith you will handle this well. Please call me if you need me to send any help. I know you're adjusting still, and I'd hate to come down hard on a man whose wife is expected to give birth any day now." She laughed, all traces of strict CEO Maryssa gone and replaced by genuine friendliness. "Okay. Good day, Mr. Korvick. Take care."

After she hung up, she stretched long and loud, throwing Andy a cheeky smile. When she was done, she stood and crossed the room in quick steps, snaking her arms around his neck. "That was one of our new branch directors. He really thought it was an acceptable excuse to say that he didn't have enough hindsight to hire more packaging staff in order to meet the shipping dates. He was late by two days. Can you believe that?"

"Honey, I don't have the skills to organize *anything* effectively," Andy deadpanned with a grin. He pulled her closer to him by her waist. "Honestly, I would have been twice as late shipping those out—and that's if I really tried! So maybe he's not doing so bad."

"Some people rely on those boxes to eat every day, Andy. They need to be on time," Maryssa said, rolling her eyes. She smiled and leaned in for a quick kiss. "This is why you will never work at my company, by the way. Have I ever told you that?"

"Like, ten thousand times."

"Good. This makes ten thousand and one."

Andy laughed. "I missed you," he murmured, drawing her in for another kiss. It was longer but still just as sweet, lingering on enough that Maryssa hummed a sound that was almost a moan.

She pulled away before he could deepen it, seemingly unaware of his intentions. "Oh, Andy, they're beautiful!" she said, obviously addressing the flowers. She trotted over to them, thumbing the petals of a lily and smelling it. Her smile widened as she turned to look at him, those pretty eyes gleaming so gorgeously. "What did you bring them for?"

Andy's heart jumped and bounced in his ribcage. He smiled, too. "Just wanted to show my wife how much I love her," he said, taking the few steps needed to join her. He nuzzled her neck and wrapped his arms around her waist, propping his head on her shoulder. "Wait, am I allowed to do that? Or do I have to call and set up an appointment with you for even something as basic as bringing you flowers?"

Maryssa giggled. She playfully smacked his forearm, tightening his arms around her. Andy grinned. Maryssa turned around and pecked him softly before she sauntered back towards her desk. She began to clean out the papers messily spread about, evermore radiant. Jesus, Maryssa was so fucking beautiful when she was happy.

Beautiful all the time—but especially like this. Especially when I'm the reason.

"I don't see any food with you. Did you come by just to say hello? You have to pick up Flynn from preschool, right?"

Crossing the distance between them again, Andy wound his arms around her as he had moments earlier, kissing the back of her ear. He held back his grin as she shuddered.

"Mmm. In a bit," he murmured, dragging his lips down her neck.

Maryssa giggled and tried to step out of his grasp in order to put some papers away where they belonged, but Andy instantly caged her in, forbidding her escape. Her breath hitched and Andy burned harder with desire. He was pretty sure that he would have smiled if he hadn't gotten so worked up at the mere sound alone.

Andy mouthed the back of her neck, the crook of it where it met her shoulder, and tasted her skin with his tongue. He scraped his teeth over the wet spot, needing to make sure his intentions were clear.

Maryssa's breathing got heavier. Andy's belly churned. He'd bet anything that her cheeks were flaming red, right now.

"Not just to say hello, Maryssa," he murmured, slipping a hand under her shirt. He felt up her warm skin. "For this, too."

Maryssa hummed and arched her neck for more. She closed her eyes, breaths growing even choppier.

Andy smiled. Good. So she had been feeling the effects of their dry spell, too.

She reached back to cup his chin, the faintest moan leaving her. "Oh… Is this what the flowers were for?" she murmured.

Andy snorted—wanted to laugh, really. Only he was too full of lust. Too worked up to be able to manage. He merely continued to mouth wet kisses where he could reach. Maryssa's fingers tightened around his nape.

Only Maryssa could ask such a naive question. She was so laughably innocent in the eyes of many, strict of a boss as she could be. His wife was known to be kind and gentle, the perfect picture of a loving mother and dedicated wife… unless you screwed up when it came to her company. *Cook with Maryssa* was her long-and-hard-fought dream, one she'd had for over a decade. Maryssa would tear even Andy apart if he dared do anything to it.

God, Andy loved his wife so much. She was amazing.

"When have I ever used flowers as a way to get you to have sex with me? I just felt like getting you flowers today, babe."

He raked his teeth over her neck, pressing his fingers against her hip as he pushed his hard cock up against her ass. She moaned and blushed, but still, ground back against him.

Yeah. Definitely haven't been the only one missing this.

"Andy… I know it's been a while but… my office…"

Her mouth was saying one thing, but her body another. Something differently entirely, really. It pulled him closer, her ass rolling slowly against his cock… as though it was trying to pull any friction it could from the connection.

"Your blinds are shut. Your door is shut. I've been here enough times to know that no one ever bothers you when the door is closed," he murmured, mouthing her neck. Her breath quickened and he bit down on her skin hard enough to make her gasp. He groaned. "All we need to do is keep as quiet as we can… Come on, Maryssa. It's been seventy-one days. Don't tell me you don't feel it too…" He slipped his hand down her side, unzipped her tight-fitting pencil skirt. Andy dropped to his knees and mouthed the skin revealed to him.

Maryssa whimpered, grabbing his hair tightly. She delved both her hands through his locks, pulling at them softly. "God, Andy… I…"

The way she said his name had him rising up once more, spinning her around to capture her mouth in a hot, sensual kiss that he would bet probably made her toes curl. At least, his did. "Maryssa… Please…"

Maryssa deepened the kiss and wrapped herself around him, pushing his hardness closer between her thighs. Andy groaned, hands spanning her form and drawing little sounds from her as he squeezed this body of hers that he loved so much, *missed* so much. He loved the fact that she had actual meat on her bones—that touching her was never hard, never bony. She was all softness and curves, all velvet skin, and warmth. She had the best damn body he'd ever set his hands on.

Just kissing her already, Andy felt like he was on fire. He burned for her. Yearned for her. The fact that she was his wife never failed to amaze him every day. How was it that he was able to keep her? To make her so happy? To have her love so genuine and earnest? He was the luckiest man alive.

And the horniest, right now.

"What's it going to be, Maryssa? Are you going to allow us to take the next fifteen minutes or so to fuck like we haven't been able to in over two months? Are you going to let me bend you over that desk and make you moan so much you'll have to muffle them with your hand?" Andy asked. "Cause' I want to, Maryssa. I really want to. I want to, *so much*." He dragged in another hard kiss, his brow furrowed. His hand slipped underneath her tight bra to grab her breast. He growled. "Don't you miss my cock inside you? Rubbing parts of you that you didn't even know existed before we found each other? Don't you miss how good it felt when I came inside of you? How hot my cum was for you?"

Maryssa moaned, kissing him harder. She squeezed her thighs around him, creating friction between them that was heavenly for their pent-up lust and sexual frustration.

"I miss trying for another baby," Andy murmured, running both hands down to her ass. He squeezed firmly, groaning. "God, I miss filling you up so much. Until I knew I couldn't fill you up another inch…"

That was another thing that made it worse. Before their sexless streak, they'd recently decided to start trying for another baby now that Flynn was old enough to attend school. They felt ready to expand their family a little more, felt like they had a great handle on parenting and would be ready to face the challenge of another child—until the board of directors decided that Maryssa's company was ready for an extension, and that they wanted to do it now.

It had been cruel for the world to build up his excitement so much only to take it away.

Dipping his hands beneath her skirt, Andy felt the heaven that was the plushness of her thighs, his chest rumbling with a groan. Fuck, he wanted them wrapped around his head right now. He missed going down on Maryssa so much. But did they even have the time? Did either of them even have the patience for it?

"God, Maryssa… You have no idea how much my cock missed you. How much *I* missed you. How many times a day I think about you naked, wonder if you might be doing the same…" He licked her ear with his tongue, sucking the sensitive part of it at the back and slipping his hands underneath her panties to feel her ass directly. He let his eyes fall shut, cheeks burning. "Wonder how wet your pussy might be for me. If you were ever touching yourself. Right here, even. In that very bathroom. Fantasizing about having me between your thighs, eating you out until I left you breathless like I do every time. Every day, I think about how much I want that tight pussy wrapped around my cock, how much I want to taste it on my tongue…"

"Andy, please… *please*…"

Andy's blood soared right out of his head and towards his dick. He growled, taking one of her dainty little hands to press over his pants right where his stiff girth was. Maryssa moaned, loud enough that he clasped his hand over her mouth. Her eyes glazed over, tongue darted out to taste his hand. Andy twitched and was sure Maryssa felt it. The way such fire swept over her features guaranteed that much.

Seemingly unable to help herself, Maryssa scrambled to undo the opening of his jeans, diving her hand past the waistband of both his pants and underwear. Andy sucked in a breath, a rush of bliss flashing across his spine as her warm fingers wrapped around his rock-hard cock. He fought back against the urge to close his eyes, overcome with the sensation.

Fuck, he'd missed this. Missed those perfect fingers wrapped around him, expert in their knowledge and softer than his own could ever be. Andy couldn't wait to re-familiarize himself with her wet, perfect cunt.

"Jesus, you're so hard," Maryssa gasped, reacquainting herself with the feel of him in her small hands. Her lips twitched as she ran her thumb over the head of him and felt his precum leak out, but Andy suspected she was the same as him—unable to truly muster up a smile because of all her yearning and desire.

His eyes slipped shut, hips bucking against her hand. "Of course I'm hard. I've been hard for weeks," he groaned. "Waiting for us to make time again…"

"God, Andy… I'm sorry. I'm sorry I've been making you wait so much," she said, moving her hand on him with just the pressure he liked best. Jesus, God fucking bless his wife for having never forgotten his preferences.

Andy kissed her hard. He tangled his fingers in her hair, tugging possessively. "Don't be sorry," he rasped, biting her lip. "Never be sorry for taking care of your dream. I want you to be happy. Always." He let out a brief, strangled laugh. "Even if my dick hates me for it sometimes."

"Not right now it doesn't," she retorted back breathlessly, and they both laughed.

He pushed her down so her back was on the desk and began unbuttoning her blouse. At every inch of skin revealed, Andy hungrily tasted it, his chest rumbling as Maryssa moaned and wrapped her legs around him. Andy barely had the sense to understand the encouraging things she murmured, too worked up, simply knowing this was happening at last.

He was going to fuck his wife. In her office. After seventy-one days without sex. He was finally going to see her cum again.

The thought had him groaning, teeth raking against her nipple over her pretty bra. He cupped both swells of her wonderful breasts. That was another thing with her. She had the most wonderful fucking tits he'd ever seen and touched in this world. The tits of his dreams. Her whole fucking body was a godsend.

They were both startled when her office phone rang, one of them moaning a complaint. Andy wasn't sure who. Maybe they both had.

Ever so dutiful in her role, though, Maryssa shifted and rolled on her desk so she could answer, giving Andy a torturous view of her ass in her pretty panties. Her skirt was still all bunched up high over her tummy, so tight that Andy was sure it had to be uncomfortable.

"Maryssa Lafont speaking."

Professional. Incredibly. Andy was honestly impressed. He was sure if he tried speaking right now, he'd sound like a wolven beast or something. That's how full of desire he felt.

As if to prove that point, Andy reached out instinctively and grabbed the hem of her unzipped, bunched-up skirt. He started pulling it down, hungry to see her out of it.

Maryssa smacked away one of his hands, briefly throwing him a glare as she gestured to give her one minute. Andy bit back a lecherous grin.

He didn't listen.

"Oh. Yes, two o'clock. That's right. I have it marked down," Maryssa went on, eyes falling shut. She bit her own lip as he dragged down her skirt over her hips and down her legs, briefly clasping a hand over her mouth. "And one at three-thirty as well. Yes. Thank you, Azah. Enjoy your lunch now, okay?"

The second she hung up, Andy's mouth was on her ass, biting it. Maryssa cried out, head falling against her arms. Andy palmed the span of her thick, perfect thighs, hungrily taking in the bare skin. He didn't waste another moment before sliding off her panties, too, groaning at her sweet, musky scent.

Christ, he needed to taste her so bad.

Maryssa seemed to think so as well; she ever so shyly parted her legs and whimpered, face still hidden in the crook of her arms.

"Andy… Andy, please."

Andy snapped. Snarling a string of incoherent words, he flipped her around and drew her legs over his shoulders, burying his face into her sweet, wet cunt. Maryssa gasped, throwing a hand over her mouth to bite back a cry. She snatched her hand in his hair with the other, moaning his name and pleas to keep going. Andy groaned in return, hungrily working his mouth on her clit in the way he knew she loved. He sank two fingers into her depths, his dick so painful in the restraints of his pants he wanted nothing but to reach down and relieve some delicious tension.

Still, Andy ignored it.

Not long later when Maryssa was close—or so he suspected as she started quivering and thrashing the way she always did when she was on the brink—she pulled on his hair and panted, urging him back up. Andy obliged. And though he wanted to finish her off, have her cum on his tongue and break apart right on that desk, as soon as she looked at him with her misty eyes thick with love and bliss, Andy was a goner.

He knew he'd give her anything she wanted. Anything she asked. So there was no way in hell he'd have been able to deny her what she wanted when she whimpered her next words.

"Andy, not like this… *Please*. Please, I need you. Inside me. I need you now, Andy," she said, tugging ever more insistently on his hair.

Andy was up to his feet in seconds, yanking down his pants as quickly as he could manage. When they were out of the way, he pulled his lovely wife by her hips until she was hanging off the edge of her desk. He licked his lips, the blood roaring in his ears growing even louder as she wrapped her legs around him tightly, dragging their lower halves as close as she could get them.

Somehow, it tore a smile out of him. She wanted him to be inside her just as bad as he wanted to. She was just as desperate to be close to him as he was to her. She'd been just as affected by their dry spell, emotionally and physically.

Andy wasn't going to let it go on for a single moment longer.

Taking his cock in hand, Andy guided himself to her warm, wet opening, heart pounding away like drums. They both held their breath when he started pushing in, Maryssa even arching her back and jerking him closer with her legs in an attempt to push more of his girth inside. It worked a little.

Andy groaned, thrusting shallowly until he was deeply seated within her perfect pussy. His eyes swept shut briefly, waves of bliss rolling over him. He let out a string of curses once he opened them again and met his wife's gaze. She hadn't looked this turned on in ages—perhaps in forever. Her eyes blazed like a wildfire, pooling lust so hot in his stomach that it felt like lava.

The sight alone had him picking up his pace. Andy pulled her up to meld their mouths together, threading a hand into her beautiful hair. Maryssa grabbed his hips, silently begging for more as she kissed him back harder and dug her nails into his skin. Andy obliged, moving his hips in quick little pounds that had her moaning, panting, moving desperately to try and meet his thrusts.

"Andy… *Andy*, I missed you so much," she gasped between hot, fevered kisses, dropping both hands down to his ass. "God, I missed you. Oh *God*, I really missed you."

Andy groaned. He broke from her and bit down on her neck, fucking her harder.

"Yeah?" he rasped, sliding his palm over her breast. He squeezed it aggressively. Hungrily. "D'you miss me—or the way my cock feels inside you? I bet you just missed the way it makes you moan. How good it fucks your wet little cunt. Look at how much it's dripping for me. I can feel how slick you are. You're probably dripping on your office floor." Keeping her close with his other hand, he leveraged himself with her weight to maintain the pace and strength of his thrusts. He licked his lips. "Is that what you want, Maryssa? For me to fuck you so good that you drip all over your pretty little office floors, so your cleaning crew finds out their boss came all over her desk? You dirty minx. I bet that's what you want. I bet you want to squeeze all the cum from my cock and have it drip all over the floor so everyone can know how filthy you can be. So they stop seeing you as the sweet, innocent CEO. So they can take you seriously like you wish they would…"

"No," Maryssa whined, burying her face in his neck. She quivered around him and jerked towards him to meet his thrusts, though, and Andy knew that meant the idea seriously turned her on.

"I'd never—That's so—"

She cut herself off and buried herself closer, so much he would bet anything that she was flushed from ear to ear. Still, she kept moaning, meeting his thrusts eagerly, too needy to let her embarrassment stop her.

Before long, Maryssa began nipping his ear, panting. She whimpered, biting him hard enough to make him hiss. "I swear, you have such—Such a dirty mouth," she gasped, tongue coming out to taste his lobe.

Andy ground against her roughly, tearing a cry from her mouth. Maryssa yanked him closer by his ass, one hand flying out to the edge of the desk to brace herself against it. Andy grinned devilishly, pride swelling within him. Drawing back to catch the look on her face, he captured her lips with his in a feverish kiss, dizzy. He groaned as her walls pulsed and closed in on him—a tale-tell sign that she was close.

"You love this dirty mouth," he whispered, tugging her lip with his teeth. "You love it so much you're about to cum right now. Like you always do. I can feel how much you love it when I talk dirty to you, honey."

Maryssa's breath caught, the red on her cheeks darkening to an even more gorgeous shade. Andy's mouth curled into a grin. He kissed her once more, tugging her body even further off the desk until she was practically hanging off. He grabbed both of her warm, soft thighs, thrusting with even more fervor.

The cry Maryssa let out right then was so sharp even into their kiss that Andy could only be thankful that his mouth had muffled most of the sound. Someone would have surely heard her if it hadn't—and Andy couldn't even fathom the idea of being interrupted while he was about to make his wife cum for the first time in much too long.

Troubled by the thought, Andy braced one hand against her desk, too, and moved faster, harder. The sturdy piece of furniture began to rattle with violent force, so much that some stacks of paper and a plastic cup of pens fell off. Andy didn't allow himself to care, though. He panted and groaned, losing himself to his pleasure. Mind clouding up with bliss, he focused on nothing but holding out for Maryssa—needing her to cum more than anything else. More than himself.

It didn't take long. Maryssa dipped her hips and curved her back to get an angle she wanted, and that was it. Half a dozen thrusts and she crumbled into a mess of muffled cries, trembling. She came apart so beautifully that Andy quickly found himself wishing he could have seen the look on her face. With a hard bite to his shoulder—hard enough she might have drawn blood—she muffled a series of high, carnal sounds that went right to his cock. They sent him tumbling over the edge with her, blinding his vision white.

Together they ground out their blissful releases and held each other close. Wanting to prolong the intimacy of the moment and ensure every drop of his cum filled her as deeply as possible. Or so Andy believed.

His heart melted with the weight of all his love. "Fuck, Maryssa… I missed you so much. Missed being close to you like this," he murmured, drawing back to lock gazes with her. He thumbed her cheek, such softness and warmth filling his heart, and smiled, capturing her lips the most sentimental kiss. "Missed filling you with my cum. Did you feel how much I gave you? That's only for you, honey. No one's ever made me cum like that before. Best pussy I ever had."

Maryssa seemed to shudder, but still she pouted against his mouth. She broke away and buried her face in his neck, holding him tight. "Okay, enough with the dirty talk," she mumbled. "I already came. No need to work me up again."

Andy chuckled, kissing her collarbone and sighing blissfully. He propped her back more comfortably against the desk, figuring the edge digging into her so much probably wasn't very comfortable, and smiled. Maryssa seemed to appreciate it—even though the movement had him slipping out. She sighed and kissed him slowly.

"You love it," Andy murmured between a kiss. "But fair enough. Sorry, I'll stop now." With one last kiss, he swept her beautiful hair over her shoulder. His heart was so full as he stared at her. He pressed his forehead against hers, keeping their gazes locked. "I love you. And I really did miss you. Not just the sex.

You've been so busy lately…" He trailed out, and shook his head against hers. "No, *we've* been so busy. I'm proud of you. I never want you to feel bad about putting your career before our sex life."

Her lips curved, at first just a little. But then suddenly, with such tenderness and love that it was breathtaking to watch, they quirked further up into a full, utterly exquisite smile. Andy's heart skipped a beat. His mouth parted.

Christ, his wife was so beautiful. Time and time again, it never failed to escape Andy how lucky he was to have Maryssa at his side. Amazing inside and out. She was ten times the person he could ever hope to be.

Maryssa cupped his jaw with her slim fingers, pulling him in for a sweet kiss. Andy's heart thundered, a blush spreading to his cheeks the moment she lowered her hand on his chest, to the space over his heart. She smiled even wider, pressing their heads together again. She was so damn lovely.

"I love you, too, Andy. So much." She paused. She tucked a lock of hair behind her ear, her flushed cheeks turning a shade redder. "But um… Do you think you could maybe help me make all this look presentable again? It's… well, kind of cluttered. And my legs are shaky."

Because you've been well-fucked, Andy thought, and didn't realize he was grinning until Maryssa shot him a dangerous—if still somehow amused—look. Andy laughed, too pleased with himself. Maryssa shook her head and smiled, muttering something under her breath he didn't hear. Still snickering, Andy kissed the top of her head before bending down and picking up her skirt and panties for her. He handed them back out.

"Course'. Anything for my wife." Crouching back down for his pants, he pulled them on, too. "Just need to clean up first. Do you want me to get you some tissues or toilet paper from the bathroom while I'm at it?"

Smiling brighter, Maryssa nodded. She pecked him and hopped off the desk to begin re-dressing, legs indeed a little wobbly. The sight swelled the silliest but most incredible pride inside his chest. He hurried off towards the bathroom, shoulders high and straightened.

When Andy came back, Maryssa was buttoning up her blouse and still skirt-less, presumably so he could help clean up the mess between her legs. She looked back when she heard the bathroom door and smiled. Tucking her hair behind her ear, she finished buttoning up her blouse.

"Thank you, sweetie," she said when he made his way to her, stretching out a hand to accept the items.

Andy didn't hand them over, though. He simply dropped down to his knees and carefully started wiping her down with the toilet paper he'd run through water, cleaning up any evidence of their encounter. The appreciative hand Maryssa put on his head swelled tenderness inside him, enough that he couldn't resist wrapping his arms around her and burying his face in her belly.

"Think we did it this time?" he murmured, closing his eyes.

Maryssa threaded her hand in his hair. Her other cupped the back of his neck, lovingly. She sighed, contently. "I hope so, Andy. I really hope so."

Andy heaved a long breath, pressing his lips over her stomach where their child might be. He smiled and looked up at his amazing wife. "Man, I really hope we have a girl this time. Don't you?"

Maryssa blinked quickly, and then she laughed. "What, you want to play teatime with a bunch of stuffed animals?"

Andy grinned. "Sounds amazing. Will you bake us cookies?"

Maryssa's laughter quickly died, stunned silence replacing it. Then, she smiled, so damn beautifully his heart actually hurt seeing it. She urged him up wordlessly; Andy obeyed. Maryssa wrapped her arms around him, kissing him slow and sweetly.

"For teatime with our little girl? Always."

Andy's heart had never felt so full.

Story 5 - Cherry Chapstick Lips (First time lesbian)

Sophie stirred awake to her head pounding, beating against her temples like a tribal drum in the midst of a ceremonial dance, powerful like no other instrument could be. But her hangover was far from anything to be celebrated or admired, however—especially with how nauseous it was making her.

What was cause for celebration, though, were the arms wrapped around her right now: dark brown, slim, and unbearably familiar. So beautiful in contrast to Sophie's pale, creamy skin. Undoubtedly, Sophie knew who these arms belonged to. They were Hazel's, her roommate.

Sophie wanted to groan. She should have realized that getting trashed with Hazel when she had the biggest lady-boner for her would end up with the two of them passed out in bed. Cuddling. Especially since she and Hazel had been flirting since the first day they met. (It felt like flirting to her, anyway. With girls, it could be so difficult to tell when teasing banter carried more weight.)

It didn't help that the two of them had even made out on a few occasions—mostly when they were tipsy on Natty Light and screwdrivers, surrounded by equally tipsy college students. The two of them had always brushed it off, though. Or, well, Sophie did to be sure. She'd never known how Hazel felt about it all. Sophie always blamed it on the alcohol and Hazel never seemed to disagree, so if neither of them attempted to bring it up even now, then surely it meant that Hazel was cool with it, too, right?

Yet, Sophie's stomach still twisted uncomfortably at the thought. Whether with doubt or worry—or something else. Something like longing. It wasn't quite that she wanted to *be* with Hazel, but Sophie still wanted it to mean more, be more, than drunken fumbling. She didn't want for either of them to have to take vodka doubling as a cleaning agent to tempt them to kiss the other. Sophie certainly didn't need it, anyway. She never wanted to go back to pretending her attraction to girls wasn't real.

"I told you to buy blackout curtains and better blinds," Hazel mumbled behind her, eliciting a flinch from Sophie. "These are so shitty they barely keep any light out."

Sophie swallowed the lump in her throat. "You're just a vampire," she replied.

Hazel laughed, the sound rough with sleep. "No, you simply can't manage to pick out any quality products—like, ever."

Sophie's lips twitched but she feigned a gasp. She poked Hazel's arm too gently to be anything but playful. "Hey! Do not."

"Do too."

Hazel poked her back—a bit less gently—and Sophie yelped. But when Hazel's lips curved into a smile, her brown eyes softening, she couldn't help smiling, too.

"Remind me… who was it that complimented the dining table that I picked out yesterday?" Sophie asked, wiggling in Hazel's hold until she was facing her. She tapped a finger to her lips. "Oh, right. You."

Hazel snorted. "You did *not* pick that out. Your mom did." She rolled her eyes.

"So I did. By proxy. *Burn.*"

Hazel stared at her, deeply unimpressed. "What year is it, 2010? Who even says 'burn' anymore?"

"Only cool people," Sophie quipped. She started to grin but winced as her head started throbbing harder, fingers coming to rub at her temples. "Ugh. Please tell me you have a hangover this time."

Hazel's mouth lifted at the corners. "You want me to lie to you?"

Sophie groaned, moving her hand across her eyes. It didn't actually help to lessen her headache, but at least it blocked out the sunlight. Maybe Hazel had a point about the blinds.

"Seriously? What the fuck. That is so unfair. Why do you never get them? You're not human."

"Great genes, baby."

Sophie erupted into giggles, her cheeks reddening. Her amusement faded quickly when her temples pulsed more violently, protesting the laugh. It was still worth the pain, though. Kidding around with Hazel trumped any hangover, no matter how awful. "Right. Screw you. Shut up now or you'll make my head explode."

"I'm not the one who refused water when the bartender offered it to you, and I didn't make you drink all those tequila shots," Hazel reminded her.

"You didn't stop me either," Sophie muttered.

Hazel huffed. "Honey, I'm not your mom. I didn't pick out that dining table. Don't go blaming me. Take responsibility for your own choices."

Sophie's lips quirked up again, fondness rushing through her heart. God, that cheeky, no-nonsense demeanor. Sophie loved it. It could make Hazel so unbelievably attractive, sometimes. But then, she always was.

Sophie peered down at Hazel's shirt, drawn in by the cartoon print of Tweety Bird. They were both in pajamas, but as far as Sophie could recall, they had gone to bed dressed in their club clothes. It was hard to forget falling asleep in a skintight bodycon dress that cut off her circulation, and Sophie couldn't remember waking up and changing into her pajamas. Only that they'd watched *Dirty Grandpa* and eaten leftover Chinese food. Had she and Hazel made out before they crashed? Had they undressed each other? Had they had *sex*?

Oh, God. I hope we didn't have sex, Sophie thought. Her first time with a woman and she'd have no memory of it? That was a mortifying concept—and concerning. If she'd been wasted enough to blackout then she was way too drunk to be having sex and that applied to Hazel, too.

"I swear I can see the wheels spinning in your head. What are you overthinking this time?" Hazel asked.

Sophie could feel her cheeks burning hotter. "Um. Nothing."

"Liar."

"Am not!"

"Then why are you staring at Tweety bird like your brain is about to fry a circuit?"

"I wasn't—" Sophie kept her mouth shut. Okay, she was. Hazel wasn't blind *or* crazy, and as a Black woman, she particularly hated when people tried to make her believe otherwise.

Sophie relented with a sigh. "I'm just… trying to puzzle something out."

"Uh-huh." Hazel stared at her. That was Sophie's cue to go on.

She ran a hand over her face. "We slept in the same bed."

"Yep."

"In our pajamas."

"Mhm." None of this seemed to bother Hazel, as though this was an everyday thing with them—and it very well wasn't.

Sophie bit her tongue. "But last I can remember, we weren't *in* our pajamas when we went to bed, Hazel."

"The first time, yeah," Hazel replied, nonchalantly stretching out her arms over her head.

"The firs—" Sophie sucked in a breath. She rubbed her forehead and rolled on her back. "Did we sleep together? Like…" Sophie gestured vaguely with her hands, like she was playing the world's most awkward game of charades.

Apparently, she wasn't very good at it because Hazel tilted her head and asked, brow raised, "What is that supposed to be?"

"Oh, God. You know what—Never mind!"

"Was that supposed to mean *sex*?"

"Jesus Christ. Just—Just forget about i—" Sophie clammed up, nausea returning and gripping her violently. Oh, *shit*. "I'm gonna throw up," she warned with a near-whimper, scrambling out of bed and towards their shared bathroom.

She barely made it to the toilet before dropping to her knees and heaving all of last night's Chinese food. Sophie's world blurred over, a mess of stinky vomit that still smelled a bit like tequila, tears blurring her vision, and thoughts of regret running rampant across her mind. She thought she heard someone saying something too, but she wasn't sure, too focused on throwing her whole life up.

When it was over, she realized someone was holding her hair. Hazel, definitely—because who else could it be?

This had to be the unsexiest thing ever. "Why do you have to keep seeing me at my worst?" Sophie asked, bemoaning her luck. Figures that the first night she slept in the same bed as her crush, a hangover would ruin everything. Oh well. At least she felt better already. Despite the still-lingering headache, spilling her guts out seemed to have helped her overall state.

Hazel snorted. "Hello? We live together."

"Remind me why again?"

"You do my laundry."

The words left her mouth so naturally that Sophie's head snapped up to throw her roommate a dirty look. Her cheeks warmed as Hazel smirked back. "Har har. Very funny," Sophie said, rolling her eyes.

Hazel puffed out a *psh* noise and replied, "So are you. You know why we moved in together after leaving our dorm. We're attached at the hip."

Sophie grumbled. "Yeah, I know. Sorry. Can you get me a glass of water?"

Hazel made it to the kitchen and back, bearing the promised water, in less than a minute. She handed Sophie the cup, but Sophie was so dizzy that when she accepted it, her fingers shook so badly that half the contents spilled on her shirt.

"Did you forget how to drink, too?" Hazel asked, sniggering.

"Hazel," Sophie whined. "Shut up."

"Here, let me help you get that off."

Sophie nodded, blushing, and let Hazel help her out. Part of her was a little panicked; though Hazel had to know that Sophie wasn't wearing a bra, and Sophie was sure she had seen many breasts in her life and never blinked an eye, something about right now still felt so different. They weren't just two women changing in the locker room or walking in on the other naked in the public dorm showers. They were Sophie and Hazel, two openly bisexual girls who had made out on multiple occasions and were clearly attracted to each other—and they had just slept in the same bed, cuddling all night.

Once the shirt was off, Sophie's nipples stiffened instantly from the chilliness of the room. She held her breath, watching Hazel's gaze dip to her chest. Sophie was sure she wasn't imagining things as Hazel's pale, almost golden eyes ignited with desire. Her insides practically melted. She swore she even saw Hazel's tongue peek out and run subtly over her lips.

She wanted to tease Hazel. Wanted to snap her out of her reverie and ask her if she liked what she was seeing. But Hazel was staring at her with such heat that she was finding it hard to breathe. How cliche was that?

"You know you have an amazing rack, right?" Hazel said.

Sophie's mouth dried. Her cheeks turned redder. Still, she lifted her chin with feigned confidence and put a hand on her hip. "They're pretty good, yeah. Nothing compared to yours, though."

Hazel's lips twitched higher. Her brow rose as if she was challenged. And maybe she was, Sophie admitted.

And so she nodded, as though it was her whole point. "Maybe you should take off your shirt too and we could have a more direct comparison."

Hazel's not-quite-golden eyes gleamed brighter. They bore into her own, burning as though they could set fire to anything they touched, should they want to. They fell down and carefully mapped out her breasts again, their hunger growing. Like she wanted to put her mouth on Sophie's nipples and memorize their shape with her tongue, over and over again.

Sophie nearly shivered at the thought alone. *Do it. I dare you. Please.*

"Maybe," Hazel said, eyes flickering up to hers again. "That's not a bad idea at all."

Sophie's brain barely had the time to process the words before Hazel asked, "You know what? Why don't you take it off for me?"

Through all their years knowing each other, Sophie had always thought Hazel's smirks were sexy. But the one that formed on her lips right now? The one so cocky and full of silent, repressed desire—all of which at this very moment was solely meant for her? It had her stomach flipping, the warm space between her legs dampening instantly.

She gawked and stood so very still as Hazel stepped closer, guiding Sophie's hands to the hem of her pajama shirt. She lifted it up some, bunching it all up around her hips. She stared expectantly at Sophie with an air of confidence Sophie knew she could never have. Not like her.

"Well?" Hazel urged, quirking her brow.

A fire rose in Sophie's chest, her competitive side. She grasped Hazel's hips briefly, eyes narrowing. She quickly yanked Hazel's shirt off, her hands instinctively settling on her newly bared breasts.

This is it, isn't it? This is finally happening, Sophie thought, amazed. *Two years of yearning for her and not wanting to ruin the close friendship we have, and we're actually facing all this sexual tension between us.*

Sophie wasn't sure whether or not this was a good idea. She loved Hazel but she wasn't *in love* with her. She didn't know if Hazel felt the same, too, but it was likely that she wasn't in love with Sophie either. She had seen Hazel in love. It was nothing like this. But was it really such a smart thing for two close friends to sleep together when they lived together?

I'm sleeping with Zeke all the time and he's my best friend. Neither of us have any feelings for each other. So why should this be any different? Because she's a girl?

Sophie shook her head, earning herself an amused look from Hazel. She smiled cheekily, uttering a quick, "Sorry—overthinking brain again."

Hazel huffed, her eyes crinkling at the corners. She pushed Sophie's hands closer, squeezing them around her fantastic breasts. "Stop thinking so much and touch me already."

Sophie struggled not to grin, circling both of her dark nipples before stepping away. She put a finger up before Hazel could protest. "Give me a minute to brush my teeth and use some mouthwash? I don't think anyone wants to kiss someone with hangover breath."

Hazel laughed, moving aside to allow her to get to the sink. "Okay, yeah."

Beaming, Sophie proceeded to the tiny washbasin, gathering her things. She couldn't believe she was about to do this. Not ten minutes ago, she was hurling over the toilet with a hangover so strong she could barely think. But now? Now her whole body felt utterly consumed and overtaken by lust, only a faint headache lingering in the background—easily ignored. On any other day, Sophie might have spent a good few hours in bed, vowing never to drink again. But not today.

Not today.

Expecting Hazel to get out and maybe fetch them some coffee or possibly even surprise her naked in bed, Sophie was startled to find her instead wrapping her arms around her waist, lips smoothing over her skin to plant slow, delightful kisses on her shoulder. Those lips made a path to her neck, hands cupping the weight of her breasts, getting to know their curves before they started playing with her hard peaks.

Sophie let out a shuddering breath and strangled hum, sagging back into Hazel and nearly choking on her toothbrush.

Hazel cracked up, exclaiming something like, "Come on, girl, don't die on me now. We're just getting to the good stuff."

Sophie had never been motivated to brush her teeth so fast in her life.

By the time she was finished barely half a minute later, she was in all but her underwear all thanks to Hazel and her wonderful hands. Hazel was still kissing her neck, holding one of Sophie's breasts in her hand while the other hand busied itself between her thighs. It had been doing wondrous work rubbing Sophie's cunt over last night's sexy, barely-there thong—which was considerably damp at this point.

It was driving Sophie insane. But something about all this was making her nervous—no, no… more like *clueless*. She'd done all this so many times with a man before today, but right now, with Hazel? Everything felt so different. New—but all in familiar ways, as odd as that sounded. Did all women like to be kissed behind the ear as she did? Did Hazel? Did they all like their clit rubbed in circles?

Probably not, right?

"Earth to Hazel. There are those gears again," Hazel hummed, nipping her earlobe. "What are you overthinking now, babe?"

Turning around in her arms, Sophie wrapped her arms around Hazel's neck and drew her into a long kiss. Her lips always tasted so good. Soft and never dry, the faint flavor of honey-melon always clinging to them. Was it Hazel's body wash? Her shampoo? Sophie would have to check what kind she used the next time she took a shower. Hazel always carried such an amazing smell, amazing everything—which was better than all these college men who consistently sprayed themselves with Axe rather than bathed.

"Honey, what's wrong?" Hazel said, gently breaking away from her. "You are so in your head. What's going on? Are you a virgin?"

Sophie gaped. "What? Are you kidding me? You heard me have sex like three days ago when Zeke was here!" she exclaimed, flustered. Like, seriously! How could she even say that? Sophie ran a hand through her hair, slowly becoming more red-faced. "That is legitimately the stupidest question I think you've ever asked me."

Hazel's brow lifted, and she tugged her closer by her hips. "Okay, let me rephrase that. Are you a virgin *when it comes to lesbian sex*?"

Sophie's mind went blank, if only for a few seconds. Her mouth dropped open wider—which she didn't even know was possible. She couldn't even find her voice; a good thing, as Sophie found there was nothing more that she wanted than to vehemently deny Hazel's assumption. Even if it was true.

She didn't really understand why.

Hazel's face softened with sympathy and Sophie winced. Letting out a heavy sigh, her shoulders slumped, and she ran her hands over her furiously blushing face, recognizing when she was defeated. "...Yes. Okay? I've made out with tons of girls before—and you know this, you've been one of them! —but I've never... well, never slept with one. Or gone further than making out. So..."

Sophie tried to cross her arms and avoid Hazel's gaze, but Hazel wouldn't let her. She stopped Sophie in her tracks and trapped her back against the counter, her eyes gleaming. God, she was close. So close that Sophie could feel her breath, could easily just lean forward and take Hazel's lips with her own.

"Cute," Hazel murmured. "Sophie, it's not a big deal that you are. I'm not a guy. As far as I know, most women don't cower away from other women who have only slept with the opposite sex. I certainly don't. If anything, I'm excited to show you how great lesbian sex is."

Lesbian sex. There it was again. Sophie was nervous but it seemed like every time she heard the word *sex* and *lesbian* coming from Hazel's mouth, she grew ever more excited. Sex. Lesbian sex. With Hazel. Her longtime crush—if only for fantasies.

She was getting wetter and wetter simply thinking about it.

Getting ever more riled up, Sophie surged forward, kissing Hazel with all of the dizzying lust within her. Hazel made a sound of surprise but kissed her back, never wasting another moment to run her hands all over Sophie's body. Sophie was of a similar mind, hungrily exploring Hazel's body as though she never had before, paying particular attention to her ass and amazing breasts.

Never breaking away, Hazel started guiding her out of her bathroom and towards their living room, where they collapsed on the couch together. Hazel settled on top of her, caressing her thighs and the edges of Sophie's racy thong. Sophie could only be glad she'd decided to wear sexy underwear when going out clubbing last night. And even though she always knew Hazel would be more of a top, she still found herself surprised by the amount of initiative Hazel took.

There was no hesitation on her part. Hazel knew what she was doing and what she was going to do next. There was no uncertainty, no cluelessness. She was clearly experienced—well-versed in the knowledge of handling a woman.

That, in particular, became very clear when Hazel's hand slipped down her panties and started touching the most sensitive part of her. Sophie gasped into their kiss, deepening it and raking her fingers through Hazel's frizzy hair. Hazel murmured something Sophie didn't have the brains to process, possibly dirty words or perhaps a question about what she liked.

All that Sophie had the brains to process was the pleasure—brought to her by Hazel's wonderful fingers. She couldn't believe how different it felt to be touched by another woman. Her touch was so good—so damn *fucking fantastic*. Men's fingers were nearly always more reckless, unless they already knew what their partners liked, and they touched with a sort of urgency, like speed was the only technique to her pleasure.

It wasn't. And Hazel knew that. Hazel was the complete opposite, even, touching her exquisitely slowly but with unhurried, hard rubs that had Sophie shuddering again and again. All she could do was kiss Hazel, and kiss her some more. She opened her thighs wider to give Hazel more access— embarrassingly often. So much that it was obscene and, worse, desperate. But somehow, that only made it better.

Until one abrupt moment, Hazel's fingers stopped moving. Sophie's mind kept spinning—unpleasantly, now.

"Do you like fingering?" she asked as she pulled away from their kiss. She radiated such smugness that Sophie figured she must have mourned the loss of friction with a needy noise or something.

God, she could barely think because of how badly her head was spinning right now. "Um—Yeah. I mean— when done right, that is. I mean—" Sophie reddened, turning crimson all the way up to her roots and snapping her mouth shut. *Fuck. I can't believe I—When done right? Did I really have to add that?*

She could have instead clarified that she preferred it a certain way—saying it like *that* was a one-way ticket to offending someone.

If Hazel was annoyed, she didn't show it. Her eyes merely glinted. "Don't worry about that, honey. When you've been with as many women as I have, you *know* how to use your fingers."

"How many women have you been with?" Sophie asked, curious.

Hazel tilted her head, frowning. "Is that really important right now?"

"I guess not…" Sophie mumbled. She gasped and arched her back when Hazel started stroking her once more, her hands taking a mind of their own and caressing Hazel's back, her shoulders… all the way down to her breasts. She dug her teeth down into her lip, winding both arms soundly around Hazel's neck and pushing up to kiss her. "You can—Yeah. Whenever."

Hazel snickered against her mouth. "Eager now, are we?"

Sophie gaped. "You're the one who asked!" she protested.

"I'm not in any hurry," Hazel said, her eyes gleaming. "Seems like you are, though."

"I—Your hand is in my underwear. *On my clit.* Of course I'm a little worked up and eager!" Puffing her cheeks, Sophie buried her face in Hazel's neck to kiss and bite where she could. She threaded her fingers through Hazel's gorgeous hair again, scratching her nails against her scalp punishingly.

A smile lifted her lips when Hazel shuddered, clearly not as composed as she liked to pretend. That made Sophie feel much better for some reason.

"Okay, yeah. Maybe we've been waiting long enough to sleep together," Hazel gibed, letting out a breathless laugh. Somehow, it only served to work up Sophie even further.

Sophie locked one ankle behind Hazel's back and dragged her in for a deep kiss. "Glad I wasn't crazy and that there really was all this sexual tension between us these past two years," she panted out between two very involved kisses, goosebumps prickling her skin as Hazel's fingers inched further down, circling her entrance.

Slowly, they pushed inside and started setting up a nice, steady beat, wrenching a sweet moan out of her.

Sophie moaned when Hazel pushed her fingers in, setting up a slow, steady beat.

"What could you possibly mean?" Hazel asked, her voice wry. "We're just *friends*. Friends finger each other. That's what gal pals do."

Sophie laughed, the sound broken by gasps and little blissful noises. Hazel kissed her for it, bracing herself against her free hand and picking up the pace with the other. Sophie whimpered and tried to drag Hazel closer with the ankle around her back, only to end up throwing Hazel off her balance. Hazel crumbled flat on Sophie's body, knocking her chin against her collarbone and sending the pair of them groaning.

Apparently, Hazel was completely justified in calling her a virgin, because she hadn't been this clumsy with sex since her first time.

"Sorry…"

"You know what? Maybe we should move to the bedroom before we get too far," Hazel said, stroking her jaw and wincing. "That way if anything like this happens again, neither of us has the chance to tumble to the floor and get hurt."

"Agreed," Sophie said, grimacing as she rubbed her own injury, too.

Hazel got up first, naturally, then held out her hand. When Sophie took it, she felt how wet Hazel's fingers were—wet from her cunt. As if she needed anything to turn her on more. Hazel led her down the hall to Sophie's room, guiding without forcing. The moment they stepped inside, Hazel maneuvered her to the edge of the bed and lightly pushed her onto it. Softness settled around her, the mattress plush beneath her weight, a luxurious warmth spreading over her from head to toe.

Sophie scrambled back on the bed. She chucked off her panties while Hazel shimmied out of her pajama shorts and blue undies, briefly mourning the fact she never got to take them off Hazel. Sophie would have liked to have bitten that ass, so much fuller than hers could ever be. Her breasts were modest, but her ass lacked some serious juice. At least it didn't stop her from getting laid, though.

Hazel was over to her in seconds, hand reaching between Sophie's legs once more. Sophie propped them up on the bed and opened wide, yanking Hazel to her level for a hot kiss, full of teeth and tongue. She kept kissing Hazel with all the frenzied passion within her as Hazel slipped her fingers back inside her pussy and gradually set up a relentless pace. It tore raw sounds from Sophie's lips, most of them muffled against Hazel's mouth.

It was clear that Hazel knew what she was doing. With her fingers curved *just* to reach that spot within her that most men never found, the buildup to her orgasm was quicker. Stronger. Even compared to when she was by herself. She'd spent so many nights craving this, Hazel playing her body like a violin, and tried in vain to ease that ache on her own. Now she knew exactly how far short her fantasies fell from the real thing.

"Keep going. Just like that. Gonna cum," she puffed between a kiss, panting in staccato beats. She nipped Hazel's lush bottom lip roughly, keening a delighted cry.

Hazel didn't say anything, maintaining that punishing rhythm with expert fingers. She clearly had no plans for a magical finishing move, because she knew it wasn't necessary. A woman who could work a cunt like that could skip the bells and whistles, and besides, Sophie had told her exactly what she had to do. What she had to keep doing in order to make her come.

It didn't take her long to get there.

Crying out sharply, Sophie dropped one hand against the sheets and tightly gripped onto them, blinding white wiping her mind. She snatched Hazel by the back of her head so she could kiss her with all the ferocity her tiny body could ever contain. Whines broke through their messy, fiery exchange, but Hazel didn't seem to mind at all. In fact, judging by the smirk that Sophie felt curling Hazel's lips, she enjoyed every bit of it.

"Cum good, honey?" she asked, a little arrogantly.

It made Sophie smile—if however lopsidedly. Her smile was one that conveyed how very blissed-out and dazed she was, but it was genuine, nonetheless.

Cupping both sides of Hazel's neck, Sophie kissed her sweetly, prolonging it for as much as she could in order to silently show her appreciation. Hazel chuckled, her fingers leaving her wet cunt to travel up her thigh, side, and over one breast. She flicked Sophie's nipple, tongue meeting Sophie's own with enough heat that Sophie couldn't help whining again. She reached out to grab Hazel's ass, loving the delicious curve of it. God, she wished she had an ass like that. But Hazel probably wore it better than Sophie ever could.

She smacked one ass cheek at the thought, loving the way Hazel's breath hitched.

Sophie grinned. "Definitely not surprised that you like being spanked," she said smugly.

Hazel guffawed and bestowed her a challenging stare. "Yeah? What other kinks did you suspect that I have?"

"Is that really important right now?" Sophie teased, recalling Hazel's earlier words.

It was Hazel's turn to grin. "I guess not," she returned, just as teasingly.

Sophie rolled them over so she was on top, slanting her mouth on Hazel's for a long, all-consuming kiss. She trailed her fingers down to Hazel's neck, over her shoulders, and across her collarbone in a path towards her breasts. She broke away and left a trail of hot kisses along the same path, enveloping a hard, peaked nipple when she reached the same destination. Hoping Hazel's preferences were similar, she sucked and nipped at the tender bud much how she liked it done on hers. Briefly, she recalled Hazel sharing when she was drunk how much she loved having her nipples pinched, so Sophie did that, too.

"Not bad for a newbie," Hazel commented, breathless. Sophie glanced up to find her biting her lip, her not-quite-golden eyes so pleasure-hazed that Sophie was sure she would be blushing if it were possible. God, Hazel was always so stunning. But like this? She was even more so. "Listening to your instincts?"

"Trying out tricks that work on me… and remembering things you said you liked having done to you," Sophie said, returning her attention to her breasts and carrying on with sucking, licking, and gently biting them.

"When have I ever told you that?" mumbled Hazel, running her hands through Sophie's hair.

"When you were drunk," Sophie said, laughing. "When else? You're so loose-lipped when you're hammered."

"And you're always horny."

Sophie grinned. "You've noticed?"

Hazel tugged her up to kiss her. "Hard not to. Why do you think we always ended up making out?"

Sophie kissed her harder, smiling against Hazel's lips. Touching Hazel everywhere, she worshipped her toned body and reveled in how good she felt in her hands, wondering if her cunt felt just as good, too. With Hazel's help, she bet she could give her a really nice time, just like Hazel had given her. Her cluelessness couldn't be any worse than when she first tried touching a guy's dick—at least with women, she knew what spots to start with.

Determined, Sophie slid one hand along Hazel's smooth leg, catching Hazel's lip between her teeth. But before she could reach her goal, Hazel rolled them over and started kissing her way down Sophie's tiny body, causing her heart to skip a few beats. Sophie suddenly felt self-conscious for the first time in a very long time. Her body had never been very soft, always more on the bony side—no matter how much she tried to gain weight and fill out her figure. The only part of herself she felt truly proud of was her boobs, which so many people assumed to be fake.

She wondered if Hazel did, too. And if perhaps her body was all hard lines and unpleasant to kiss— something she never wondered before Hazel. Hazel said nothing, though, so hopefully that meant she must have been okay.

When she realized Hazel was heading somewhere in particular, however, she just about yelped and jumped out of her own skin.

"Wait, are you—?"

"Yup. Eating pussy is a favorite hobby of mine. Mind if I indulge in it right now?"

Sophie could only blink, jaw dropping. Hazel watched her closely, those honey eyes flashing as she sank her teeth into Sophie's taut belly. Jesus, she was so damn sexy.

"But you just—I mean, you haven't even cum yet."

"Orgasms aren't always the goal for everyone. Honestly, if we stopped right now, I'd still be happy with what we did."

"I wouldn't," Sophie countered, which earned her a downright cackle from Hazel.

"Don't worry, babe. I'll take care of you," she replied, licking her lips.

Sophie didn't even have the time to think about anything to say in return. Hazel immediately buried her face between Sophie's legs, mouth immediately going for her clit. Sophie's breath caught in her lungs so sharply she almost choked, and she moaned, snatching out to grab fistfuls of the pillow behind her. Hazel chuckled, sending exquisite vibrations that thrummed against her overly sensitive nub. Holy hell, Hazel was a fucking godsend.

Using her lips and tongue in ways Sophie had never experienced from anyone else, Hazel's prowess became transparent when it came to knowing what women liked. Within seconds, she had Sophie thrashing, quivering in the sweaty sheets; crying out in octaves never reached before, climbing heights she never knew existed. Sophie didn't know if her practice came from Hazel's own experience receiving oral or from any feedback she might have gotten after performing it, but she didn't care. Enjoying the ride was all she wanted to do now.

And what a ride it was. Sophie couldn't be sure what Hazel was even doing between her legs, but whatever it was it worked like a motherfucking charm. Every flick of her tongue and strong suck had her shuddering, twisting needily, and begging for more. It was even better when her fingers joined in, delving back into her depths to curl at that spot that drove Sophie wild. She couldn't understand how she ever doubted that women would be better than men when it came to this. Of course they would. Women had to know better than men for most things when it came to sex—except maybe for penis-related tricks.

"Hazel… *Hazel…*" Sophie chanted, wailing her bliss incessantly. "Hazel, oh my God. *Fuck*. I'm gonna cum. I'm gonna cum, baby, I'm gonna—"

Hazel hummed some kind of acknowledging noise and Sophie cried out, pinching her nails so sharply against Hazel's scalp that she was sure it had to hurt. Holding her mouth steady against her cunt, Sophie ground out her waves and moaned with all the wanton lust within her, her world shifting into a blurry mess. Hazel groaned, sending more delightful vibrations through her, but she kept going and helped Sophie ride out the bliss with slower, tender strokes and sucks that prolonged her orgasm beyond what she was used to.

She erupted into bits of laughter when Hazel planted a few last kisses on her inner thighs before removing herself from between them and collapsing beside her, causing Sophie to immediately clasp a hand over her mouth. She hadn't meant to react this way in response to such sensational oral, and it occurred to her how offensive it could be. But then Hazel hauled for a sweet kiss, propping her head against her hand, and Sophie relaxed. Hazel smiled as they pulled away.

"That good?" she asked.

Sophie blinked, mouth parting. She was astounded that Hazel seemed to understand everything going through her head right now. How did she do that?

Sophie's cheeks reddened and she nodded, smiling shyly. "It was just… wow. I think—I mean I always enjoyed it when men went down on me but… I think—no, I *know* that this was the best oral I've ever had. Who taught you all this?"

Hazel smirked, both pleased and decidedly unsurprised. Jesus. She was so hot. "Mix and match of experiences. My first girlfriend had a lot to do with teaching me what fantastic oral is like, though. She was the queen of it."

"Well, thank you Hazel's first girlfriend," Sophie acknowledged, melting into the bed, completely sated. Her eyes were droopy, still dazed from the strength of her orgasm, her body utterly blissed out. She hesitated before asking, "So… was that all foreplay?"

Hazel snorted then tapped Sophie on the nose playfully. "Nope. That, my lovely Sophie, is what we call lesbian sex."

"Really?" she asked, dubious.

Hazel's eyes crinkled at the corners, lips lifting faintly. "Contrary to popular belief, sex doesn't begin at penetration. Sex is everything before it. From the moment you're having foreplay, you're having sex, honey. Heteronormativity has led people to believe otherwise for most of their life."

"I don't know if I like that way of thinking. If I accepted that, I would have lost my virginity at thirteen instead of fifteen," Sophie mused aloud.

Hazel snickered, tugging her in for another kiss. Sophie responded—at least, she started to before realizing that she'd been the only one who came yet again.

"Wait—don't you want to—?"

Hazel shrugged. "Like I said, it's not everyone's goal to cum. I got more out of this watching you cum twice than I would have if I'd had an orgasm. Plus, I've been fantasizing about going down on you for *so long*. You have no idea how satisfied it makes me to have finally heard you moaning my name and begging me over and over."

"I didn't beg you," Sophie protested, but nagging doubt set in before the words even left her mouth. "Oh shit, did I?"

Hazel preened, looking like the cat that ate the canary. "You can't even remember. God, you have no idea how smug that makes me feel. So worth not having an orgasm."

Sophie smiled. She yanked Hazel close and smoothed her lips over hers, feeling up and down her wonderful dark chestnut-toned body. They kissed like that for a while, spent and blissfully content (at least Sophie was) but full of lazy passion. They cuddled afterward, too full of loving hormones to deprive themselves of the occasion.

It wasn't long before it started hitting Sophie that this might have been a horrible idea. She didn't love Hazel. Well, she *did*, but she wasn't *in love* with her. They were great friends, had been for two years—had they now ruined everything by not talking about what this was going to mean from the start?

She didn't want to date Hazel.

Or anyone, really. She never even wanted to date Zeke, and he was her best friend. They had been best friends *with benefits* for a few years now.

But things weren't messy with him, so maybe there was hope for her friendship with Hazel, too. No two friendships reacted the same way to similar situations, though.

Sophie bit back a sigh. This whole thing was already starting to give her a headache. Or maybe that was simply her hangover coming back into focus now that all the bliss and lust was wearing off. She'd barely noticed it since the moment she and Hazel started seducing each other. Although she wasn't sure she could have so easily forgotten it if she hadn't thrown up beforehand.

Jesus. Had she really just had sex after waking up feeling like such a pile of garbage? The thought was laughable.

Nausea crawled back up her throat. Sophie closed her eyes. Now she wasn't sure if she felt like vomiting because her fragile stomach still wasn't done being angry at her or if it was because this entire friendship was about to crumble into ruins.

A hand swept over her side and the slight curve of her ass, and Sophie shuddered. She chewed her bottom lip. Pushing herself away from Hazel to meet her gaze, Sophie cleared her throat and licked her lips. Hazel blinked back at her, bemused.

"Hey, so um… this might get awkward," Sophie began. "But I think I need to put this out there in case you might be starting to think otherwise right now…" She paused, biting the inside of her cheek. She was tempted to look away, but she kept their gazes locked anyway. A sigh left her mouth. "Okay. Hazel, I think you're really hot and I adore you. You're amazing. But—Well, I don't want to date you. This has kind of… only been a release of sexual tension for me. I don't… feel anything romantic, you know? Like. I'm attracted to you, but I don't—"

Hazel began to crack up and she shook her head. "Sophie, relax. I get you. Know why? Cause' I feel the same. Honestly, if I didn't know you were down with this kind of thing, I probably wouldn't have let you seduce me earlier."

"This kind of thing?" Sophie asked, brows rising. Then she poked Hazel's shoulder. "And hey! We were both seducing each other. In fact, I'd argue that *you* started it. You offered to take my shirt off."

"I was genuinely just trying to help you out. You got yourself all wet."

Sophie scowled. "Yeah right!"

Hazel's grin was edged with mischief. "Okay, maybe I wasn't being totally selfless."

"See! I knew it."

Hazel laughed again and Sophie did, too.

She was so glad that everything turned out okay and that they would remain friends after everything. Friends who fucked and still had the most fun together outside of the bedroom. Who knows, maybe Hazel could even teach her how to give such fantastic oral. Then she could give tips to Zeke—who was the best she'd had when it came to men, but only after some heavy teaching on her part. She didn't realize how much better oral could still be until Hazel.

Sex with a woman was so awesome. In some ways, even better.

Maybe people were actually right. Maybe they really weren't lying when they said lesbians were the best lovers out there.

Women knew what made other women feel good, after all.

Story 6 - Love Me Hard, Love Me Better, Love Me Dirty (Hot Wives, Anal and BDSM)

Bringing a man to bed with her that was not her husband was always an exciting thing. Especially one she'd been eyeing for a while. Alana had spotted Joey at the gym for several weeks now and his stolen looks had not gone unnoticed. How could they—especially coming from such a delectable man?

He was some Chris Evans lookalike type. Light-brown hair, a strong jawline, and not overly bulky, but packing firm muscles, those of which had Alana wanting to lick every single one of them up— particularly the ones on his lower abdomen, pointing like an arrow to his dick.

Naturally, she told her husband about him after a few days of unsubtle glances. Arthur's interest was piqued.

"How old is he?"

"In his early thirties I think?"

Arthur's mouth had lifted. He'd looked back down to his novel, flipping the next page. "You do like robbing the cradle, my love."

She'd smacked his arm playfully. "I'm only forty-seven! That's not exactly a May-December romance. Besides, you're older than me, smart-ass."

"Yes, by two whole months," Arthur had said without looking up, his voice dripping with sarcasm. She'd smacked him again, bringing out the smile he'd been trying to repress. He'd leaned over to kiss her temple fondly. "Bring him over next week when I leave for Vancouver. I'll set up the camera stream."

Alana loved her husband. Loved his openness and his implicit trust. While their marriage had first started off entirely monogamous, Arthur's many travels presented far too many obstacles in their sex life. Arthur was often too tired and jetlagged from his long trips. His stamina was sometimes not up to par, often leaving her hanging. Their phone sex calls were interrupted by business lunches, dinners, and meetings, doing more harm than good.

Alana quickly grew more and more sexually frustrated. She regularly went weeks without sex and fulfilling orgasms, the weight of her unsatisfaction eventually starting to get to her. But when she'd shared the matter with Arthur, instead of being bitter about it or requesting her to be patient like she was sure he would have, Arthur suggested something far more surprising than anything Alana could have imagined: to open up their marriage for her sake, as long as they told each other everything. She could sleep with other men as she liked and get more than her fair share of orgasms, she had been missing in his time away—just as long as she never kept anything from him. He wanted in on the details, wanted to know everything done to her.

Other men probably would have felt jealous. Or maybe even secretly resentful. But Arthur enjoyed her stories—so much so that they made their sex hotter than it already was. Which was saying something considering what kinks they were into.

"You sure your husband is okay with this?" Joey asked as she led him to bed, yanking off his sweaty gym shirt in one fell swoop

"Okay?" Alana's brow lifted. "No, honey. Arthur *loves* this. That camera I told you about in our room? That's not for me. That's so Arthur can watch wherever he is. He loves seeing his wife get fucked by other men. Loves to know how desirable I am. Loves to see me getting all the satisfaction that he can't give me all the time. He's away so often… and he hates to see me left out. Plus, it makes him feel more competitive and like he has to fuck me better than all those other men did… including you." She dragged her hand down his pants and over his cock, feeling him stir from such a simple dose of her attention. "So, be a dear and fuck me like you've never fucked anyone before, won't you?"

"Don't have to tell me twice," Joey said, roughly. He leaned in and kissed Alana hard, hauling off her shirt, too, and cupping her breasts. When he bit on them, Alana leaned back and grasped his hair (lighter than Arthur's salt-and-pepper, but not as thick) and guided his face deeper against her chest.

She thought about what Arthur was doing right now, if he was on the other side of that camera observing them through the stream, or if he was too busy, instead saving the show for later. She hoped for the former. Hoped he was there, gaze unquestionably set on her, lips lifting every time she made sweet, pleased sounds.

The thought alone had her pussy throbbing harder. God, if he was there, she prayed he was taking note of how Joey was touching her. Prayed he was getting himself all worked up, growing ever more competitive. She couldn't wait for him to come back home. To find out how he'd react to some thirty-something man fucking his wife, seeing her handling a cock that wasn't his.

For now, she was with Joey, though. And she'd give him all of the attention that she could. Suck his gorgeous dick like he was *her* king and hope he would be kind enough to return the favor. She always loved oral—especially if she got to sit on their face and ride it.

"Do you want me to be on top?" Joey asked as he slipped off her pants. His brow was furrowed. He was such a good-looking man. Had such nice lips. Such a beautiful fucking body.

Alana caressed his cock through his gym shorts. He was so hard already. "Whatever you want, baby. I just want that magnificent cock inside me."

Joey's eyes flared and his chest rumbled in response. He spread her thighs wide and cupped her cunt, cursing at how wet she was. Alana tipped her head back and reached over her head to take hold of her pillow, exhaling a hot breath. Her lips split into a blissful smile when he broke away from her and kissed down her neck, traversing all the way to the valley of her breasts, past her belly button, and further below.

Alana bit back a sigh, sliding her hand through his thin hair. Goodman. Most of her suitors seemed averse to perform oral on a woman, perhaps because of their lack of skill. But Alana never expected any of them to be wizards of the tongue. She simply enjoyed having a man's mouth down there, even if he didn't know what he was doing. The sight of it was always so sexy, enough to have her cunt running like the river Nile within minutes.

Fortunately for Alana, though, Joey soon proved that he did know what he was doing. Someone had clearly taught him some good tricks, good enough that it had her turning into a panting, writhing mess. What was better, he also seemed to really enjoy it.

"Just like that, baby," Alana gasped, tugging on his hair. "Keep doing that. Right there. I'm gonna cum all over that pretty mouth."

"Would rather you do it around my cock," Joey replied, drawing away from her sopping wet pussy, features dripping with smugness as he crawled up over her form and fitted himself inside her in one solid thrust.

Alana wrapped her legs around his back, locking him inside. Though she was mildly disappointed he hadn't finished her off with his talented mouth, she still closed her eyes and focused on murmuring encouragement and praise into Joey's ear, raking her nails over his skin as he started pounding her into the mattress.

"Say my name. Say my name so your husband knows who's fucking you," Joey grunted, kissing her sloppily.

And say his name Alana did.

It was late Friday that Arthur came back home, dragging his feet through their front door at seven forty-eight just as Alana had settled into the couch to watch one of the playoff matches of her and Arthur's favorite hockey team. She'd barely noticed he was home until the hall light came on. She dropped her popcorn bowl, but managed to catch it before it hit the floor.

"Red Wings are on. Playing against the Rangers tonight," she called.

"Score?"

"Zero to zero. A bunch of shots, though."

Arthur appeared in the living room door frame, in the process of stretching his neck. He smiled when he spotted her, grey eyes gleaming with a mix of fatigue and happiness. He was exhausted, clearly, but overjoyed to finally see his wife again. Alana's eyes softened and she smiled back, offering him the bowl of popcorn.

Arthur dropped his travel bag by the corner and then made his way to her, slumping on the couch and taking the spot directly at her side. His arm immediately opened as she nestled herself against him, plopping the bowl of popcorn in his lap. They murmured a sweet greeting and offered each other a few lingering pecks. Then they settled more comfortably and cuddled, contently.

"How was your night with that gym guy?"

"Joey?" Alana frowned and peered at him, disappointed. "You didn't see the stream?"

"I did," Arthur corrected, kissing her temple. "I just want to hear it all from you."

Alana's cheeks flushed adorably and snuggled him closer. "After dinner? Let's watch the Red Wings kick ass for now."

"You were waiting for me for dinner?"

"Of course. You didn't eat, right?"

Arthur tapped the middle of her forehead, a gentle gesture he reserved for moments of quiet, loving connection. "You know me too well, my love."

Some hours later, when the Red Wings had won and dinner was had, the two of them shuffled into the laundry room to put in another batch, hang the last one, and fold the clothes that were dry. Alana tried to shoo away her tired husband, but Arthur would have none of it and insisted on helping.

"So," he began to say, drowning out the sound of the faint music playing on the radio in the background. "About this Joey."

Alana's lips twitched. "He was a good sport. We had a lot of fun. As you saw," she said, folding the shirt in her hands. She threw him a flirty look, one that she was sure brought a fire to his loins. "What do you want to know? If he gave me better head than you do?"

"I very seriously doubt that," Arthur said dryly. The stare he set on her in return had *her* burning up inside, now. "No, I was thinking more… How you seduced him. How easy was it to get him on board? Did he know about me?" He gave her a lopsided grin, waking one of his dimples, eyes blazing. "Did his dick feel good inside you? So good that your eyes rolled to the back of your head?"

He was self-inserting, there, and Alana knew that. Arthur had never let it slip his mind the one time he made her cum so hard her eyes rolled to the back of her head in the height of her orgasm. She bit the inside of her cheek and took a pair of sweatpants next, folding them neatly.

"You know that's only you," she mumbled, cheeks reddening.

A moment of silence passed, but then Arthur wrapped his arms around her waist, planting a slow, seductive kiss on her neck. "You didn't answer the rest of my questions."

"Oh?" Alana hummed. She closed her eyes and arched her neck to give him space. "Remind me what they were again? I can't remember."

"Bullshit," Arthur growled. "Don't play coy."

Alana giggled, the sound cut off by Arthur shoving down her shirt to kiss and lick her shoulder. "Seducing him was easy. All I had to do was ask him to show me how to work this machine… and he was putty in my hands already. He'd had his eyes on me for weeks, you see… He didn't waste time letting me know what he wanted."

Arthur's hands clawed possessively at her stomach, teeth sinking a little deeper into her skin. Alana closed her eyes but didn't stop him. Wouldn't dream of it. She'd been waiting with bated breath for this ever since he left.

"You're sure you're not too tired to do this, honey?" she asked, biting her lip as he unbuttoned and unzipped her jeans with nimble fingers. She sighed when they slipped past her panties, seizing her heat. She hoped to God he would say he was never too exhausted for this.

"I'm the one asking questions," he reminded her, his tone hot and authoritative as it always became in moments just like these. "And you better start answering them all before I punish you, Alana."

Alana whimpered, hunching over the washing machine when he began to rub her firmly. He parted her legs, causing her pussy to start throbbing, begging to be filled and used already. God, she was so needy. But she knew it would be a while still before he gave her what she wanted most. Arthur was always such a tease, especially when he took the reins. No one would ever guess that her kind, mellow husband dommed his wife behind closed doors, and Alana loved it. Only she ever got to see this side of Arthur, and no matter how many other men she fucked with his blessing, she never gave the gift of her submission to anyone besides him.

"He knew about you. He knew I was married," she gasped, eyes shutting tight as he rubbed her clit in perfect, expert strokes, mouthing messily at the nape of her neck. "He didn't believe me at first when I told him about—our little arrangement. But then I kept insisting. I kept saying he could call you. Or text you. Or see you in person when you came back. And he was so surprised."

His hand pressed more fiercely, rubbing her in vicious circles that had her trembling. She started to widen her thighs, but Arthur smacked her ass smartly and said, "Keep your legs together so I can get these jeans off you. Don't move until I tell you to, and don't speak unless you're spoken to."

Alana held perfectly still, wanting to follow her husband's instructions, to please him—and herself—by yielding. Yet the temptation to disobey was nearly irresistible, because taunting Arthur and flouting his authority in bed (whether an actual bed was involved or not) always led to the most delightful chastisements, those of which Alana could never get enough of.

She fought that impulse, though, like a good sub, and didn't move a muscle until Arthur told her to step out of the pants he'd jerked down to her ankles.

She felt him press a deceptively innocent kiss against her hip. His breath warmed her skin when he said, "There. Now tell me more about Joey."

"It was funny, actually," she went on, picking up the conversation right where they'd left off, as if Arthur hadn't just silenced her. Such a simple order, but Alana knew things wouldn't stay simple for long. She could hardly wait for more. She was too full of lust already, and they had just gotten started. "He almost bailed when I brought him home. Kept asking me if I was sure you were okay with this. If you really knew. If you were really on the other side of that camera, getting off on this." Her breath caught in her throat when Arthur got back up to his feet and dove between her thighs once more, finding her clit with ease. He pinched it. "I think half of him expected you to walk in on us in a rage—"

Arthur huffed a laugh, but he played with her more roughly. "I knew he looked a little hesitant."

"Maybe we should have gotten a better camera," she breathed. "So you could hear everything…"

"Sweetheart, all I need is to hear how loud he makes you moan," Arthur returned.

He flipped her around and manhandled her onto the washing machine. Alana instantly wrapped her legs around him, carnal in her desire. But after one long kiss, Arthur withdrew, separating their bodies completely. He leaned back against the wall and crossed his arms, that air of dominance returning with even more intensity. Alana's heart raced faster.

"Take off your panties and touch yourself."

A shiver ran up Alana's spine. When she hesitated, Arthur's eyes narrowed. "Now, Alana. Don't make me wait. You'll only get punished worse."

It always fascinated her how different Arthur became when sex was in the picture. He was such a loving husband and golden-hearted man, always smiling at everyone and listening quietly. But during sex, a whole new side of him came out. One who loved to worship her even while he was throwing orders at her. It was always there in his eyes. The confidence, the fire. The love.

He was never degrading. Neither of them were much into humiliation, after all. But there was always something in his tone of voice that made Alana feel so desired; so powerful—as ironic as that was. There was an astonishing freedom that could be found in submission, with the right partner. And no partner could ever be better for her than her husband.

Obeying Arthur's command, Alana lifted her hips and slid off her panties, keeping her gaze locked with her husband's. She opened her legs for his view, reveling in the way his eyes dipped to her wet pussy. She ran her hand down with excruciating patience, keeping her lascivious gaze carefully set on him. She played magic on her clit, touching herself in firm, unhurried circular strokes. Arthur wanted a show, and she was going to give it to him.

Arthur's hand curled at his side, but he did nothing. He only said, "Good. Keep playing with yourself. *Slowly.* Keep your eyes on me. Are you ready to answer more of my questions?"

Alana nodded, eager to do as she was told, to be good for him. Arthur's gaze flared hotter.

"How much did you like his cock inside you?"

"I liked it a lot. It was great. Thick… Hot. Reminded me of yours," she replied, a little breathless. "It was *fun.*"

"Did you beg for it?"

She bit her lip, shaking her head. "No… No, I didn't."

Arthur frowned and strode forward until he had her caged between his arms. "Now what did I say before I left?"

Cheeks reddening, Alana leaned forward to capture his lips in a fierce kiss, but he evaded her by recoiling away.

"What did I say, Alana?" he repeated, grabbing a fistful of her hair.

He tugged—just sharp enough that it hurt, but not so much that the pain would overcome her pleasure. Her eyes flew shut, a raw, keening sound passing her lips.

Arthur tsk-ed. "And now you've stopped looking at me. You're being extremely disobedient today. How should we handle your punishment?"

Alana opened her eyes again to stare at him pleadingly. She knew it wasn't going to work, though. But she still loved it. "Please… Please, Arthur."

"No," he said, with the ease of a man who thrived on her supplication. "Not yet. Not for a long time."

Alana whimpered. Arthur freed her from his grasp and stepped away, returning to lean against the wall. He stared her down.

"I want you to go upstairs, strip naked, bend over the foot of the bed, close your eyes and spread your legs wide. When you do, I want you to stay like that. And wait for me. You will not touch yourself. You will not open your eyes and glance around to pass time. You will not do anything but stay exactly as you are and think about what I might do to you next."

"How long will you make me wait?" she asked, her voice small and needy.

"However long it pleases me. You don't get to have a say. This is the first part of your punishment."

Alana whined, stroking herself faster. The thought of waiting there for him, spread open for his perusal and sopping wet, was so cruel and torturous in the best ways. She ached for him already. Ached to know what he would do to her when he joined her.

Arthur stepped forward and stilled her hand, forcing it away from her body. His stare was commanding, even as he let her go and brushed some hair from her face. "Upstairs. Now."

Alana scampered off to do just as he'd asked, breaths heavy with desire. She paused at their staircase to glance back at her dom, her husband, and bit the inside of her cheek as she found he had followed, arms casually crossed over his chest. She swallowed and stripped off her shirt, leisurely climbing up the stairs as she dropped the garment over the railing. Her bra was next, leaving her bare as the day she was born and completely at his perusal.

Arthur didn't react, but he didn't take his eyes off her either, his stare only becoming more intense. He was pleased.

"Don't make me repeat myself again, Alana," he called, as she lingered too long, and Alana hurried on with her path.

Her heart was pounding as she followed his instructions. By the time she reached their bedroom, her cunt was so wet it was probably dripping onto the floor. Alana was surprised to find that the most difficult part was keeping her eyes closed. Torturous as the cool air was on her very aroused and wet pussy, accentuating how empty it felt and how much she yearned to have *some* kind of friction, it was the lack of visual stimulation that had her growing antsy more than anything else. Her mind had to fill in on what her eyes could not, haunting her with fantasies and expectations that had her growing even wetter. Had her aching to touch herself and soothe some of her burning desire.

What was Arthur up to as he made her wait? Was he getting ready in the bathroom, stripping naked as well? Was he pounding his cock with thoughts of her, picturing her as she was right now? Was he watching from their camera feed, making sure she obeyed his every direction?

The last thought had her burning up tenfold, the image of this possibility igniting every nerve in her body. She didn't know how she managed not to touch herself. It was all she wanted to do, all she could think about.

Alana had no idea how much time passed before she heard Arthur's voice break the deafening silence of the room at last.

"Good girl. You did exactly what I asked. You can open your eyes, now." When their eyes met, Arthur nodded. "Perfect. Now lie down on the bed and open your legs for me. But keep those hands to yourself, you hear me? I'm not giving you permission to touch yourself yet."

Alana opened her mouth to complain but swallowed her words down as she reminded herself what was at stake, heart racing even faster as she did as he asked. Once she was settled, she chewed the inside of her cheek and waited for his next commands, her pussy aching for him.

Still fully dressed, Arthur merely made his way over to the side of the bed, tracing his finger on one of her peaked nipples. Then he reached into one of their nightstand drawers—the one that kept all their toys and sexual necessities. She whimpered at the realization alone, a sound that instantly drew his attention. His eyes softened and he smiled, brow rising as he started taking out her favorite toys.

"Help me figure out something… Is your good behavior enough to make up for all of your disobedience this week?" he asked, using her hot pink vibrator to trace a path from her breasts to her stomach, going down, down… Only to stop just at the edge of her pelvis. "Do you feel you should be rewarded right now? I'm tempted to allow you to pick out the toy I'll use for your next part of your punishment…"

He moved the beloved hot pink vibrator away as the last words left his mouth, leaving her so needy that she stamped her foot against the mattress. Bratty and willful, but Alana was beyond caring. She could only imagine what Arthur saw when their gazes met again; she felt so feral that she wouldn't be surprised to learn her eyes conveyed as much.

"Arthur… Arthur please…"

Arthur's eyes crinkled at the corners. He shrugged. "Maybe you shouldn't be rewarded after all. You haven't been obeying any of my orders since I left."

Alana moaned in despair, but her pussy pulsed with even greater veracity and longing, so desperate for some kind of friction that she began rubbing herself on the sheets.

"You'd think that since I left, you haven't been with anyone with the way you're acting…" he murmured, observing her with brazen grey eyes. "Like that guy's cock wasn't enough. Like you didn't get what you needed. And that's not what our little arrangement is supposed to be, my love… You're supposed to be satisfied. Always."

"He was, I swear," Alana said. "It's just… you… You drive me insane."

Arthur's lips curled higher. He reached up and cradled the swell of one breast, tracing the reddened, peaked bud. "You better not be lying to me, sweetheart."

Alana wanted to insist that she wasn't, but Arthur pinched her nipple enough to make her cry out, and she writhed helplessly. He soothed the pain by leaning down and giving her a loving suck, his tongue rolling around the tender nipple in sweet strokes. She caught hold of his hair and Arthur snatched her hand away.

"Hands off," he ordered. "You're at my mercy."

With another man, playing by different rules, that might be frightening, but not with Arthur. Never with Arthur. God, he was so hot when he was like this.

Arthur gave her breast a few last sucks before releasing her. Alana stayed obediently compliant in her silence, staring at him with pleading eyes. Arthur wound his hand in her hair tightly, yanking on it just enough to hurt, exactly as she liked.

"You're being a good girl. Maybe you do deserve to get rewarded tonight. How would you like to get your ass fucked? I know how much you love that."

Alana's breath hitched and her desire flared higher. It took her everything not to frantically nod and start panting like a bitch in heat. It wasn't that Arthur wasn't big on anal sex, but he had to be in a particular mood. And that mood didn't come as often as Alana would like it to. It was a special treat to be rewarded with such an offer—and though she knew her suitors would probably enjoy fucking her ass, she only ever trusted Arthur enough to care for her properly. As much as they flirted with pain play, and as authoritative as he could be, Arthur was first and foremost always most concerned with her pleasure.

There was only one problem, though.

Arthur chuckled. "Look at you. Getting that look in your eyes like there's nothing else you could ever want more. Such a dirty girl. I'll fuck your ass tonight, my dirty girl. I'll fuck it good and hard—"

"Wait—Teletubby, *teletubby*!" Teletubby was their safe word. Nothing could possibly throw off their mood more than bringing up the alienish child show creatures who were the centerpiece of so many parents' nightmares.

Arthur instantly stopped, utmost worry gracing his features. His grip loosened on her hair, turning softer and kind instead. "Are you okay, my love?"

"I'm alright," Alana said softly, warmth flooding her heart. She tucked her hair back. "Arthur, if you're serious about this… I didn't prepare. Would you mind if I slipped in the bathroom and made sure everything is clean and ready?"

Arthur cradled her cheeks between his hands and smiled. "Take all the time you need. And while you're busy, I'll get a couple of ibuprofens for you. I don't plan on going easy tonight, darling… I'll leave you feeling good and raw. Everywhere."

Alana blushed. She nodded meekly and whispered a shy thank you, offering him a sweet peck as he helped her off the bed. She hurried to the bathroom to ensure that everything was as hygienic as could be and in proper shape, unable to stop thinking about what would ensue tonight.

God, how long had it been since they last had anal sex? Arthur hadn't been in the mood for quite a while. They usually reserved this for special occasions, but lately, even this year's special occasions hadn't moved him enough. It couldn't have possibly been a year since their last time, could it?

"Everything okay in there, honey?" Arthur called, just outside the bathroom door.

Alana grinned. "Be out in a minute!"

Arthur chuckled. There was a pause, and then he said—no, *ordered*, "A minute and not a second longer."

Alana pressed her lips together tightly to keep from giggling, practically vibrating from all the excitement.

She fluffed up her hair and finished in the bathroom. When she came out, she blinked in surprise at what she found. Arthur had set up his laptop near the foot of the bed and was waiting by a chair, holding toys and lube that he evidently intended to use.

He smiled when she met his eyes.

"Ready?"

Alana nodded, the anticipation making it hard for her to stay still. She managed, though. Arthur's somber, authoritative stare took over, inducing a shiver from her body. God, he was so fucking hot. She loved her husband.

"Walk over to me," he commanded.

Swallowing, Alana did as he asked, making sure to keep her shoulders straight and her head high. Naked, she stood dutifully in front of him as quiet as a mouse, shyly meeting his gaze. Arthur leisurely ran his eyes over her, his face never revealing anything. He locked their gazes again and stared wordlessly for a short moment, the urge to squirm rushing through her. She refrained, though.

She wanted to ask what the laptop was for, what he had planned for them, but remembered his earlier words.

"I'm the one asking questions."

She knew he wouldn't answer them now, either.

"Bend over the foot of the bed."

Again? Alana thought. Still, she followed his command. She would play along with his game.

She wasn't expecting to come face to face with a paused video—the one their camera had recorded and streamed for Arthur just a few days ago. The one of her and Joey. On the screen, Joey was in the middle of going down on her.

Alana blushed to her roots. She opened her mouth to say something, but Arthur beat her to it.

"You've never actually seen any of them, have you?" he whispered, parting her legs and firmly running up and down the curve of her ass with his hands. He dipped one hand to her cunt, tracing the length of her folds lightly. Once. Twice. Then once more, more firmly. "You've never watched yourself fucking these other men. Seen the way you react to what they do to you. Never seen yourself as you enjoy someone who is not your husband."

His fingers rubbed her clit now, so tenderly it was torture, and Alana squirmed back against him.

"Play it," he said firmly.

Alana did as she was told, but she was more fixated on trying to intensify the pleasure his fingers brought. Arthur was quick to catch on.

"Pay attention to the recording, Alana. Or else I won't fuck your pretty little ass," he warned. He wasn't helping, though, touching her clit harder and working her in ways she liked.

Alana whined, but she obeyed, forcing herself to focus on the home movie playing on the laptop. She quivered seeing Joey going down on her, remembering how good his mouth felt on her pussy. Never better than Arthur, but he was one of the more skilled men she'd had. Some never even wanted to—selfish cowards that they were.

"God, your pussy tastes so good. And you love it so much drenching my mouth. I could stay here for hours, making you cum again and again."

Two fingers slipped inside of her, mimicking the two that Joey had used when Alana was getting closer to her orgasm. Joey's fingers had been slim but rough, calloused from perhaps construction work or maybe musician skills. Arthur's were softer, thicker—having only ever known office work and piano keys. She liked her husband's infinitely better. Liked their thickness, and how Arthur knew exactly where to curl them, exactly what pace she needed most to cum—

"He didn't touch you like this, did he? Did he finger your cunt and hit this spot right here?" He crooked his fingers, rubbing firmly against her g-spot. "I bet he didn't. I bet he tried to go as fast as he could. These young men always think faster is better. But I know you, Alana. I know how you like to be fucked. With my cock, my fingers, my mouth… I know all your places. But he didn't find many of them that night, did he?"

Alana shook her head, moaning and bucking against his fingers. Arthur huffed, pleased. He added another finger, keeping the steady but firm pace just as she liked it for a slow build. Alana grew dizzy.

"I asked you a question, Alana," Arthur ground out.

Alana whimpered. "No…"

Arthur rewarded her with a thumb to her clit, rubbing circles in time with his thrusting fingers. Alana gasped, feeling the knot within her winding tighter.

"Eyes on the screen. Or I'll stop what I'm doing," she heard him warn in her haze. Alana hummed and gathered all of her energy to do as he asked.

"Good girl," he said, moving deeper, reaching all the way within her where she liked most. "Tell me what was going on through your mind right then. He hadn't made you cum when he went down on you, had he? Were you disappointed? Even though his cock was inside you?"

"I… Yes," she admitted, watching herself moaning on the screen as Joey fucked her, maneuvering her legs over his shoulders in order to go deeper. It wasn't long before she was coming, shouting his name as she grabbed his ass, though she remembered feeling slightly off-put by how he'd never gotten her off with his mouth. "I really wanted to cum on that face. You know how much I love to."

"I know how much you love to cum all over *my* face," he corrected, withdrawing his fingers from her needy pussy.

Alana mewled helplessly at the emptiness he left her with. Oh no. Had she said the wrong thing? Had she made him feel less special? He was torturing her and leaving her unattended to punish her, wasn't he? God damn dizzy brain—

The pop of a bottle cap filled the room and Alana's breath hitched, desire flushing her all over again. That was their lube. Most definitely. She'd know that sound anywhere, as pitiful as that was.

A wet, careful finger rubbed around her puckered opening, sending a shiver up Alana's spine. Goosebumps prickled her skin, breaths falling heavier as Arthur rubbed more firmly, quickly arousing the sensitive area. The cap of their lube bottle popped off again and Alana's heart pounded up a storm, anticipation practically shaking her bones.

She could barely register the sound of her and Joey in the recording, especially as Arthur began to play with her opening again, slipping one finger into her ass. The sensation was foreign, but it was one she always welcomed anyway—one that excited her more and more for the promise of what was to come.

As he worked her, Arthur played her clit with his other hand and murmured, "You didn't cum after that, did you? That was your only orgasm. You tried so hard to cum again, but you knew you wouldn't get there before he did. So you faked it, didn't you my love?"

Alana squirmed against his hand, breath catching in her throat. "How—How did you know?"

"Because I know you, sweetheart. I know how you sound when you cum. I know how your face gets all twisted up. I know how you tremble, how your head always tilts back…"

As if on cue, the sound of her heated moan ripped through the room again—only her recorded one. Her faked orgasm. Jesus, had time passed by so fast as Arthur worked her ass? Had Alana really lost herself this much to everything? Or had her time with Joey been shorter than she remembered?

Arthur paused, took his hand away from her clit briefly, then carefully inserted another lubed-up finger, cutting her breath from her lungs. He paused to let her grow accommodated, murmuring a genuine, "Too much?" to which Alana replied with an enthusiastic headshake.

"Sure you don't need more lube?"

Alana smiled dazedly, then ground back against his hand. She reached down to play with her clit. "Not yet…" she reassured him. "I'm okay."

"I didn't tell you that you could touch yourself," Arthur warned, tugging her wrist away with his free hand.

"Arthur…" Alana complained.

"I told you to cum while I was gone. And you didn't listen. Now you don't get to cum until I say so."

"I want you to cum twice while I'm gone. Not by yourself. You'll bring this gym guy over. Let him fuck you so good you can't walk the next day. You'll think of him. Not me. And you'll let him make you cum twice before he does and not any less. You'll be a good girl for me, won't you?"

Alana moaned again, too turned-on by his words. Even if she knew that it meant she would probably have to beg him later, that he was probably going to deny her orgasm again and again, it still rendered her a mess of lust.

God, she missed him. Missed how intense their sex was, how intense Arthur could be. Missed his cock in her mouth, her cunt, her ass—everywhere.

When Alana heard the zipper of his pants come down, her pussy throbbed so fiercely she swore she could feel her heartbeat through it. Arthur's fingers paused, free hand fumbling to no doubt free himself from the confines of his pants. He led himself to her wet, dripping folds, rubbing his cock against them before leisurely slipping inside. Alana was so wet that her pussy offered him no resistance, accepting him as easily as a hot knife through butter. Arthur groaned, unabashed.

"Look at how wet you are. You're drenching my cock… Feels like I'm buried in silk. Is that all for me, Alana? Or did you get wet seeing yourself be unfaithful to your husband?"

Alana shook her head vehemently. "No—For you," she hissed, pushing her ass back against him and gripping the sheets. She blindly reached for the laptop with one hand, shutting it. She didn't think Arthur would mind at this point. "Always for you. No one else can have me wet like this."

Arthur growled, anchoring his free hand against her thigh and setting up a lazy beat. "I bet if I pulled out right now, you'd drip all over the floor." Alana whimpered, locking her ankle behind his to try and keep him from doing so. Arthur chuckled gruffly. "Don't worry, sweetheart. I missed your cunt too much while I was away. Leaving it is the last thing on my mind."

Moaning, Alana quivered around his cock so much she simply had to plunge a hand between her legs and touch herself. She moved in a frenzy on her clit, crying out in protest when Arthur forced her hand away and pounded his cock into her, moving his fingers in tandem with his thrusts with such delicious force that Alana quickly found herself teetering on the edge. She wailed her husband's name with reckless abandon, crying out short, succinct encouragements and trying in vain to meet his thrusts, desperate to topple off that blissful edge—

"Are you going to cum, Alana? Are you going to cum all over this cock like a good girl? Tell me whose cock is pounding into you. Tell me whose name you're going to scream when you cum all over this cock—"

"*Yes*. God, yes. Arthur, Arthur, *Arthur*," Alana chanted, moans growing in octaves with every thrust. She started whimpering as her end became clearer, her arms trembling so much they could hardly hold her up...

And then Arthur stopped. Just like that. Stilled both his fingers and his cock, steadying her with a single, strong hand. Alana's bliss-filled sounds went somber, lamenting the orgasm that was just beyond her reach. She wanted it so much.

"I told you. You don't get to cum until I say so," Arthur said, slipping his fingers out of her to rub circles around her slickened, puckered entrance. Tears of frustration stung her eyes, still reeling from being so close to relief. "You disobeyed me while I was away. Now you need to learn how to follow my commands again."

"I know how," Alana complained, slipping an unsteady hand between her legs. She sobbed in discontentment when Arthur stopped her from reaching her aching destination. "Please, Arthur…"

"You know how?" Arthur echoed, maintaining his grip on her wrist. He slapped her ass hard with his free hand, still slickened with lube, and Alana cried out. "So you chose to ignore my orders?"

Alana buried her face in the sheets, making some noise of denial. Still, she couldn't find her words as Arthur slipped his perfect fingers into her ass again, working them just the way she liked, which had her quivering around his cock and turning into a panting mess once more.

"More?"

"Yes," Alana answered frantically, rocking back against his hand. She needed more than his fingers now. Wanted his cock—but she knew she wasn't ready for that yet.

His fingers withdrew once more, only with the promise of something else to come. It was the most challenging thing for Alana to be patient, having just had her orgasm torn away from her—one which felt like she had been waiting for all week. Even with the great sex she'd had a few days ago, nothing was ever as fulfilling as sex with her husband. Only he could fulfill her true needs—physically and in all other ways.

Something hard pressed against her back end and Alana shivered, biting down on her bottom lip. Arthur rubbed one full cheek tenderly, murmuring, "Ready?"

Alana nodded, taking a deep breath as he started pushing the toy in. It was a butt plug, she was sure—the toy she preferred to use, sleek and all black, just wide enough to make her feel that deep pressure she so loved.

"All good?" Arthur asked, as always most concerned about her pleasure—or at this moment, rather, her level of pain or discomfort.

There *was* some pain but none Alana couldn't handle or didn't like, so she shook her head no, taking the moment Arthur paused to suck another deep breath and exhale slowly, forcing her body to relax. She gasped when the toy was fully settled within, squeezing around it instinctively.

Her head spun and her body throbbed, squeezing around Arthur again and again. She couldn't even hear what he muttered while he ground his hips in a rough circle.

Alana bit the back of her hand, grinding back into him. She only realized he was talking when he growled, "Alana. Pay attention to me. You don't want me to start punishing you again, do you?"

One of his hands inched closer to her ass, a clear warning about what he would do if she did not comply, and Alana snatched out behind herself to touch him anywhere, needing him to know she was all ears for him.

"Good. Turn over and play with yourself while you suck my cock."

Alana shuddered, but she scrambled to do exactly just that, heart beating out of her chest. She reached for him before she even dipped a hand between her legs, licking her lips at the thought of finally having her mouth on him again.

Arthur chuckled but the sound was quickly followed by a groan, mixing the two together. He gently took hold of her hair before harshly tugging down on it, drawing a moan from her that created vibrations against his rock-hard dick. Another groan slipped from his mouth, hand guiding her rhythm vigorously. Alana settled her free hand on his backside, holding it tightly. She squeezed his ass over and over again, every push and press full of need and pure love.

"My dirty girl… you missed my cock, didn't you?" Arthur murmured, tugging on her hair once more. She hummed, pleased. "Missed the taste of me. Makes me want to cum all over your tongue and make you swallow it all. Every. Single. Drop. Spank you for every one you missed."

Alana whimpered, mouth full of him. She rubbed her clit eagerly, sucking him harder, lapping up the pre-cum leaking from his slit. He groaned again, more fiercely, tugging her closer and choking her on his thick girth.

"*Yes*. God, yes," she moaned, words muffled by his cock. She rolled her tongue around his crown like she knew he loved, looking up at him with the most pleading, tempting eyes—or so she hoped. "Please. *Please*. Cum in my mouth, Arthur. I want it. *Please*."

Arthur stared down at her, never once stopping bobbing her mouth over his cock. His intoxicating little grunts and groans persisted, dampening her cunt even more. But he was considering and that gave Alana hope. Hope that he would give in, that he would let himself go and fuck her mouth till her eyes teared up, growling her name as he would cum messily all over her tongue—

"No," Arthur said, removing himself from her mouth so suddenly that she shouted in frustration.

Arthur threw her a warning look and she quieted instantly. She glared back at him, a pout forming at her lips.

Arthur's lips quirked, just barely. "Watch the attitude, Alana."

Alana softened up and swallowed, averting her gaze to convey her submission to her dom. It worked; Arthur let out a pleased huff and kneeled down on the floor, bringing her legs over his shoulders. Alana's heart quickened.

He didn't waste time lunging between her legs and setting his mouth on her wet cunt, cutting the breath from her legs. Alana tilted her head back against the sheets and clung to them with her hands, panting as Arthur took her clit in his mouth and sucked it rhythmically, just the way he knew she loved it.

With how worked up she was, it didn't take her long to see her end in sight and quickly start approaching it. But Arthur, the tease that he was, never let her reach it—pulling away and denying her orgasm every time it seemed within reach. Punishing her and driving her to madness with a fire of desire and need.

"Arthur, please. Let me come. *Please*," she begged as another orgasm neared. She needed it. So much. So, so much that she thought she might cry if she didn't get it.

But Arthur kept on with his punishment, removing himself from her completely once more. Alana shouted, driven up the wall and desperate, but Arthur rose up and climbed over her in bed to capture her lips in a harsh, demanding kiss.

I'm the boss, it meant. Alana kissed him back, tears pricking her eyes because she was so worked up that it actually hurt. God, it was so easy to forget how much she loved her husband's torture.

Arthur settled himself between her legs. He paused, just for a moment, then tilted her hips up further— until her ass was tantalizingly close to his cock. Alana's heart stuttered, breath hitching then falling heavier with excitement. She bit her lip when he gently started removing the toy, barely managing to hold back her relieved sob when it left her body.

Arthur met her gaze and smiled, if faintly, before his features slipped back into seriousness as he reached for their bottle of lube. He wet his cock very generously with it, coating his fingers again to ensure her ass was still sufficiently slicked up.

He caught her gaze for her silent approval to go on with the next step and whispered, "Don't play tough. Let me know if you think we need more lube, okay?"

Alana meekly nodded. A shiver ran up her spine as the head of his cock tapped her small, puckered hole. She nodded and reached for her husband, whispering back, "As always. Just take it slow, okay? We should be fine."

Arthur rubbed her thighs up and down twice, then seized one of them firmly and used the other to help push his cock inside. He glanced up at her, gauging her reaction, pushing in one tiny inch at a time—always peering back up at her to try and capture any hint that he should stop.

But Alana didn't give him any.

Although she was uncomfortably full and overwhelmed, she felt no inclination to tell him to stop. She liked the sensations—adored them. Felt like she couldn't be any slicker; Arthur had done a good job lubing them up. Maybe had even gone overboard—but going overboard with lube when it came to anal was highly recommended as opposed to not putting enough.

"Okay, my love?" Arthur asked, all traces of authority gone and replaced by his deep, genuine love. He took hold of her other thigh, adjusting his grasp on them so she was more secure against him.

Alana nodded, throwing her arms over her head. She needed more. But they needed to go slow. No matter how much she wanted to beg him to pound her ass until she couldn't even stand upright. Not letting her body accommodate his cock was a sure way to get torn. Or bleed. Or both.

It took a few minutes before he was fully fitted inside. The moment he was, they both moaned in turn, reveling in the moment together. Experiencing different kinds of pleasures. Arthur, likely in heaven because of the tightness of her ass around him. Alana's, though, was more mental—the unbearably full feeling of him, the borderline pain, the intensity of the room. She felt like she could cum already, like she was right there at the wonderful edge and needed just a little something more.

"Fuck. I always forget about how good you feel like this," Arthur muttered, running his hands up her thighs, her sides, then settling over her breasts. He palmed and squeezed them firmly, his eyes full of appreciation. He finally met her gaze.

Alana felt so overwhelmed and full of desire she was sure it was visible. Especially with the way Arthur's eyes softened.

"I'm okay," she reassured him, grabbing one of his hands and squeezing it. "Don't you go mushy on me now. I thought you said you wouldn't take it easy on me tonight."

Arthur's lips quirked briefly and then his eyes darkened. His chest rumbled with a sort of low growl. "You're asking to be tied up talking to me like that," he warned.

Alana grinned and Arthur reached behind him for the pair of handcuffs he'd set aside earlier along with the lube and butt plug, locking them on her wrists tightly. Maybe even a little too tightly.

Still, Alana didn't say anything. Especially not as Arthur pressed the chain link down into the bed, holding it there to lock her in place and restrain her movements.

"Still remember the safe word?"

Alana's stomach quivered, breaths falling choppier from all of the anticipation. "Yes."

"Good. Cause' that's the only word you'll be allowed to say until I'm done with you. That and my name. Nothing else."

Oh, God. Yes. Fuck yes.

Alana's eyes grew wide. Her pussy quivered in need but it would find no reprieve this time. Not in the way it wanted. Her mouth opened to say something—she didn't know what—but she never got the chance to speak.

Arthur started moving, at first slowly—no doubt letting her body grow more accommodated to him. Then, his pace picked up; gentle but fast little pounds that had her gasping and mewling at every turn.

It wasn't long before those turned into firm, punishing thrusts. Alana moaned, barely able to catch her breath between cries of his name. She tried to rise up to kiss him, but he held the chain of her handcuffs firmly down, keeping her just out of reach. Alana complained. Arthur moved more fiercely, bracing himself against his captor hand so he could deliver a hard slap on her ass. Alana cried out, squeezing around his cock as she teetered even closer to her end.

"Arthur," she said, itching so much to touch herself and reach that release. She sobbed, hands clenching in the sheets as she writhed, desperate for more. "Arthur, *please*—"

Arthur clasped his hand over her mouth but didn't relent, pounding into her roughly. His grey eyes lit up like wild embers as he growled, "What did I say? My name, the safe word, and nothing else."

Alana whined against his hand, the words winding the knot in her belly even tighter. She shouted over and over again when he started hammering into her with even more ferocity, intensifying all of the already overwhelming sensations and bringing tears to her eyes. She was so close it was painful. Alana stared up at her husband pleadingly, in the hopes that he would understand how badly she needed him to finally allow her to cum.

How much she couldn't handle another denial, another punishment.

Arthur bent down and kissed her feverishly, bracing himself on the hand holding her to the mattress so he could drop his hand between her legs and rub her clit. She barely lasted a few slow, delicious rubs, going off like a rocket. Breaking away from their kiss, she screamed, unable to think about anything at all, her whole world blurring over in white.

She hadn't even been aware she'd been murmuring until she started coming down from her high. With both hands somehow buried in his hair and holding his face to her neck, soft encouragements and croons of Arthur's name spilled from her mouth as her husband grunted and continued thrusting away.

He came a moment later, groaning into her hair. Alana held him, relishing in the feeling of him grinding and spurting his hot, thick cum inside her ass, a shiver running up her spine. God, she'd missed the sensation so much. While she loved the overwhelming, too-full side of anal, this still had to be her favorite part.

Or maybe this is, Alana thought, as Arthur began to pull out so very carefully, the sensation making her tremble and ache—in the best way. She bit her lip and closed her eyes, holding on to every second, and sighed when he finally left her body vacated.

Arthur chuckled and Alana's eyes blinked open, seeing bliss-dazed grey pools staring down at her. His lips were curled; amused. He lifted her handcuffed hands from around his neck and let them fall onto the bed, bowing to kiss her deeply. She felt him unlock the too-tight restraints, and as soon as her hands were free, Alana cupped his face and kept kissing him, still reeling from the strength of her orgasm.

"Feeling okay, sweetheart?" he asked, gaze full of love and care. He traced her cheekbone and thumbed her chin.

Alana smiled. "Mm. Feeling perfect," she whispered back, raking a hand through his short hair. "I really missed you, Arthur. No matter how many men I have in bed when you're away… I'll always miss you."

Arthur smiled too, his features softened with more than just his post-orgasm bliss. It was love. Plain and simple. Alana knew it. "Because of how good our 'welcome home' sex is?"

A giggle fell from her mouth. She shook her head, considered his question, then shrugged. "Well, partly. I guess." She began to crack up again at the grin that formed on his lips. She traced his jawline, kissing it tenderly. "Because I love you. And nothing and no one can beat the sex we have for that reason alone. No matter how much bigger their dick might be than yours."

Arthur huffed, then kissed her nose. "Oh, how I love your compliments, wife of mine," he teased, eyes crinkling happily at the corners. He captured her lips again, lingering sweetly. "I'll run a bath for you and get you some water?"

"And a snack, please," Alana added with a wry grin, rubbing her sore wrists.

As Arthur got up, she looked around for the ibuprofen he'd gotten for her earlier and heard him call from outside their room, "Pills are on the dresser."

Alana laughed. "I love you!"

"Love you more, sweetheart."

Story 7 - Elevator High (Forbidden Fantasies)

There was that laugh again. The one that tore Violet Reed right out of her focus zone, each and every time. Violet's eyes snapped over in its direction, cheeks warming at the sight of the lean, scruffy-haired man standing over with two of her coworkers a dozen steps away from her. He was grinning, teeth pearly white against his tawny-beige complexion, large black glasses, and navy three-piece suit.

Sebastian Lam; CEO and founder of LEI. He'd been her boss for about two months now, and Violet still couldn't believe she was working for such a hunk. When she'd met him for the first time on her final interview day, she thought he might have been a branch manager of LEI—not the highest-ranking boss of the whole company. She'd assumed that role would have gone to a fifty or sixty-something-year-old businessman, as it typically did. Besides, people didn't usually meet their CEO on one of their entry-level job interviews, either.

But Sebastian Lam proved he was different from the start. He was so committed to his company and its work environment that he wanted to be included in even the little steps. He never let his busy schedule get in the way of getting to know his employees, ensuring they were thriving. His door was always open for those who needed to talk about any work-related issues, yet he still kept clear boundaries conveying that his friendliness and kindness had limits; that there would be consequences to anyone trying to take advantage. He was a kind, charming man, but he took no bullshit. Violet found him too enchanting to watch.

So did all the other ladies in the office, frankly. They all seemed to be crushing on him or fantasizing about the type of sex they could have with him. But how could Violet blame them? She was one of them too, now. Sebastian Lam was the Asian equivalent of a White Knight—the kind of man their Asian grandmothers liked to brag about at get-togethers with friends and estranged family members they only saw once every few Chinese New Year's.

"I'm telling you, if that man was mine, I would never let him out of the bedroom," Jiang, her desk mate, professed matter-of-factly. Her tone had Violet's lips beginning to curl up.

"I don't think you're the only one who thinks that," Violet replied, eyes flickering briefly to some of their other coworkers staring dreamily at their boss. She brushed her sleek black hair over her shoulder and returned to inputting information from a stack of client files on her desk, trying her best to ignore Mr. Lam's wonderful laugh as it rang through the room again.

It was impossible; her gaze still shifted over to him to catch his grin, and Jiang caught her. She grinned. Violet threw her nearest pencil at her, struggling not to laugh as Jiang squeaked in surprise.

Jiang tossed it back. "Of course I'm not the only one! You do, too," she said, sticking her tongue out.

"Do not," Violet lied, throwing the pencil at her again.

Jiang was more prepared this time, though, giggling as she flung it back to Violet. "Do, too!"

"Do not!"

"Liar!"

"I'm not!"

It went on like that, the pencil being tossed back and forth as she and Jiang argued and started cackling together. The two stopped and blushed, however, as their boss's friendly voice sounded across the entire room.

"Having fun, ladies?"

Violet and Jiang ducked their heads shyly. "Sorry Mr. Lam," they chorused, transparently embarrassed, but Mr. Lam simply chuckled and wordlessly brushed them off.

Mr. Lam's gaze lingered on Violet for a split moment, his friendly smile growing as he waved her hello—something which he'd been doing since the first day she started working at LEI. It was platonic; simply something he did to help her to feel welcomed, Violet knew. Still, the gesture had her blush worsening twice-fold, which she hoped he wouldn't be able to notice from where he was as she waved back.

"Lucky bitch," Jiang muttered, urging Violet to shift her attention to her once more.

She found Jiang pouting comically, leaning her cheek into her hand. Violet bit the inside of her cheek to keep from smiling.

"For what?" she asked, going back to her tasks. "Didn't he do that with you, too, when you started? You said he always waves at every new employee for a while."

"For a while," Jiang agreed. "But not *this* long. What did you do? Blow him in the bathroom?"

Violet stiffened, her mouth dropping open. She reddened like a tomato and threw her eraser at Jiang, a garbled sound leaving her. "What?! No way!" she hissed, looking around the room in panic. No one seemed to have noticed her little outburst. Good.

Violet relaxed, swallowed, and ran her hand through her hair. "He's probably just impressed with my work ethic, that's all."

Jiang smiled, sympathetic. "You're right. I'd be surprised if he hadn't noticed all the overtime you do. Probably helps out a lot with our backlog of paperwork."

"Of course he does. He was the first person I asked when I was coming up short on rent, you know? He's really nice. Always makes sure I get the money I need on time."

"Sebastian Lam, the lifesaver," Jiang concurred. "Thank God he exists."

The both of them raised their cups of coffee as if they were vodka shots and cheered to the rare, amazing bosses out there. Then, they went back to work.

She ended up having to work overtime that night again when her little brother Jaxon texted a little before her shift was over that they had forgotten to pay this month's phone bill. Violet groaned, but she powered through and lamented the loss of a hopefully relaxing night. Jiang gave her a sympathetic look and smile, patting her shoulder, and suggesting she take a bath after going home, then bid her goodnight.

Fortunately, Violet's overtime passed quickly. Within three hours, the giant stack of financial papers her manager had provided her before leaving with everyone else had diminished, until nothing but a dozen files remained. Violet briefly considered finishing it, but her growing headache pounded persistently behind her achy eyes, protesting the idea, so she decided against it. She had done enough for the night, she reasoned, sighing as she rubbed her temples. She needed to go home and decompress. Draw herself a bath, maybe—like Jiang had suggested. That sounded so good right now.

Nodding to herself, Violet gathered the remaining files, got up, and dropped them on her manager's desk with a note. She went back and collected her things, stretching her limbs out, stiff from being at her desk for so long. Gosh, the office was so quiet right now; almost eerily so. It was always so odd being here when most of the lights were out and no one else but her was around. Violet was so used to hearing keyboard taps, chatting coworkers, and phones ringing that she never realized how oddly comforting the sounds were until they were gone.

Shaking off the discomfort, Violet headed for the elevator and smiled, thankful to finally be heading home. When the doors opened, she got inside and leaned against the back wall, yawning. She stretched her limbs again, rubbing the back of her neck. The elevator doors closed, but Violet was surprised it started heading up—called by someone else.

Probably the janitor or something, she thought. Though she hadn't seen him clean her floor yet. Had he decided to work his way backward today? Maybe he wanted to switch things up a little.

When the elevator rang and opened its doors again, though, Violet's mouth promptly fell open. Her brown eyes widened, heart pounding up a storm. Because standing right in front of her was Sebastian fucking Lam, the man haunting the wet dreams of every woman working at this building. Including hers.

Mr. Lam was dressed up in a sleek formal gray suit, his hair combed back in a neat hairdo—taming his usually wild locks with class. Her pussy dampened her panties in an instant. Her mouth went dry.

Violet was not the only one surprised.

Blinking out of his momentary jolt, Mr. Lam smiled warmly and made his way inside. He greeted her amicably and Violet's heart stuttered inside her chest, even as he stood a respectable distance away. The elevator doors slid shut and it started heading down, finally.

"Working overtime again tonight?" Mr. Lam asked, his eyes crinkling up at the edges.

Violet stood stone-still, still unable to recover from the suddenness of his appearance. Why was he still here? Why was he all dressed up? Did he not have the chance to go home because he had too many tasks to finish, but still had to attend an event of some sort? Holy shit, he looked so good.

Good enough she wanted to tear his clothes off and beg him to fuck her right here and now.

Shaking off her daze, Violet thankfully brought back her wits before Mr. Lam could suspect anything and she cleared her throat. "Uh—Yeah. I'm—The phone bill—" She clammed up, growing flustered by his sheer gorgeousness. "Oh God, I am *so* sorry," she stammered out, clasping a hand over her mouth. "I didn't know you'd be—I mean, I—"

Words dying on her tongue, her embarrassment barreled into her with enough force to make her dizzy and Violet covered her face with her hands. Jesus, she was such a ditz!

"You're… sorry for being in the elevator?" she heard him ask, clearly confused.

She peeked through her fingers to find him looking at her quizzically, one perfect eyebrow raised. Violet wanted to groan. She just realized how stupid that sounded. How stupid *she* sounded. Why did her boss have to be so damn handsome and dazzling right now? It was screwing with her brain and her ability to think.

"Um… I guess?"

Mr. Lam's black eyes gleamed brighter. His lips curved up with a smile. He chuckled and shook his head, directing his attention to his reflection in the shiny elevator wall so he could readjust his tie. Violet didn't know why it needed adjusting when it already looked perfect.

"I admit I was surprised to see you here, Violet, but I'd never be angry at an employee of mine simply because they happen to share an elevator with me so late at night."

Violet bit her lip, and she hung her head. "Um. Y-Yeah. Sorry. I guess it sounds totally dumb when you put it like that. Sorr—" She cut herself off, cringing. "Jesus. I apologize for apologizing so much, Mr. Lam. That must be really annoying by now…"

Mr. Lam smiled, all friendliness, charm, and warmth as usual. God, he was so nice. So good. It was unfair how much more attractive it always made him.

"It's alright. I've been there, too. Before I started my own company, of course. I remember how it was. I'm the big boss who can fire you for breathing the wrong way, right?"

Violet tucked her hair back, looking away. "Uh… Yeah. Something like that." *And the fact you're stupidly fucking hot and I want you to fuck my brains out right now,* she finished in her head. *I would drop down to my knees and go down on you at the drop of a dime—Oh my God, shut up, brain!*

The damage was done, however. As she looked at Sebastian Lam in all of his gorgeous glory, she couldn't help picturing herself sinking down to her knees right this moment and undoing his pants with greedy hands, Sebastian's thick fingers sinking into her hair as she freed his cock and sucked him for all he was worth.

Her face burned with such intensity she could barely stand to think, the space between her legs growing considerably wetter. Her panties were probably soaked by now. In front of her fucking boss. Jesus Christ. She needed to get herself together—to change subjects *now*. Anything to keep from focusing on her perverse mind.

"Do I look okay?" Mr. Lam asked, prompting her to peer at him. She found him adjusting his tie, still, frowning like he was nervous.

Violet hoped it wasn't to impress anyone else. Not romantically, at least. As far as she knew, Sebastian Lam wasn't married or in a relationship, but who knew? Maybe he secretly had his eye on someone.

The thought made her stomach ripple with possessiveness, brought a fire to her chest. She wanted to sink down on her knees that much more, to prove herself worthy and suck his cock like no one ever had before, to make him *see* her—

Violet mentally shook the thoughts from her head. She had no right to think like that. Mr. Lam was her boss. He could lose his job, ruin his company's reputation. Why would he risk all that for her?

But, God, what she would give for just one night of hot, dirty sex with him. For ten minutes where they'd both be free of any consequences; where he could just pick her up and fuck her whichever way he wanted, ram his cock inside her wet cunt until she screamed—

Fucking *hell*, she needed to get laid. Soon. She couldn't keep thinking like that about her boss.

Swallowing the tight lump in her throat, Violet cleared her throat once more. She ran a hand through her silky black hair. "Um. Yes," she managed to answer at last. She hoped she hadn't been quiet for too long. "Very ha—very dapper, Mr. Lam."

Mr. Lam blinked, glancing away from his reflection in the wall and back at her. He tilted his head, eyes sparkling with transparent amusement.

Shit. Had he caught on to what she'd almost said?

His lips twitched up in a kind smile. "Thank you. I'm supposed to be meeting this big potential partner tonight. I hear he looks down on anyone with poor style. So naturally, I need to look perfect."

You already do, Violet thought. She bit the inside of her cheek to keep from saying so, swallowing the words down. "As I said, Mr. Lam. Very dapper," she repeated. She hoped he didn't notice how her voice got a little hoarser.

Mr. Lam's smile widened. "Thank you, Violet. And please, call me Sebastian outside of work. There's no sense always keeping formalities."

Violet's cheeks reddened again. She wiped her hand on them instinctively, as though that might make her blush disappear. It didn't, obviously. She ducked her head timidly. "Aren't we at work, though?"

Sebastian shrugged, his eyes continuing to sparkle. With one last look at his reflection to check out his hair, this time, he peered back at her and winked.

Violet's heart began to perform a series of dangerous acrobatics and she was rendered speechless, unable to even think. Oh my God. Sebastian Lam was so perfect. It wasn't fair. Violet had never wanted anyone so much.

The elevator dinged and the doors opened again. A confusing mix of relief and disappointment rushed through Violet and neither of them moved to get out. Finally, Sebastian gestured in invitation for her to leave first and bowed a little, though Violet wasn't sure if it was a playful gibe or simply the manners of a well-raised man. Still, she obliged.

When she passed him by, Sebastian said, "Good work, by the way. Mr. Lei told me that your overtime is really making a difference. Come by my office sometime this week and we'll talk about getting you your first raise."

Violet stiffened, freezing in place. Mr. Lam didn't seem to think anything of it, passing her and offering her a bright smile and a chirpy, "Good night. Rest well. You deserve it," and then trotting off to the limousine waiting for him outside. He patted the shoulder of the limousine driver who opened the door for him, then disappeared inside the car.

Violet remained speechless. Her heart pounded. A raise already? How was Sebastian Lam so fucking perfect?

When Violet got home, she first checked on her little brother to make sure he had eaten dinner, cleaned up the empty beer bottles on the living room coffee table by her snoring father, then went upstairs and drew herself a bath—like Jiang suggested.

She hesitated, then decided to light up some candles and throw in a lavender bath bomb. As she waited for her bath to set up, she went to her medicinal cabinet and got some Tiger Balm to soothe her headache. She brushed her teeth and washed her face, then applied the Tiger Balm to her forehead and temples, a relieved hum leaving her lips at the familiar scent. Once that was all done, she undressed, hopped in the bath as it was still filling up, and sighed as the hot water barely immersed her tired muscles but instantly started unwinding her from her long day.

Violet closed her eyes and tilted her head back against the bathtub wall, then started to drift off. Thoughts of Sebastian filled her mind not two breaths later, remembering how amazing he looked tonight, dressed in all of his fancy glory. Her breath caught in her lungs, imagining what unbuttoning his dress shirt from his body might be like. God, if she had her way and life was in her favor more often, how things would have gone differently tonight…

"Working overtime again tonight, Violet?" Mr. Lam asked as he got in, kind and friendly as ever. His smile was respectful, and so was the distance he kept between them—but his eyes, however, roamed her form in a way that was impossible to miss.

Violet's mouth dried and her cunt throbbed. When he noticed she hadn't missed him checking her out, he politely looked away, throat working on a swallow.

Violet bit her lip. "Yes, Mr. Lam. I hope that's okay," she said.

"Nonsense." Mr. Lam replied, forcing a cheeriness into his tone. "Why would it not be? And please, call me Sebastian. We're off the clock. You can treat me like you would treat any other friend."

I don't want to fuck any of my friends, though, Violet thought. Still, she tucked her hair back and said, "Sebastian, then." Violet savored his name on her tongue. It sounded so good. She wanted to moan it all night long, over and over again.

Sebastian's gaze lit up with even more intensity, and Violet blushed. She licked her lips, heart racing and skipping beats as his eyes followed the move. Her stomach churned. "T—Thank you, Sebastian."

Sebastian's eyes were so heated that Violet felt like they were burning her up from the inside. "No problem at all, Violet," he said, enunciating every syllable of her name in a way that made her pussy instantly wet. Her throat bobbed, thighs shifting together as subtly as she could to relieve herself with some friction.

She stopped breathing when Sebastian noticed, eyes dipping down and flaring hotter before looking away. They stood in silence in the elevator, tension so thick not even a diamond hammer could break it. Violet bit her lip again to keep from whimpering, belly twisting in such tight knots it continued to take her breath away. At this rate, he'd have her panting by his hungry stares alone.

Jesus. If he could do that with just a few hot looks and one slow, delicious enunciation of her name, what could he do to her with his cock?

"How do I look—honest opinion. Would you be impressed by this? I'm meeting an important potential partner tonight. Apparently, he's very high on style. Won't waste his time on people with standard fashion."

His eyes flickered her way, still smoky and blistering. Violet nearly shivered, a thrill running up her spine. She swallowed thickly. *How do you look? You look perfect enough that I would cover you up in chocolate and lick every inch of your body,* Violet thought, licking her lips. But she couldn't say that. Not even with the way he was looking at her. She was still his employee. Maybe he was only testing her willpower?

Instead, she settled on saying, "You look incredible, Sebastian. Very handsome."

Violet thought it was respectful enough to be harmless as a compliment. But when Sebastian's stare shot to her once more, her eyes widened and her heart stumbled at the pure heat she found emblazoned in his gorgeous black eyes, inciting her jaw to drop. Violet had never seen anyone look at her like that before— like it was taking all the restraint in them not to pin her to the floor and fuck her senseless. The attraction was undeniable. One look like that from her ex-boyfriends, and they would have never gotten out of bed for days; insatiable with their lust.

Violet's knees shook. She glanced away, fingers beginning to fidget anxiously. Her breaths got choppier, her eyes remained wide. What was going to happen next? Was he going to call her out on the impropriety of the situation, no matter how much he wanted her? Because he did want her—if at least for that moment. But he was her boss first and foremost, and he could never risk his whole career just because she pushed his buttons. Right?

The elevator doors *dinged,* but neither of them moved to get out. The tension grew higher, higher—until Violet felt like it swallowed all the air between them. When it grew intolerable, Sebastian stepped forward—but not to get out, like her rapidly deflating heart thought. Instead, he stepped towards the panel, pushing the button for his office floor. And then the ones to close the doors.

Violet's heart skipped a beat. Neither of them said anything as the elevator barred their only exit, locking them with their thick tension once more. Sebastian stepped back again, closer to her than he was before. The elevator started going up.

Violet's throat was so dry she barely managed to swallow. "D-Did you forget something, Mr. Lam?" she asked, a little raspily.

Sebastian's gaze snapped over to hers, his black eyes liquid embers of pure desire. Violet's pussy pulsed louder, demanding to be filled.

"Yeah. My head," her boss replied, his voice rougher than sandpaper.

Violet's mouth opened, but she didn't have time to say anything as Sebastian grabbed her waist and whirled her back into the elevator wall, slanting his mouth possessively over hers. Her toes curled in her shoes, a sound of surprise leaving her in a breath, but she was all too quick to respond. She wrapped her arms around his neck, pulling him closer, and moaning softly. Sebastian shoved his knee between her legs, parting them slightly before hiking her up on the wall, drawing a gasp from her. Violet tilted her head back, gaze clouding over as he started rubbing her through her clothes, aiming right for her sweet spot. She whispered encouraging approvals, already riding up the clouds of bliss when none of their clothes were even off.

She barely had the mind to register when the doors of the elevator opened again to his office floor, but thankfully Sebastian did. Not that she really thought she would have minded fucking him in the elevator at this point. He could do whatever he wanted with her. It felt too good to have him like this. Not just because she hadn't gotten laid in a while, but because her attraction to him was also insanely powerful, making her more and more miserable every time she saw his smile, his sparkling eyes. Especially when both were directed at her.

But now she had him.

Sebastian hauled her up around his hips again, and Violet wrapped her legs around him, eliciting a groan from his lips. He carried them both down the hall, stopping a dozen steps away to push her against another wall. His hand plunged between her legs, cradling her wet cunt and hissing something about her being so fucking wet. He rubbed her over her pants, and she began to whine, thrashing and making a mess of his perfectly coiffed hair.

She pulled back and dragged him into a deep kiss, the act squishing his thick, squared glasses against her face. Neither seemed to care, though. Sebastian only kept touching her, rubbing his palm over clothes, creating friction against her clit. Violet rocked against his hand, making pleased sounds and panting.

Good work today, by the way. The words flashed across her mind. Violet's skin prickled. She shuddered, biting down on her lip. *Good girl. You did so good today,* she imagined he said, biting her tongue as she rocked back harder against his hand. *So good I want to bend you over my desk right now. So I could fuck you in front of everyone to show them how much you're my favorite.*

She keened a low cry, scratching her nails against his scalp. She broke away from their kiss harshly tugging on his hair, pulling him back so he would look at her. Sebastian's chest rumbled with a low growl, his eyes hooded with burning want.

"Tell me I'm a good girl," she whispered, so full of need she wouldn't be surprised if she was looking at him pleadingly. "Tell me I did a good job and that I'm your favorite. Tell me—"

Sebastian dove forward and captured her lips in a fierce kiss, breaking away to pull roughly on her bottom lip with his teeth. He grinned. "Praise kink, huh? Don't worry, we'll take care of that, my dirty girl."

Giving her one last harsh kiss full of teeth and tongue, Sebastian wrapped her around him and carried her down the hall some more, soon stepping inside his large office. Violet was sure he was going to carry them both to his desk and start tearing off each other's clothes to carry this thing forward, but instead he walked them both to the end of the room and pressed her into the huge glass window displaying their beautiful city lit up in all its glory.

Violet gasped, taking it all in. She didn't know why that of all things made her think about the event he was missing out on. "Shoot, Mr. Lam—"

"Sebastian," her gorgeous boss corrected with a growl, cutting her off. He lifted her shirt up and pulled her bra down to suck and lick one nipple; already hardened to a peak and rendering her dizzy.

She panted and mewled, tilting her head back against the window. "*Sebastian*. The… The thing you were going to…"

"I'll be late. Who cares," Sebastian replied, snapping off her bra and sinking down to his knees. "No one is on time for these things anyway." He yanked her pants down, and then her panties—with enough force that Violet nearly fell over. Probably would have, too, if it wasn't for his hand holding her steady at her waist.

Her breath hitched as he drew one leg over her shoulder and bit the inside of her thigh, mouth coming closer. "For now, I just want that pretty pussy to cum all over me," he murmured hotly.

His mouth plunged between her legs and drew a cry from her mouth, sucking and licking hungrily like he hadn't eaten in days. Violet grew so light-headed she felt as though she'd lost her mind for a moment, chanting his name like he was her God. She only started coming back to her senses when he undid his pants and freed himself, hiking her up again around his hips. Positioning his cock at her entrance, he slipped inside her slowly and began to rock into her with shallow thrusts. Once he was sure she was good and ready to be fucked, he picked up his pace and rammed his cock deeper, harder.

Soon, his thrusts were so ruthless and good that Violet was shouting time and time again, moaning his name and muttering how good he felt inside her cunt, how much she'd dreamed about this. Sebastian groaned and fucked her with even more fervor, kissing her so sensually she could have come right there.

But then Sebastian lifted her leg carefully over his shoulder, his stare attentive as he watched her face, as though wanting to catch any sign of pain that might tell him to stop. It was a little difficult and stretched out her muscles to the point of discomfort, but Violet didn't let on, too into this to even think about wanting to stop. Her pleasure far outweighed her ache, anyway.

"Fuck. Should have known you'd be flexible," Sebastian murmured. "Such a dirty girl. My good girl. You have no idea how much I've been thinking about this. Thinking about you between my legs, sucking me off on lunch breaks. Thinking about bending you over that desk and fucking your brains out. You're the only one who makes me hard. I've been wanting to feel this pussy around me so badly." He groaned, slowly building up a faster rhythm and grunting his bliss. "Such a good pussy. I love your pussy, Violet. I love how good you feel—"

Violet tightened her good leg around him and snatched both hands to his ass, guiding him in a faster rhythm. She moaned feverishly and smacked one cheek, digging her nails into his skin as her high climbed to heights she never felt before.

"Cum in this pussy then," she breathed, meeting his thrusts frantically. "Fuck me until you fill me up. I've been dreaming about it for so long, please, *please*—"

Sebastian grunted and he flipped her around, trapping both of her hands against the glass and crushing his back to her chest. He moved harder, faster, fucking her like an animal. "Not until you do, sweetheart," he growled.

Violet cried out, reaching between her legs to touch herself. Sebastian's hand got there first, however, and her hand shot out to his hip instead to grab on for dear life. She sang his name over and over, reciting it like it was a mantra. Building pleasure fogged up her mind, at last reaching its breaking point.

Shattering into his arms, Violet let out a breathless cry as white spots danced all over her eyes. Or maybe those were just the blurred-out city lights. Either way, it didn't matter. She didn't care. She just cared about the blissful waves, the blinding, electrifying pleasure coursing through her veins. Nothing else mattered to her—nothing else but the way he panted into her neck, groaning and grunting out his own race to relief. She shuddered and ground against him when he came, banging a fist against the window and letting out a string of curses, his hot sticky wetness spilling inside her in hot spurts.

Breaking from her reverie, Violet bit down the back of her hand and muffled her shout, grinding against her hand. She ground out her high, prolonging the waves with expert strokes as she recalled Sebastian's last words over and over again.

"God you feel so good. Take it all, my good girl. Take all my cum. Take it all in that good, pretty pussy."

When her bliss started waning, a sluggish smile curled her lips. Violet imagined him cradling her in his arms and carrying her to his desk chair, imagined them both slumping into it together and cuddling for hours. Imagined they murmured conversation and loving confessions, free of consequences from the world.

A sigh left her mouth, reality sinking back in. What was she even thinking? Mr. Lam was her boss. This could never happen. Their love would never be permitted, would ruin the image of his business. He probably hadn't even thought about her this way, and here she was exploring a vivid fantasy. This was wrong. So wrong.

At least I got the best orgasm ever out of it, she mused, slumping deeper in the water. *From the ones I've given myself, anyway.*

Would she ever be able to look at him in the eye again without thinking about all the things he said in her fantasy, though?

Shit. That could be a problem, she thought, running her hand through her wet hair. She slung her arm over her eyes, defeated.

…Oh well. You win some, you lose some.

www.ingramcontent.com/pod-product-compliance
Lightning Source LLC
Chambersburg PA
CBHW080917190726
48293CB00011B/2677